3D20

SERIES ANTHOLOGY

ALLYSON LINDT

ROLL AGAINST TRUST

ONE

"I'm not sharing a cramped inn room with two orcs, a halfling thief who keeps stealing my panties, and a sweaty paladin. He hasn't taken off that armor in a freaking month."

Ryan draped himself across the couch to lay his head in my lap. Brown eyes so dark they were almost black crinkled at the corners when he laughed up at me. "C'mon, Tash, join me in the bath. We'd save water at the same time, and that kind of conservationism should do something for your druid sensibilities, right?"

"My character's name is Ardra," I corrected him out of habit, not irritation. It had only taken me a couple of weeks of campaigning with him to realize he was just going to use my real name, regardless of whom I was role-playing as. I made a half-hearted attempt to push him upright. "And aren't you supposed to be celibate?"

"Absolutely not. As of now, I serve a god of orgies and wine. Dionysus, maybe?"

Seth looked up from behind his dungeon master screen, eyebrows raised. "He's not in our pantheon." His mouth twisted in thought. "Then again, sure, why the hell not? Roll against your charisma."

3

I laughed in disbelief. "I'm not taking a bath with him, water conservation or not." Even as the protest passed my lips, my imagination crept in to taunt me. My druid character might prefer the plague over rubbing skin with his paladin, but I wouldn't mind watching Ryan strip down. Or Seth, for that matter.

They were as different in personality as appearance. Ryan was one of the few guys I'd ever met taller than my five-eleven, and he was as thin as a blade. His short hair was the same shade as his almost-black eyes, and his deep voice always sent shivers down my spine.

Seth, on the other hand, was only an inch or so shorter than me. He kept his blond hair in a ponytail, his broad shoulders reflected how dedicated he was to his gym time, and his attention to detail was why we always let him run our Advanced Dungeons & Dragons campaigns.

The two of them lived together—Seth rented a room from Ryan. All three of us had become quick friends when I'd started working for the same company as them about two years earlier. I'd gotten over my crushes on both early in our friendship.

A decision made easier by the fact I'd married and divorced in my early twenties, and learned from the experience not to trust myself or my partner in a long-term relationship. I was that bad at reading myself and the people around me. But that didn't mean I had a problem with looking. Or, on occasion, letting fantasy run rampant through my thoughts when I was alone and wanted more than just batteries to help the vibrator do its job.

Dice clattered against the table, and Seth let out a sharp, "Ha!" He looked at Ryan. "You've failed to seduce the fair maiden."

"Not even possible." Ryan sat up, frowning at the dice. "I want a re-roll."

"Nope." Seth shook his head. "No mulligans. Pick up a bar wench, or you'll have to hit the sack alone tonight."

If I squinted, I could make out the red letters on the microwave in the kitchen. Almost two a.m. This had become a ritual for the three of us at our weekly role-playing sessions. Even after everyone else threw in the towel and headed home, we'd stay up long into Saturday morning, waiting to see who would fold first and either fall asleep or call it quits. Tonight we'd been sillier than usual, so we'd be here a while longer. I was fine with that. I was enjoying the evening too much to be the person who tapped out.

"I'm not tired," Ryan announced. "So, after my bath, I'm going for a walk in the woods."

Seth looked up at me, pale eyes hauntingly captivating in the dimly lit living room. "Are you going with him, my lady?"

"Forget that. The bath is free. I'm rinsing off the grime."

"Boring!" Ryan winked at me, no malice in his tone. He gestured to himself. "You could have had all this if you hadn't waited."

My gaze traveled over his lithe frame: the way his T-shirt hugged his torso, the jeans with as many tears as fabric. A throb nagged between my legs, accompanied by a brief flash of letting him strip me down and joining him in an actual bath. I nudged the daydream aside to save for later, trying to keep my expression neutral. "I'll live. I'm sure."

"All right, mister 'bath time is boring now'." Seth tapped his pencil against the table. "What are you doing in the forest that's more interesting?"

Ryan shrugged. "I'm alone for the first time in a month. I've left all my mates in the inn room or bath. I'm jerking off."

Heat flooded my skin thanks to the enticing mental image of freeing Ryan's erection from his torn jeans and stroking his shaft, and I was grateful it was dark in the room.

Seth snorted with laughter. "Roll against your stealth."

Ryan was so screwed. He hadn't put any points into dexterity. Said there was no reason for finesse when he could kill anything with his massive sword.

"What? Why? I left my armor in the room," Ryan protested.

"And you're a klutz even without it. Roll."

Ryan tossed the dice and groaned at the result. "Damn it."

Seth shot me a look I couldn't interpret, and scribbled some notes on the pad in front of him. "You find a nice, empty clearing in the forest, and start to beat one out. Our lovely druid, Ardra, is almost done with her bath when she hears a disconcerting noise outside. She grabs her dressing gown, and races to investigate."

"I don't get dressed first?"

Seth smirked. "No. And you don't hide, or check for traps, or anything else. The only thing out there is the mighty paladin, Galahad."

If there had been anyone else still around, or I hadn't been silly tired and a little turned on, I might have argued that if I already knew who was out there, I wouldn't need to go investigate. But giddiness, and the daydream-induced dampness between my legs, let boldness have its reign. "All right, I'll go investigate."

"You rush through the small patch of woods behind the inn, dressing gown threatening to tear free on the wild growth, and stumble to a stop at the edge of a small clearing, agape at what you see."

I made a flash of decision and rushed forward with my response before I could talk myself out if it. If we were going to role-play this ridiculous scenario, and neither of them was going to balk, I wanted details. "Which is...?"

When Ryan met my gaze this time, something dangerous laced his teasing expression. "Just because I couldn't have you in the bath doesn't mean I'm not fantasizing about it. I'm leaning against a nearby tree, breeches around my ankles, and cock in my hand."

I liked this. Dampness grew in my panties. "And I'm properly impressed. The paladin is well hung."

"Roll against getting caught." Seth's command blended into the delicious tension in the room instead of destroying it.

My ability to move silently through the forest was higher than Ryan's charisma. There was no way I was risking staying hidden in the shadows. I let my impulse continue to drive. "No need. I'm so shocked and compelled by what I see, I gasp and step into the clearing for a better look."

A wicked smile tugged up the corner of Ryan's mouth, and I swore he looked like a big bad wolf about to devour me. In the most delicious and ravenous way possible. "Your appearance catches me off guard, but I've never minded putting on a show. I slow down when I realize your gown has fallen open. It drapes off your tits, and shows me a perfect patch of red fuzz hiding in the V between your legs."

A teeny tiny part of me said I should correct him. I hated my copper-colored hair, so my character was blonde. I wasn't interrupting this, though. In the dim room, with just our voices and his captivating eyes, I could slip into the fantasy we were painting, and it had me wet. "I stare as you stroke up and down. I've never seen such an impressive man before."

"I don't have to be doing this alone, you know." He licked his bottom lip. "You're welcome to join me. I bet the trees you usually fuck don't spread you open the way I would."

There were times when Ryan's direct comments embarrassed me. Now wasn't one of them. "I'm too dumbstruck to leave. I can't stop thinking about letting you have your way with me."

"I close the distance between us in just a few steps, and nudge your robe farther to the side, exposing one fleshy, soft breast. I glide my hand up your ribs, cupping the mound, and dragging a callused thumb over your already rock-hard nipple."

My own nubs twinged in response, aching under my bra as the phantom touch flicked over one. "I let out a soft moan and step closer until your…" I fumbled for a moment. Could I actually talk like this out loud? In the context of the game, yes. "Until your manhood presses into my leg."

His dark stare held me captive now. Watching his lips move as he painted his character's desires. Hearing his seductive voice. "I squeeze and pinch at the pink temptation in my hand, and you squirm under the attention. I trace my mouth down your chest, dropping to my knees as I move to your stomach. My fingers part your pussy. My gods you're wet. I flick my tongue out, and groan at your incredible taste."

Oh gods was right. My thighs squeezed together at the thought of him buried between my legs, licking. "I whimper and tangle my fingers in your hair. This sensation is new and incredible."

"I trace ancient runes over your clit with my tongue as I slide two fingers inside you. You're tight, but slippery. I want you wrapped around my cock before the end of the night. I lick and suck, letting your gasps guide me while I finger fuck you."

This was the single most erotic fantasy I'd ever delved into, and I knew it was because it was all vocal and shared. Something was even more arousing about the fact Seth was still listening to us, and not interrupting. I wanted to be riding Ryan by the end of the night, too. Err, my character did. "You're good at this. Apparently there's some truth to the rumors the village girls spread between each town."

He smirked. "They spread more than rumors. But none of them taste as incredible as you do. You're intoxicating. I devour your pussy, nipping with my teeth as you get more vocal. I want you to come."

I might just from his words. Not really, but maybe. "I'm so close. You hit a spot inside and pleasure explodes through me. I clench around your fingers until my legs are weak and everything is too sensitive to touch. But I want more."

"I help you sink to your knees and sit on the ground in front of you, dick harder than it's ever been and standing at attention. I wonder what your perfect, full lips would feel like wrapped around my cock, but I can't wait for that. I know how soaked you are and I need you riding me. Your pale skin is flushed as you straddle me. With one hand on your hips and the other on my rod, I guide you into place. I want to take this bit slow, but your heat is too tempting. I thrust up, plunging inside you."

I almost arched my back at the thought of him impaling me. My panties were soaked, and I was going to see this through. Wanted him—his paladin, whatever—to come hard because of me. "You're so big it hurts, and I love it. I try and measure your pace by rocking up and down slowly against you."

"I want to stretch this moment out. I glide my hands up your chest, cupping your perfect tits and thumbing your nipples. Your skin is gorgeous in the full moon."

A new voice interrupted the conversation, but Seth's smooth

tone wasn't jarring. It added to the dreamlike quality of the entire moment. "The two of you have made too much noise and the innkeeper is coming to check and make sure everything is all right. He hesitates at the edge of the clearing, dumbstruck and amazed at the scene before him. He's instantly hard at the sight of two bodies intertwined with each other, panting and glistening."

TWO

If I had been turned on before, it was nothing compared to what ratcheted through me at the new arrival. My fantasies had always been about one or the other of them, never both men. I didn't know which I liked more, the thought of Seth getting off by watching us, or the idea he might join in. "Are you simply a passive observer?"

Ryan gripped his leg hard enough I saw the cords and muscles in his arm strain in the dim light, still watching me. "I see the curious interloper over your shoulder, and slide my hands to your back. Raking down your spine, I cup your ass and pull your upper body forward, never letting up on the steady rhythm. I want to pound you hard and fast, but I think you want this more."

Seth picked up the dialog without hesitation. "I drop my breeches as I join you in the clearing. I kneel behind you, and you jump then sigh when I run my hand down your perfect ass. I slip my fingers between your legs from behind, amazed at how incredible you feel. I stroke his cock while I coat my hand in your juices."

I hid a wince. Please don't let that ruin it. Seth was bisexual, and Ryan was as straight as I had ever seen. But the slip in narration didn't break things up. I didn't even know if I could speak at this point. My mouth was dry with anticipation. I didn't have to worry about coming up with a response, though.

"I use your arousal to lube my dick." Seth's voice wasn't as deep, but it still had a hypnotic effect. "I nudge your ass with the head, and in your almost frenzied state, you let me in with little resistance.

Both of them inside me at the same time? My hands twitched and I forced them not to actually move to my breasts and pleading clit. "Gods, this is amazing."

"Filling you with two hard, thick cocks has made you even tighter," Ryan said. "I finger your clit, and you almost come from the contact. As you lean forward, I raise my head up to suck on one of those exhilarating pink nubs that's taunting me. Taking it between my teeth, I nibble and flick at it with my tongue."

"I won't last long," I manage to keep the breathlessness out of my voice. It was true. If we did this much longer, I might not be able to keep my hands out of my pants. Or theirs.

"Your enraptured shouts milk me better than your tight hole," Ryan said. "And as you come a second time, I pound you hard. I grunt at the feelings, and spurt deep inside you when I climax."

"I pull out," Seth added. "Beating my cock, stroking it when I watch the two of you grind, and cover your backside with my orgasm."

"We all collapse on top of each other, spent." There was a hint of strain to Ryan's voice. "After we catch our breath, none of us says anything. We extract ourselves from each other and make our way back to the inn for some of the best sleep we've had in months."

A silence descended on the room. Had we just made a mistake? Were they actually imagining me in that scene the way I had with them, or had this just been a random game?

"Okay, then." Seth finally shattered the still. "Wow. Fortunately, the druid is protected by her gods, and we don't have to deal with pregnancy during this raiding party."

"Good call." Ryan sank back into the cushions with a small exhale.

And just like that, the moment was over. We laughed and joked a little more, but it wasn't much longer before one of them—I wasn't even sure who, or maybe it was both—decided to call it a night.

"It's too late for you to drive home, Tasha." Seth disappeared from the room and returned moments later with a pillow and blanket. "Stay here."

I wasn't going to argue. It was as common as anything for me to crash on Ryan and Seth's couch. I made up my temporary bed, and they said their good nights.

As the house fell silent, sleep evaded me. I stared at the ceiling, images still teasing me, and unresolved need still begging for my attention. Were they both asleep yet? I listened to the house creak, wondering if each new noise was one of them getting up.

I slid a hand under my shirt, hidden by the blanket, and pinched my nipple. I had to bite my lip to keep from letting out a groan of pleasure.

I tweaked and pulled harder, letting snippets of the off-course game roll through my mind. My other hand slid down, unbuttoned my jeans, and dipped under my panties. I really was wet.

I stroked myself slowly, trying to draw out the moment. Something creaked, like footsteps, and I froze, breath catching in my throat. The noise paused nearby. Would they know I wasn't asleep? Was I breathing too loud? Not loud enough?

Would I prefer to get caught, and let whichever of them it was watch, and maybe help? I liked that idea. My clit trembled in response. Seconds later the footsteps resumed, and I heard the bathroom door swing shut. A faint light moved a few inches across the other side of the room, but petered out before it reached me.

A soft grunting drifted toward my ears. I couldn't tell which of them it was, but heat and arousal burned through me when I realized it was the sound of one of them jerking off.

Knowing I wasn't the only one impacted, and part of me hoping to get caught, I resumed my self-attentions. I closed my eyes and let the faint sound from the bathroom penetrate my fantasy. I stroked my swollen button as I imagined Ryan pushing himself deep inside me, while Seth watched, stroking his own cock.

The sounds from the bathroom increased in pace and volume,

and so did my masturbation. I was so close. I worked myself faster, moving my other hand from my tit to slide two fingers inside me. The penetration was enough to push me over the edge, and I arched my back as I came.

Seconds later, the grunts from the bathroom grew more frantic and then abruptly stopped. The toilet flushed, the footsteps crossed the room, and a bedroom door closed.

I sank back onto the couch, mentally and physically spent, and drifted into a solid sleep.

I NEEDED coffee in a serious way. Who made people come into the office at six-thirty for a conference call? Besides my boss, apparently. I had a laptop, a cell phone, and a perfectly good pair of PJ's no one would have noticed I was wearing. I could have taken the call from home just fine.

In contrast to when I'd arrived an hour and a half ago, all the lights on the floor were on now, and people were filling the desks. I rubbed my eyes to try and wake myself up as I wove through the maze of cubicles back to my own.

The one nice thing about the early meeting had been that it took my mind off what happened over the weekend with Seth and Ryan. It was just a spontaneous thing, but ever since Friday night, fantasy and images had teased me, most of them involving being pinned between both guys, and feeling hands in more places at once than should have been possible. The reminder sent heat rushing through me, and an insistent throb echoed between my legs.

Now was definitely not the time to be entertaining those thoughts. Not in the middle of the office, knowing the entire thing had been a game to both of them. Especially after I'd run out of the house this morning without any makeup and no time to do anything with my out-of-control curls besides pull them back and hope my hair didn't frizz. I just wasn't feeling the sexy those fantasies required.

I dropped into my chair with a heavy sigh, but a trace of my exhaustion vanished when I went to log into my computer. A cup of coffee sat in front of my keyboard, with TASHA scrawled on the sleeve in Seth's familiar block-letter handwriting. Above my name was a pair of horns, with a halo falling off one. Despite my Monday morning grumbles, a smile overtook my face. He didn't always do things like that, but he'd known I had an unreasonably early meeting today. Maybe everything was back to normal between us after all.

I sent him a quick thank you over messenger, wishing I had time for more chatting. But there were deadlines to meet, and clients to please. I had only officially been a project manager for about six months, and this was my first solo assignment. So far, everything was going smoothly, and I intended to keep it that way. I dove into double-checking the project milestones to make sure we were on track, and quickly lost myself in time.

My cell phone rang, and after a brief glance at the "Unknown Number", I ignored it. I'd learned too much from years of fighting off bill collectors for debts my ex-husband had raked up in my name. One of the big lessons was to never take those calls in the office, especially during months I couldn't afford another payment.

I dropped back into what I was doing. The morning noise faded into the background as I worked.

"Hey, Tash." Ryan's greeting dragged me back to the here and now, and his playful tug on my ponytail sent an unexpected, but pleasant, flicker of want through me.

A brief image flashed in my head of him pulling my hair hard while he slid inside me from behind. I banished the thought before my panties could get too damp, and spun to face him. "Morning."

He pulled up a nearby chair, and dropped into it. He studied me for a minute. The attention lasted long enough for concern to flit in. Had I spilled coffee on my sweater? Did I look that bad without any mascara and eyeliner?

"You look good today." A grin broke his serious expression. "It's the blue top with your eyes or something."

"Thanks." The compliment caught me off-guard and heat rushed under my skin. He was just being polite, right? Not like I was going to ask for clarification. I'd take the compliment for what it was. "What's up?"

His brows furrowed for a moment, then his casual demeanor slipped back in, and his voice dropped in volume. "Kitner says Zedophap has an issue with their config."

It might have sounded like a secret code to anyone else, but to me, Mark Kitner was in senior management and in charge of our department, Zedophap was the client account I was managing, and as the business analyst on the project, Ryan was in charge of working with them to make sure we configured our product to their specifications. And I knew for a fact, after that morning's phone call, there were no issues or concerns. "Nope. You're clear."

"You're the best." He hopped to his feet. "You joining me and Seth for lunch today?"

"Only if we go somewhere fast."

"You'd enjoy it a lot more if we took our time." He trailed his fingers lightly along the back of my neck, sending pleasant tremors racing over my skin.

My nipples tightened at the light touch, and my belly clenched. It took every ounce of my restraint not to lean into the teasing gesture with a sigh. This kind of joking wasn't new for us. I needed to bring my hormones under control. "I'll see what I can do."

"Killer." He gave my ponytail a final tug, and seconds later dropped into his own cube.

As I shifted in my seat to get back to work, the lace of my bra slid across my breasts, making my nipples harder. How had that one little moment turned me on so much?

"Natasha." Mark's sharp tone squashed my growing arousal. "Do you have a few minutes?"

I'd always hated that question, especially when it came from my boss. If I said I had time, did that mean I wasn't working hard enough? But if I said I was busy, would it sound like a brush off? Besides, its vague nature frequently meant bad things. I always just settled for, "What did you need?"

He nodded into his office. "It'll be fast."

That sounded bad. Mark waited until I was seated in one of the chairs across from his desk, before closing the door and taking his own seat. He clucked his tongue against the roof of his mouth. "We have an issue."

Shit. I let my concern leak onto my face. "With Zedophap?"

He nodded. "I just got off the phone with their VP of marketing. Apparently, they started doing some basic user acceptance testing first thing this morning, and nothing is working like they want it to."

A million possibilities raced through my head. Bad programming, poor data entry, mismanaged client expectations. Where to start? Oh, right. "They said on the call everything was going fine."

He sighed and leaned forward, forearms resting on the edge of his desk, and fingers interlocked. "That's part of the problem." His tone was grave, and his forehead bunched into wrinkles. "They're not comfortable bringing this up with you, because they say you haven't handled their concerns in the past."

My stomach clenched, and indignation rose inside me. I tempered it as best I could. "I didn't know there was anything outstanding."

"When I gave you this job, I warned you that a project manager has to be the bad guy sometimes."

I remembered that conversation distinctly. As I sat in front of him now, racking my brain, I couldn't think of why that was relevant. "You did."

"If there's someone on this team who's not pulling their weight, I need to know."

My insides wrenched a little more. Did he have someone specific in mind? "As far as I know, everyone's doing great."

He sighed, and looked at his hands for a moment before meeting my gaze again. "I'm trying to be polite about this, Natasha. This is a big client, and we can't afford to lose them. I understand working as a team, and camaraderie and all that. I'm not asking you to hang someone out to dry with the client, but if you're having an issue, and you can't deal with it, you need to tell me who's causing the problem."

He took a deep breath, eyes never leaving mine. "If we lose

Zedophap—if they do something like sue us for breach of contract —someone is going to lose their job. I don't want it to be you if you're not at fault. If it's someone else, and we can fix this now, I'd rather do that. I don't want to have to let anyone go."

I swallowed the bile rising in my throat. I might have wondered how idle the threat was, but I'd seen it happen before on botched implementations. The bigger issue was I didn't know what was wrong. How was I supposed to discipline someone if I didn't see a problem? "I understand."

"I knew you would. I'll forward you their email. Let's track this down quickly and deal with it quietly."

"Yeah. Completely."

His smile returned, and he turned to his computer. "Thanks for your time."

I was numb as I headed back to my desk. I was already living on floated checks and past-due promises. I couldn't afford to lose my job. There had to be a way to make things right. Someone must be overreacting. I'd find the problem, we'd deal with it, and everything would be fine.

I opened Mark's email as soon as I sat down. For the next few hours, I pored through everything related to the complaints, and my chest ached more and more as I dug. All indicators pointed to Ryan. And it wasn't just a little screw-up. It was jaw-dropping, contract-violating, facing-off-a-beholder-who-just-decided-to-tentacle-fuck-us huge.

I didn't want to have this conversation. I didn't have a choice.

THREE

"Ready for lunch?" Seth stopped on the other side of my chest-high cubicle, resting his arms on top.

My stomach growled in response, and I mentally told it to shut up. I didn't have time for lunch. Maybe I shouldn't have said yes to Ryan's invite so easily this morning. Then again, when I'd talked to him I hadn't known my work world was imploding. I opened my mouth to tell them to go without me.

"You have to eat." Ryan slid into the empty spot next to Seth. "Vending machine food doesn't count."

Then again, maybe this would be the perfect chance to ask him what was going on with Zedophap. We could lessen the sting over food and then fix everything when we got back. The snippet of a plan didn't completely ease my tension, but it helped. I grabbed my purse and locked my computer. "I'm in. Where we going?"

"Fresh Mex," Seth said as we made our way toward the elevators. "Fish taco day."

Ryan snorted. I rolled my eyes. We all joked and laughed as we walked across the street to the dive that made some of the best food anywhere near the office. Any lingering doubt I'd had about things being awkward after our vocal session over the weekend evaporated.

We were all predictable with our orders. Seth would get the daily special, Ryan would want a smothered-pork burrito, and I always opted for the tortilla soup—cheap and hearty enough to get me through the day without starving. They let me order first. I handed over my debit card. A twitch throbbed behind my eye when the cashier swiped it, waited a few seconds and then frowned.

She gave me a nervous smile. "Sorry. Let me try again."

There was nothing to worry about. It was just a register screw-up, it would be—

She handed the card back to me. "I'm sorry. It's declined. Do you want to pay some other way?"

Shit. I gave her my most confident smile, and rifled through my purse, pretending to look for cash I knew wasn't there. It had only been a couple of days since payday. I'd just dropped my rent check off that morning, so there was no way that had cleared yet, and even if it had, I should have had plenty of money left. Embarrassment mingled with my creeping panic.

A hand rested on my shoulder, the familiar heat drawing me from my spiraling thoughts. "I've got it." Ryan's whisper was barely loud enough for my ears. His voice returned to regular volume. "We're together."

I gave him a grateful smile as we staked out an empty table and waited for Seth. "I'll pay you back. I don't know what happened. I just have to call my bank. Thank you so mu—"

"Don't worry about it." He cut me off before my panic made me ramble out of control. "Chill. Enjoy your lunch. We're even."

"You all right?" Seth asked as he dropped into the empty seat, and set his order number on the edge of the table next to ours.

I forced a smile into place. I wasn't discussing my money problems with either of them. It had taken me months to even tell them I'd been married once upon a time. "Typical Monday, you know? Sucky here and there and everywhere. It'll pass."

Seth studied me, pale eyes trying to pry into my soul, and I turned my attention to chasing the ice in my drink with my straw. A heavy silence fell over the table. Someone set our food in front of us, but I was too distracted to dive in. I needed to ask Ryan about the Zedophap project. Just spit it out.

"Split the difference?" Ryan cut into my hesitation, even though the words triggered an instinct that told me he wasn't talking to me.

Seth took a moment to respond. "He is pretty cute."

Irritation crawled under my skin. Great. Not this. I followed their gazes toward a couple on the other side of the room. She was short and curvy with straight, blonde hair—basically the exact opposite of my physical appearance. He was okay. Not gorgeous, but better than average, and so immaculately dressed I wondered if his T-shirt was pressed. They were scowling at each other in some sort of silent-argument, death-match-stare-down.

The point of Ryan and Seth's *split the difference* was to find an arguing couple, be the friendly stranger with a shoulder to cry on, and if they did things right, Ryan would go home with her number, and Seth with his. My aggravation bubbled up, carried by the tensions of the day. "Could you two not do this? Just this once? Could you maybe let the arguing couples of the world try and work things out on their own for the day?" I winced at the edge in my own voice. *Way to blow things out of proportion, me.*

Two heads whirled in my direction. Seth studied me, brows furrowed. "Are you sure you're okay?"

Ryan's eyes narrowed and he turned back to his food. "Hormonal."

That single word, even though a tiny part of me knew he was teasing, broke something inside. I let out a soft growl and turned my attention to him. I adored everything he did for me, and I felt bad snipping at him since he'd just saved me at the cash register, but sometimes it was as if he just didn't pay attention. Which, now that I thought about it, had to have been what happened at work. "What's going on with Zedophap?"

His jaw opened and then snapped shut again, and his brow furrowed. "Um… stuff? You tell me. You're in charge and you said nothing was wrong."

Not helpful. "Except apparently their configuration is completely screwed up." I didn't want to handle things so aggressively. I needed to dial it back, but the morning had destroyed a portion of my control. I had to fix this. I couldn't lose my job.

"You told me this morning they were cool. Also, not even possible." He turned his attention back to his food. "I double and triple checked. Everything is in order."

And now he was brushing me off. More of my hesitation evaporated, replaced with annoyance. "Are you sure?"

He finally gave me his full attention. "You don't trust me?" A sliver of hurt lingered behind his stare.

I pulled my gaze away first. How could those dark eyes fill me with so much guilt over something that wasn't my fault? This wasn't getting me anywhere. How was I supposed to fix it if he wouldn't even own the problem? Frustration and ambivalence clawed at my skull, making my head ache. I stared at my soup, not daring to focus on anything else. "Just forget it."

"Oh, sure. You throw my reassurances back in my face, and I should just forget it?"

"Something's definitely wrong." Seth cut into the tension.

I whirled on him. "You think?" I shouldn't be taking this out on him at all. I needed to stop now. But worry was gnawing my gut alive. If Ryan didn't take responsibility, my job was at risk. I could fix the problems, but I couldn't hang him out to dry. I also couldn't let it happen again. I dropped my face into my hands. Gods this bit. "Did I mention the sucky Monday bullshit?"

"But you were a little scarce on the details." Seth scooted his chair closer, and tilted his face until it was under mine. "Boo."

A smile slipped out without my permission at his antics. "I'll fix it. It's not a big deal." I didn't know how I'd do it, but this conversation wasn't getting me anywhere.

"You sure?" He traced a line up the top of my leg, drawing away some of my tension. The light contact teased me with ideas that had nothing to do with fixing the issues at work. Of working off all this stress by finding a hidden corner with him. Of letting those skilled fingers roam over me.

What was wrong with me? Lusting after both of them in a single day like this. And still I couldn't stop staring into Seth's pale eyes.

A loud screech cut through the moment, chair legs sliding on tile against their will. "I have to get back to work." Ryan was on his feet. He only looked at me for a moment, jaw set. "Apparently, I'm not doing something right."

The accusation in his tone pulled out my guilt. "I didn't mean—"

"Yeah, you did."

Damn it. I slouched in my chair. I knew his temper well enough to realize I couldn't go after him right now. I looked at Seth again. "Can you pin him down long enough for me to apologize later?"

His smile vanished, too. His, "sure," was flat.

Now what? I rolled the last few minutes through my thoughts, and while it was true I'd started to lash out at Seth, I'd reeled that in quickly.

And then, just as quickly as it had appeared, his sour expression evaporated. "You know I will. Besides, we're going to that thing tonight. He's not going to miss it, and you can apologize then."

"Thing...?" We didn't do stuff on Monday nights.

"OT?"

Original trilogy. That jogged my memory loose. I couldn't believe I'd forgotten about it. A local movie theater was doing screenings of the extended edition Star Wars movies, one a night, all week long. They were showing them in the order they'd been released, instead of in the order of the stories. The tickets had been expensive, so I'd had to pick which one I wanted to see. We'd agreed on Episode IV. Ryan had offered to pick up the rest for me, but I couldn't let him do that. The reminder tugged in more guilt and confusion over what just happened.

Seth nudged me with his shoulder. "I can't believe you forgot."

"I guess I'm more distracted than I realized."

He moved his chair even closer. "Turn. Back toward me."

Curious, but not in any kind of mood to argue, I did what he said. When his fingers dug into my shoulders, a soft groan slipped from my throat.

"You need to chill." His voice was soft. He kneaded away the tension. "You're so tight."

The innuendo-laden words, combined with his warm breath against the back of my neck, slid under my skin, and tempted me. When I closed my eyes, I could picture the vivid scene we'd painted on Friday night. Or better, I could wrap myself in what was happening now and take it a step further. Imagining his hands sliding lower. Cupping my breasts. Pinching my nipples through lace while he sucked on my shoulder.

Wetness pooled between my legs as his fingers dug deeper, and the fantasy grew more detailed.

I forced my eyes open and tried to pull away without jerking out of his touch. I couldn't do this with either one of them. I couldn't destroy friendships because I was daydreaming about guys who didn't see me as anything more than a gaming buddy. I pushed back from the table. "I should get back. I have so much waiting for me."

"No worries. I've got stuff to do too." His smile looked forced. Or I wanted it to. I must be projecting. I knew from experience how horrible I was at reading men.

We were halfway back to the office, neither of us saying much of anything, when my stomach growled and reminded me I'd completely ignored my food. It was a tiny thing, but it was enough to pull all my frustration back to the surface. What was I going to do? About Seth and Ryan, about work, about money? About anything.

FOUR

When I got back to my desk, my work and cell phone showed twin missed calls. I would have suspected an overambitious bill collector, but there were voicemails to go along with them. It took me a minute to recognize the number, and my gut sank.

I dialed into my cell phone quickly, any thoughts of missed lunch evaporating as I listened to the message. My landlord wanted me to know she'd called to verify funds on my rent check, and was told I couldn't cover it. I muttered every curse I knew as I wandered toward a more private part of the building, already calling my bank.

My balance was twenty-two cents? What the hell? Yes, to speak to a teller. I tried deep breaths to calm myself as the phone rang. It wasn't a big deal. I'd find out it was a data entry error. My money was still there, right? My gut turned in on itself, already knowing better than my head that I wouldn't be that lucky.

Someone finally answered, and I swear my heart leaped into my throat. I gave her my name and account number. "I need to find out what this twelve-hundred dollar withdrawal is on my checking account."

"Sure, I can help with that." Her cheer set my teeth on edge.

Keys clacked over the phone, and she made a couple of "hmm" sounds. "Can I have you hold for a minute?"

"Uh, sure?"

She had to answer a question for someone else, right? It wasn't anything to do with me. There was no hold music. Just a click that echoed over the line every fifteen seconds or so. Which, I decided after too many of them, was definitely worse.

"Natasha?" My chest almost exploded when she came back on the line. "Sorry about that. I had to double-check something."

"Of course." I couldn't keep the strain from my voice. "Is everything all right?"

"It looks like the withdrawal is an electronic debit from a First Check Central."

One of his post-dated checks. Shit. In the case of judgments, at least I got a warning, and lawyers tended to be easier to deal with than bill collectors, as long as I was willing to pay something.

But with the post-dated check places, since the check was the collateral, their contract allowed them to go directly to the bank account for their money if they didn't get paid. I just hadn't expected any of those loans to still be outstanding.

I wanted to scream and yell and toss out every vulgar word in existence. But it wasn't her fault. Goddamn my ex. "Can you give me the number of who it came from?"

"Sure. But we can't reverse the charge."

"No, of course not. I understand."

I scrambled to find a pen and paper in my purse, and wrote down the information she gave me. Panic welled up inside. I was broke, I didn't get paid for almost two weeks, and my rent was already late. Did I have enough ramen and macaroni and cheese in the house to eat until payday?

I leaned against a nearby wall and forced myself to not lose it. Freaking out wasn't going to help me. I grasped for strands of reason and broke the problem down logically. What bills could I shift to next paycheck?

Things would be tight, and I couldn't eat out for a few weeks, but I could make the money balance. I could plead with my land-lord. I could get an extension on my next car payment. Hopefully.

I made my way back to my desk, rolling the better parts of my plan over and over in my head, certain I could make this work. As long as I didn't linger too long on the not so great bits of my idea—like missing a couple of meals and skipping the coffee—it felt like I had a solution.

I hadn't even had a chance to sit yet when Mark poked his head out of his office and caught my eye. "You have a minute?"

Something told me I didn't want to have this conversation. But it wasn't as if I had a choice. My paycheck was the only thing keeping me from living on the streets, and even then only barely. Speaking of, I still needed to call my landlord. Beg her for more time. She was kind, but I also knew she was tired of my excuses.

The situation jumbled in my head as I made myself comfortable in Mark's office. Solutions and problems and two weeks of cheap starch-for-meals taunted me. I had a jar of change, right? It had only been a couple of months since I cashed it out, but there were probably ten or twenty bucks of coins in there. I could buy oatmeal and some other basics.

"I need to know what's happening with Zedophap." Mark's severe tone dragged me back to the now, and I realized the door was closed once again. Whatever this was, he didn't want eavesdroppers.

At least I had an answer to this. Mostly. "I've got it under control," I assured him. "I know where the issue happened, and I'm putting steps in place to make sure we can resolve it and still meet our milestones." My gaze drifted absentmindedly to a stack of papers on his desk. I tended to read whatever was there upside-down, just to see if it was interesting. It was a habit I always felt bad about, but had never managed to break.

This definitely ranked on the interesting scale. It was a copy of our configuration document, but not the one Ryan had handed to me. Even at a glance, I could tell it was so different from Ryan's, there was no way things would have worked the way the client expected.

He nodded at his monitor, and the email on the screen. "I'm

afraid it's more serious than that."

He had to be kidding me. Was this the universe's day to shit on me? "How did we go from fine on the call this morning to more serious than just making things right?"

He shifted the papers around on his desk, sliding the curious document underneath other things, but not before I caught the name of a different business analyst up top. So odd.

"Their legal contacted us. They're talking about arbitration and possible breach of contract."

Whoa. That didn't happen. Not in a single day for sure. People tossed the threat around all the time, but no one acted on it. "What do we do?"

"Do you know where the breakdown happened?"

"It was Ryan, but we're fixing it." The words tumbled out as I dug through my thoughts for solutions. "We can show them an updated timeline by the end of the day. If I talk to the data group, they'll put in a couple extra hours to make sure the existing issues are fixed." I hated to call in that kind of favor from Seth, but I knew he'd help me out. I'd have to owe him a drink. Sometime next year.

I just didn't know why Ryan had so seriously dropped the ball. "No one's losing their jobs, right?"

Mark's face pinched. "I hope not. But your group isn't the only team that's had problems with this account. Marketing hasn't delivered, the call center made promises they can't possibly keep. You need to know how critical this is. And I should warn you, it's not usually the 'grunts' who take the heat for things like this. Since you're managing this part of the implementation, if layoffs happen..."

It would be my head on the chopping block. I didn't need him to finish. "I get it. I'm on it, I promise."

My feet felt like they were boxed in concrete as I trudged out of Mark's office. I had a plan. I could make it all work. As long as I told myself that over and over, there was no room in my head for doubt.

Ryan looked up from his desk when I crossed the room, but I couldn't meet his gaze. And I still needed to call my landlord. Damnit damnit damnit damnit damnit.

FIVE

I couldn't get ahold of my landlord, so I left her a rambling, probably convoluted, explanation-apology-plea-for-forgiveness, and hoped for the best. Fortunately, we'd bought the Star Wars tickets months earlier. I considered scalping mine but decided instead to give myself one last luxury. I got to enjoy the show on the big screen, surrounded by fans who cheered when the opening text scrolled, and hushed the moment the THX logo grew quiet, the way Lucas intended.

By the time the movie ended, it was almost midnight, and most of the stress of the day had slipped to the back of my mind. I could deal with it all in the morning. There was nothing I could do before tomorrow except enjoy the night.

We stayed through the closing credits, and were some of the last people to leave the theater. My philosophy at the movies was if we had been in a rush, we wouldn't be there. Waiting a couple extra minutes meant we didn't have to fight traffic leaving the parking lot. Not that there would be much tonight. This had been the latest showing in the place, and while the theater had been packed, it was still just one out of twenty-four.

Our conversation was casual as we pushed out a side door,

and more of my stress ebbed. Whatever weird tension had happened at lunch was in the past. We joked and talked as we made our way to the far corner of the parking lot. Seth liked to park way out there because...well, he said it was because it wouldn't hurt us to walk. But I knew it was more because his BMW was his baby, and he felt like it was safer away from the other cars.

As we drew closer, the darkness closed in around us, and I realized the parking lot lights in the entire section were out. "Ooh, dark and creepy. What if there are bad things hiding in the shadows?"

"Don't worry, we'll protect you." Ryan tossed an arm around my shoulder, his voice sliding into the same false bravado he used when he was playing his paladin.

It was just a friendly gesture, like so many hundreds he'd made before. But the part of my mind that had been out of control all day honed in on the warm contact. The familiar security and at the same time, bold assumption in the gesture. I was too drained from the day to completely suppress my response. I teased back, "What if you're the big-bad I need protecting from?"

We'd reached the car, and there was no one else nearby. All the other filmgoers were parked far enough away their voices barely reached us. Even then, most of them were already gone.

"You've got a good point." Seth grabbed my wrists loosely and tugged them behind my back. I could have broken away if I wanted, but the heat of his palms against my skin held me captive more than his grip. His hot words caressed the back of my neck. "It's dark enough no one will see us."

I didn't want to hold back the fantasies. Need coursed through me, driving my response. "So what's to stop you from taking advantage of the situation?"

Ryan stepped closer, pinning me between the two. "Only you."

Hesitation wormed up inside. These were my two best friends. Even if I had been dreaming about Ryan yanking my hair and screwing me hard, or Seth sliding his fingers inside me, it didn't mean I was willing to surrender our current bond over it. "I still have to look you in the eye in the morning."

"That wasn't a problem after Friday night." Seth's lips glided over my skin.

A whimper slipped from my throat, and my heart threatened to hammer out of my chest. "That was just a game."

"So's this." Ryan traced a finger over my bottom lip, and my mouth parted at the sensation. "One where everyone wins, and then we go on with life the next day."

"Say the word and we won't play." Seth's thumb stroked the tender flesh on the inside of my arm.

Every inch of me ached for more. A kiss, a touch. Given how wet I was, if I shifted my weight, I'd slip and slide. Had they planned this? Did I care whether the moment was spontaneous? "Let's play."

Ryan pressed against me, and dipped his head. His teeth skittered along my throat and the hollow below. "I've been thinking, ever since Friday night." He dropped his fingers below the waistband of my jeans enough to tease, but didn't move lower. "How much I'd like to make that scene real. To fuck you hard and fast until you scream my name, while Seth watches, stroking his cock."

Oh geez. My knees wobbled, but the two of them were pressed close enough they'd hold me up if I stumbled. I didn't know which turned me on more. The thought of Ryan buried inside me, or the idea of being a private peep show for Seth.

"Still want to play?" Ryan's fingers skated over the top of my hip, and I thrust toward his touch before I realized what I was doing.

I managed a breathy, "Yes."

"You sure?" He gave me a wicked grin. "You're not just being polite? How do I know you mean it?"

My panties were practically soaked; that was a reasonable indicator. I worked a hand free from Seth's grip, and slid my fingers down the back of Ryan's arm, nudging it lower. "Check for yourself."

His hand moved down the front of my jeans, and I gasped when his fingers brushed my mound.

"You're so wet." He spread my pussy lips and dipped between.

When he nudged my swollen clit, a shock of pleasure ripped through me. What if someone caught us? The idea heightened my arousal. We'd have to be careful.

With his free hand, he undid the button on my jeans and dragged down my zipper. He stroked my slit slowly, methodically, drawing near my aching sex, but not touching it again. I rocked my hips in time to the rhythm, pushing for more with each pass.

"So hot." Seth's breath caressed my skin. He let go of my other wrist, and slid his hands under my shirt. His rough palms against my bare stomach were another enticing point of contact. When he pushed one breast out of my bra, the sensation sparked across every inch of me. He tweaked my nipple and I pressed my ass back against him, grinding against his hard length. His groan mingled with mine when he rolled my pink nub between his fingers.

I found the bulge in Ryan's jeans, and he sucked in a sharp breath through his teeth when I stroked him through the rough fabric.

I inhaled sharply when he finally found my aching clit again. I rocked between the two as Seth pinched hard, and Ryan caressed. Every time I rolled toward the edge of climax, Ryan eased off. I caught my bottom lip between my teeth, and fixed a desperate gaze on him. "Please?" The word came out breathlessly.

He gave me a wicked grin. "Please what?"

"I'm so close," I whimpered.

He caught my earlobe in his teeth, voice a low growl against my skin. "Beg me, Tash. Tell me what you want."

I couldn't say that. Not here. Even in the privacy of a house, I'd have a hard time with it. I shook my head.

"It's easy," he coaxed as he dragged his nose up the edge of my neck. His fingers dipped near my opening and then pulled away to tease my clit until my hips bucked, and he eased off again. "You don't have to scream. That can wait until we get home."

Oh gods, he had more in mind? The thought short-circuited my brain, and I pushed out the plea. "Please, Ryan. I'm so close. Let me come?"

He plunged his fingers inside me with a sudden thrust, and I had to bite the inside of my cheek to keep from crying out. His thumb found my clit, and he rubbed hard and fast, drawing tight circles. Orgasm rolled through me, and I ground against his hand when I came. My legs wobbled, but I had been right, the two of them kept me upright.

Ryan eased off down below as he pressed his forehead to mine. "We need privacy. Your place is closer."

I nodded, not sure I could speak.

"You ready to put on a show?"

"Oh, fuck yes." Seth's whisper echoed in my head, and he tugged me back into his stiff cock one more time before letting me go.

SIX

I t took the last of my focus to fumble with my keys long enough to let us into my apartment. The moment we were inside, Ryan kicked the door shut and pinned me against it, arms over my head. "Now, I want to hear you scream."

I was going to argue the neighbors might not like that, but just then I didn't care. The entire ride home had been a series of exchanged teasing gropes. Me sliding my hand along Seth's inner thigh and stroking him through his jeans. Ryan reaching up from the back seat to cup my breasts.

Now that we were inside, Ryan held me in place, lowered his head to my neck, and sucked the sensitive flesh, biting hard occasionally and making my head swim. His voice low but commanding when he finally let up. "See, Seth doesn't tell anyone this, but he's a voyeur." He let go of my wrists to yank my shirt over my head. I was certain something tore in the process, and positive I didn't care.

Heat and desire flooded me when two pairs of eyes raked over me.

Ryan continued. "But I don't think you're like that. I think you like the idea of being watched."

33

So much more than I'd ever realized before about an hour ago. "Maybe."

"Good." He followed my spine with a series of tantalizing taps until he reached my bra. More fluidly than I think even I was capable of, he twisted the clasps and snapped the lingerie open. He dragged the straps down my arms. I didn't think it was possible, but under his attention, my nipples got even harder. I heard a zipper drag down, and behind him I saw Seth drop into an easy chair, dick in hand, and slowly start to stroke. He really was well hung. What would it feel like to have that inside me?

Ryan trailed his lips down my collarbone and flicked a tongue over a hard pink nub. He grabbed my other breast, kneading one while he nibbled the other. The sensation was incredible, but I wanted more. I tugged the bottom of his shirt, and he broke away long enough for me to pull it over his head and toss it aside. He was so slender. I traced my fingers up his sides, marveling at every dip and nuance against my touch. When I dragged across one dark-brown nipple, he inhaled sharply and flicked his tongue fast and furious. I used my thumb to imitate his pace, and he moaned against my skin.

My other hand dropped to his crotch, and I found his erection again, stiff and eager through denim. I teased the bulge, and he jerked back with a grunt. He grabbed both of my wrists again. The rough gesture sent a spike of need through me.

Ryan pushed me toward the couch. "I'm so glad I bought condoms this morning."

Part of me wanted to read something into his comment, but I was focused on other things. When he spun me away from him, I caught Seth's gaze. He was still slowly stroking his cock, breathing heavily, and tiny smile played on his lips. Seeing that made me even wetter. I wanted him to get off watching us.

Ryan's front pressed into my back, and he made quick work of the button on my jeans. The zipper groaned open on its own when he yanked my bottoms to the ground, cotton and denim drawing friction as they were pushed aside.

He rested a hand on the middle of my back and pushed me forward. "Lean over the back of the couch."

I did as I was told, feeling more exposed than I ever had, and thrilled by every minute of it.

"I've always loved your ass." He gave it a light slap. "It looks even better bare."

The sting of his palm drew a new gasp from me.

"You like that?" He chuckled. He slapped one cheek again, harder this time. The pain was balanced by the pleasure of my pussy lips sliding together and vibrating around my engorged sex. He spanked me four or five more times.

As much as I enjoyed the new sensation, I wanted more. I forced the words out, loving the way they tasted rolling over my tongue. "I want you to fuck me."

His hand cupped a butt cheek and slid forward, fingers dipping in my wet, anxious opening. "I like the sound of that."

Me too. From behind, I heard his buckle clang, a zipper slide down, and the rip of foil. My anticipation spiked. My breath tore out in anxious, jagged pants. His fingers slid along my slit one more time, before the head of his cock nudged me.

He pushed inside with a single, hard thrust, and I cried out.

"Jesus." His words glided on my skin. "I'm not going to last long. You feel so good. So fucking tight."

I wanted to reply, but every time I managed to find the words, he slammed into my G-spot, slapping against my still tender behind with every grunt.

I was so close. I rode the edge of climax, head growing light and every sensation blurring into one another. When he found my clit again, it was like flipping a switch. "Oh, gods, Ryan, yes." I couldn't believe what was tearing from my throat, but it felt so intense. The orgasm flooded me, peaking again when his grunts reached my ears.

"I'm going to come, Tash. You're so tight. You fit perfectly on my cock." The words trailed off in a series of groans and frantic pounding. In the background, I was vaguely aware of Seth moaning, too.

Then everything slowed to as stop, and silence crashed in around us.

Ryan slipped out of me. He wrapped his hands around my waist and helped me stand. I wasn't sure my legs would support me, but he held me up. His cheek rested against my back, and his thumbs traced over my ribs. "Fuck, you're amazing."

I wanted to echo the sentiment, but I couldn't find the breath. I leaned into him, memorizing every lingering touch, and letting it meld with the bits of me that still stung pleasantly. "Ditto."

I woke up the next morning to a warm body pressed against my back, and an arm draping over my stomach. I inhaled deeply, searing the memory of Seth's aftershave mixed with sex into my mind. Had last night really happened? After we'd all caught our breath, any remaining clothes came off, and I sucked Seth off while Ryan screwed me from behind again. Yeah, that had really happened. Wow.

Seth's hand glided up my stomach and brushed the bottom of my breast. "Morning, Tasha."

"Mmm…" I arched my back at the teasing contact, and need throbbed between my legs. I wasn't going to dwell on if this was awkward or not. We'd agreed last night it was just fun and games. A pang echoed inside at the idea this wouldn't happen again, and I pushed it away. I couldn't get attached to them, partly because I'd never be able to choose, but mostly because I wasn't going to scare either guy off by being *that girl* who didn't know the difference between sex and love.

That didn't mean I was in a rush to extract myself from Seth's arms. Or that I could ignore the hard length pressed into my back, and how wet I was getting as he drew closer to my nipple, but never quite touched the rigid nub.

"We have an eight a.m." Disappointment tempered his tone. "Otherwise, there are so many things I'd like to do to you. Hell, I'm tempted anyway."

Damn it. Why did work have to be so…consistent? I wiggled my ass against his erection as one final tease and reminder and then reluctantly rolled away. "I guess you're right."

As I climbed out of bed, he grabbed my wrist and pulled me back to my knees on the mattress. He sat up in front of me, and rested a hand at the back of my neck, light eyes locked on mine. "Even though it was *just a game*, I had an incredible time last night."

Did he sound disappointed the night before hadn't meant anything? Before I could question the hesitation in his statement, he pressed his lips to mine. The soft kiss seeped into my senses, searing my thoughts. I leaned into him with a groan. Electricity danced along my skin when his tongue dove into my mouth. His dick dug into my bare stomach, tempting me. I trailed my fingers along his chest, seconds away from moving my hands lower. He held my head captive and deepened the kiss, crushing my lips into my teeth.

Every inch of me was on fire with need. We could miss our meeting, right? I nipped at his bottom lip, and let my palm slide down.

He broke away with a gasp, stopping me before I could wrap my fingers around his cock. His hooded gaze swept over me, his voice an octave lower than normal. "So, so tempting."

I'd have to settle for that. It was still a fantastic way to end a fantastic fling. I caught my bottom lip between my teeth. "Had to try."

Something occurred to me, and I strained my ears for a second, listening for any other sounds in the small apartment. Nope, nothing. "Where's Ryan?"

Seth's shoulders slumped. "Early meeting. He had to jet."

"Oh." I needed to keep the disappointment from my voice. It's not as if I could expect him to wake me up. Hell, I was lucky Seth had stuck around. I shifted my weight and the slickness between my legs was obvious. I was *really* lucky Seth had stuck around.

"Yeah." He scrambled to his feet.

With the morning light peeking through the blinds, I got to see what had been shadowed the night before. He really was gorgeous. Just the right amount of muscle tone, handsome face, and—my gaze

37

paused on his crotch—as well hung as his roommate. The thought flushed my skin.

I really needed to get ready for work, and if I asked him to join me in the shower, I was sure that would cross a line, and make us both late. "Do you need me to drop you off at home?"

"Sure." His enthusiasm sounded forced.

Had I missed something?

SEVEN

Would things be different with Ryan this morning? Conversation with Seth had felt forced in the car, but he assured me several times we were fine. By the time I dropped him off, he'd relaxed enough I believed him. Would I have to go through the same ritual with Ryan? He wasn't at his desk when I got in, and a trickle of disappointment joined my paranoia.

I forced myself to sit and finish prepping for our meeting. It was another client call, this one with the entire team. I'd sent my updated timeline to Mark yesterday afternoon, and even though he hadn't signed off, he would.

"Hey, Tash." Ryan tugged a few loose strands of my hair, and relief rushed a smile onto my face. "Sleep well last night?"

Pink flooded my cheeks. "Better than in a long time."

"Glad to hear it. " He moved back to his own cube and dropped into his seat.

That seemed to go okay. Nothing to worry about, we were all still friends. Except I knew my fantasies were going to be vivid and rampant and involving one or the other or both of them for a long time. But that was only barely different from before, right?

Seth walked in with just minutes to spare before the meeting, and gave us both a weak smile as we all took our seats in the conference room. I was surprised to see Mark already there, his laptop hooked up to the online meeting and projector. Normally that would be my job. Worry leaked into my thoughts.

No big deal. He was just making sure Zedophap knew we were serious about fixing the situation; that was all. And he had another business analyst in the room because he'd recruited someone else to help us with the work. That had to be it. I repeated the reassurance enough times I almost believed it.

After brief introductions on both sides—that wouldn't have been necessary except they had members of their upper management on the phone, never a good sign—we launched into the call. As the formalities and basic repetition dragged on, I remembered just how little sleep I'd gotten the night before.

When Mark pulled up the adjusted timeline, my gut sank further. It wasn't the one I'd presented to him. It was far more aggressive, and completely implausible. I literally bit my tongue to keep from calling him on it in front of the client, but I was already composing my response in my head for when I could speak to him off the record.

"What about the configuration problems? How do we know those won't happen in the future?" That was one of Zedophap's VP's.

"Our project manager has tracked down the problem. I can assure you Ryan Coleman is being pulled from the project and someone new who's been brought up to speed on the sensitive nature of this project will be taking his spot for the duration."

My head shot up, eyes wide, and my gaze locked on Ryan's across the room. His jaw clenched and he gave an almost imperceptible shake of his head before he looked away. Bile rose in my throat. Fuck, that wasn't how this was supposed to go. My right eye twitched, and I rubbed my temples to try and stave off a headache.

Ryan was the first out the door when the call was over, and I hurried after him. "Ryan, wait, please?"

He kept walking, brushing past a couple of pockets of our coworkers, and not pausing until we were in the empty break room.

He whirled on me, eyes narrowed. His voice was low enough only I would hear it. "What the fuck was that?"

"I don't—"

"No." He held up his index finger. "You threw me under the bus."

"I didn't." This wasn't right. It didn't mesh with what Mark told me yesterday. None of it clicked. I really had sold him out and I hadn't even realized it. "I'm sorry. This wasn't supposed to happen."

"You know what? I don't care." His angry tone wavered. "Just don't talk to me right now, okay?"

He brushed past me without making physical or eye contact. I just needed to let him cool down. This would pass, and then I could apologize. Except no matter how many times I tried to tell myself that, there was a part of me whispering about how devastated I would be if he didn't forgive me.

He already had his head down, typing furiously, when I got back to my desk. He didn't even glance in my direction. I needed to talk to Mark, but his door was closed. And the voicemail light on my phone was blinking. The caller ID said it was my landlord.

Please let just this one thing go right for me. I dialed up the message.

"I'm so sorry, hon, but I can't afford to keep having this happen. I have bills I need to pay, too. Your deposit will cover the rest of the rent for the month, but I need you out after that."

I was being evicted? Nausea rolled through me as I hung up the phone. I was going to be ill.

My messenger chimed, with a note from Seth. *You couldn't have at least given him a heads-up he was about to be crucified?*

Oh gods.

The email from Mark in my inbox should have made me feel better. I think it was meant to. *Sorry I couldn't warn you, but you did great. We've don't have a choice on the updated timeline, but I know you can make it work.*

But the email from Ryan in my personal inbox was worse. It wasn't addressed to me; it had gone to our entire AD&D circle. It just said, *Can't make Friday's game. Maybe not again. Find another venue. I hope this is enough warning.*

I dropped my head in my hands, trying to keep my fractured thoughts from pulling my skull apart and spilling out my forehead. Tears stung my eyes and every inch of me ached with frustration. I couldn't do this. I didn't know how I was going to make any of this right, let alone all of it.

EIGHT

I worked through lunch, telling myself it was because I had so much to do and didn't want the peanut butter and jelly sandwich I'd brought. Really, I couldn't have stomached food even if I had time.

Neither Seth nor Ryan talked to me the rest of the day. I tried to initiate conversations when I passed by, but I never got more than a grunt in response. I wanted to believe they were being babies about this, but given how heavy the threat had been for me to make the project right again, they were probably under similar pressure.

I spent that night scouring the Internet and want ads for cheap apartments. My current one bedroom had been a fantastic deal, and I'd be lucky to find a cramped studio basement for the same price. Especially since I couldn't pass a credit check, and I'd be breaking my wallet to afford any deposit at all. There was no way I could manage something like first and last month's rent.

The next day at work was a repeat of the previous, with Ryan even turning and walking out of the break room in the middle of me saying hello.

I spent half the workday staring at my monitor. I needed to be doing something. Working, figuring out the housing problem, something. But every time I tried to redirect my thoughts, they drifted back to how to get Ryan to forgive me. Or at least, how to set things right for him. Even if I'd screwed things up so bad he never spoke to me again—an idea that gnawed me from the inside out—I'd never forgive myself if I'd done something like destroy his career.

My cell phone vibrated against my desk, jerking me from my rambling panic. My landlord. At least for the next couple of weeks. Dread made every inch of me feel like I was made of lead as I extracted myself from my chair. I didn't know if I had the strength for whatever this was about but ignoring it would only make things worse, if only because it would send my stress sensors into overload.

"Hello," I was already talking as I locked my computer and strolled to a more private part of the building to take the call.

We made small talk for a few moments. Her polite attitude and the underlying apology in her voice made some of my tension evaporate. "I'm sorry to bother you at work, hon," she said. "And I hate to ask this. I haven't put your place on the market yet, but some friends of the family are looking, and they're interested in your apartment. Is there any chance I can bring them by in the next couple of days? Feel free to say no, of course. It's still your place."

For now. My shoulders slumped and I rubbed my temples. I needed to start packing anyway. This sounded like an extra dash of motivation. "Sure. Anytime this weekend." Especially if our AD&D game was off, maybe forever. "Just give me a little warning first."

We said our goodbyes and I slunk back to my chair. I didn't like these feelings of impotence and frustration. I was used to being in control. To having a solution. But now? I couldn't see anything past the fog of negativity in my brain.

I dropped in to my chair with a soft, "Oof." Irresolution clawed at my throat, and stung my eyes with unshed tears. I would not break down in the middle of the office. That would be one misstep too many.

I breathed deep through my nose to try and calm myself. There were answers. I just needed to stop wallowing and spinning my wheels and find them. First things first. I didn't want to be homeless at the end of the month.

Opening a web browser, I typed in *cheap cash only housing*. I didn't think it would get me anywhere, but nothing else had either, so I needed to try a new approach. My eyes grew wide at one of the paid search results that popped up. I knew the image, and the logo. I drove by the motel every night on my way home from work.

But that was just it. It was a motel. I needed something long term. I clicked the link anyway, mind whirring to catch up with solutions I couldn't quite grasp. As I scanned their page—weekly rates, discounts for storage, small cash deposit—hope crept in.

It was a little more expensive than what I was paying now, but considering the cost included utilities, cable, and internet... It would give me a place to crash until I could save a little more money.

I felt better than I had all week. I still needed to figure out what to do about Ryan and Seth. But now I could focus exclusively on them.

ON THURSDAY, my gut sank when Ryan's desk was empty. The clock ticked past nine, and then ten, and he still didn't show up. Had I really cost him his job? The possibility made me want to retch.

I shouldn't think like that. His own inability to take the project seriously had done this. Still, I could have given him more warning. Tried harder to make it right. And something told me I didn't have all the facts. Too bad he wasn't giving them to me.

By the time lunch rolled around, I was too ill with imagined scenarios to have any interest in the sandwich I hadn't touched on Tuesday or Wednesday, either. I needed answers. Since Ryan was ignoring my texts, I'd have to go to a different source.

I said a brief prayer Seth wouldn't make me raise my voice to have this conversation, and stepped into his cubicle. I fumbled for words I probably should have composed before I got there.

He looked up from his computer, brows raised. "So we're finally going to stop this?"

"I— Yes?" I should feel relieved, but the lack of anything but irritation in his voice set my nerves further on edge.

"Good." He grabbed his sunglasses and kept his voice low. "Get your purse, we'll go to lunch, and you can tell me why you're not eating, why you're looking for a new apartment, and…" He glanced around, gaze pausing on Mark's open office door. "Other things."

I wasn't going to tell him about the first two. No way in hell. And the twenty-two cents in my bank account wasn't going to let me eat out. But I did want to have the "other things" conversation. "I was thinking we could just go outside for a little bit. Enjoy the sun. Chat. You know."

He sighed as he stood. His hand at the small of my back summoned wants I shouldn't have, but I couldn't bring myself to pull away. He reached over the top of my cubicle, grabbed my purse, and handed it to me. "Lunch is on me. No arguments."

We made our way outside, and I dropped into his passenger seat when he held the door open for me. I twisted my fingers in and out of each other, trying to compose my story. He'd ask me again about skipping lunches, I knew he wouldn't drop it that easily, but I could skate over the details. Tell him it was nothing and I had it under control. Then we could talk about Ryan.

A knot formed in my chest when he pulled into the parking lot of my favorite pub. They had the best steak sandwiches anywhere, and I was suddenly painfully aware of how little I'd eaten over the past few days. He still didn't push for any information as we were seated. We both had our regular lunches, but I couldn't ask him to spend that kind of money. I scanned the menu for something inexpensive.

When the waitress arrived, he placed his order and I asked for a large bowl of the soup of the day.

"No." Seth cut me off before I could finish. "She'll have the rib eye on sourdough, onion rings, not fries, and a diet Coke. And we need another of those sandwiches to go."

Embarrassment raced through me. Great, now I felt like a starving orphan or something. I couldn't look at him.

"Hey." The irritation was gone from his voice. Under the table, he nudged my shoe with his. "Tell me what's up, please?"

"I'm fine." The lie was harder to force out than it should be.

Suddenly, every inch of me desperately wanted to spill my guts. But I couldn't unburden myself to him. "A little short on cash until payday. Nothing big. It happens."

His lips drew into a thin line. "You've been drinking work coffee —which I know you hate—instead of bringing your own from home. Your lunch bag has sat untouched on your desk for three days, and you hide a long string of apartment listings anytime someone walks by your desk. Tell me, please?"

His expression was so sincere, the edges of his blue eyes soft with concern. Something inside gave under the uncertainty and tension, and I spilled everything about my money problems. Being broke, being evicted, ignoring calls from creditors who weren't mine, and dealing with judgments. It felt good to finally have shared, but it still didn't jar any solutions loose.

Wrinkles creased his brow. "You should have told us. We could have helped. You could probably borrow money from Ryan."

Just the mention of that was enough to make me ill all over again. "No. Nuh-uh. I can't."

"Why not?"

"First of all, I can't do that to our friendship. Even borrowing fifty bucks would hang over my head, and I'm so much further behind than that. Second, he hates me. Third, he's not even here today. He didn't get fired, did he?"

Seth let out a slow breath. "No, he didn't get fired. He just decided he could take a day off since his schedule has cleared up recently. He called in sick." He made air quotes around the word *sick*.

Relief coursed through me. At least he wasn't unemployed.

But Seth wasn't done. "Speaking of, though. He doesn't hate you, but the fact you completely screwed him over is going to hang over your head a lot more than asking for a couple hundred bucks that I can almost guarantee he'd never want you to pay back."

"I didn't know that he was going to be fed to the Zedophap dogs like that." All the rationalizations I'd told myself over the past few days rushed back, but they sounded weak now. Still, I pushed them out. "I tried to ask him about the issues, and he brushed me off. You were there." Even to my own ears, I sounded more as if I was trying to convince myself than him.

"Three years ago, Ryan slept with Kitner's wife at the company Christmas party."

Whatever I had expected Seth to say, Ryan getting it on with the boss's wife was nowhere on the list. If I'd counted out to one hundred, it might have landed somewhere around a serious, *We're KGB sleeper agents, and now I have to kill you because you know.* Jealousy surged inside with the news, and I wasn't sure how to react. "He never told me that."

Seth raised an eyebrow. "You never told him your ex-husband bankrupted you."

Touché. "But... I mean... I know he screws around, but an affair?"

"To be fair, she told him she was the new girl in accounting. He had no idea she was even married until he saw them arguing at the end of the party. And Kitner's marriage was already on the rocks. That was just one of many catalysts."

The story hit me hard, not because of the nature of it, though that was heavy too, but because it pointed out how little I knew about both of them. And I wanted to know more. Not just best friend stuff, but everything. "I didn't realize."

"I know. You also probably had no idea Kitner is screwing your new business analyst. The one who took Ryan's place on the Zedophap account."

Shit. The pieces started to slide into place. Mark wanted a new job for his girlfriend; he made things up to make it happen. Except... "The config really was wrong. And I tried to ask Ryan about it and he brushed me off."

Seth shrugged. "I wish you'd trusted him. I don't know what happened, but he didn't screw this up. You know that, right?"

Part of me did, and that was a large bit of what had me feeling so horrible. I'd let stress override common sense and friendship. "I have to apologize. You have to tell him to hear me out. Please?"

"I will. Anything you want." His smile had a trace of sadness I didn't understand. "Follow me home after work, and I'll sit on him if I have to."

The imagery made me giggle, and it released a load of tension, making my chest lighter. Nothing was solved, but life didn't seem hopeless anymore. Even if Ryan forgave me, I still wasn't asking to borrow money, but one step at a time.

NINE

I managed to make it through the rest of the workday on fifty percent concentration. I kept coming up with new variations on how I'd apologize to Ryan. Would he even hear me out?

And my mind kept drifting back to lunch. Why did something feel different talking to Seth? There was an odd kind of comfort, but at the same time a sadness I'd never felt from him before. I had to be projecting. Letting stress get to me. But I couldn't get past the idea I was still missing so many pieces, both with him, and with the project at work.

That evening, I parked my car next to the curb in front of their house as Seth took his spot in the driveway. The nervous apprehension I'd been trying to fight all day surged forward with a vengeance as I followed him up the walk to the front door. When we pushed inside, Ryan was on the couch, Xbox controller in hand, entire body ducking and weaving with whatever he was playing. He looked up when the door creaked, and his grin faded when his eyes met mine.

He tossed the controller on the couch and stood. "I'll be in my room."

Seth stepped forward, but I pulled him back. This was my

mistake. "Wait, please." I tried to keep my voice firm, but a waver snuck in.

"What, Natasha?" At his use of my full name, something cracked in my chest. "You didn't listen to me, why should I do any differently for you?"

My carefully crafted apology evaporated, and the words spilled out before I could consider them. "I'm so, so sorry. I didn't know. Based on what I saw, what was I supposed to think? And I shouldn't have done it anyway, you deserve better than that. I just didn't know what else to do. And I—"

"Stop." The single word snapped through the room. "I can't. You never realize. It doesn't matter how obvious it is. How in your face it is, you don't get it."

Something told me we weren't just talking about work anymore.

Seth stepped around me, crossing the room with rapid strides, and stopping nose to nose with Ryan. His voice was the same low, controlled tone he'd used earlier today, but with an angry roar lining it. "Don't yell at her. She made a mistake, and she's apologizing for it. But you... This last week has been a game for you. You've even said so. Your exact words. You're using her affection for you. She's wanted you since she met you, and it's just a tumble to you."

My words stuck in my throat. How did he know that? I always thought I'd hidden it so well. I should be humiliated that the truth was coming out now, but it felt good. I wanted Ryan to know. I just wished it was under different circumstances, and that it didn't mean pushing Seth away in the process. Gods, please don't let me lose Seth over this.

Ryan's voice was low, but it carried through the entire room. There was no mistaking the threat in each emphasized word. "Walk away now."

"Fuck you." Seth's calm vanished with his reply. "You don't give a shit about her, not like I do. You don't even care about me the way I do you. Now that this is all over, and you got off, you'll move on."

My brain hitched and stumbled over the words, and despite my trepidation, warmth spread inside at the realization. Had he just said...? He had. Seth cared about me. About Ryan. How had I not seen that? "I—"

Ryan held up a hand, never looking at me, but it was enough to silence me. He rested both palms on Seth's cheeks and kissed him hard. One of them moaned—or maybe it was both of them. I expected to feel a pang of jealousy, but instead pure liquid heat filled my veins. Gods, that was hot. I wanted to be a part of the desire flowing between them as Seth traced the visible bulge of the erection straining against Ryan's jeans.

Ryan finally broke the kiss. The anger in his tone had been replaced with breathlessness. "You're wrong. I love you both so hard, and I don't know what I'd do without either one of you."

Love. The word bounced in my skull, feeling both terrifying and right at the same time. How had I never seen that? "I had no idea." I clamped my jaw shut when two heads swiveled in my direction, and I realized I'd spoken out loud.

Ryan moved to stand in front of me, and nudged a curl off my forehead. "No kidding." He nodded over his shoulder in Seth's direction. "He wasn't supposed to push this, either. We both agreed we wouldn't pressure you. That if you made up your mind somewhere along the way, we were fine with it. But seriously, Tash. I'm tired of dancing around this." He nipped my lower lip, and my chest almost burst. "I don't want you to pick. I want you, and I want him. I'm selfish."

The blood had rushed from my head, leaving me a little stupid, and incredibly turned on. "But you're not..."

"Gay?" His mouth twisted in amusement, and he trailed a finger along the edge of my ear. "Nope. But you have to admit, Seth's hot."

"I'm not going to argue with that."

"It took the two of you long enough," Seth teased.

Ryan laughed, his attention still on me. "I've been thinking about it for a while, and Friday night kind of pushed me over the edge. Monday cemented it for me. But you still didn't get it. I had to walk away. Get some distance from you. Figure out what I was going to do if you really weren't interested."

So that was why he hadn't been talking to me? "I'm so interested. I thought you were mad about work."

"I am. I'm furious." His roaming hand fisted in my hair, and he yanked. "But I also get it. And we'll deal with it."

His kiss was as incredible as Seth's had been the other morning, but in a very different direction. Instead of safety and security, this was heat, and want, and everything nasty I tried to pretend I didn't dream about. Rough sex and handprints on my ass and sleepless nights I'd do again and again if I had the chance. He tugged my hair back, and his teeth lightly scraped along my throat. He bit into the fleshy, sensitive part of my neck, and sucked until I swore I might come just from the hickey. I shifted against him, and the friction built.

He finally pulled back, holding my head captive and looking me in the eye. "Mine."

I had never wanted to be possessed before, and now it felt right. "Yours," I repeated.

He grabbed my fingertips and tugged me toward the back of the house, where the bedrooms were. My pulse seared with flames under my skin, making my nipples ache against their prison. Damp need grew between my legs.

He sat on the edge of his bed and then let go of my hand. Confusion flitted in as he stared up at me with expectation.

"Take off your clothes," Seth commanded from behind me. "Slow. A piece at a time. Every eye in the room is on you."

Gods, the two of them were going to kill me, and I was going to die happy.

TEN

Bold mischievousness coursed through me, and I stepped out of Ryan's reach. A glance over my shoulder told me Seth was near the doorway. I pushed a hint of teasing into my voice. "If I'm putting on a show, then that's all it is. No touching."

Ryan smirked. "We'll see."

My fingers glided down the front of my shirt, undoing each button along the way, but not pulling the sides apart. The two pairs of eyes on me lit my every nerve ending on fire. I moved to my skirt next, undoing it and letting it fall to the floor. Stepping out of it, I kicked that and my heels aside.

I stood in the middle of the room, shirt barely covering my panty-clad ass and hinting at what lay underneath in front. My pussy ached for attention, and my breasts strained against fabric, begging to be touched. Ryan's hand drifted to his crotch, rubbing lightly through denim as his hungry eyes traced over my body.

Seth moaned, and I wondered if he was doing the same. I was too lost in my light striptease to look. I let my shirt slide to the ground, and moved my palms to my bra. I cupped each mound through the lace, squeezing enough to draw out my own sigh, but not sating the desire. I wanted more.

My fingers trailed down my stomach, past the top of my panties, and to my wet mound. I slid the crotch aside enough to give a peek and stroked my slit lightly. My eyes closed at my own touch. It still wasn't what I wanted, but knowing the impact it was having on both men made me lightheaded.

I was so lost in the moment, my heart jumped when Seth grabbed me from behind. "Another day." His voice was low. I leaned back, and his bare skin met mine. When had his clothes come off? I wanted to spin and take him in, but he held me captive. He shoved up the bottom of my bra, and the rough elastic bit into my skin.

I whimpered for more and he obliged, lips tracing light lines along the back of my neck while he caressed my skin. He kissed along my ear. "Don't get me wrong, I like watching." He trailed his tongue over my skin. "But sometimes, I want to participate. I need to know what it feels like to be inside you."

"Me too."

He stripped off the remainder of my clothes and moved in front of me. Ryan stood, putting him only a few inches from Seth. The two stared each other down, and the seconds ticked away. Ryan's hand glided down Seth's chest and wrapped around his sheathed cock. He kissed Seth hard, a hungry snarl rising between them, and pulled back again just as abruptly.

"Be good to her," Ryan warned.

Seth gave a light laugh and shoved him aside. "Trust me, the rough stuff is more fun to watch. It's all yours."

Ryan gave me a wicked wink and slid out of sight.

Seth sat near the edge of the bed, dick at attention, and pulled me toward him. "I want to watch you ride me."

I licked my lips and straddled him. I wrapped my hand around his cock, and he closed his eyes with a sigh. I slid the thick head along my slit, before slowly impaling myself. "Gods, you're so big," I moaned.

I rocked slowly against him, our breathing shifting until we were in perfect sync. His hands roamed up my chest, softly cupping my tits, and his gaze never stopped roaming my body. Every time I tried to increase the pace, he'd slow me back down. One hand dropped, and his thumb brushed my aching sex.

"Please?" I begged.

He smiled. "I'm not him. You can't beg me for hard and fast." He trailed circles around the swollen nub, exposing it and stroking it at the same rhythmic pace he glided in and out of me.

He shifted his attention, and rubbed my clit harder. An abrupt spark raced through me, stealing the air from my head, and I plummeted over an edge I hadn't known I was on. I clenched around his cock as I came, panting and grinding against his hand.

A pair of fingers slipped between my legs from behind, trailing through my juices and drawing the slick wet back. I gasped with a new kind of pleasure when Ryan's finger glided along my asshole.

"You like that?" Hand on my back he pushed me forward.

Seth guided me down until my chest was pressed against his, still rocking inside me.

Ryan's fingers glided along my slit again, and this time one slipped into my ass without a problem. "I'll be gentle this time." His seductive tone rolled off my skin. "Just relax."

Something nudged my back door, and I moaned at the push.

"Tell me if you want me to stop."

"Gods, no." There was pain, but he eased in slowly, and being stretched out from both sides felt amazing.

Ryan laughed. "I so completely adore you." His hands gripped my hips, and both men resumed rocking, one slamming into me from behind, and the other driving deep into my pussy.

Seth took one nipple into his mouth, and sucked hard. Ryan's fingers dug into my pelvis hard. Would he leave bruises? I hoped so. The multiple points of contact penetrated every one of my senses. I was so close to coming again. I lost track of the specific sensations. I was moaning both their names, sinking into lightheaded ecstasy as they fucked me at the same time. This time climax crept up slowly, washing over me in waves that mingled with everything else.

Seth grunted and his attentions to my breast paused. He threw his head back with a groan, pushing hard and fast until he was spent inside me. I recognized similar sounds from behind. Moments later Ryan slipped out with a quiet, "Fuck, Tash. Just… Fuck."

I giggled at the sudden release of tension in the room, and buried my face in Seth's muscular chest. My words were muffled. "I love you both. You should know that. Intensely and deeply, and I can't believe I was so dim."

Seth lifted my head enough to press his lips to my forehead. "Not dim. You just need to learn to trust yourself."

Seconds later, Ryan dropped onto the mattress next to us, tugging me back into him. He kissed my shoulder blades. For the first time since I could remember, he didn't say anything. He just held me.

ELEVEN

Thank the gods it was Friday. Finally. This had been the longest week of my life. A smile played on my face as I rolled onto my back and found Ryan's bedroom ceiling above me instead of my own. And I would do it again in a heartbeat. I'd take the bad with the good, if it turned out like this. The sound of the shower running provided background noise to my contentment. Last night had been amazing.

I wasn't even concerned about my looming eviction. I had the inklings of a plan. It wasn't much, but it was a start.

A warm weight rested on my legs—the familiar sensation of flesh against flesh teasing me—and seconds later Ryan's face appeared over mine. He pinned my hands above my head, and traced his lips along my neck. His words vibrated against the sensitive skin when he spoke. "You're going to be late for work, sexy."

Right, I couldn't lay here all day. And I should probably tell him to un-cancel the AD&D game before tonight. Something popped into my head without permission, and I realized what it felt like to have the light bulb go off. "How long has Mark been screwing around?"

Ryan pulled back enough for me to see his frown. "I'm going to draw a line right there. It's not a turn on to talk about any kind of sex from the guy who wants my job so bad he probably beats off to the fantasy."

I reluctantly nudged him off me, disappointment rushing in to take the place of his body pressed against mine. I sat up, latched onto my growing idea. "I'm serious. How long?"

"I don't know. A couple of months. Seth said they were having problems, but I guess he read them wrong."

Oh motherfucker. I really was dim. "And you swear to me you filled that config doc out exactly the way the client said?"

His mouth twisted in disbelief, and his brows rose. "I'm pretending you didn't ask that."

I rolled forward on my knees, and brushed my lips over his. "I need to go home and get dressed. I'll see you in the office."

He tangled his fingers in my curls and pulled me in, deepening the kiss. When we broke apart, I struggled to find my breath. I hoped I never got used to that rush. I gave him a shy smile and scooted to the edge of the bed. I plucked my shirt from the floor, and frowned when I realized last night's activities had covered the silk in something that was probably sticky once upon a time, and was now just kind of hard.

He nipped my earlobe. "Sorry about that." He didn't sound the least bit sorry. Seconds later, he was holding something over my shoulder. "Wear this."

I tugged his T-shirt over my head, inhaling deeply at the faint traces of his cologne mixed with laundry soap. "If you insist. And seriously, I need to go."

He laid a tender line of kisses along the back of my neck. "I guess."

I reluctantly pulled away, picking up the pace when I saw how late it was. I was in such a rush to make it to the front door, I collided with Seth when he emerged from the bathroom in nothing but a pair of boxers. I smacked into him, palms resting against his firm chest. "Sorry."

"Don't worry about it." He kissed me. His erection dug into my leg, making me regret even more we all had places to be. He stepped behind me and gave my ass a light smack, pushing me toward the front door. "Go."

THERE WAS a cup of coffee waiting for me on my desk when I got to work. TASHA written on the sleeve in familiar block letters, and what I think was a goblin to the right of it. Both my guys were already at their desks, heads down and working. *My guys*—I adored the sound of that. I dropped into my chair and dove into work.

Almost three hours later, I had a stack of log files, and all the proof I'd been hoping to find.

My messenger pinged with a note from Seth. *Lunch? No money isn't an excuse.*

We'd still have to talk about that. As much as I liked the idea of letting my boyfriends spoil me—and loved the plural—I wasn't going to be the leech my ex had been. But for today, I'd let it slide. Besides, with any luck I'd have news in exchange for the meal by the time noon rolled around. I sent back a quick, *I won't argue, just this once,* and then locked my computer and made my way to Mark's office.

He looked up when I knocked. "Natasha, come on in."

My nerves bunched in on themselves, and I hesitated. No, I needed to do this. I closed the door behind me. His brows rose as I took a seat and set my stack of papers face down on the desk. "We need to talk about Zedophap."

His back went rigid, and his jaw clenched for a moment. His casual, "Sure," defied every tense inch of his posture. "But I have a meeting in five, so it'll have to be fast."

"I'm sure we can cover what we need." I hoped I sounded more confident than I felt. This might all still blow up in my face. It could cost me a job I couldn't afford to lose, which would obliterate my half-formed plan to not be homeless. But I also needed to do this. Letting it slide wasn't right.

"Great, so what can I do for you?"

I flipped the documents over, and slid the first one across his desk. "This is the log from the configuration interface, showing that on Sunday afternoon, someone with administrative rights logged into the system and changed almost everything associated with Zedophap."

I pushed the next page to him. "This is from the source control software, showing that early Monday morning, someone replaced all of the documentation from the then business analyst with something entirely different."

I slid the next print out toward him. "This—"

He rested his hand on the papers. "Where are you going with this?"

My hands shook, and my heart was threatening to tear from my ribcage, I was so nervous. I pushed the words out. "This tells me Ryan isn't responsible for the screw up earlier this week. But someone with your login might have been. Possibly someone you're close to. Someone you're sleeping with?"

"There aren't any company rules against fraternization."

Thank the gods for that. I was feeling both more confident and more terrified as the conversation progressed. "No. But I don't think upper management would be too thrilled with your girlfriend sabotaging a major client to worm herself into a better position."

"Where's this going?" An edge crept into his voice. "Blackmail? Extortion? None of that's going to fly."

I hadn't even considered something like blackmail. The guys were right, I was a little dim. But I was fine with it in this case. I didn't want to be *that* person. "Gods, no. I was just thinking you'd tear up Ryan's write-up, you'd apologize to him for the mistake— you don't even have to do it publicly—and then we make sure this doesn't happen again."

Mark's eyes narrowed. "You don't think big, Natasha. That's always been your problem, and I suspect it always will be. This creates a rift you don't want in your career."

"I can handle it. I've seen what it's like to be on your shit list." I nodded at the paperwork. "And I know how to cover my ass if it happens again to me or anyone assigned to any of my projects."

His lip pulled into a sneer. "I have a meeting. You've made your point."

"Have I?" I didn't want to push him too far, but I had to be sure this wasn't just lip service.

"Yes." His bark filled the room. His tone returned to normal when he said, "we're done here."

Sick giddiness flowed through me as I sat back at my desk again. Things wouldn't drop as easily as it seemed like they just had, but I'd meant what I said about being able to cover my own ass.

There was a text from Ryan waiting for me when I got back to my desk. *Game's back on tonight. You know Ardra missed me.*

Why hadn't he emailed the group? My stomach fluttered at the teasing. He was just a few desks away, but this was low-key and playful, and not something I wanted anyone overhearing. Well, except one person. I sent back a response, and added Seth to the thread. *Galahad set her expectations high. Sure he can keep it up?*

A soft snorting laugh filtered through the cubicles, and seconds later, I had another text. *I'm having a hard time doing anything but keeping it up, and that's just from thinking about your bare ass.*

Heat flooded my cheeks, and I squirmed in my seat. Maybe work wasn't the best place for this. *We're talking about the game.*

Bullshit we are.

A giggle slipped past my lips, and I winced and clamped my mouth shut.

A new message from Seth interrupted the banter. *Some of us are trying to work.*

I raised my eyebrows at my phone. Was he really pissed off?

Seconds later, he followed it with, *Unless there are pictures. I'll drop everything for pictures.*

Goodie. Bossman wants to talk to me. Ryan's message killed my cheer in instant. I wanted to send him a quick *good luck*, but he was already walking away from his desk.

Please, please don't let me have made things worse. I swore the fifteen minutes from the time Kitner's door closed behind Ryan, until it re-opened, were the longest of my life. I'd taken a risk with what I'd done, but the full impact didn't hit me until I was stuck here waiting, without answers.

When Ryan re-emerged, he didn't look at anyone. He cut a straight line to his desk and seconds later, disappeared into the hallway leading to the back stairs.

A few moments later, my phone buzzed with a new text, and I thought my heart was going to explode out of my chest from the tension. It was from Ryan, and just said, *Take a break and meet me by the tree?*

Sure.

I tried to keep my pulse from tearing out of my veins, and my pace even and slow, as I followed a similar path to his. There was a tree with a bench near the office. We ate lunch there sometimes when the weather was good. And now I couldn't believe it was almost a five-minute walk. My nervousness was cranked up another notch by the fact I could see Ryan pacing long before I got to him.

As I drew closer, he crossed the last several yards between us, tangled his fingers in my hair, and kissed me hard.

I groaned and molded against him. I hadn't expected that, but I wasn't complaining.

When he broke away, he rested his forehead against mine. "It was a really stupid thing to do."

Shit. Had he been fired after all? I hadn't been bluffing with Kitner, I would make the information I had public, but I hadn't expected to have to. "I didn't—"

He cut me off with another brief kiss, nipping my bottom lip before he pulled away. "You're going to have to tell me what you said to him, because he was practically spitting venom when your name came up. But whatever it was, it worked. He destroyed my write-up."

I exhaled in relief. "You scared me."

He pushed a loose curl off my forehead. "Serves you right. Fill me in next time. Fill me in this time. And you know your life just got miserable at work, right?"

I nodded, agreeing to all three requests at once. "It was worth it. What he did was bullshit. And it'll cost him his job eventually."

He wrapped his arms around my waist, and I rested my cheek against his chest. His words vibrated through my ear when he spoke. "Just make sure it doesn't cost you yours first."

"That's the plan."

He traced tiny circles along the small of my back. "Good. Text Seth. Tell him early lunch. And you can give us all the juicy details."

I smiled, though he couldn't see me. "Yes, sir."

WHEN I PULLED up in front of Ryan and Seth's place, I thought it was odd there wasn't a single other car there yet. I was never the last one to arrive, but a couple of our players were consistently early. Maybe it had been too short a notice for everyone to show. Which was a little disappointing, but it would mean fewer people had to leave before we had the house to ourselves.

That made me pause. Were we telling anyone about our relationship? Even more important, why had we un-canceled game night when we had an entire weekend to explore this incredible new thing between us?

Well, maybe not the entire weekend. I still needed to pack up most of my stuff, move it into storage, and figure out how little I could get away with keeping on me and still be comfortable in my motel room. But that could wait at least a little while.

The door swung open before I could knock, and Seth stood on the other side.

I gave an exaggerated glance around me, pretending to look for someone else. "Expecting someone?"

He stepped in, rested a hand on the small of my back, and his mouth crushed down on mine. I intertwined my fingers at the back of his neck memorizing every inch of him pressed against me. The rough stubble of a five o'clock shadow, his hungry lips devouring mine, the hardening length digging into my stomach.

His free hand slid up my arm, and disentangled it. He pressed something hard and small into my palm before he finally let me go.

I studied the key with a frown. "What is it?"

He kissed me on the tip of the nose. "A house key."

"I know that, but why?"

He tugged me inside. Ryan was lounging against a nearby wall, arms crossed. "Why do you think?"

A hopeful bubble rose inside me. I didn't want to want this, or assume it was what I thought, but I couldn't help it. Still, this was one thing I was going to make them spell out. "You're going out of town, and you want me to water the plants?"

"You know that's not what it is," Seth said.

"Maybe." I couldn't fight my smirk, and my giddiness threatened to break loose. "But pretend I really am that dim."

Ryan kicked away from the wall, spinning to face me completely. "Even if you weren't having problems with your landlord—"

"That was between us." I shot a glare at Seth

"No." Seth shook his head. "We're not playing things that way. No more secrets."

"What he said." Ryan slipped a hand into Seth's back pocket. "And anyway. Even if it weren't the case, we don't want you to have to go home at night. Any night. I mean, obviously, you have to be okay with it, and pride isn't a good reason to say no. We'll all split the rent and such, so that's not even a valid excuse."

They'd already taken the wind out of my objections, and I had to admit, I didn't like the idea of going home at night either. "I'd love to."

It occurred to me, they were being awfully affectionate, with each other and with me, considering there would be a small crowd of people in the house soon. I felt a tug of relief we were going to be open about this. I didn't know how we were going to explain it, but I also didn't like the idea of hiding it.

Speaking of, where were all the other people? I glanced around the living room, realization sinking in. "There's no game tonight, is there?"

Seth gave Ryan a thoughtful look before turning back to me. "I don't know. We could role play *something* if you wanted."

Ryan nodded. "Locking the princess in the dungeon, for instance."

My cheeks warmed and anticipation spread through me. "Then rescuing her?"

Ryan seemed to consider this for a moment. "Probably eventually. I'll only keep her in chains until she's spent."

I liked the sound of that. Being bound and at his mercy.

"Hey," Seth interrupted. "Sometimes the innkeeper is going to want to be chained up too. This is only *mostly* about the princess."

His implication made me laugh, and added a new layer of fantasy to the growing list of possibilities in my head. I was really looking forward to what the future held for us. "Druid," I corrected them. "She's a druid."

ROLL AGAINST REGRET

ONE

I logged onto the game and loaded my character, ZaneyPixie. The assassin elf waved, before the character screen faded and the world took its place. At the same time, I connected to the live-chat channel I shared with my boyfriend, Jackson, and our in-game party mate, DarkAngel.

"Hey, gorgeous." DA's deep tenor tickled my ears. "Ready to slaughter a dragon?"

"I'm in." Jackson's voice joined the three-way chat. He sat on the couch across from me, just a few feet away. We were in his apartment to play together, but I could only hear him over my headset. If I didn't wear noise-canceling earphones, the echo made my head spin. "You weren't going to pillage without me. Were you?" he said.

DA laughed. "I was thinking about it, Fiend." TattedFiend was Jackson's character. "You're welcome to watch, though."

"You and Pixie? I'd watch that in a heartbeat." Jackson met my gaze over the screens of our laptops, heat lingering in his eyes. His blond hair was spiked, and the glow of his display added an eerily sexy cast to his pale blue eyes. Even with him hunched over his computer, it was clear he was tall and wiry.

A flush spread over my skin, and a tease of imagery danced in my mind. I had no idea what DA looked like, but his voice reminded me of an ex-boyfriend I had, so he always took on Carter's face in my fantasies. When DA and Jackson started joking like this, those fantasies frequently involved being pressed between them, two sets of hands roaming over my body. I tucked the thoughts away, for when Jackson and I weren't logged in. "Do I get a say in this?" I asked.

"Absolutely," DA said. "You can say if he watches or joins in. You're the boss."

Tough call. Jackson had been pretty direct about the fact he wouldn't mind watching me with another guy. Two months ago, when we hooked up, the idea had terrified me, but I had a new perspective on a lot of things these days. Both possibilities sent flutters through my belly and tingled between my thighs. I dragged myself from the lust-filled daydream. We were supposed to be forming a raiding party. "We're still talking about slaying the dragon, right?"

"If that's what you want to call it." Jackson winked at me.

Men. I rolled my eyes and shook my head. "As much fun as this is, the event ends tonight. We doing this or not?" The event ending was just an excuse for hurrying. As much as fun as DA was, he wasn't here. Jackson had greeted me this evening with a mind-numbing, panty-soaking kiss. He'd slid his hands down to cup my ass, pulled me close enough his hard-on pressed into my stomach, and then moved his attentions back up to roll my nipples between his fingers. He pulled away abruptly, reminded me we had an in-game date, and he and I would have to finish once we were done conquering.

I squirmed in my seat. Focusing wouldn't be easy, but it would be worth it.

"We're doing this." Was that disappointment in DA's voice, or just a glitch in the connection?

"Adding our party to the queue," Jackson said. Seconds later, a message flashed on the screen, warning us this mission was meant for a four-person party or larger, and asking if we were sure we wanted to proceed. His avatar cast a series of protection spells on us.

Jackson clicked 'Yes,' and an on-screen timer counted down from sixty. DarkAngel fell into a battle pose, axe at the ready, I drew my daggers, and a transparent shield radiated out from Jackson's TattedFiend to encompass all of us.

The screen flashed to black, and the cut scene started. The red dragon swooped in from the skies, and hit the earth hard enough to shake the world. Flame spewed from its nostrils and jaw when it roared.

I tucked the last of my arousal aside and leaned forward, ready to battle. "Dark. Minions, approaching from the west."

"On it." The joking was gone from DA's voice, and his avatar fell into line.

"South." Jackson barked the single word.

"Going for the wings." My Pixie sprinted forward, weapons at the ready.

The next ten minutes were a mishmash of the same. All of us knew our roles—DA drew enmity, Jackson kept us alive, and I dealt damage. None of us spoke more than a few words at a time, mostly to announce our intentions, to keep from stepping on each other's toes. Spells flew, hit points dropped and were magically replenished, and the dragon's HP bar dropped lower and lower.

The dragon let out one final roar and dropped to the ground. I exhaled, pushing out the tension of the last fifteen minutes, as the 'You Won' cut scene played.

"Fuck, yeah!" DA's cheer echoed in my head, drawing a smile.

"Owned!" Jackson threw his arms in the air in celebration.

I wasn't sure I could find better words for it. Fights like that always pumped excess adrenaline through me, and sapped me of my ability to think. We spent the next fifteen minutes or so divvying up the drops and making random small talk.

"I hate to cut this short"—Jackson caught my attention visually again—"but we've got plans tonight."

"Without me?" DA's whine was exaggerated. "Not sexy plans. Right?"

"That exact kind."

Jackson's confirmation heated my cheeks. Even as comfortable as I was, joking with DA, I was still getting used to how honest and direct Jackson could be. Especially when it came to our love life.

"Sorry I have to miss it. We still on for tomorrow?"

"Totally." Jackson said.

I'd almost forgotten. When we'd discovered DA lived in Salt Lake City, same as we did, we agreed to meet in person. There had only been one rule. No photos and no real names exchanged, until we saw each other in person. We didn't want anything but our existing friendship waiting for us in the coffee shop.

We finished saying our good nights, I stripped off my headset, shut my laptop, and set it in its resting place, on Jackson's coffee table.

Seconds later, Jackson stood in front of me. He grabbed my hand and pulled me to my feet with a swift tug. The air pushed from my chest when I pressed against him. Our relationship was new enough I still felt a rush every time he touched me.

He pushed up the hem of my T-shirt, and his fingers danced along my spine. "You make it so hard to keep my hands to myself." He traced his lips along my collarbone, and followed the line of the vine tattoo snaking around my neck. The ink was new. Something I'd always wanted to try, but never dared until Jackson. He'd helped me get past a lot of the reservations that had held me back in the past.

"I thought that fight would never end," he said.

I trailed a nail down his chest, past his navel, and tugged at the waistband of his jeans. "We didn't have to play."

His erection dug into my hip when he held me closer. "We did. Dark is important."

"He'd also understand."

"We still have the rest of tonight." Jackson nipped at my lips, and then deepened the kiss. He moved one hand to the back of my head, and tangled his fingers in my hair.

A vise squeezed around my chest at the intensity in his kiss. Elders, I loved that feeling. He pushed his tongue into my mouth, and it danced with mine. His free hand glided up my chest, brushed the bottom of my breast, and then flicked over a nipple. I groaned into his mouth.

He broke away and met my gaze again. "I'm so lucky to have you, Zoe."

"Me too. I mean... You know what I mean." The sudden compliment raised my arousal another notch. I trailed my fingers down to his crotch, and traced the outline of his cock through denim.

He jerked against my touch. His laugh was shaky when he grabbed my wrist and raised my hand to his lips. He kissed each knuckle. "I'm serious. I don't ever want you to think otherwise."

"I know." The intensity in his words made my heart stutter. Why did something so sweet set me on edge? "Are you okay?"

He slid a hand into my back pocket. "I'm good. Perfect, even. I've just been thinking."

It felt like he was dragging the conversation out. Hesitating to say something. That probably made me more nervous than his words did. Jackson didn't hold back. "About what?" I asked.

"You know how I think it would be hot to watch you with another guy?"

The reminder tingled over every inch of me. I nodded.

"I'm not trying to jump to conclusions or anything." He kissed up my jaw and caught my earlobe in his teeth. His voice was low, vibrating against my skin. "And I know there's a really good chance it won't work out this way, so really, this is just me fantasizing. But" —He breathed deeply—"what if that guy were Dark?"

I bit the inside of my cheek as the words sank in. My brain struggled to process the idea, while my body reacted on its own. My nipples tightened, and an ache grew between my thighs. I wasn't sure if I was turned on at the prospect, or terrified we were one step closer to it becoming a reality.

"Pixie?" Jackson lifted my chin and forced me to look him in the eye. "Are you still with me?"

TWO

I swallowed and nodded. "I'm here. I just... Dark? Really? What if he's..." I had no idea where the question was going. The longer the thought lingered in my head, the more I latched onto it.

"It's just a fantasy right now, Pixie." He'd given me the nickname, and I loved the way it rolled off his tongue. It was why I used it in-game.

Jackson stripped my shirt over my head. His gaze raked over me and left need lingering on my skin. He drew his tongue down the curve of my neck. He unsnapped my bra, and tossed that aside too. "It may not ever be more. It never has to be, if you're not comfortable with it." He lowered his head to one breast and drew a swollen nub into his mouth. He alternated a light biting with flicking his tongue back and forth. The feelings tugged an invisible string that traveled through all of me. If I'd been wet before, I was soaked now.

"It's not that." I hooked my fingers behind his head, holding him in place. I whimpered when he dragged a thumb over my other nipple. "I'm not saying no. It's more that I'm saying I don't know."

His palm glided down my stomach and over my jeans. I gasped when he brushed my already tender mound through denim. "Stay with me for a minute or two, then." His voice was smooth, almost hypnotic. He pressed harder against the seam of my pants, grinding the fabric into my swollen clit. My hips bucked in response.

"Say we click with this guy in person." He continued to rub, pushing me near climax but not over the edge. "He's just as much fun as online, and we hit it off." Jackson stopped his attentions, and anticipation joined everything else churning inside me.

"Then what?" I hated that I was hung up on the logistics, but I couldn't help myself, even knowing it might spoil a good fantasy. "You say, 'Hey, wanna fuck my girl while I'm in the room?'"

He made quick work of the button on my pants, and then the zipper. "More or less. And he says yes. We come back here, and I watch him strip you down, a piece of clothing at a time." He dragged the rest of my clothing down my legs, letting friction build. He dropped to his knees, and kissed along my thigh.

I wasn't prepared for my own response to the suggestion. The images he painted were as enticing as his touch on my skin. A new wave of lust spiked through me at the idea of Jackson watching me. Being aroused by me with someone else. Someone we trusted. "And you just sit in the corner?" I asked.

"And stroke my dick." He drew closer to my aching sex, but never touched it, before kissing back down the other leg. "Watching him kiss you for the first time would make me hard." He reached up and cupped my ass. "Seeing you yield to his touch would make me stroke faster." His mouth brushed my lower lips, and I groaned.

"Watching him penetrate you, knowing how wet you get… That would almost be enough to make me come." His warm breath on my damp skin sent chills through me. "And when you screamed in pleasure. Fuck, Pixie. I'd blow my wad."

He finally dipped his tongue between my folds and licked up to my aching button. I let out a whimper, and tangled my fingers in his hair. He trailed back down, and plunged inside me. I thrust against his face, too lost in the images and sensations to say anything. When he found my clit with his thumb, orgasm tore through me, and I cried out.

He eased off, then pressed forward again, drawing me back from the edge and pushing me over it a second time. My knees wobbled, and I pulled away when his touch became too much.

He guided me back toward the couch, and helped me sit. I pulled his face to mine and kissed him deeply, enjoying the taste of myself on his lips. I helped him shove his jeans to the floor, and his cock sprung to attention the moment it was free.

"I think you'd like it." He dragged the swollen head of his dick over my slit. Going without condoms had been one of the first, and easiest, concessions we made in our relationship.

I scooted my butt forward on the couch until I was more hanging off than sitting. "I might." That was an understatement. It was the hottest fantasy I'd ever had.

He thrust his hips forward, and drove inside me. I threw my head back at the feeling of being spread open. He half knelt, half leaned his weight on his wrists, as he drove inside me. "Fuck, I love that idea."

"More than watching me pleasure myself?" I grabbed my breasts and kneaded, pinching my nipples as he pounded me.

"Say it right." His command was punctuated with short bursts of breathing.

I only hesitated for a second, knowing exactly what he wanted to hear. "More than watching me fuck myself with my own fingers? Play with my pussy, while you're hands off?"

He kissed me hard. "And people think you're so sweet and inno-cent. God, you've got a filthy, sexy mouth." He shifted his angle, and this time his thrust hit a sweet spot inside me. "And it's two very different kinds of hot. Don't make me choose."

I screamed when I came again, and clenched around his cock, milking him. His speed increased, and I recognized the frantic pants of his nearing climax. He thrust a few more times and spilled inside me, hot and hard. He pulled out, and collapsed onto the carpet.

I slid from the couch. "I definitely won't make you choose."

He wrapped me in his arms, and trailed his lips over my shoul-der. "Good. I meant what I said. I don't ever want to scare you away. Nothing you're not comfortable with." He flicked a thumb over my nipple, and I groaned, not sure if it was too much or just enough of a tease.

The words bounced in my skull and tried to tug an old memory loose. One I'd buried more than five years ago. I wouldn't let him uncover that, though. I wouldn't dwell on the last time a man had said something similar to me, and the regret I had over it. That was then. I'd learned my lesson since, and this was the new, carefree me. The Zoe who wasn't afraid to admit she had kinks. The woman who didn't dwell on the past.

I snuggled closer, and wrapped myself in the now. 'Then' didn't matter.

THREE

I hated Mondays. I didn't use to be one of those people who dreaded the end of Sunday night. Being a data analyst wasn't for everyone, but I was good at my job, and up until a few months ago, I'd liked the people and the culture at work.

I grabbed a Styrofoam cup from the break-room counter, filled it with coffee, and tried to force the sleepy fog from my brain. It didn't help that I'd been up past midnight with Jackson. The memory was enough to warm my skin and send a pleasant jolt through me. That was almost better than coffee. I poured milk and enough sugar in my drink to jump-start a small engine. When I turned to head back to my desk, I almost collided with a coworker. "Sorry about that," I said.

Ryan didn't return my smile. His narrowed his eyes, pursed his lips, and stepped around me.

The fact the interaction was status quo these days didn't stop my mood from sinking a notch. "See you around," I called over my shoulder, trying to keep the cheer in my voice.

I sank into my desk chair with a sigh. A few months ago, before I met Jackson, I'd made a big mistake—or a string of them —and I was still paying the price. I brought it on myself, and karma was exacting its fee. Which was the entire reason I needed to make things right. Ryan wasn't making it easy. Not that I blamed him.

I'd dated one of the managers. It had been a stupid decision for a lot of reasons, but Mark Kitner was all the suave, seductive things I thought I wanted to sweep me off my feet. Mark had used our relationship to convince me to do a little bit of after-hours work for him. I hadn't thought it was a big deal at the time, until I realized he had me sabotaging Ryan's job. I was furious, told Mark we were through, and cut him out of my personal life.

Too bad doing the same at work wasn't an option, unless I found a new job.

I'd tried to apologize to Ryan, but he'd blown me off and said the damage was done. I didn't blame him for being pissed, so I tried not to push the issue.

"Got a minute?" Tasha stood on the other side of my chest-high cubicle, a manila folder in her hand. "It's about Zedophap."

The account I'd unwittingly stolen from Ryan. It's not that we made more based on the clients we worked with or anything, but the work I'd done had made him look bad. Tasha was the project manager, and knew the truth of the entire debacle. She'd brought it all to light. Fortunately, she'd forgiven me. It surprised me, since I was pretty sure she and Ryan were an item—or the closest friends ever—but I wasn't complaining.

I pressed the lingering unpleasantness of Monday to the back of my mind. "Sure. What's up?"

She handed me the folder. "I don't know why I can't do this over email, but Kitner..." She blew a red curl off her forehead. I envied her hair. My straight blond locks were so blah in comparison. "Anyway. These are all the data documents the records say you've got going for Zedophap. Can you give them a look, and fill in any missing or out-of-date information with printouts?"

I frowned and grabbed the paperwork from her. "I'm sure it's right. I've put everything in the document system. Won't this throw the versioning out of sync?"

She twisted her mouth and rolled her eyes. "It won't, once you go back into the system and update everything. Don't hate me. This wasn't my decision."

"Update from the printouts?"

"Yes." She met my gaze. "Welcome to the busywork side of being on Kitner's shit list."

Elders, that man was a childish asshole. "Got it. Due date?"

"It's critical." She drew out the word 'critical' and smothered it with sarcasm.

Of course it was. Because the snide looks, silent treatment, and whispers behind my back weren't enough. I swallowed the bitter response. I'd brought this on myself. "I'm on it."

"Thanks." Tasha sounded sincere. "I'll take the heat off you wherever I can."

I STEPPED into the familiar coffee shop, and the scent of fresh roast washed over me. Jackson already sat at a table in the back. He grinned the moment I approached, and met me halfway to the booth. He wrapped an arm around my waist and kissed me hard. "You look drained."

"I'm better now." I dropped into the seat across from him, and pushed the day to the back of my mind. "I'm not late, am I?" Now that work was behind me, I was free to focus my thoughts on meeting Dark. The nervous anticipation sliding through me combined with memories of the fantasy I shared with Jackson last night.

"Dark called about thirty seconds before you walked in. He took the wrong exit, had to loop back, and got stuck in rush hour. He's going to call when he gets closer, and I'll go out and make sure he can find the place."

The little cafe was tucked away in a strip mall that looked all but deserted from the main road. Basically, unless someone knew it was there, they wouldn't look. I had no idea how they stayed in business, but they managed.

Jackson raked his fingers through his hair, dragging the combed and ordered blond into a mess of spikes. He loved his job as a trade broker, but hated the dress code. I wasn't surprised he'd shed his tie already—it was probably in his car—and undone the top two buttons on his shirt. He reached across the table, covered my hand, and stroked his thumb over my knuckles. "Was work that bad?"

"Same as usual."

"Sorry to hear it." A heavy-metal bass riff drifted from his phone, and he grabbed it with his free hand. "It's Dark. Back in a few." He kissed me on the cheek, before striding toward the front door.

I fiddled with my phone, and then dropped it back in my purse. It would only take them a minute or two, and it felt rude to be staring at a digital screen when they came back. Besides, nervous energy hummed inside. Sure, I knew more about Dark than I did about most people I saw every day. He'd been by our side in game, not just for raiding parties, but for personal crap as well. Offering an ear. Occasionally asking for one. In a way, I was worried this meeting would ruin that. I'd hate to lose a friend because the medium changed.

"Look who I found." Jackson's voice startled me and dragged me back to the now.

I looked up, and my nervous laugh died on my lips. I stared into an eerily familiar pair of gorgeous brown eyes. My vocal chords refused to form words.

Recognition shone on his face, too. His gaze locked on mine.

"This is Zoe—ZaneyPixie," Jackson said.

It was him. Bad choices aside in life, dating, and work, he was the only thing about my past I truly regretted, no matter how much I told myself to move past it. I forced a weak smile to the surface. This explained why his voice sounded so familiar in game. "Hi, Carter."

FOUR

"Carter? Really?" Jackson gave a short bark of a laugh, and dropped onto the bench next to me. "What are the odds?"

He never sat on the same side of the table as me when there were bench seats. This was just because there was a third person. It had nothing to do with possessiveness or jealousy, or the fact I'd told him about large portions of my past. I was just overthinking… everything. My mind kicked into overdrive the moment I saw Carter.

"City of two million, and she and I both still live here? I'd say a million to one." Carter slid into the seat across from us. Unlike Jackson's, his shoulders were broad, and his chest defined enough to do justice to his fitted T-shirt. His dark hair was longer than I remembered, and pulled into a ponytail. "You know who I am, so the advantage is yours."

I dragged my gaze away. I wouldn't stare. "This is Jackson." I spit the words out, not sure where my mind was going, or if my mouth could keep up. "He's my…" Boyfriend. The word stuck in my throat. What was wrong with me?

"Your velvet-voiced wolf in sheep's clothing. I get that." Carter's gaze raked over Jackson. "At least you've still got good taste in men."

Heat flooded my skin, though I wasn't sure if it was arousal or embarrassment. Both, probably. Regret, and knowing Carter still lived in the same city, meant I'd played out a lot of awkward scenarios in my head about what would happen if he and Jackson ever met. Not a single of those involved one hitting on the other. Though Carter was the only other guy I'd ever met who was as open about his bisexuality as Jackson. Maybe I shouldn't be surprised.

"I could say the same." Jackson's tone was light and friendly. He intertwined his fingers with mine and shifted his weight on the bench, putting us closer together. "Don't worry. She only says good things about you."

Carter clenched his jaw, then relaxed it again so quickly I thought maybe I'd imagined it. An easy smile slid back into place. "You've got one up on me. She's never told me anything about you."

Was the air getting thicker, or was it my imagination? "Should we get coffee, since we're here?" I asked.

"Good call. My treat." Carter stood. "It's late, so vanilla steamer for you." He glanced at me for a second, before turning to Jackson. "And you?"

"Double shot Americano."

"Be right back." Carter turned away.

Jackson draped an arm around my waist, and trailed his nose up the side of my neck. "Do you want to go?" His whisper caressed my ear.

I leaned into him. This was ridiculous. I wasn't going to fall into whimpering and hiding behind niceties. I couldn't change my decisions from back then, but I still liked the life we had now. There was no reason to destroy that. I rested my hand on his thigh and squeezed. "I'm good. We're good. Aren't we?"

"Always, I hope." He nipped my shoulder with his teeth.

Carter returned a few minutes later and set our drinks in front of us. "Apparently, I don't know as much about the two of you as I thought." The creeping animosity had vanished from his voice, and his tone was casual now. "Where'd you meet? How'd you fall in love? Is the ink as new as it looks?"

My hand flew to the tattoo on my neck, and I rubbed the line with my thumb. "Online. It just kind of happened. And if it looks like it's still healing, then yes."

Carter leaned his head back, exhaled loudly, and then focused on us again. "You look happy."

"We are." I didn't want to be mean, but honesty was important.

"What did she tell you?" Carter asked Jackson.

My pulse kicked to a painful trot. I'd been as straightforward as I could, and I trusted Jackson, but that didn't stop trepidation from galloping through me over his answer.

"Said you were the love of her life when she was in her early twenties." An edge lined Jackson's voice. He cleared his throat. "That you wanted an open relationship, to invite other people in, but only if she was willing. That you promised not to pressure her into anything she wasn't ready for."

That was almost an exact summary of what I'd told Jackson. So why didn't hearing it take the edge off my mood?

"Did she tell you why she left?"

"I'm right here. You could ask me." I winced at the irritation in my voice. I hadn't meant to snap, but the third person thing was crawling under my skin.

"I could"—Carter looked at me—"but I already have a pretty good idea what you said. Sweet, honest, self-sacrificing Zoe. I remember. I wanted to know what he'd say."

"So, she really left you so she wouldn't get in your way?" Jackson asked.

"Yup." Carter reached across the table, nudged my fingers away from my drink, and slid his hand under mine.

A shock of familiarity flooded me, tingling in my gut. I pushed the memories aside.

"We're cool now, right? It was a long time ago. We were still finding ourselves. I forgave you already." His jaw worked up and down, as if he wanted to say something else, but he snapped his mouth shut.

At his reassurance, some of my tension evaporated. I squeezed his hand before pulling away. "Yeah, we're fine now."

"Good." He slouched a few inches in his seat, and his smile looked more casual and genuine. "Wow. Wasn't expecting that."

"Right?" Jackson laughed. His grip on my hand eased, but he didn't let go. "I'm just glad we cleared the air."

"Absolutely," Carter said. "Though I am curious what it took to strip your filters off, Zoe. I knew Pixie sounded like you, but the things that came out of her mouth… Not that I'm complaining. Just curious."

I tried to squash my embarrassment. Letting go in a virtual world, or around someone I trusted not to judge me, was one thing. Owning up to the foul language and innuendo in real life was something I was still adjusting to. I nodded at Jackson. "Someone helped me shed a few inhibitions."

Carter's smile wavered. "That's great."

This conversation needed to be somewhere else. Somewhere that didn't focus on my life then versus now. Somewhere neutral. "So what are you doing these days? What's DarkAngel into?"

"Besides spending my nights playing games?" He wasn't completely relaxed, but he was getting there. Even all these years later, I saw it in the tilt of his head and the angle of his back. "Contract work, mostly. Still play guitar when I'm not screwing around online. I'm even with a local band. We do gigs occasionally."

The waver of tension in the air dissipated during the next few hours. Somewhere along the way, the guys started tossing random questions back and forth at each other. I wasn't sure if it was more game or a bizarre kind of challenge, but it was fun.

"Your turn." Jackson had finished his coffee over an hour ago, but still tapped the empty cup back and forth.

Carter furrowed his brow for a moment. "Who's your favorite Avenger?" He looked at me. "You first."

"I don't know." I was familiar with the franchise. They just all had their own good and not-so-good qualities. "If I have to pick? Tony Stark."

Carter smirked, and Jackson stopped knocking his cup around, a frown shadowing over his face before disappearing. "I'm actually not picking, unlike some people." The teasing was back in Jackson's voice.

"That's not an answer, it's a cop-out," Carter said.

I enjoyed the banter. It was similar to in-game, and it was pleasant to see them getting along so well.

Jackson's sigh was exaggerated. "Tom Hiddleston."

"Loki isn't an Avenger."

I felt a bit like I was watching a verbal tennis match.

"I didn't say Loki. God, that accent. I'd go gay for that."

Carter laughed. "That implies you're straight now."

"Busted." There was no embarrassment in Jackson's retort. He draped his arm around my shoulders. "Though, there's no way I'm giving up this amazing woman so I get a quickie, even if it's from Tom Hiddleston. But that doesn't stop me from fantasizing about sucking him off."

"I think that's fair," Carter said.

"Your question, you have to answer now. Favorite Avenger."

"Since the two of you are going all physical attraction"—Carter pursed his lips in exaggerated concentration—"Steve Rogers."

"Chris Evans?"

"You suck at this. I said Avenger, not actor. Steve Rogers is a sexy package of wholesome American beauty." Carter raked his gaze over Jackson. "Blond, tall, good looks, and completely corruptible. I'd give him something worth kneeling for."

The blunt conversation had me flushed with embarrassment. Hearing them talk like this over chat was one thing, but in person put it on an entirely new level. I guess I hadn't expected the conversation to still be so direct. "The two of you are crass." I made sure to keep the teasing in my voice. I didn't want them to stop, even if it was a bit over the top.

"And you're not complaining." Carter turned his attention back to me. "Tony Stark, really?"

"I'm with him on this," Jackson said. "The dude is all ego."

"And a lot of brains. And confidence—completely hot." Neither of the men I was sitting with had any issues with either of those.

"And secure enough in his masculinity that he lets the woman he loves run his company. Because he's completely incompetent about it."

Jackson squeezed my fingers. "I think she's got a good point."

"Of course you do. She goes home with you at the end of the night." A strain crept into Carter's voice.

The conversation shifted, and the miniature bump of tension vanished. As we wound things up for the evening, I felt better about the past than I had...ever. The coffee shop employees had to shoo us out at closing time. We laughed and joked on the way to our cars, and then said our good nights.

Jackson hung over his car door. "Stop by my apartment tomorrow. I'll text you the address. The three of us will play in the same room, no headsets. Zoe's staying the night anyway."

"So, you're not living together?" Carter's expression became an emotionless mask.

"We've only been together two months," I said in lieu of an explanation. "Two good months, but still."

"Really." Carter's tone went flat. "Two months, and he's changed you this much? Kind of wish I knew his secret."

My gut sank. So much for things going smoothly. I didn't know how to respond.

"Tomorrow night it is, then." Carter slid into his car, started the engine, and pulled out without waiting for a response.

FIVE

I didn't want to part ways with Jackson after Carter left, but I needed sleep after the Sunday we'd had, and Jackson had an early meeting.

Too bad sleep didn't happen, once I got back to my apartment. I spent half the night tossing the coffee shop conversation over and over in my head, wondering if I could have handled things better, questioning how this would change the synchronicity we had with Dark. When I did manage to drift off, my imagination taunted me. Not with nightmares. With overlapping visions of Jackson—hands running over me, teasing, caressing, kissing—and Carter, who had been more aggressive in bed but just as incredible, pushing me back, ripping off my clothes, and leaving me breathless.

The alarm tore the seductive dreams from me, but not the feeling they left behind. The combination of memories blended and danced in my still-drowsy mind, tingling over my skin and begging for attention between my legs. I shoved my T-shirt up, and kneaded one breast, pinching my nipple until it ached. I slid my other hand lower, under my panties, immediately zeroing in on my clit. I was already wet from the dreams. My fingers wrapped easily around my swollen button, gliding up and down and stroking with frantic need.

I arched my back, gasping pants tearing from me when I came. I kept rubbing, even though I was tender and raw. I didn't stop until I couldn't take anymore, and then collapsed back onto the bed with a sigh.

Please let me make it through this. I didn't even know what *this* was, but I needed to survive it and come out the other side sane.

Exhaustion loomed, as I got ready for work. By the time I dragged myself to my desk at the office, the coffee was kicking in but only enough I didn't have to pry my eyes open with toothpicks. That the sensual dreams still danced on my skin didn't help. My head was in the most pleasant cloud ever, and didn't want to emerge for nasty realities like work.

I checked my email to make sure nothing critical was happening, and then dove back into the paperwork Tasha handed me yesterday. I hadn't been at it for long, when I was interrupted.

"Sutton." Mark Kitner's voice sent daggers of irritation through me. Since I'd broken up with him almost six months ago, we'd managed to keep ninety-nine percent of our interactions over emails, or through third parties like Tasha. Why was he approaching me now?

I spun in my chair, fake smile freezing in place when I saw who was with him. I searched for a polite way to ask Carter if he was following me, but for the second time in twenty-four hours, his wide-eyes said he was as surprised as me.

"This is Carter Erikson." If Kitner had any inking of our shared awkward stare, it didn't show. "He's our new data analyst. Contract to hire. I need you to show him the ropes."

What? I didn't train new people. It wasn't that I had a problem with the idea, but Ryan had always taken that job in the past. He'd been here long enough he knew all the obscure stuff. "Did you want me to teach him anything specific?"

"Yes." Kitner snagged an empty chair from a nearby cube, slid it next to mine, and gestured for Carter to sit. "Fill him in on all things Zedophap."

"I—" My protest died in my throat. I'd be professional about this. "We can start him on something more generic, like data structure. Maybe spin him up with a new client."

"No." Kitner was already turning away. "Bring him up to speed on Zedophap, and then we can get him familiar with other accounts."

We didn't have enough staff to cover new clients, let alone double people up on existing ones. What was going on? I dropped my face into my hands. A nasty thought nudged the back of my mind, and I pushed it aside, refusing to give it enough attention it could form into actual words.

"No, I'm not following you." Carter's teasing tone disrupted my descent into frustration.

I shook aside the cobwebs and focused on him. Not on the light stubble that said he hadn't shaved in a day or the faint earthy scent of his cologne. He'd always worn just enough it wasn't noticeable unless someone was close—it was more a suggestion than a smell. No, I wouldn't take notice of any of that. "I'm good. Data analysis, huh?"

He shrugged. "It's not where I started after college, but it's where the contracts ended up taking me. I have more of a knack for making the numbers say pretty things than presenting them to the people in charge."

"I get that." None of that explained why I was supposed to catch him up to speed on my clients, but I was already on thin ice at work. Rehashing a fancy-meeting-you-here conversation wouldn't be the best use of my time. "So, um…let's dive in, and stop me when you have questions."

"Hmm… Bossy Zoe." His comment barely reached my ears, even though he'd leaned in. "I could get used to that."

I wouldn't blush. I didn't care he sat close enough his heat brushed my arm. This was the perfect chance to prove I'd gotten over him. "You'll have to, at least until you know this stuff." I pointed at the document list. "This is our version control system."

The next several hours went smoothly, if I pretended I didn't notice every time Carter brushed my arm or whispered something meant only for my ears. He was good at what he did, and caught on quickly.

When a Human Resources person pulled him away to fill out some paperwork, I drew in a deep breath. I could do this. So far, so good, but I needed a drink. Too bad I didn't trust myself with anything stronger than soda. I wandered into the break room, stretching my legs and trying to shift my mind into a neutral spot.

Ryan was already at the vending machine. He flashed me a smirk. The biggest acknowledgment I'd gotten from him in months. "You pissed off the big guy, huh?"

I should be demure and polite, but I'd used the whole of my reserve already that morning. "You think? When I told you, way back when, that I left him because I didn't like what he did to you, did you think I was making up stories?" The words came out sharper than I intended, but it felt good. I was tired of Ryan scowling at me.

He raised his eyebrows. "Not making up stories. More like… sugar coating things, to make you look better."

I didn't need this. I stepped around him and dropped my coins in the machine. "Glad you've got such a high opinion of me."

"You were screwing the boss."

I whirled back to face him. "So you assumed I was a bad person?" I should have had things out with Ryan ages ago, but guilt had kept me from rocking the boat. I'd apologized, and it was up to him to accept that. "Besides, you hooked up with a project manager." I hid a wince. Maybe I shouldn't have dragged Tasha into this.

He glanced over his shoulder at the door, before looking back at me. His voice never rose. "It shows, huh?"

"A bit, yeah. I mean, it's not obvious, but something's changed…"

"A lot's changed. And what she and I have isn't the same."

I searched his face and the casual mask he'd put up when I brought up Tasha. What was he hiding? "How is it different?"

"I don't know what your reasons were for hooking up with Kitner, but since you've split, I can guess a few things. We're

93

different because I love Tasha and S—" He snapped his mouth shut.

The unfinished sentence stuck in my head. He loved Tasha and she loved him...? And stuff...? What had he meant to say? "I'm happy for you two." I made sure to keep my tone sincere. "And yeah, I meant it when I said I was sorry and I made some mistakes."

He shrugged. "It's all right. I should have let you off the hook sooner."

Elders, what an ass. "Glad to hear we're better. I have to get back to training the new guy."

"Zoe." The word landed against my back. "I'm sorry Kitner's making you train your own replacement. Grudge or not, you don't deserve that."

Replacement. The word sank like a stone in my gut. The words I'd refused to let myself think. This wasn't an exercise in busywork, to keep me from getting my other tasks done on time. This was Kitner's move to push me out the door. "Thanks for that." I headed back to my desk, a new kind of dread spilling through me.

Carter was already waiting, lounged in his chair, casual smile in place. "What time's lunch? Kitner told me to coordinate with you."

I was surprised Mark hadn't told him to just do whatever he wanted, to see how I'd react. I also hadn't realized how late it was. "Now, I guess. Be back in an hour?"

"Let me treat you."

"Carter."

"Stop." His voice had dropped in volume again. "We decided we were cool last night. If the three of us are going to keep hanging out, we may as well figure out how to get past the awkward alone time. Right?"

Stupid logic. "Yes."

"So pick a place. Lunch is on me."

"No." I grabbed my purse. "We split the bill."

He leaned close enough his breath brushed my skin when he whispered, "Yup, I think I like bossy Zoe."

I couldn't fight the flush that time, so I ducked my head and cut a straight line for the door, hoping he'd follow.

SIX

We stepped through the front door of the little restaurant I'd navigated us to. A wash of chatter and the scent of curry greeted us.

"Really?" Carter sounded pleased. "Spicy food? You?"

I knew he'd like the place, and was surprised he hadn't heard of it before. "No. They make a wimp version of an amazing mango curry."

He shook his head, but was smiling. We were seated at a table and given a simple menu, along with instructions I'd heard many times. That the heat level ranged from zero to ten, but if Carter had never been here before and liked it hot, he probably wanted to start with a three.

He raised his brows at the implied challenge. "What if I want to start with ten?"

The waitress smirked. "I'll bring you a three, and if it's not hot enough, I'll take it back and get you something else."

"How about a four? And be prepared to take it back."

She grabbed our menus. "If you want. I'll bring extra ice water." She moved to the next table.

ALLYSON LINDT

Carter turned his attention to me. "I'm not stepping on your toes at work, am I?"

"No." The reassurance flew to my lips without thought, and I paused. "I mean, yeah, you are, but it's not your fault."

He drummed his fingers on the table. "I had a feeling. You looked almost as surprised to be training someone as you were to see me."

Was I really so transparent, or did he just know me that well? "It's not a big deal."

"It is. I'll find a new contract."

The concern warmed me, but my chest tightened at the same time, as if a fist squeezed my heart. Where had that reaction come from? The answer struck me. I didn't like the idea of Carter vanishing from my life again, even though he'd only been back in it for a day. I also didn't like that the idea of him scared me, but I couldn't ignore the trepidation filling me. "I appreciate it. But Kitner will bring on someone else, if you leave, and the next person probably won't be as understanding."

His gaze lingered on my face for a moment. "Is there a story there, or is Kitner just as big a jerk as he appears on the surface?"

The nature of the question caught me off-guard. Most people liked Mark Kitner on first meeting. It took a while before he dropped the pretenses, and even then, only if he was pissed off. "Why did you take the job if you don't like the boss?" I asked.

"A boss may or may not make a job, but the offer was good, and I thought I'd try it out. Why did you dodge my question?"

Hiding things from Carter wasn't going to be easy, unless I put some more effort into it. I wasn't sure if that was a bad thing or not. "I started here a year or so ago, and he wasn't my boss then. So when he hit on me and said all the sweet, flattering things a girl likes to hear, I decided to give things a try. Except then he pulled a few strings to get me into his department, and I discovered he'd broken a lot of corporate rules and threatened someone else's job, to put me there. Turned out he'd done it to get back at the other guy, not for me, but that didn't change the situation any in my mind, so I left him."

"And then came Jackson."

Not quite where I'd expected Carter to go. I twisted my mouth in frustration. "We can't keep coming back to this."

"We also can't keep ignoring it's there."

"What do you want from me, Carter?"

He slouched in his seat and interlocked his fingers. "I'm not trying to be a jerk. I just want the full story. I mean, given how we ended…"

He probably did deserve the truth. When we dated, five or so years ago, Carter encouraged me to break out of the tight, conservative shell I'd formed growing up in a religious environment. Some of the things he suggested excited me, but others were terrifying. The kind of stuff I'd been raised not to think about. Like bringing another person into our relationship, to experiment—male or female, he left it up to me.

However, he'd also told me he wouldn't pressure me. That he loved me and we'd do those things when I was ready and not before. The longer we stayed together, the more I realized he wasn't going to be happy with just me and plain old boring sex. I couldn't be what he needed, so I left him to explore life the way he wanted.

I took a deep breath and collected my thoughts. "After we broke up, I kept coming back to *us*. To what you wanted. To what we had together. I struggled to accept that I could ever be those things. That I had any interest in something like… being with two people at the same time." I pushed the words out more easily than I expected. "It was always in the back of my mind. Time passed, it had been a few years, and I realized I'd become more comfortable with the idea, but it wasn't like I could just go find you again."

Carter's attention never left me, and his expression was soft. "Why not?"

I stumbled on the question. "Because relationships don't work that way. I wasn't going to be the girl who crawled back and begged for a second chance from a guy who had moved on. I didn't think it was an option. I met Mark, and I thought I was being naughty. It was an office romance, forbidden-love kind of thing. Except dating coworkers isn't against the rules here. But still, we fooled around a few times in his office after everyone went home. There was a little rush, but not quite the spark I was looking for."

I had no idea why I was being so open with Carter about any of this, but it felt right. I knew I could trust him. "After I split up with him, I met Jackson. He was bolder and more direct than anyone I knew—except you. He calls me out on what I'm thinking, gets me to share what's on my mind, coerces fantasies from me I don't know I've got…"

I trailed off when I realized Carter's expression had shifted. The corners of his mouth and eyes tugged down. He shook his head, and a smile flitted back in. "I can tell he's really good for you."

"He is." It didn't matter what other confusion or frustration was in my mind. Jackson and I were incredible together.

"I'm glad. I don't begrudge you that. You deserve to be happy."

"So are we actually okay now?" I asked. "Not this phony let's-be-polite stuff?"

"We're actually okay now."

It sounded like he meant it this time. We'd still have obstacles, but maybe we could actually be friends.

Our food arrived, and the waitress watched closely, while Carter took a bite.

"You want it hotter?" she asked.

A thin sheen of sweat broke across his forehead. He hesitated, and then shook his head. "No, I'm good. Thank you."

She shook her head, a tiny smile threatening her face. "I'll check back on you."

We spent a few seconds shifting dishes, and taking a taste. "Fantasies, huh? Care to share a couple?" Carter asked, open curiosity in his tone.

It was tempting. Probably more than it should be. If all three of us were online, when he was just Dark to us, it's possible I would have. "Not between just us. Maybe if Jackson were here."

"Of course. He's always invited to watch."

The words stuck in my head, and I worked to shove aside the thoughts they tugged at—the memories of two nights ago with Jackson. I wouldn't let myself connect the dots. I wouldn't draw any conclusions or make any suggestions. Carter and I were just about to move into a more comfortable, friendly place.

"Speaking of watching, when's your band's next gig?" A rapid change in subject was the only out I could think of. "We'd love to see you perform."

Carter smirked. "I'd like that too. Area Fifty-One. You should definitely both come."

"Do you write their songs, or is that not your thing anymore?"

"I write some of them."

"Sing me something?" I let the hope slip into my request. Carter had an amazing singing voice. He could wail like a heavy-metal god, or slip into a love song without issue.

He sang a sweet ballad. I'd never heard it before—I assumed it was one of his songs—but I found myself keeping beat with the song after only a few lines. We shifted our focus back to lunch and I found myself more and more drawn into the conversation, and leaving my apprehension behind. Maybe I could actually find a balance with Carter that didn't involve romance.

SEVEN

I parked next to Carter's car, in the guest parking lot, and made my way toward Jackson's apartment. The rest of the work day had been more of what the morning offered, but at least the tension wasn't as high with Carter. By the time five rolled around, only the occasional stumble interrupted us. I'd been halfway out the door, when Mark called me back and asked me to finish some last-minute tasks. I told Carter to go without me, and ended up spending the next hour on more of Mark's bullshit tasks. I hadn't even bothered to go home and change, so I still wore my blouse and skirt.

I walked into Jackson's apartment without knocking. I didn't have a key, but he left the door unlocked on nights he knew I was coming over.

Carter had already staked out a spot on the floor near the far window, and his laptop sat on the coffee table. He'd had a chance to change into something more comfortable. He looked like that had always been his spot, as he leaned back with one leg propped up, wrist resting on his knee. He flashed me a warm smile. "Are you following me?"

Jackson stepped between us, wrapped an arm around my waist, and pressed his lips to mine. He held me tight, entire frame pressing against me. My pulse soared, and the gesture chased away more of the day. I sighed and rested my forehead against his, after we broke the kiss.

"Coworkers, huh?" Jackson let me go, but I wrapped myself in the lingering comfort of his greeting.

"Better." I looked at Carter, who was staring at his laptop, not doing anything. "Did you tell him the rest of it?"

Carter's head flew up. "Uh, no. I thought I'd let you do the honors."

"Thanks." I stuck my tongue out at him. I was going to keep this casual and fun, regardless of what it took. "He's being groomed to be my replacement."

Jackson clenched his jaw, and a growl rumbled from his chest. "You know Mark can't do this."

"I know he's got a lot more influence and pull than me, so I'd better have actual proof for accusing him of trying to push me out, before I pursue any complaints." It was an old disagreement—one I didn't expect would go away until either Mark or I quit. "Besides, the guy I'm training is nice. He feels bad about it. And there's nothing we can do tonight, so let's play."

Jackson nodded to the chair against the wall, where I usually sat. "Plug in. We're already on."

I woke my computer up, and stopped halfway to plugging my headset in. Right. I didn't need to do that. As with the night before, in the coffee shop, it didn't take long for the conversation to shift to the familiar banter we were used to online. Even though we started our game clients, none of us made it past the character login screens.

At some point during the conversation, we logged off the game one by one, and closed our machines. Apparently, half the time we were only playing to talk to Dark. Now that he was in the room with us, we could eliminate the middle-man.

I relocated to sit next to Jackson on the couch, Carter took my spot in the easy chair, and still the conversation stayed light and fun. At some point my eyes drooped shut, and I snapped my head back up with a jolt.

"Still a morning person?" Carter asked, sympathy in his eyes.

"Especially when we keep her up too late, too many nights in a row." Jackson tucked a loose strand of hair out of my face. "Go to bed, Pixie."

I shook my head. "I'm good here a little longer." A yawn threatened to split my jaw. "But I might lie down."

Jackson patted his leg, and I shifted so my head rested on his thigh, my legs tucked up behind me. I risked a look at Carter, worried he might be wearing that same almost-sad expression I'd seen too many times in the last day, but he was still smiling, looking fine with the whole thing. Good. It would be fine. Everything would be fine.

I struggled to keep up with the conversation, but the small part of my brain that was still conscious knew I wasn't grasping any of what was being said.

The next thing I was aware of was a sharp pain in my neck, and the discomfort of prying open dry, tired eyes.

"Hey. Welcome back." Jackson helped me sit up.

I stretched my shoulders and struggled to grasp the world around me again. Carter and Jackson still sat in the same spots, but something was off about their postures. The clock on the wall told me I'd only been out about an hour. "What did I miss?"

"Nothing." Jackson's answer came too quickly. Or my brain was moving too slowly. "Random shit. Guy stuff."

No, there was definitely something off about his tone. "What does that even mean? Guy stuff?"

"We were talking about you," Carter said.

My gut twisted. Why did I assume that was bad? "Because I was snoring?"

"No." Jackson's laugh was forced.

Carter started. "Because he thinks you didn't—"

"Don't." A heavy warning hung in Jackson's voice.

My uneasiness grew, and I shifted my weight enough to look at Jackson. "Don't what?"

"Nothing."

"No. That's bullshit." I wouldn't have delved too far into questions, but even half-awake, I knew Jackson didn't close off like this. "You don't think I what?"

Jackson narrowed his eyes, and directed the glare at Carter. "Not what we agreed to."

"No secrets, dude." Carter's satisfaction was tinged with an uneasiness I didn't expect.

Jackson turned his attention back to me, and his expression softened. "I know you still care about him. That despite what you say, there are still regrets."

Wherever this was going wasn't right. "We're dealing. He's still a friend, and we can make it work."

Jackson's smile didn't reach his eyes. "I don't want you to have to do that. I promised you this relationship was as much about exploring your wants and needs as it was mine. If that's Carter, then that's the way it is. It'll hurt like hell, but I'll let you go."

A giant void grew inside, aching and gnawing at my every nerve. "What? You'd give me up just like that? For a random guy you barely know and a situation you've only just touched the edge of?"

"No. Not just like that." Jackson trailed his thumb over my cheek. "I'll be honest—it'll all but kill me to let you go. But you have to do this for you."

"Fuck you." I spat the words, hiding my hurt under venom, and summoning rage to burn away the ache in my bones. "I mean, oh yay, how sweet of the two of you to decide what it's okay for me to do. At least you did it while I was in the room, even if I was passed out. But you know what? That's my decision. Not yours. I made my choices; I live with them. And even though you're seriously making me waver on one of them right now, you and I are together unless our reason for splitting is us, not some random third party."

"But it's not that easy"—A raw edge crept into Jackson's voice— "because I don't think you want to get over him."

The reality of his words sank in. It was easier for me to ignore what I felt for Carter when he wasn't in my life, but with him right in front of me... Jackson was right, and I hated him for knowing that about me. Even more, I hated myself for not wanting to admit it. "You don't get to say that."

"Why not?" Carter cut in. "It was okay for you to do it to me five years ago, but not for him to do it now?"

"It's not okay." I whirled on him. Tears stung my eyes, and I blinked them back. "It was stupid of me then. It's stupid of him now."

"You know that, but you don't want to take it back?" Jackson asked.

Holy fuck, why were they teaming up on me? I struggled to keep my thoughts afloat amid the turmoil flooding my heart. I wasn't going to deal with this. I stood and backed away from Jackson. "You know what? Fuck you both. You can stay here and fight or negotiate or fuck or whatever, as long as I'm not the bargaining chip. I'm going home."

EIGHT

I had my hand on the doorknob when someone grabbed my arm. I recognized the control in the grip before I registered Carter's face as he spun me toward him, so my shoulder was to the door and Jackson was behind me. "That didn't go the way it was supposed to. I'm sorry," Carter said.

Tears tinged my vision. I dragged my hand across my face, and the friction burned my cheeks. "How exactly is something like that supposed to go? 'Hey babe, I love you, but bye'?"

Carter's laugh was bitter. "Stings, doesn't it?"

I shook my head and jerked out of his grasp. "I'm leaving."

He didn't reach for me again, but his voice was enough to make me pause. "Talk this through with us."

I sniffled and summoned the last of my composure. "I'm sorry about all those years ago. I really, really am. I loved you completely, and yeah, it hurt like hell to make a decision that stupid. But I'm not that person any more. I've dealt with my past. I'm with Jackson now. He helped me shed so much of what held me back, he pushes me more toward that every day, and I like to think I give him something in return. He wasn't the impetus for my changing, though; I would have done that regardless. He just gave me the safety I needed to let it happen. Don't you dare take that away from me."

I didn't dare look behind me. Couldn't stand to meet Jackson's gaze, after a speech like that. So I kept my attention on Carter. He was the guy I was pushing out.

"I get it," Carter said. "I can tell you're happy together. And I know you do the same for him that he does for you, because he told me. I'm not trying to... Okay, that's a lie. I was trying a little to break you up. It doesn't matter how good you are together—it doesn't stop me from missing you. But I meant it earlier, that I can put that behind me. I'm bummed I never got to see this kinkier, less reserved side of you."

"Pixie." Jackson's voice sank into the cracks in my frustration, and soothed me in a way I didn't want. "Do you remember what I asked you about, a few nights ago?"

The question summoned memories I didn't want just now. Arousal. Desire. Diving into Jackson's fantasy about me being with another man. I struggled to draw a breath amid the conflicting emotions. I didn't know if I was more turned on or pissed off that he'd bring that up now, of all times.

"Are you still interested?" Carter asked.

I pursed my lips. I wanted to grab onto more betrayal, but it was sliding away behind want. "He told you."

Carter shrugged. "Jackson's more comfortable sharing his fantasies with me than you are."

Jackson's hands rested on my hips, the heat from his touch melting more of my frustration. "What if that was actually an option? You and Carter get another chance. Not at *you*, but at a no-strings version of what you never got."

This was so ridiculous, I didn't know why I was still there. It certainly wasn't because part of me clung to the suggestion. "It's not no-strings, because of this entire conversation we just had. Were the two of you listening? How did we go from the me-choosing-and-everyone-understanding bullshit to no-strings sex?"

"Guy stuff?" Carter suggested.

"He wasn't supposed to lead with that." Jackson tightened his grip enough his fingers dug into my hips. I tried not to dwell on the possessiveness in the gesture, but I needed the reassurance. It was the one thing I expected in this mess. "That was supposed to be a plan B, to make sure you had an out, in case you didn't go for the first idea."

"That's ridiculous. You're both insane." I poured emphasis into the words, as much to reinforce the notion in my head as anything.

Carter traced a finger over my ear. "Is that a no? You're not interested?"

Damn them.

"It is ridiculous"—Jackson's breath was hot against the back of my neck—"but the entire situation is completely, implausibly ludicrous."

"It's a bad idea." Fantasy and memories of both men weakened my resolve with each passing minute, nudging aside my reasons for arguing.

Carter trailed his finger along my jaw and over my bottom lip. "It's closure. I don't expect you to come back to me, after. It's really fucking obvious where your heart is." He swallowed. "This is only sex. If our only regret is we never got to try this, now's our chance."

There was so much more to the situation than that, but if I kept arguing, I'd lose the chance. Saying yes would come with new baggage, but not a lot more than what already existed. The tension was already there, between Carter and me. And if I said no, I'd hate myself for it. "All right."

"You're sure?" Jackson trailed his lips along the back of my neck.

I wasn't, but when he pulled me closer and his erection dug into my butt cheek, the remainder of my hesitation slunk away behind how much I wanted this.

"I'm sure."

Jackson nipped at my ear with his teeth. "I love you," he whispered.

His hands still rested at my hips, when Carter closed the distance between us, captured my face between his hands, and crushed his mouth to mine. Reason evaporated, and I groaned against his mouth. Cool air met my back. Carter slid one hand up, to tangle his fingers in my hair, and tugged my head back. His teeth scraped along my throat, to the soft spot where my shoulder met my neck. The day's worth of stubble on his chin and cheek left a delicious burn on my skin. I dug my fingers into his chest when he sucked and bit at the sensitive skin, marking me.

He dragged his gaze back to mine, and held my head captive. A wicked smirk had replaced his casual smile, and my heart hammered against my ribs.

"God, I missed the way you yield." Carter claimed my mouth again.

He slid his hand down my arm, intertwined his fingers with mine, and led me toward the bedroom. He stopped me in the middle of the room, a foot or so from the bed, and stepped in front of me again. I registered Jackson sinking into a chair in the corner, and the sound of a zipper sliding down.

I expected the sight to make me hesitate, but a new surge of desire rushed through me when Jackson worked his cock free and wrapped his fist around it.

Carter raked his gaze over me, devouring me even though I still had all my clothes on. I shivered under his attention, as anticipation built inside. He rested his palms on my neck, and then moved lower, his caress gentle on my skin. He reached the collar of my shirt and grabbed both sides. He yanked hard and ripped my shirt open, sending buttons clattering everywhere and my pulse screaming through my veins. My senses flared at his attention, nipples straining against lace and wetness growing between my legs.

"Fuck," Jackson muttered.

Carter stepped in and wrapped an arm around my waist. "Getting there." Gravel lined his voice.

I managed to find my voice. "That was silk. And expensive."

"I'll replace it." Any of the negotiation that had been in Carter's voice earlier was gone.

And, Elders, I wanted him to own me for the night.

He shoved up one bra cup, forcing elastic over my already pert nipple, and then dragged a calloused thumb across the hard nub.

I reached for him. Something to grab. Needing to touch more of him.

"No." His single word stopped me. "Hands to yourself. This is my game tonight."

I dropped my arms back to my sides. "What am I supposed to do, then?"

He massaged my breast, as he lowered his mouth and sucked hard on the sensitive flesh. Pleasure spiked through me at the rough handling, and I leaned into him. He pulled away and blew on the damp skin. The combination of cold and hot drew a gasp from me.

Carter looked me in the eye. "If I do my job, you're supposed to enjoy yourself as much as I'm about to."

NINE

Carter shoved the other side of my bra out of the way, and alternated his attention between sucking and tweaking my nipples. The blood rushed from my brain, leaving me lightheaded and euphoric.

It was a struggle to keep my hands by my sides. I pressed into him instead, shifting until my hip rubbed his erection through his jeans. I slid my knee up his leg, and my skirt crept higher, as I pushed for more contact.

He stepped back with a hard laugh. "Not what I had in mind."

I liked nudging these boundaries. When we were together before, I'd been timid, not trusting myself with what Carter really wanted. Now I was willing to erase that line. If I only had tonight, I wanted the Carter I'd blocked out before. "You should have been more specific."

"My mistake." In a single swift move, he grabbed my hips, twirled me, and lifted me onto the middle of the mattress. He straddled my legs and pinned my arms above my head, trapping me between him and the bed.

Jackson grunted, and his breathing grew heavier.

My teasing laugh died in my throat when I met Carter's gaze

again. Lust, desire, and something more serious I refused to recognize stared back. "Keep your eyes on mine." He forced one knee between my legs. Denim rubbed my thighs, raising sparks and making me squirm with need. "I want to watch your eyes when you come. Want to see the gorgeous expression on your face."

I bit my bottom lip, my short pants of breath making it hard to speak. He dropped his hand lower and shoved my skirt out of the way. He found the source of my need in seconds and pushed the crotch of my panties aside. I thrust closer to his touch when he rubbed my slit with rough fingers. I wanted to close my eyes, sink into the sensation, but his gaze held me captive.

I moaned and ground against him, orgasm driving in quickly. The sights around me bled together and stopped making sense. I cried out as I came, frantic and hard. Instead of easing off, he forced three fingers inside me, and hooked up. I couldn't look any more. The sensations were too much. I closed my eyes and let the pleasure wash over me, as I slammed against his hand.

The frantic rhythm slowed. The pressure on my wrists eased, and I forced my eyes open, a lazy smile playing on my face. He lowered his head and laid a row of kisses along my face and up to my ear. "I need to be inside you." Despite the tender touches, hunger dominated his whisper.

"Fuck me hard." I pushed extra pleading into my voice, and made sure Jackson heard me.

"Filthy, naughty Zoe." Carter pulled a condom from his back pocket, unzipped his jeans, worked his cock free, and sheathed it. "I fucking love it."

He startled me by sliding a finger inside me again. He withdrew, and then thrust his dick in to the hilt, spreading me open. I clenched the sheets, and arched my back, diving into the sensation.

Jackson's groans matched Carter's grunts as he pounded me hard. I knew from Jackson's voice he was close to peaking, and my arousal climbed another notch at the familiar sound of him coming. Carter slid his still slick finger in my ass, and I gasped at the new feeling. I'd never... the thought faded in another wash of climax.

My pussy clenched around Carter, and his pace increased, drawing out my orgasm.

His grunts were near primal, and he gripped my hip with his free hand, hard enough to leave a mark, as he finished. He took his time slowing and easing me back from the edge of pleasure.

I still couldn't focus my thoughts, when he leaned in and kissed me before pulling out and rolling to the side. Silence flooded the room, punctuated only by heavy breathing. I wasn't sure how much time passed before Jackson helped me sit.

Carter climbed to his feet to go wash up. I grabbed his hand. "You're not going home yet, are you?" I didn't know where the question came from, but I couldn't bring myself to take it back.

His expression was unreadable. "No." He turned away and headed toward the bathroom.

Jackson drew me close, his voice low. "I was right. That was one of the hottest things I've ever seen."

A new rush of heat flooded me, and I buried my face in his chest. "It's okay, right?" I couldn't be specific. I was pretty sure I meant the entirety of the evening, but I might have meant more. "We're okay?"

"Always, Pixie." He brushed his lips over mine.

I curled up against Jackson, the way I normally did when we first climbed into bed, and rested my hand on his chest, our fingers intertwined.

Carter slid into bed behind me, chest pressed against my back, and draped his arm over mine, covering both our hands.

A nagging voice in the back of my head reminded me this wasn't how no-strings worked. This wasn't closure; it was going to be a new kind of pain in the morning. I smothered the doubt. Right now, it was exactly what I wanted, and I didn't think Jackson or Carter minded.

I WOKE up before the guys the next morning. Without the haze of desire clouding my thoughts, reality rushed back in. How were we going to walk away from this? Or maybe I was the only one with a problem. Neither of them had seemed fazed by much of what happened yesterday. I steeled myself against a wave of doubt. I could be cool about this. Sever ties with Carter and make the night before exactly what it was supposed to be.

I extracted myself from the pile of limbs, careful not to disturb either one of my—the guys. I kissed them both on the cheek, grabbed one of my spare T-shirts from Jackson's drawers, and cut a straight line for my car. I could have gotten ready for work here, I had enough stuff at Jackson's place, but I needed time to compose myself. A breather, to cement my resolve.

By the time I made it home, I had convinced myself this was good. Last night had been amazing—I didn't question that. Even amid everything else, I didn't regret it. And I was fine this morning. There were amazing memories, but nothing else had to change. Things would be great.

I had finished showering and getting dressed, and was on my way back to my car, when Jackson texted me.

Missed you this morning.

I smiled at the sentiment, and sent back a reply. *Too much to do at work. Sorry I had to run out.*

He got back to me seconds later. *No worries. Don't let Mark give you any shit. You coming over tonight?*

That was a good idea. It would be part of getting things back to normal. Just like pasting on a smile for Carter at work, and dialing everything between us back to 'friendly.'

Absolutely, I wrote.

There. That had been status quo. Nothing had changed. We'd all be good. And if I said it enough times, over and over in my head, it would make it true.

TEN

I settled into my desk a few minutes early. My mind was hopping a million miles a minute now, still working over everything I tried not to think about. I was wired now, but I'd be dragging by this afternoon. I hoped things went as smoothly with Carter, once he got here, as they had with Jackson. Which made me wonder how they'd gotten along this morning, waking up in the same bed.

In a way, I wished I could have seen it.

"Hey, boss." Carter pushed a chair into my cubicle, and dropped into it. He still hadn't shaved. I wouldn't focus on how sexy that was on him. Wouldn't let it summon memories of the stubble burning against my skin.

I slid a smile into place more easily than I expected. I was happy to see him, even with the conflict raging inside. "Morning." Would he be obnoxious? Push some kind of confrontation about last night? Was I hoping for that? Because backing down wasn't the Carter I remembered. Then again, I'd changed. He had to have, as well.

"What's on the docket for the day?" He stayed at a reasonable distance—not too far away, but not close enough for me to sense him.

"I assume more of the same, unless someone told you otherwise."

He leaned in, and his barely-there cologne teased my senses. He whispered, "I missed you this morning, but I get it. And thank you for last night."

Ambivalence spiked my heart. So many things I could say. I could ask… I didn't even know. All my options would draw out the situation. "Same for me."

He straightened again, and leaned back in his chair. "That's non-specific."

I shrugged. It was, but I didn't have anything better. Was the whole day going to be like this?

"Erikson." Mark's bark carried halfway across the room, and several heads turned toward his office. "Conference room O-49. Reception can tell you where it is. I need you in the Granwald launch meeting today.

I'd held my tongue with Mark Kitner for months now, never arguing in public, and only rarely rocking the boat over email or through third parties, but I was tired, and this was bullshit. I stood. "Granwald's my account." I made sure my voice reached him, not caring who heard. "I worked with sales for months, to secure them."

"Sutton, my office. Erikson, fourth floor, window side, O-49."

Carter shot me an apologetic look, and his hand shifted toward mine. He flexed his fingers, and then turned away without making contact.

I ground my teeth and kept my back straight, gaze locked on my target, as I marched into Kitner's office.

He closed the door behind me and nodded to a seat. "You don't want to do this in front of everyone."

I didn't sit. "Why not?" Apparently exhaustion had zapped more of my filters than I realized. "It's not like they're not all talking about it anyway."

Expression calm, Mark sank into his chair and leaned back, one ankle propped on the other knee. "We don't typically give new clients to analysts who are falling behind with their old ones."

I knew this ploy. I'd been on the other side of it when he'd pulled it with Ryan. But I'd watched my back and made sure I couldn't be set up. "All of my work is in and accounted for."

"You're sure?"

Fuck, what had I missed?

"Because the Zedophap audit is tomorrow, and I was just in the file share. It's not looking good."

The wheels in my brain wobbled, and bile rose in my throat. "Audit?"

Mark widened his eyes. "The one I told the entire team about, two weeks ago? They don't like the way we've handled their account, and have ordered a full internal audit of our records with them to date."

I would have argued that maybe if he stopped swapping out analysts because he was a petty asshole who took his personal problems out on employees, they might not have an issue with the way their account had been handled. My mind still whirred over the claim I'd known about this for weeks. It was definitely the first time I'd heard about it. "What do I need to do?"

"Go through their documents and make sure all the most recent versions are checked into the system. The normal work. It just has to be done by tomorrow, but I know you're on top of it, so that won't be a problem."

"Of course." Sugar dripped from my voice. "We'll be fine."

Eyes were on me when I stalked from his office. I didn't care. Any obstacle Mark threw at me, I'd climb and conquer. When I left this company, it would be on my terms, not because he forced me out of my job.

I settled in front of my computer and grabbed the folder Tasha had handed me the other day. I would have finished the project yesterday, but I'd been training the new guy. Not that any of this was Carter's fault. Irritation burned away the lingering traces of sleepy, confused fog in my brain, and I honed in on my work.

I kept on top of these things, so it wasn't like I'd be here all night. Being done by tomorrow would be a piece of cake.

I opened the document management system and clicked through to the Zedophap files. My insides twisted in on themselves at the chaos that greeted me. Locking errors, file missing warnings, and out-of-date alerts.

He'd had to fuck me one last time. No. I breathed deeply through my nose and forced myself to exhale slowly. I would handle this and still get out of here on time.

I couldn't ignore the minutes ticking by, as I worked my way through individual files. For the audit, every document stored had to be the most recent one, and match exactly between the email archive and here. Contracts, data configurations, everything. Some looked okay. But I had to open most individually and do manual comparisons, to make sure the correct version was saved in both systems. It wasn't as simple as just picking the email version and saving it over again, because the timestamps and digital date trail had to match as well.

As the clock crept up on noon and I wasn't even a quarter of the way done, I had to admit a sliver of defeat. Not that I was giving up, but something would have to go. I sent Jackson a quick text. *I'm going to be very late tonight. I'm sorry.*

It took a few minutes for him to reply. *It's okay. Can I bring you dinner or anything?*

That would be nice. Take a break, spend some time with him, and get back to work. But I knew I wouldn't get anything done that way. It would be too tempting to let work slip. *I'd love that, but no. The faster I finish, the faster I'll be there.*

Seconds later, my phone rang, his picture smirking at me from the screen. "Hey." I answered with a smile, locked my computer, and strode toward a more private part of the building.

"You can't eat vending-machine food for dinner."

The concern in his words warmed me. "It wouldn't be the first time. It'll be a nice complement to its twin lunch."

"Is this really work, or just a specific coworker?"

Ice rolled through my veins at what he was implying, and a retort died in my throat. I didn't even know how to respond to that.

"I'm sorry. I didn't mean that," Jackson said.

"The two of you are such good friends now. Why don't you invite him over tonight?" I struggled to keep the bitterness from my voice, and failed. "Put your mind at ease, decide more of my future while you're at it." I didn't want to fight with Jackson, but I wasn't letting a comment like that slide.

"Pixie, no. That was the wrong thing for me to say. I don't want to argue."

"I have to go."

"Wait. Come over tonight, no matter how late you are. Even if it's three in the morning. It'll be just you and me."

I could tell him no. Make him suffer a little longer, for the bullshit jealousy, but it meant he cared. Besides, maybe I'd call in tomorrow. Let everyone else deal with the audit I hadn't been told about. Sleep in. Spend the day with Jackson. I knew I wouldn't—we were both too responsible to skip work like that—but it was a nice fantasy. Still, I did need to see him. "All right. I'll be there."

ELEVEN

One by one, the desks around me emptied, and people called their goodnights to each other. Office lights clicked off, half the overheads dimmed, and the ambient chatter of phone calls faded. I'd made it more than halfway through my document list. It was only a mess because someone had sabotaged it, but I didn't have the time to prove that and still finish before tomorrow.

As it was, I really might not make it to Jackson's until three in the morning.

Tasha, Ryan, and his roommate Seth stopped at my desk. "You're here late." Tasha sounded sympathetic.

"Prepping for the audit tomorrow." I couldn't keep the exhaustion from my face. "How long have you known about it?" Come to think of it, why wasn't she panicking and rushing to finish things last minute?

Tasha shrugged. "A couple of weeks."

The information added another layer of tiredness to my brain. Maybe I'd actually missed the announcement. "I didn't find out until today."

She frowned and leaned forward, arms on the cubicle. "Kitner

ALLYSON LINDT

said he was handling it, or I would have told you. Gods, I'm so sorry."

Of course he had. "Don't worry about it. Karma's a bitch, right?"

Ryan held his hand toward Tasha. "I rode in with Seth this morning. Are you okay to leave me your keys and go home with him?"

She handed them over without question. "Absolutely. You're staying then?"

"I'm stubborn, not cruel. I'll see you at home." He kissed her on the cheek. It was the most obvious affection I'd ever seen between the two of them. Elders, I hoped Jackson and I could keep that. When he squeezed Seth's hand too, I widened my eyes but kept my mouth shut. That was too tender a gesture to be between just roommates.

Seth and Tasha left, and Ryan dragged over the chair Carter had been using. "Tell me where you're at, what you're doing, and how I can help."

"Why?" I shouldn't be challenging the offer, but considering he'd all but ignored me until a few days ago and someone had helped Kitner set me up, I had to know.

"Because otherwise, you'll be here for the rest of eternity?"

He was right, but it didn't answer my question. "No. Why help me? I'm not dim. I know what I did, even though I didn't mean to do it. You're not the only one paying the price, and Tasha is struggling too."

"Work shouldn't be personal," Ryan said, as if it were the most obvious statement ever. "Kitner makes it that, and he's wrong. You shouldn't have to pay the price for doing what was right."

I scooted my chair aside, to let him see my screen. "I'm doing the most tedious task on the face of the planet. Now's your last chance to back out."

"Nope. He deserves to suffer as much as you shouldn't have to. Give me the bottom half of what's left."

I grabbed the last sheet of paper from my folder and handed it over. "Thank you." I didn't spend time explaining what I

120

needed—his job was the same as mine, he was familiar with the details.

"No worries." Seconds later, I heard him sit at his own desk, and his mouse clicks joined mine.

My mind chewed on something while I worked, but I wasn't sure what. It nagged at the back of my thoughts, trying to force its way past document comparison. Something about Ryan. What, though? Not that he was helping, though I definitely owed him lunch for that. And probably Tasha and Seth too.

My thoughts skidded to a stop, a mini loop playing over and over. Ryan saying he loved Tasha and S— It was Tasha and Seth. No. I shook the thought aside. People didn't do things like that. Especially not Ryan. The entire reason Mark hated him was because he'd slept with Kitner's ex-wife at some company party, years ago. Ryan was as completely hetero as anyone I'd ever met. And that meant Tasha…

I couldn't wrap my brain around the logic. This wasn't the time to puzzle over it, anyway. I dove back into my work and tried to obliterate my rambling curiosity, but it gnawed at me.

Ryan's chair creaked, and seconds later, he stood in front of my cube, holding out a sheet of paper. "Next?"

I swapped out his lists, and couldn't help studying him. Was I missing something? Not like it would be written on him somewhere, but I needed information he had.

He snapped his fingers. "What's up?"

I shook my questions away. There was work to do. "Nothing."

He dropped back into his seat, and clicking resumed. "It didn't look like nothing. Do I have ink on my face?"

It was almost eight, so no one was left in the office. That meant, even though he sat several desks away, we could talk in a normal voice, without being overheard. "No. I was just thinking…"

"I figured."

I worked while I dragged up words, operating on auto-pilot. "You and Seth are close?"

There was a long pause before he replied, hesitation in his voice. "We're best friends. Besides, you live with a guy long enough…"

I knew where the unfinished thought was going, but I wanted confirmation of what was underneath, even if I didn't know why it was so important to me. "But the whole hand-squeeze thing is more of an intimate gesture."

He gave a short laugh. "You caught that."

"Never before today." I clicked open the next file and started the automated comparison.

A long silence filled the room. Had I pissed him off? I didn't want that, and not just because he was helping. It was nice to finally be on speaking terms with him again.

I almost jumped when he finally replied. "Because it's not something we tell anyone about. Hint, hint."

All the pieces were in front of me, so why couldn't I put them together? "I thought you and Tasha..." The puzzle formed and clicked. "All three of you? How's that work?"

"Amazingly well." He spoke so quietly I had to strain to hear him. "It takes twice as much work as a two-person relationship, but it's worth it."

"I completely get that." Did I? I couldn't imagine sharing Jackson with anyone. "I couldn't ever do it, but I have total respect for it. Also, it's just between us. I promise."

"Thanks." Relief lined his voice.

"You're lucky you've got that." Odd thing for me to say. That was a given, right? But then I realized what I meant. "I don't think I could temper two people at once. And... do you worry about what people say?" Saying the words sent an unexpected rush of sadness through me, and I gasped at the sharp pain it left in its wake.

"There's a reason we keep it quiet."

My grief twisted another notch. "That must suck. To love them and not be able to shout it from the rooftops."

"Really?" He sounded surprised. "You can't imagine being in a relationship like that, but you can image proclaiming such a thing to the world. Walk a mile in my shoes, Zoe."

"You're right. But you're still lucky." Silence descended again, as we dove back into our work .The conversation still spun in the back of my head, but with my curiosity sated, I could ignore it for the most part.

It was almost midnight when I stepped into Jackson's apartment. My brain might as well have been made of oatmeal, and I'd had to swap my contacts for glasses just to be able see on the drive.

Jackson looked up from his spot on the sofa and immediately shut off the TV. He crossed the room, wrapped me in a hug, and just held me. Elders, I loved that feeling.

"I didn't mean what I said earlier." His lips moved against my hair when he spoke.

I'd almost forgotten about that. Somehow the conversation with Ryan had taken up residence in my head instead. "It's done. It's over." Though I meant the phone conversation with him earlier, I had to fight the compulsion to clarify that was all I meant. Weird.

He tugged me toward the couch, cringing when he extended his arm.

"Are you all right?" Concern filled me at the pain in his expression.

"I'm fine." He rolled his neck, smile not masking his grimace. "I had a golf date with a prospective client today. Last minute, this afternoon. I think I pulled something in my neck."

"Sit." I knelt on a cushion and patted the spot next to me. After the day I had, it would be easy to give him crap for whining about having to spend the afternoon in the sun. But he didn't like golf, he wasn't actually complaining, and my bad day shouldn't be his.

He positioned himself with his back to me, and I kneaded his neck and shoulders. He tilted his head forward with a happy groan. "You're an angel, Pixie."

The nickname was as comforting as the comment. Though neither of us spoke for several minutes, it was reassuring.

He reached back, grasped my hands, and pulled them forward. "Much better, thank you."

I draped my arms over his shoulders, slid into a sitting position, and pulled him back into me.

"I'm sorry," he said.

"We already covered that. I forgave you."

He shook his head. "I mean for last night."

Did he have regrets? My doubt and confusion from earlier flooded back, free to roam now that I was in a safe place. Stupid feeling of security.

"Hear me out." His sharp words interrupted my thoughts before they could gain momentum. "Last night was amazingly... Wow. I didn't know it could be that good. I don't mind sharing you, if you want to do that again. But what I said about you choosing—about me being okay with you going back to Carter over me? I'm not ever giving you up without a fight. I love you too much for that." The gravelly possession in his words warmed me more than I thought possible.

"I meant it when I said I'd already chosen."

He grasped my hands in his and held them in the middle of his chest. "I know. But you needed to hear that from me anyway."

He was right. I did. We shifted positions until I was leaning against him. Elders, I was tired. And for the first time since Sunday night, I felt like everything was right with the world.

"Still"—Jackson's single word threatened to shatter my calm—"it's kind of a shame Dark is Carter. If he were just Dark, I wouldn't mind seeing what else we could get up to. If you wanted."

My eyes snapped wide open, exhaustion evaporating. Why did that statement wreak havoc on my entire body?

TWELVE

Seeing Mark's door closed and his office light off the next morning filled me with giddiness. If there was an audit, he'd probably spend most of the day schmoozing with Zedophap representatives, instead of finding new ways to screw with the rest of us.

I still had deadlines, but the looming dark cloud of work that had been there all week felt lighter with him distracted otherwise. I shuffled through the messy stack of paperwork from last night's cram session, straightening it out. I should probably put that back in order, in case Mark decided he wanted some additional kind of proof I'd done my work.

First, I fired off an email to Ryan, thanking him again and telling him I owed him and his friends lunch for ruining their night —he just had to name the time and place.

His reply arrived a few minutes later. *We'll figure it out. Did you see those notes I made on the contracts versus invoicing last night? Nothing big. Thought you should take a look.*

Weird. I shuffled through the paperwork, found the pages Ryan was talking about, and then pulled up the corresponding documents. He was right. At a glance, it wasn't a big deal. Contracts had been archived with different dollar amounts on them than on the invoices, but they'd been adjusted since.

Except—I clicked through a few more cells in the spreadsheet—it wasn't that simple after all. Something wasn't right.

I heard rolling-chair wheels and the squeak of a seat, but it was background noise. I clicked through cells and pulled up additional invoices. There were a lot more than a normal project would involve, but that was because Zedophap had continuously upgraded along the way, adding more new features every couple of weeks.

Right?

"What are we looking at?" Carter's question startled me.

My heart hammered into my throat, and I laughed at my own skittishness. I gave him my attention. The night before, with Jackson, made it easier to push aside my gut response to Carter, but it didn't completely erase the desire that thrummed under my skin and kept my pulse racing even after the startled feeling faded. "Training you, unless you're swooping away to another kick-off meeting or some other glamorous thing." My curiosity about the files would have to wait.

"And next up on the docket is whatever has you so engrossed?"

I needed time to sort things out on my own. No reason to drag Carter down with me, if this was another nail in my job's coffin. "Nope. Probably making sure I answer any questions you have about yesterday."

"Zoe." Carter's sharp tone made me spin the rest of the way and meet his gaze. He kept his voice low. "You know you still can't lie to save your life. Don't you?"

I was seriously never-ever, *ever* again working with a guy I'd dated. "I was working late last night, cleaning up some files for today's Zedophap audit. Found some unusual stuff I need to revisit later."

"You should have called me. I would have come back after my meeting."

Jackson's jealousy flashed through my mind. "No. I couldn't have. Leave it. Please?"

Carter clenched his jaw and slid his chair back a few inches.

"You're doing a good job of being vague about this considering it's something I'm supposed to be learning. What's going on?"

I nodded at the few files I had open on my screen, and scooted out of the way for him to look. "Tell me what you think of these. No context, beyond what you already know."

I wasn't trying to trick him. Carter had always been analytical, picking things apart ad infinitum. If there was something there, something that might trigger the auditors' suspicions, I hoped he'd see it too. More, though, I wanted it to just be my imagination. To be able to put this document mess behind me and move on to the next obstacle.

He flipped back and forth several times, without saying a word. Seconds ticked into minutes, and my uneasiness grew. There was nothing there, was there? He'd already decided it was clean, and was making sure I wasn't testing his knowledge?

He pushed back several feet, and stood. "I need caffeine. Is it too early to take a walk down to the gas station?"

A couple blocks from the office, there was a convenience store a lot of us used as an excuse when we needed a short break. At least he was learning his way around quickly. The idea calmed me. I liked that Carter fit in so easily.

That didn't make his sudden request any less odd, though. "Let's go," I said anyway.

Neither of us spoke until we were outside and had cleared the parking lot. No one else was in earshot when Carter said, "What was I looking at? You saw something. What was it?"

He could have asked me that inside, if it were nothing. I hadn't imagined it. "Someone's embezzling money and using a bad string of record keeping on the Zedophap project, to cover their tracks."

"So I didn't imagine it."

I would have been amused Carter's words echoed my thoughts so closely, but the situation had sapped my humor.

"That explains why we're being audited." He shoved his hands in his pockets.

"Which is why I need you to review your notes from yesterday. I'm not trying to brush you off. I need to focus on this."

He grabbed my arm and spun me to a stop, so I was facing him. I inhaled sharply through my teeth at the arousal flooding me. A half-formed smirk twitched into place on his face and then disappeared. "Why would I let you tackle this alone?"

It took concentration to keep my voice steady. "I asked for a second opinion. I appreciate you giving me one. It wasn't an invitation, though. You're not familiar with the business. Even if I wasn't worried about taking other people down with me, if this goes bad, you don't know enough to help me root this out."

He dropped my arm. "I knew enough to give you a second opinion."

"The answer's no." I couldn't budge on this.

"God damn it. You never used to be this stubborn."

The words sparked an irritation I hadn't know was there. "I don't know how many more ways I can tell you. I'm not that person. I'm not the Zoe I was five years ago."

"I know you're not. I see it in everything you do and say. You've... 'Changed' isn't the right word. You've grown. You're not my Zoe anymore; you're Jackson's Pixie. Except you're not. You're your own person. Amazing. Strong. Standing on your own."

The acknowledgment warmed me, but it didn't solve any problems. "Then why do you keep doing this? Why do you keep comparing me to her?"

He turned away and started walking toward the gas station again. "Don't worry about it."

"I *do* worry about it, Carter"—I felt like stomping in the middle of the sidewalk—"Because you're not stopping."

He tilted his head back, as if only the sky had answers for him. "I keep doing it, because that Zoe loved me. I don't even know if this one likes me very much."

"I l—" My response choked off. I'd been about to say 'like,' right? "I like you just fine."

He clenched his jaw and looked at me again. "Then let me help. I'm a second set of eyes. I don't know what I don't know when it comes to the policy structure here. You need to have an answer before the auditors find this, and two sets of eyes are better than one."

"No." I turned away. "Go back to your desk, work on your new client, and learn your job. Don't touch mine." I didn't want to shut him out, but the alternative wouldn't work. I'd relax, I'd let him in, and then we'd be back to awkwardness and jealousy and petty arguments about the past in the middle of gas-station parking lots, when things like jobs were on the line.

"What if I dig into things on my own?"

"I can't stop you. But it doesn't change my decision or win you any points. Or fix anything." I didn't stay to hear his answer. I was already walking back to the office, struggling to keep myself from feeling anything.

THIRTEEN

I t took the last of my restraint to keep the conversation with Carter from playing on a loop in my head. I settled back into my desk and pulled up the Zedophap files. I wouldn't linger on what I'd just done. There was no reason to admit I'd turned down help I really could have used, because I still struggled with my past.

I swallowed all of the doubt and immersed myself in research. Carter came back about fifteen minutes later. He didn't look in my direction, but he did approach Ryan, introduce himself, and ask if Ryan was available to answer questions if needed.

Ryan sent me an IM, asking what the deal was with my trainee going somewhere else. I ignored it, not sure what to say.

I hadn't even been at what I was doing for half an hour, before my phone rang. I grabbed it, but didn't recognize the extension. "This is Zoe."

"Ms. Sutton, this is Greg Oliver. Will you join me and the other internal auditors in conference room I-32?"

My stomach dropped to my shoes. "Of course. Do I need to bring anything?"

"Just yourself, Ms. Sutton."

"I'll be right there." As soon as I could force my legs to work and get back the thought in my brain. This was status quo, right? I'd never been through an audit before, but they were probably talking to everyone involved in the project. It didn't mean anything that Mark hadn't warned me. I forced my feet one in front of the other toward the room number provided.

When I got there, the room was lit, despite there being a projector on. Two men and a woman sat at the far end of the oblong table, paperwork spread out around them. All three heads swiveled in my direction when I hesitated in the doorway. The man in the middle stood. "Ms. Sutton, I'm Greg Oliver. Close the door and have a seat anywhere, please."

He was probably the same age as me, but his posture and flat expression made it difficult to tell. I swallowed, but the lump in my throat refused to go away. My mouth felt like it was stuffed with cotton. I took the seat at the far end of the table from them. Nowhere seemed appropriate, but it was closest.

"Ms. Sutton, is it true you're currently the responsible party for document control, in regards to the Zedophap contract?"

"Yes." I noticed he didn't bother introducing his colleagues. Was that significant, or just their means of being efficient? All three made notes as I spoke, none of their expressions shifting. It gave me the impression I was on trial.

"Thank you. And can you explain why almost every single digital document related to that account has been accessed in the last twenty-four hours?"

These were standard questions. They had to be. Of course they'd want to know that information. I collected my thoughts as neatly and quickly as I could, and explained it had been in preparation for the audit. From there, the questions flowed into an explanation of how I'd verified versions; why Ryan's log-in information was on several of the files, when he'd previously been removed from the project for incompetence; how the file structure had gotten to be a mess in the first place; and everything in between.

I was half surprised they didn't ask what I'd had for breakfast that morning, and if it had impacted my decision to keep the Zedophap files up to date.

It was almost two hours later, when Mr. Oliver finally nodded at the door. "Thank you for your time, Ms. Sutton. You may go now."

I gave my polite goodbyes and shuffled back to my desk. I felt like I'd just been wrung out. How could something as simple as answering a series of questions leave me so exhausted? The journey back to my desk took me past Carter. From the corner of my eye, I saw him swivel his head toward me, but I couldn't meet his gaze. The last thing I was up for right now was another conversation. With anyone. About anything. But especially with him. My filters were all but gone, and odds were too high I'd say something I couldn't take back.

I managed to get back into my research, though at this point I wasn't sure why I tried. The auditors would find it or they wouldn't. I'd explained myself—did it even matter what I uncovered? The clock crept toward noon, and I'd never been so relieved for lunch time approaching.

I was about to wrap up everything and take a much needed break, when my phone rang again. This time I recognized the extension as belonging to one of the women in human resources. "This is Zoe."

"Hi, Zoe. This is Jennifer. Do you have a minute to talk to me, in my office?"

"Of course." My hand shook when I cradled the phone. This was nothing. Just like the auditor's questions. Nothing at all. I kept a brisk pace across the building. The faster I got this over with, the faster I'd know nothing was wrong. This was about... I didn't know. Something normal and ordinary.

The bottom fell out of my world when I saw Mark Kitner leaning against the windowsill behind Jennifer, who sat at her desk. A loud buzzing grew in my ears, and my head spun, as they asked me once again to close the door and have a seat.

The next fifteen minutes were the most surreal of my life. Jennifer explained they were letting me go. Kitner added I was lucky it wasn't worse. The auditors had concerns about my numbers, but there was no reason to believe I was responsible for anything. Jennifer took back over and told me I shouldn't expect legal ramifications if I hadn't done anything wrong, but I should be aware it was being considered.

I wasn't sure exactly what I said, but I forced myself to be polite. I wouldn't be the person who screamed and raged about being fired, despite the voice in my head insisting this wasn't fair. I signed termination paperwork, shook both their hands, and didn't miss Mark's smirk when he wished me good luck with my career.

A security guard waited outside Jennifer's office. My face burned hot as he walked me back to my desk—my former desk. My computer had already been turned off, and a box sat next to everything else. I was allowed to take anything obviously mine. The reference books. The picture of Jackson and the two stuffed wizards he'd given me to watch over me at work.

I had to leave all the paperwork behind. Every eye in the room had to be on me. As security escorted me toward the door, Carter rose from his desk. I shot him a look. I wasn't even sure what I was trying to convey beyond *don't*, but he had to have gotten the message. He frowned and sank back into his seat. The guard stayed by my side until I was in my car, and even then waited for me to pull out of the parking lot. I finally saw him head back into the building in my rear view mirror.

The numbness evaporated as I left the property. I didn't even make it as far as the gas station, before tears flowed down my cheeks. I pulled into the same parking lot I'd argued in with Carter hours earlier, found the furthest spot from the road, and shut off my engine. I couldn't hold back the sobs. They wracked my body, until my chest ached and I couldn't breathe. It wasn't like it had been the best job in the world, but I had done it right, and the thanks I got was to be dumped at the front step and humiliated.

My crying finally slowed, and I managed to wipe most of the tears away. I sent Jackson a short text, not trusting myself to call him. *I was fired.* I almost broke when I swiped out the short note.

Ten minutes later, I pulled into my building's parking lot and dragged myself up to my place. My apartment had always felt lonely to me. A place I went to sleep when I wasn't with Jackson, and to grab fresh clothes when the need arose. It never felt this empty before, though. I sank into an easy chair, tucked my legs under me, and stared at the wall. The tears were gone. The only thing left was dry eyes and an empty hole in my chest, trying to figure out what I was supposed to do next.

FOURTEEN

I wasn't sure how long I sat there, staring into nothing. I'd intentionally avoided the clock and stashed my phone out of reach, because I wanted to feel the blankness and live in it. A bit of me knew it was melodramatic, but that was fine with me.

Someone knocked. I didn't have the energy to answer. Missionaries, probably. Or a lost pizza guy. They'd get the hint. Seconds later, the latch snicked open, and Jackson walked in. Maybe I should have locked that.

He stopped next to my chair, nothing but concern in his eyes. "I'm so sorry, Pixie. What can I do?"

Instinct told me to fall into his arms. To lose myself in the comfort, the way we always did with each other. It wouldn't help, though. Hugs couldn't fix this. "Nothing. There's nothing to do."

"I took the rest of the day off." He sounded so kind. So sympathetic. "We'll go wherever you want, even if it's just here."

No. I didn't want here to be a place I was comforted. This wasn't *ours*. Something snapped inside me. Days and months of holding back. Being diplomatic. Trying to figure out which way was up, and how to right a series of mistakes that weren't meant to hurt anyone. At work and in my personal life. It was all a mess, and every time I tried to make things right, I made them worse. So maybe the answer was to stop trying so hard. "I want for this to not have happened. I want Kitner to rot in hell for setting me up."

Jackson rested a hand on my shoulder. "That's fair. Since it's not an option though, what do you want to do instead?"

Irrational irritation flooded me. He was working to help me. To calm me down. It was kind and thoughtful, and so very Jackson. And I didn't want to be reasonable. "Fuck it all, Jackson. What I want is for you to be furious alongside me. I need to rage over this. To vent and scream and hate the world. I don't want you to wrap me up and tell me it'll be okay, because right now it's not okay, and I can't see past now. I want you to get angry. To lose your cool. To tell me what you're actually thinking, instead of glossing over this in that fucking calm voice of yours."

I should take back the last few words. Even if he hadn't cringed, I'd know that. But the words were out there, and I didn't know if I wanted to cover them up again.

Jackson stepped back. "I'm sorry if I offended you."

The sterile apology. The patronizing calm. It snapped something inside. "Stop being fucking sorry. Sorry won't fix this. Sorry isn't vengeance. Hate my boss for setting me up, hate a system that trusts computers that can be tricked over people who know their jobs. Hate me for not getting over Carter. Be pissed about something."

"I'll come back later. Once you've chilled out." Jackson spoke through clenched teeth.

"Fine. Do that." I was being cruel. I was being completely unreasonable. Part of me knew I needed to back up now, or things would break and change forever, but it wasn't enough to stop me.

Jackson shook his head, spun on his toe, and stalked toward the door. He paused, hand on the knob, and whirled back to face me. Fire danced in his eyes—a fury I'd never seen from him before. "You know what? I am mad. Pissed off as hell. You want rage? You want me to stop trying to paint sunshine on things? This thing at work isn't your fault. You tried. This firing you thing? You got shafted. But I hate what you have with Carter. I'm tired of pretending it doesn't bother me."

Of course he'd latch on to what I said about Carter. That was the perfect way to fuck things up completely. My laugh was bitter. "Thanks for your support."

"You wanted to make this personal. You wanted a verbal punching bag, and I'm here for you when you need a shoulder, but I didn't sign on for what you're doing now. So you're in the mood to use getting fired as an excuse to lay this all on the line? Let's do that. Spew it all out into the open. Make some new scars. Reopen some old wounds, because you can't cope with grief."

"Sorry we can't all be zen masters like you." I needed to stop talking. To plug this out-of-control demon spewing from me. But I didn't know if I could. It was as if a cord had been yanked, and I knew now that we'd started, if this didn't all come out with Jackson, it wouldn't matter if we backpedaled and I apologized. Things were never going to heal between us.

"Carter wouldn't be here right now. He'd be back at the office, screaming at Mark Kitner on my behalf." I bit back a wince as soon as the words were out. That had been too much.

"Would he?" Jackson asked. "He watched you leave, right? Do you think your big, bad protector is doing that right now? Screaming at a boss he barely knows, for something he never has to be involved with? Is that even what you want? You'd willingly go back to being the girl who lets everyone else make her decisions? Who regrets the only choice she ever made on her own at that point in her life? You still love Carter, and you knew that when you said yes the other night. You've never even tried to stop caring about him. I'm not a good enough man to pretend that doesn't devour me."

Every new word dug deeper, gouging me. And they were all true. The fire was fading from my argument, leaving me grasping for a retort. "You said you were okay with what happened. You said it was sexy and that you didn't have a problem sharing me. You suggested we go through with it."

"I'm fine with Carter as Dark. And yes, you fucking him was

one of the hottest things I've ever seen. And yeah—sharing? I'm still okay with that, if we both agree on it, but only if I know you're coming home to me at the end of the night. That's so much of what makes this work. That's *the* thing this arrangement has to have. Trust."

"And you don't trust me." I didn't have to ask. The statement was rhetorical.

"You're still second-guessing a decision you made five years ago. You don't trust yourself. How am I supposed to?"

I didn't know what to do or say. I'd just wanted an outlet for my anger at work, and now I'd opened this can that could never be closed again. "You're right. There are times I question my own decisions. If that's a problem, we're a problem."

"That's what you want. Really?"

"No, it's not." I wouldn't cry. I wouldn't cave now. "But you don't trust me to make that decision, remember?"

Jackson's frown vanished behind a stony mask. "Goodbye, Zoe."

FIFTEEN

The door closed behind Jackson, and it flipped a switch on my tears again. Except, unlike earlier, they felt justified this time. Not just the result of a long week of culminating stress, but as if I were mourning that things would never be the same again.

My entire body shook until I hurt everywhere, and I deserved it. I didn't know why I'd just picked the bitchiest fight ever with him. Each new thought dragged me further into a hole of self-loathing. I'd just been fired for suspected embezzling. What was I going to do if I couldn't get another job?

Worse—what if Jackson and I were really over?

He wouldn't be stuck with a disappointment like me anymore. I stumbled into the bathroom for some tissue. When I flipped on the lights, wide blue eyes stared back at me from my reflection. Red-rimmed, puffy, and bloodshot. It was the face of someone I didn't recognize.

I blinked, and so did the woman in the mirror.

Was that really me? I sniffled, and she did too. It wasn't my face, distorted by grief and self-pity, that I didn't recognize. It was everything else. The haircut, sweeping my straight hair back from my face and framing it in a way I'd never managed as a girl. The tattoo winding around my neck—ink I'd wanted for more than a decade but hadn't dared get until recently. My blouse. Sure, the polished cotton was wrinkled from the way I'd been sitting, but it was also vibrant, form-fitting, and complimentary. Unbuttoned just enough to hint at the figure underneath, but not so much as to be unprofessional.

Each bit of my reflection was just a visual thing. Something that looked pretty, or was meant to catch gazes. Draw attention—in a lot of cases, Jackson's attention. The name surged with a new pain inside me, and I gasped. All put together, it was more. It all represented how much I'd changed since I was younger. The differences Carter was talking about. Some of it was because of my time with Jackson, but just as much was thanks to Carter and the way he'd opened my eyes.

All of it was because I hadn't liked the way my life was going, so I'd made changes.

I turned the faucet on full-force, and splashed cold water over my face. The shock stung and helped drag me further from the pit my psyche was determined to plummet into. I wouldn't do the wallowing, self-hate thing. I refused. Things weren't going the way I wanted, but picking fights with Jackson and Carter wasn't the solution. It was time to make another change.

My mind skipped ahead several steps, before I could catch up. What hung between Jackson and me now was never going away. I needed to make things right, anyway. With him. With Carter. And I was going to get a little vengeance. If I had any say in it, Mark Kitner would go down for what he'd done to so many of us.

I took several minutes to compose myself and make sure I could speak without losing my shit. Then I dialed Jackson's number. A text wouldn't work this time. My heart flipped over when I heard the click of someone picking up. I'd been afraid he wouldn't answer.

"What?" His voice sounded as rough as I felt.

The tone hurt, but something far more serious would be wrong if it didn't. I wouldn't chicken out on this. "I'm sorry."

"Too little, too late, Pixie."

A smile slipped out at the use of the nickname. It was probably a good thing he couldn't see my reaction. "I know. I was horrible earlier. I can't take it back, and I'm not sure that would be a good idea anyway. Tell me you didn't mean what you said."

Silence met my demand. I let it spread between us.

He finally spoke. "I would have phrased it differently if I hadn't been pissed off, but I meant it."

I bit the inside of my cheek, to get an external source of pain to focus on. A target to keep me here. "I need you. And I need your help." I forced out the next words, knowing they had the potential to obliterate any headway I'd just made. "And Carter's." Technically, it didn't have to be Carter. Ryan or Tasha would probably be just as willing to help. And I might still need to ask one of them. It would be better if it came from Carter, though.

Jackson growled. "You have a really fucked-up way of trying to make things better."

"I know. I have my reasons, though, and I'm hoping we can figure it out together, if you'll give me another chance. To be what you need, to be able to trust myself, I need to fight for what I want. That means you. I'll fight to the ends of time for you, because I love you. But I also need your help proving they screwed me over at work, and there's not a lot of time for that."

"Why do you want me there?"

"Because having you by my side is better than not." There was more to it, though. "You're brilliant with numbers." He'd majored in accounting in college, though he wouldn't tell most people. "I need your eyes and mind on this."

"They already fired you. Why do you care what happens to their numbers at this point?"

"Because I meant pretty much everything I said earlier. Including that I want to see Mark Kitner burn for this, if he's behind it." So I wasn't completely past the petty me.

"If you're going into this, looking to blame him, the proof will lean in that direction. That kind of bias will only mar your results." Jackson—the voice of reason even in the face of a minor catastrophe. Another reason I loved him so dearly.

"I know. That's why I'm calling the two of you," I said.

The sound that carried over the line was somewhere between a laugh and a strangled cough. "I'm not a neutral party either. I'd see him suffer for what he's put you through. And Carter's no more objective than either of us. Besides, if you want to work side by side with me and see if we can heal, he's an obstacle."

I'd expected resistance. I wouldn't cave now. "He's not going away. It doesn't matter how much either one of us wants to pick and choose between what parts of our relationship we have with him. I bet you're almost as reluctant as I am to cut him out of your life, and you can't just have the good stuff that existed before you two met in person. Before—as you keep putting it—he became more than just Dark." I was guessing at that; maybe Jackson and Carter didn't really like each other. But something in my gut told me I was right. "Besides, he's got an eye for detail. Between the three of us, we can pull everything together, send it off to a couple of higher-ups, and let them draw their own conclusions about what Mark Kitner's been up to. Even if he's not the one embezzling funds, his personal vendetta against… well, half the company as far as I can tell, has covered it up. They won't like that."

"Wow." Awe had replaced some of the exhaustion and anger in Jackson's voice. "You've thought this through."

Not really. I'd made a lot of it up along the way, but it was working for me so far. "Are you in?"

"I'm going to try be the bigger man and let the stuff with Carter slide, but I don't promise I'll manage."

A flicker of hope split through the muddled mess of my emotional state. "Then you'll be here tonight?"

"I'll be there. It still doesn't change what was said earlier, though."

"I know." I smiled. "But you'll be here, and I'll use it as an excuse to chip away at your rough exterior until we find a new way through that too. I love you completely, Jackson. Carter or not, that hasn't changed."

JACKSON SAT at my kitchen table, laptop in front of him. I'd been wounded when he picked the farthest seat within reasonable distance from my spot, but I understood. Neither of us spoke, and there was a lot of clicking and typing, even though we hadn't started working yet.

Someone knocked, and I swung the front door open for Carter. "Thank you for coming," I said.

Carter studied me. "I'm not sure why I'm here."

"Because you're a good guy?" I kept my tone light.

"Really, I'm not." He stepped past me, and I locked the door behind him. "I'm the guy trying to steal a woman who dumped him, from a man who'd probably be his best friend—or more— under most other circumstances."

"That didn't escape me." I nodded at the open space that was my living room and dining room. "Pick a seat."

He dropped his laptop back on the kitchen table, next to Jackson's setup, and then set a brown paper bag next to it. "I brought beer, by the way."

"Jackson brought caffeine. You can put the bottles in the fridge." I didn't have to see what it was, to know it would be bottled and either imported or microbrew I settled back into my spot on the sofa and told him the same thing I'd told Jackson. "We're not cramming for exams."

"No, but we might as well be." Carter looked between Jackson and me. "Did I miss something?"

Jackson shook his head, grabbed Carter's power cord, and plugged it into the wall. "Not as much as you might think."

So far, this was almost going better than expected. Which still wasn't great, but the night was young. "Did you get it?" I asked Carter.

He plugged a USB stick into his laptop. "I filched an entire history's worth of confidential files from *my* employer, yes."

I cringed at the subtle dig that he still had a job, and he shrugged apologetically. "Let's do this," I said.

SIXTEEN

A few hours later, everything Carter and I had seen in the files this morning was coalescing into a whole picture. We didn't have account numbers, so there was no proof Kitner stole the money, regardless of how much I wanted that. But there was a distinct paper trail that pointed to his antics being responsible for hiding the numbers. To me, it meant he was either the unluckiest asshole on the planet when it came to how he'd gotten petty revenge, or that getting revenge on Ryan and me had just been a convenient excuse to hide something he was already doing.

The biggest ding against Kitner, though, was the beginning of a new trail pointing to Carter. If the audit had happened three or six months down the line, Carter would have looked guiltier than me, just like the signs now pointed to me instead of Ryan.

Except Kitner was getting careless, as far as we could tell. Some of the hints that pointed to Carter—file check ins, modifications, and other changes that had his login associated with them—had happened before Carter had even started. Pretty much right after his first interview.

Only the bank could confirm whose account held the money,

but the top brass would know what to look for, based on everything we'd put together.

The tension in the room had slowly lifted once we started working. As we wrapped up, a silly euphoria snaked in.

"Giving or receiving?" Carter asked.

"Oral?" Jackson laughed. "Giving. Absolutely."

I didn't know if I'd ever get used to how easily they slid into the explicit joking and teasing. It felt good to see them chilling out. Even if they were halfway across the room.

"I could have called that." Carter knocked back the rest of his beer. "Though, I know you're getting as good as you're giving."

Heat flooded my body. "He does do this thing with his tongue and fingers…" Was that okay to say? Was I taking things too far?

Carter held up his hand, palm out. "I don't want details unless they come with a hands-on demonstration."

"Get back to me when I'm not still trying to shake numbers loose from my skull." Jackson shut his laptop. "Answer your own question."

Images I shouldn't be lingering on taunted me. Jackson on his knees, dragging down Carter's zipper, working his cock free, and taking it into his mouth. My senses flared to life at the vivid fantasy. I could help or watch. Which would I prefer? I shook the thought aside. Definitely not an idea I could afford to entertain.

Carter stowed his equipment too. "No comparison. I couldn't even start to pick one over the other. It all depends on who's doing the giving or receiving." He winked at me and turned his attention back to Jackson. "Burying my face in a gorgeous, smooth pussy? Incredible. Then again, having the right head bobbing between my legs, full lips wrapped around my cock…"

I scooted back on the couch and pressed my legs together to try and quell the need throbbing between my thighs. A question flashed in my head and refused to be dislodged. Was he talking about me or Jackson?

"You didn't say both was an option." Jackson crossed the room and took the spot next to me on the sofa. He didn't reach for me, but having him less than a foot away was a rush of relief. It also made it more difficult to ignore the strain of my nipples against fabric. If these two were going to tease each other so graphically going forward, I'd need to learn to bring my reactions under control.

"I shouldn't have to." Carter joined us in the living room but settled onto the floor, facing us, one knee propped up. "You're an intelligent man; you could have made that decision on your own. You meant what you said."

Jackson draped his arm over the back of the couch and traced lazy circles on my far shoulder with his index finger. Just then, taking the events of the entire day into consideration, it was the most comforting sensation I'd felt in ages. Some of the tightness in my back and neck faded. My racing pulse didn't ease off, though.

"Fine." Jackson spat the word, but it had more amusement than force behind it. "Um... Boxers or briefs?"

I laughed. "Are you asking what he prefers on someone else, or what he's wearing?"

"Carter's wearing boxers," Jackson said. "I almost guarantee it. I still have those images burned pleasantly into my mind."

He meant Carter fucking me. That did anything but help me fight my arousal. "So doesn't it stand to reason, for either one of you, you'd prefer to see the same thing you wear?"

"Absolutely not." Carter leaned in and rested one arm on the couch. His elbow settled against my leg. "That's like saying you only like high-cut bikini briefs."

I didn't want this to be about me. Well, I did, but the desire spilling through me would only get worse if we stayed on that topic. "Fine, smart ass. Which do you like to see, then?"

"Strictly visual?" Carter asked.

"Yes," Jackson said.

"Commando. If we're talking pure aesthetic pleasure, few things are hotter than having a guy drop his jeans and his erection spring free, unbound. Just as hot as pushing up a woman's skirt and finding out there's nothing in the way."

I couldn't do this anymore. The need flowing through me insisted I either back-burner it now, or insist Jackson suck off Carter while I fingered myself to orgasm. "Enough." That was harder to say than I expected. "My turn. Rock concert or MMA fight?"

Two amused faces stared back at me, but Jackson took my cue. "Rock concert. No question."

Carter shrugged. "You're asking a guitarist to pick music or punching people?"

"Okay, that was too easy. I want a do over."

The back and forth continued for several more hours, until all of us were ready to drop from exhaustion. I wasn't sure who yielded first—probably me—but eyelids drooped and yawns ran rampant as the night wore on. I smiled in relief when Jackson shifted his weight on the couch, to lie down, and then pulled me down in front of him.

"This doesn't fix everything." He didn't lower his voice.

Carter raised his brows.

"I know." I leaned back into Jackson anyway.

"But I have a feeling we'll get there." Jackson kissed me on the back of the neck.

The banter died from there. They both had to work tomorrow, even if I didn't, so I let them get some sleep.

I WOKE FIRST the next morning, feeling better than I had in almost a week, despite only having had a few hours of sleep. Jackson still lay behind me on the couch, and Carter sat on the floor, arm and head on the cushion, hand resting on my ankle.

I'd have to wake them both up soon, but something in my dreams had forced consciousness on me, and I needed to process. I extracted myself from the two bodies and made my way out to the balcony. It was the first time in ages I'd woken up in my own apartment and not felt isolated.

Everything from the last five days—I couldn't believe it hadn't been longer—jockeyed in my head for attention. On top of it all was how well Jackson and Carter got along. When all of the stupid arguments and second-guessing the past got shoved aside, they joked, laughed, flirted, and just clicked like I couldn't believe.

I couldn't give up Jackson. I still didn't doubt that, even after our fight. But I also knew now I couldn't walk away from Carter. Not that it mattered unless they both chose to forgive me. Wow. How selfish did that make me?

The dream I couldn't quite grasp rushed back full-force. It had been my conversation with Ryan, the night we'd worked late. His explanation of what he had at home, overlapping some very vivid fantasies of me with Carter. And Jackson. At the same time.

I stared out past the mountains, struggling to process it all.

"What happens now?" Jackson's question startled me.

I whirled, to see him standing in the doorway. "You're asking my opinion?"

Carter was awake too, standing now, and stretching.

"I'd like to take it into consideration," Jackson said.

I brushed my thumb over the stubble on his chin. "You need to shave."

"You don't think the stubble's sexy?" He moved so quickly I didn't see it, and grasped my wrist.

It was a valid question. I loved Carter's rough whiskers burning my skin, but on Jackson, it didn't do the same for me. "You're sexy, so that helps. But I like your face smooth."

Jackson jerked his head back, nodding at Carter. "What about on him?" Jackson asked.

"It works on him. Don't you think?"

Jackson raised his eyebrows, gaze sliding over my face, searching. "Yeah, I do."

I looked at Carter long enough to confirm he was listening. His expression was flat, as if he were keeping thoughts to himself, but I couldn't tell what. I gave my attention back to Jackson. "Could you fall for a guy like that?"

Jackson snorted and glanced over his shoulder. "With the arrogant asshole who's been trying to steal the woman I love ever since I met him, five days ago?"

Hearing the word *love* sparked in my heart. We'd both been saying it for a while, but after last night... Maybe we'd be all right. As long as this went well, that was. "With the friend you never hesitate around," I said. "With the attractive, intelligent man, who has your back and doesn't mind that you have his."

A smile spread over Jackson's face. "I could."

The next question would cross a new line, but I'd already been doing that, so I might as well take things a step further. "Could you share him with me? Could all three of us work together, instead of two of us having to leave the third out?"

Carter's mask slipped, and he widened his eyes. "Do I get a say in this?"

Jackson turned so he could see both of us. "I guess it depends on what you're saying."

Carter didn't meet his gaze. He looked at me. "What if I don't want to share him with you? What if I want to be the one who has a guy to temper and bolster me, and I want to keep him all to myself?"

The question stung. It dug up an insecurity I hadn't faced yet. I knew losing Carter was a possibility, but my ego hadn't let me acknowledge just how likely it was. Still, I'd started us down this path. "Then that's what you want. I can't force you to change your mind." But I could hope and pray he would. My heart ground to a stop when Carter looked away, jaw tight.

SEVENTEEN

Carter finally looked at me again, and my pulse kicked-started again, double-time. His expression softened, and he turned his attention to Jackson. In a few short strides, he joined us on the balcony and wrapped an arm around Jackson's waist. "You didn't answer the lady's question. If I tell you I'm falling for you, do I have to share?"

Jackson turned away from me and draped his arms around Carter's neck. Elders, I liked the way that looked. Jackson scrubbed his thumb across Carter's cheek. "I'm not as forgiving about the shaving thing as she is. I've got delicate skin."

"You're outvoted. Besides, maybe you just haven't tried it on the right guy yet." Carter crushed his mouth to Jackson's and pressed him against the doorframe. Twin groans teased me, and my senses flared to life. I couldn't drag my gaze away from the sight. Desire flowed through me. I hoped the neighbors were enjoying the show too.

They broke apart, and one of them gasped. Both, maybe. I struggled to find my voice, more desperate than ever to know if they were okay with what I hinted at.

Jackson dropped one arm from Carter's neck, but held on with the other. He reached for my hand, intertwined his fingers with mine, and turned his head enough to look me in the eye. "Do you know what you're actually asking? Have you thought this through?"

I hadn't actually sat down and plotted details, but my own okay-ness with the situation told me I'd been mulling it over in the back of my head since Ryan told me about his relationship. "I know what I'm asking."

Carter scooted closer to Jackson. "I refuse to be a casual use-me-at-night-and-toss-me-out-the-next-morning kind of thing. At least when it comes to you, Zoe. And to Jackson. I want all in. I want to be your now, not just your past. Both of you."

I wanted that too. So much, it ached in my chest and lingered in my fingertips and leased space in my head. I stopped myself from saying so. Jackson needed to chime in first.

"I'd be pissed if you wanted it any other way," Jackson said.

"I don't want you to do it for me. Either of you. I want it to be because you feel something for each other," I said. Why was I objecting to my own idea? Maybe I couldn't believe it was actually working. I was terrified one of them would decide this was a bad idea.

"That's ridiculous." Carter's tone was kind. "If we weren't doing it a little for you, we'd go back to the idea where I walk out with him and leave you behind."

"No, *we* don't." Jackson pulled away from him with a teasing huff. "If that were the case, you'd leave alone. Pixie and I are a package deal. Do you come with the package?"

Carter laughed, and heat flooded my cheeks. I couldn't hold back my snicker either, despite the sentiment in the words. "I can't believe you just said that."

"Yes, you can." Jackson squeezed my hand. "You also believe I meant it exactly the way it sounded."

Carter shook his head. "I'm going to waste the last of my restraint by not responding to that the way I could." He rested his free hand at the base of my neck. "Which means, I can stop exercising self-control, and do this."

He brushed his lips over mine, a touch so feather-light it almost wasn't there. When he deepened the kiss, the rest of my doubt evaporated. I didn't think Carter's touch had ever been so tender. It wasn't the same as it had been the other night. Hunger still hid behind the gesture, sneaking in on his tongue when it danced in my mouth. Echoing in his groan. But this wasn't a frantic, just-for-one-night grasp. His scent filled my head, and he dug his fingers into my skin. This was a complement to the security I felt with Jackson. The promise that whatever happened today, tomorrow and every day after built on it.

Carter didn't so much break the kiss, as slide his mouth along my jaw and up to my ear, before pressing his forehead to mine. "I won't lose you again, Zoe. And I won't give up Jackson, either." His voice was low.

He jerked away suddenly, and I realized it was because Jackson was pushing him back into the apartment. They kissed again, a tangle of limbs and gropes, as Carter walked backwards, letting himself be guided. Even though I'd known from the start of my relationships with them that they liked men as much as women, I'd never seen either of them act on it. Which made sense, given the whole we-were-dating thing.

Watching them together, synchronous, grasping at each other, I understood exactly why Jackson enjoyed seeing me with Carter. Holy hell, that was hot.

Jackson pushed Carter's shoulders, and Carter collapsed back on the couch. Jackson dropped to his knees and traced the bulge in Carter's jeans. Carter moaned and slid lower on the couch. Jackson made quick work of the button and zipper in his way, and worked Carter's cock free.

A new level of arousal coursed through me. I couldn't pull my gaze away. Didn't want to. As I watched, I moved my hand to my breast and kneaded the flesh through my T-shirt.

Carter leaned his head back and closed his eyes when Jackson flicked his tongue over Carter's swollen, purple head, and licked away a drop of precum. Jackson took Carter in his mouth, hand gripping Carter's thick shaft.

Need throbbed between my thighs, and I pinched my nipple,

engrossed in the show in front of me. Carter tangled his fingers in Jackson's hair, setting the pace, and a whimper tore from my throat.

Carter turned toward me, and his eyes opened halfway. He smirked, before his attention was snatched from me again. His hips thrust against Jackson's face, and his breathing became a series of pants. He pushed Jackson back, his voice heavy when he spoke. "God, you're amazing. But not like this. Not this morning, anyway. We have time." Carter looked between us. He stood, pulled Jackson to his feet, and kissed him again, before turning to me.

"Bedroom. Now," he barked.

I swallowed at the command and at the slickness I felt between my legs with each step I took to obey him. I paused in the doorway, unsure where to go next. Jackson stepped in front of me. Carter placed his hands on my hips, and in one swift movement pulled my top over my head and tossed it aside. Cool air caressed my scorched skin, drawing my already hard nipples into sharp nubs.

Carter's chest met my bare skin, his cock pressing against my back. He cupped my breasts and massaged, the gentle gesture becoming hard and insistent within a few seconds. I leaned my head back against his shoulder, losing myself in the sensation and diving in deeper when he scraped his teeth along my neck.

Fingers brushed my stomach. Jackson's, I managed to register. He undid my jeans and pushed them to floor with my panties, leaving me exposed, wet, and eager, between two mostly-dressed men.

Jackson pressed against me, trapping me. He pulled my head forward again and kissed me, tongue sliding into my mouth. The same tongue that had licked Carter, the same lips that had been wrapped around Carter's dick just moments earlier.

Apparently I could be more turned on.

I reached for Jackson, caressed his hard-on through denim, and enjoyed the way he jerked against my touch.

Carter continued his ministrations on my nipples, cock grinding against my ass. Jackson slid his fingers between my legs and parted my wet folds, still holding me captive in a kiss.

I gasped into his mouth and bucked against his hand when he

brushed my clit. The sensitive nub had swollen to the point where his first touch almost made me climax. I didn't know which sensation to focus on, so I sank into all of them, letting the multiple touches wash over me. Climax surged quickly. "Jackson, you're going to make me come."

And like that, every touch stopped. Gone in an instant. Vanished from both the front and behind. I forced my attention back to Jackson, desire still pulsing hard and hot in my veins. He glanced over my shoulder, and then met my gaze and shrugged, a smile playing on his face.

EIGHTEEN

Carter spun me to face him. He pressed his entire frame against mine. The fabric of his T-shirt and jeans against my hypersensitive skin sent desire—and traces of disappointment for the interrupted moment—crashing over me. He stepped into me, forcing me to retreat until my legs collided with the bed.

"Climb in the center." His gaze locked on mine. "And lie on your back."

"And you'll fuck me? Drive your thick cock inside me and finally let me come?" The language was only partly for Jackson's benefit. I was so turned on, an entire string of dirty words was queuing to escape my lips.

"God, I love how filthy you talk." Carter scraped his palm up my chest and squeezed my breast hard enough to send a jolt of pain accompanied by need shooting straight to my sex. "But no. Middle of the bed."

I crawled on my hands and knees to the center of the mattress, making a show of keeping my ass in the air for a couple extra seconds before rolling onto my back. Calloused palms grabbed my wrists and pinned my arms over my head, erasing what would have been a seductive lip bite and replacing it with a gasp. Carter knelt above me. Holding me in place. "Don't focus on me," he said.

I turned my attention to the foot of the bed. Jackson stood there, stripping down to nothing, exposing his lean, wiry frame.

"Fuck, he's sexy." Carter growled.

Jackson's gaze trailed over my body, leaving whispers of fire in its wake but not sating me. I didn't know which part to play. The submissive girl Carter demanded, or the equal partner who bantered with Jackson. Though Carter didn't seem to have any problems with what I'd done so far, and I could tell from the lust in Jackson's eyes he was enjoying the combination as well.

I squirmed against Carter's grip as the seconds stretched on, not trying to get away so much as needing to be touched. Carter brushed the outside of my ear with his lips. "What happened to the dirty talk?" His voice was low and gravelly.

I licked my lips and turned a seductive smile on Jackson. "If you'd wanted me tied down while you fucked me, you could have asked sooner."

Jackson knelt between my legs. "Some things take experimentation."

"So, helpless little me, squirming because my pussy is wet. That makes you hard?" I teased.

Jackson pushed my thighs apart, and the head of his cock hovered close enough to my skin I felt the heat. "Helpless is one thing you're not, Pixie. But yeah, this is pretty hot."

He glided his dick along my slit, sliding easily. Any other clever words vanished from my mind when he bumped my clit. I expected him to pull away, but the pressure increased. It wasn't like the circling he did with his fingers. I lifted my head to see his hand wrapped around his shaft. He stroked himself, pressing his dick against my engorged sex.

My interrupted orgasm built quickly again but hovered right at the edge of climax. Jackson worked himself—and me—harder and faster, drawing out my pleasure.

The pressure on my wrists disappeared, and the weight on the mattress shifted. Carter knelt next to me, pinched one of my nipples, and rolled it between his fingers. With his other hand, he jerked off. He twisted the hard nub on my chest, and bliss rocketed through me. I cried out and arched my back. At the height of orgasm, Jackson thrust inside me, drawing me out to another peak.

I was half-aware of Carter's movements to my side, his rough touch on my chest and on himself. Most of me fell into Jackson's frantic rhythm. Slamming against him. The sounds and touches and all of it blending into a mind-numbing euphoria.

Carter's panting became grunts, and seconds later, he spurted across my chest—warm, sticky, covering my breasts and stomach. I don't know if it was the visual, or if Jackson was as lost in everything as I was, but moments later, he gripped my hips almost hard enough to bruise, and spilled inside me.

The haze in my head shifted to something new but didn't fade, as the world returned to normal around us. I leaned my head back with a lazy smile, and relaxed against the sheets.

Carter brushed his lips over mine. "I'll get you a washcloth."

Jackson rolled onto the bed next to me, propped himself up on one elbow, and traced a finger down my cheek. "Are you sure this is what you want?"

"No fair having that conversation without me there," Carter yelled from the bathroom.

"He's got a point." I kept my voice loud enough they could both hear. "And yes. Very much so. Not just because of the super-hot sex, though."

Carter knelt next to me again, touch gentle this time as he wiped his cum from my chest. "There's more to life than that?"

"You're an ass." I laughed. "I love you both."

"I get that." Jackson sat, gaze flicking between me and Carter. "And I'm even falling for him, so it all works out."

Carter stood. "Ditto for me. You know we're late for work, right?"

Crap. I'd forgotten. I was the only one with no plans for the day. "Yeah. I know." I sat too. "And I have a resume to update, and some files to send to my-not bosses." I looked at Carter. "You suck at pillow talk."

He dipped his head in and kissed me. "You'll have to teach me what someone is *supposed* to say during and after sex. Apparently, you've been practicing."

I pushed him away. "Go to work. I'll see you both tonight."

"My apartment may start to feel cramped real soon." Jackson brushed his lips over my cheek. "Here?"

"Here," I said.

Jackson spun back, after Carter vanished into the living room, and pulled me close. He rested his forehead against mine. "This doesn't flip a switch and instantly change everything."

"I get that," I said. Carter was right, most conversations were for the three of us now, but not all of them. Jackson and I still had a few outstanding issues of our own. "I'm in this for the long haul, but only if you're there."

"I've told you before, I always am."

"So... Yesterday—"

Jackson crushed his mouth to mine, swallowing the words. I dragged in a deep breath when he finally back. "I'm glad you brought him in. You and I are solid. It needed to be said, but I'm not bruised over it if you're not."

I smiled. "I'm not. We're solid."

After Carter and Jackson left, I lingered in the pleasant haze of the morning a while longer—hopped in the shower, took my time, and just unwound. I hadn't dared focus on the suggestion of all three of us too long before I made it. If I'd put hope into it, and it hadn't worked out...

I pushed the thought aside. It had worked out, and we'd make it keep working. A glance at my clock told me it was almost nine. I should get started. I still had to file for unemployment—if I could even qualify, given the circumstances of my firing. Had to start my job hunt. But first, I had some files to email.

I sent our files from the night before to all of the executives, along with a note saying I also had a backup of the documentation, outlining our findings, and leaving my contact information, just in case. A knot clenched in my chest when I clicked 'Send.' What if this backfired?

Too late now. I'd left Carter and Jackson's names out of things, so they wouldn't get in trouble over the fact those had been proprietary documents we'd just shared technically outside the company, after I'd already been threatened with embezzlement charges.

I set my laptop up on the kitchen table and started the next steps of my day. I didn't realize how slowly time dragged without huge, looming deadlines. Ten, and then eleven took an eternity to arrive. My phone rang. Maybe someone had already picked up one of my resumes. I chided myself for the hope. "This is Zoe Sutton."

"Zoe, this is Greg Oliver. We met yesterday?"

The name and voice seized my chest. Had that really only been twenty-four hours ago? I felt like I'd lived an entire lifetime in the last week. "Of course. I remember. Can I help you?" My voice wavered.

"I'm looking at some files you provided to upper management this morning."

"All right…" It made sense they would call me to ask questions, but I hadn't thought that far ahead. What was I supposed to say? *Good for you?*

"And you did this work last night, after you were let go?"

"I would have done it before, but I got my walking orders first." I tried to joke, but my laugh came out strangled.

"You know these are proprietary internal documents. Not meant for non-employees." His tone remained steady. How did he do that?

"I do. But I'd already seen them before last night, so it wasn't like it was new information to me."

"I see."

Saw what? I almost screamed the question into the phone.

"I'd like you to come down to the offices today, if you can. The sooner the better."

"With all due respect, Mr. Oliver, I was fired yesterday. Since you can't do that to me twice, and the police can arrest me here, if this is about the embezzlement. Everything I know is in that documentation."

NINETEEN

"What?" Mr. Oliver laughed. "I'm sorry. I should have been clearer. After looking at this, I realized there was a terrible mistake made yesterday. More than one. I want you to come work for me, as an auditor."

My eyes widened, and my jaw moved up and down, no sound coming out. I found my voice. "I'm, um…" Too bad I hadn't found my brainpower to go with it. I gathered my thoughts. "I appreciate the consideration, but there's a bit of bad blood between me and my former employer."

"I understand, and I really am sorry about that. We have policies, and they keep us from making a lot of mistakes, but something may slip through the cracks." His tone had relaxed. He almost sounded friendly. "Which is why we need more people with an eye like yours."

"I… didn't do this alone." I didn't want to admit that. I hope he didn't make me give up names.

"I see. And I assumed. You spotted the original error, though?"

"Ryan—one of the other data analysts—told me something looked off. I figured out what it was and asked for another set of eyes to confirm it." I could mention Ryan; they already knew he'd touched these files.

"That's fine. None of us operates in a bubble, otherwise the system fails. I'm prepared to offer more than you were making before, not a lot, but this department does operate on a higher pay-scale. Do you have an hour today, to stop by and meet with me? I'm sure we can work something out."

"Well..." I dragged out the word. Did I really want this opportunity? I was pissed they'd fired me, but I'd also never left before because, until yesterday, Kitner was the only thing I hated about the job. "I'm not working today, so I guess I can find time."

"Excellent." He sounded pleased. "Stop by around one and ask reception for me, and we'll see what we can do for you."

In comparison to that morning, the next few hours raced by and at the same time felt like they took forever to pass. I dressed in one of my nicer suits—though I was tempted to walk in wearing casual clothes, just to see how badly they really wanted me back—and paced my living room. I sent Jackson a text and a second to Carter, letting them know I had an interview. It felt natural to fill them both in. I left out the who details, though, wanting to get the meeting over with before I got their hopes up.

When I pulled into the parking lot, a police car sat in one of the front spots. Someone must have a friend or something who was a cop. Maybe they'd gone to lunch together. The logical scenario didn't stop me from hoping they were there for Kitner. To deal with him now that they had enough evidence. I stepped through the front doors, and a cacophony assaulted me. People lingered chattering by the elevators, the front desk, and the waiting room couches.

I got the attention of the girl working reception. I wanted to ask for details, but in my nervous anticipation didn't know if I could handle gossip right now. "I'm here for Greg Oliver."

She glanced at me for the briefest moment, gaze not quite focusing. "Right." She nodded at a conference room behind her. "He's in there. Said you can go right in."

The chatter died in an instant, and my ears rang with the sudden silence. I whirled to see what was going on, and shock poured through me. Two policemen led Mark Kitner toward the front door, hands cuffed behind his back.

"Wow." The soft word slipped past my lips. I'd meant to think that.

"Right? Anyway. Mr. Oliver is waiting for you."

And he was. He stood when I poked my head into the conference room, and shook my hand when I entered. "I'm so glad you agreed to meet with me. I'm sorry you had to see that," he said.

"No, it's okay." The smug satisfaction I expected wasn't there. Instead, I felt pity for the man who had let pettiness and greed drive him that way.

"Have a seat." Mr. Oliver nodded to a chair near his paperwork.

We spent the next half hour or so going over benefits—some of it things I already knew and others meant to win me back and make sure I knew how sorry they were for their mistake. Greg—as he insisted I call him—made sure I knew that.

I thought I'd have doubts about signing the offer, but it felt right. I shook his hand and wandered out the front door after agreeing I'd start on Monday. That meant I had the rest of the afternoon free. I sent Carter another text. *Downstairs, outside. You have a minute?*

He didn't respond. I lingered near the entrance. How long should I wait?

"Hey, gorgeous." Carter's familiar voice made me smile. He wrapped his arms around my waist, and more of my concern about how we'd all fit together evaporated. If we could keep this up, we'd be fine. "You missed the fun earlier," he said.

"No, I didn't." I filled him in on the insane happenings of the morning.

"That's incredible." He gave me a quick kiss. "Congratulations. You earned it."

"With your help. Both of you."

"That's the way it works now. Right?" He grinned. "We do everything together?"

"Not everything." I dragged out the word in a teasing tone.

"Zoe?"

162

I whirled, leaving Carter behind me, to find Ryan, watching us. "You two are...? Never would have guessed," Ryan said.

"We weren't." Carter draped his arms over my shoulders and clasped his fingers together, resting his hands on my breastbone.

"So what about... I mean, I thought your guy had blond hair?"

"The other one does," I said. "And I'll clarify that for anyone who thinks otherwise."

Ryan shook his head and reached for the door. "You're a stronger person than I am. I hope that works out for you."

I wasn't worried about it.

Carter nuzzled my hair. "What was that about?"

"Some well-timed advice." I leaned back into him. "You need to get back to work."

His exaggerated sigh vibrated against my back. "But it's so pretty out here. Gorgeous view."

"It's missing something." I spun to face him and brushed my lips over his. "But it's not bad. I'll see you both tonight."

As he headed back inside, a huge sense of relief settled in my bones. Life was only going to get more interesting now, and I was looking forward to every minute of it.

ROLL AGAINST DISCOVERY

ONE

W hen the elevator doors slid open, and I saw how many people were already packed into the car, I almost told them to go ahead without me. Someone dressed in a furry dog costume held the door, and another voice behind them said, "There's room for one more."

"I'm fine. I'll take the stairs." I waved the waiting people off with a smile.

"Come on." A friendly female voice joined in. "We'll make room." As if it were a command, a tiny path formed in the middle of the box.

Discomfort crawled through me at the seven or eight sets of eyes on me. Rather than drawing out the attention any longer, I stepped into the miniature crowd of costumed and casually dressed people. The throng closed back around me, assaulting me with heat, a dizzying array of perfumes, and early-stage body odor.

It might have made someone else wince and complain, but it drew my smile back out. This was one of the reasons I loved anime conventions, and also why I was staying in the hotel, even though home was only an hour away. The full immersive experience of fans who loved the medium as much as I did—or more—was intoxicating. Some of the guys at the call center where I worked gave me grief for being a twenty-five-year-old woman who spent her time watching cartoons. They had their fantasy football though, and I didn't see how this was any different.

If only I could get past my self-consciousness and let go, even for a few days, the way the people around me did... Then again, if I could let go of my insecurities, I might have gotten the job I wanted a few days ago, instead of being told I didn't have the personality it took to teach.

I ran my hands over my ass and down my thighs, to smooth out my costume. The skirt of my school uniform stopped halfway to my knees, so every time I moved, it felt like my white cotton panties were on display. I had a hunch I'd be reminding myself all day this wasn't the case.

If I were a bolder person, I'd have left the panties behind. An image nudged its way into my thoughts. I'd spill from the elevator with the crowds, wander into the hotel lobby, and catch the attention of some cute guy. He'd smirk as he looked me over, gaze lingering on my legs and chest. I'd pretend to drop something and bend at the waist to pick it up, giving him a private peep show. He'd introduce himself. I'd tell him I was Kathryn. Maybe we'd joke and flirt. He'd step into the elevator with me, on the ride back up. In the midst of the crowds, with people only paying attention to their own groups, he'd press close, slide a hand between my legs, and brush my bare mound.

The idea sent a naughty shiver through me, and I squeezed my legs together, to suppress the sudden pulse between them. Nope, as much as the fantasy turned me on, I wasn't that girl. I'd feel accomplished if I made it through the day without tugging my skirt down too often. My sensei at the Aikido dojo was probably right. Regardless of how skilled I was at the art, I didn't have what it took to stand in front of an entire class of people. All those eyes on me, those people expecting me to know what I was doing. The thought was almost enough to make me freeze.

We reached the lobby, and the pack around me dispersed. If I didn't stash the unpleasant memories of my missed job opportunity, I wouldn't be able to enjoy this weekend. I stepped aside, to keep from being underfoot, found a wall to lean against, and pulled out my program. What first? I wanted to visit the Dealers' Room and see what kind of neat trinkets I could lose my paycheck on, but it didn't open for another couple of hours.

"Captain." A male voice interrupted my browsing.

A second guy chimed in. "What are you doing here alone, Captain? You should have an escort with you at all times."

I looked up from my program, to see two guys standing in front of me, both apparently talking to me. Or rather, to the character I was dressed as—the captain of a submarine, masquerading as a student. My pulse sped, as I traveled my gaze over them. Guy One had almost military-short brown hair and brown eyes I could fall into, and he filled out his T-shirt to the point I itched to trace the definition of his chest with my fingers. Guy Two was just as gorgeous. Spiked dark hair, pale skin, and green eyes. The contrast made my breath catch. He was a couple inches shorter than his friend, which still made him at least six inches taller than my five-foot-four. His shoulders were narrower, but that didn't stop my imagination from running rampant, planting either one of them in my daydream from a few minutes ago.

"I'm okay, really." My response squeaked out, and I cringed. I could have played along. Told them I'd love an escort. At least gotten in character long enough to ask their names. Why did I always think of these things too late?

Guy One quirked his lips in a half-question, half-smile. "Are you sure, Captain? We'd be happy to make sure your visit's enjoyable."

Yes. Yes. *Yes.* The simple but emphatic answer struggled against my shyness, but lost the battle. "Thanks, but I'm meeting friends real soon." It wasn't technically a lie. My brother, Jackson, and his partners would be joining me after they finished work that night.

"If you're sure," Guy Two—Mister Green-Eyes—said, "we'll take our leave." They both bowed from the waist, and Guy One gave me one last glance before the crowds swallowed them.

Regret pinged inside me, though it was better this way. They were cute to look at, but they'd be happier escorting one of the women who didn't mind squealing in joy and running up to random strangers for a hug who were dressed as their favorite character.

Now back to how to spend my morning.

I meandered toward the hotel conference rooms, keeping half an eye on my surroundings as I scanned the con schedule again. I could watch something in a viewing room, but I'd seen everything currently playing, and none of them ranked high enough on my list, to sit through again.

Laughter and chatter drifted from one of the rooms ahead. There was no sign to indicate what panel started next, but according to my schedule, it was an Alternate-Reality Game. The description read, *If you're looking for a game within a game, something to keep you busy and give you the inside track during your con downtime, check us out.* I paused in front of the door and glanced in. Unlike any other panel room, this had no chairs. Small groups of people milled about in front of a makeshift stage with a podium on it, chatting and laughing.

It looked like fun but also sounded like a lot of interacting with random people. I was about to move on, when my gaze landed on two people near the front. Guy One and Green-eyes from outside the elevator. Before I could think myself out of it, I let my feet carry me into the room, but I hovered near the back. There was no harm in checking things out. I tried to summon the courage to approach them. Someone else probably wouldn't hesitate. My heart hammered at the thought of walking up and casually introducing myself, and my palms grew clammy. Why couldn't I be someone else?

At least from back here, I could enjoy the view.

Someone stepped up to the podium. A woman, maybe a little older than me. It was hard to tell. A few other people turned to look at her, but for the most part everyone kept talking. "Let's get started, everyone." The woman spoke into the microphone. The talking continued. She turned to the man next to her and gave a slight shrug. He stuck his fingers between his lips, and seconds later, a shrill whistle threatened to split my eardrums. Silence washed over the room.

I massaged my ear until the ringing stopped. This ought to be interesting. Guy Two glanced behind him and met my gaze. My mouth went dry, and I licked my lips to try and get some of the moisture back. He winked before he turned back to the stage.

This was definitely going to be interesting.

TWO

"Better." The woman at the podium smiled. "Thank you, everyone, for coming. I'm Chloe, this is Jordan, and we're your contacts for the weekend. For those of you who've played these games before, let everyone who hasn't listen. The basic concept is simple—there will be a series of quests for you to complete. As you finish each one, it will lead you to a new task, and more of the story will unfold for you. Some goals and tasks will be obvious. Some not so much. Just because a clue led one person or group somewhere, don't expect it to do the same for you, as we'll adapt according to how you play. Recruiting new people—they have to tell us you referred them when they start—is worth bonus points, as are other things. There will be a grand-prize winner. The person who unravels the answer first. There will also be a bonus prize, for whoever gets the most bonus points.

"This isn't a purely altruistic gesture on our part; you're helping us test new software. The rules are simple. Sabotaging your fellow players won't be tolerated. You're welcome to work in groups or alone, though keep in mind more minds can give you different perspectives. And all the con's policies around harassment must be followed. Questions?"

The room erupted in chaos again, but one voice carried over it all. Guy One, with his seductive tenor. "That's all well and good, but it's really vague."

I nodded my agreement. I was familiar with the idea of an alternate-reality game. Basically, it was an interactive experience that used the real world and its participants as a medium. Role playing in tandem with reality. But it still didn't tell me much about what I should be doing specifically.

Chloe's smile grew. "It's supposed to be. If I give you all the details now, there's nothing left for you to do. Unless you've really twisted your head and viewed the situation upside down, very little of this will be what it appears on the surface. That being said, your first task is simple. Go out there, take cosplay pictures, and share them online using the hashtag RINARG. Where you post them is up to you, just make sure you've got the cosplayer's permission to post. Tag everyone in your group, including the cosplayer if they want, and it counts for all of you."

"That's it?" someone else asked.

Another voice chimed in "Boring.".

"Then don't play." Chloe stepped back from the podium. "It's up to you."

I let the idea roll over in my head. If the game wasn't what it appeared, what was it? Curiosity, both for the game and the attractive guys at the front of the room, spilled through me. A familiar voice nagged in the back of my mind. The first task involved talking to people to take their pictures, and odds were it would only get more social from there. I shoved the irritating voice aside. Screw insecurity. I took a deep breath, and summoned my courage past lingering uncertainty. This was a game, right? Why couldn't I be someone else for the weekend? There was no reason to be shy, withdrawn Kathryn, who didn't dare flirt back, let alone approach people on her own. I was going to dive into this and enjoy it.

My gut protested the decision, and I told it to hush. It was time to enjoy myself. Bold-me donned what I hoped was a playful grin, and strode toward the cute guys, who were fiddling with their phones. I swallowed my doubt and forced out my greeting. "Can I be your first model?"

Instead of replying, they exchanged a look I didn't know how to interpret. I'd expected a more enthusiastic response. So much for stepping outside my shell. I should leave now, before I made a bigger fool of myself.

Guy One turned a warm smile on me, his brown eyes almost melting my insides. "I don't know," he said. "It wouldn't feel right if we didn't even know your name."

Hope and giddiness sparked inside me, and I bit my bottom lip. I was bold. I was friendly. I didn't shirk. "Sounds fair to me, as long as it works both ways. I'm Kathryn."

Guy One shook my hand. "I'm Evan. He's Trevor." His grip was warm. Firm and tantalizing and enough to summon my earlier fantasy. Desire skittered over my skin. "I'm glad you changed your mind about us, Kitten. You did change your mind. Right?"

I seared the names in my mind, wanting to remember both for a long time. Kitten. The nickname rolled under my skin, and danced in my thoughts. "I'm still making up my mind"—I let the words roll past my lips without pause. —"but so far, I like what I see."

Trevor offered his hand next, and his touch was just as enticing. "I'm glad." He pointed his phone toward me. "Pose for me?"

Pose. What was I supposed to do? Panic flashed through me. I buried it under improvisation, set my feet at about shoulder width, bent slightly at the waist with one hand on my hip, and extended my other, fingers held up in a *V*. Any awkwardness I expected vanished behind the natural-feeling gesture.

They both snapped pictures and stood on either side of me, to show me the results. Trevor settled his arm against my back, and the sharp scent of cool body wash—probably with a name like Mountain Spring—filled my head. His warm breath caressed my ear when he said, "Absolutely gorgeous."

Evan trailed a finger down my arm, drawing my focus. "Give me your user name. I'll tag you."

There was no way I was sandwiched between two hot men, both vying for my attention, and neither looking like he wanted to beat the crap out of the other. Maybe I was still asleep, dreaming soundly in my hotel bed. *If so, let it last a little longer.* I turned to Evan, my voice light. "I'll share, but only if you promise not to use it to stalk me."

He chuckled. "I prefer a much more direct approach than following someone in the shadows, who doesn't want to be followed. We like a woman who knows we're here, and who we know is interested."

My mind stumbled over the pronouns. He hadn't said *I.* I swallowed past a new lump of excitement. I wouldn't mind hooking up with either or both of them. Not that I'd ever done something like that before, but it sure sounded good in my head. No reason to get carried away, though. This was harmless flirting. An exchange of names and photos. It wasn't as if they'd invited me upstairs.

Then again, the day was still young. No reason to rule anything out. "I'm definitely interested." The words sounded awkward. Did people really talk like that? Neither of them was backing away from me in shock, so apparently it was the right answer. I gave them my user name, and seconds later received the alerts they'd both posted their photos.

"Hey, can we get a pic?" Someone new interrupted the conversation. I nodded and fell into my pose, for them and several more people. Ten minutes later, the crowd finally thinned, and then dissipated. I felt like my grin was permanent, and though my cheeks ached, the quick burst of attention had been a blast.

Happiness fluttered through me that Evan and Trevor still waited, just out of range of all the cameras.

"You're practically famous now." Evan dragged his gaze over me, leaving a path of heat in its wake. "Can we say we knew you way back when?"

"I have a better question." Trevor held up his phone, as if to take another picture. "Will you still volunteer to be our model if the next challenge involves a fan service shot?"

Fan service, in short, was a term for showing a hint of something provocative. My pulse stuttered, and then raced ahead at a full gallop, with bold-Kathryn at the reins. "Are you asking to see my panties?" I forced my voice to sound coy. At least I hoped it did.

"He's asking"—Evan stepped closer, voice low and gravelly—"to take a picture of you flashing your panties." Unlike Trevor's scent, his was a faint musk.

My bravado faltered. "Not in public." Crap. That's not what flirty, fun Kathryn should say. It wasn't that I didn't like the idea. On the contrary, the suggestion filled my head with all sorts of delicious images. The kinds of things normally relegated for alone-time with my vibrator. Putting on a private show for the camera. Knowing the guy on the other side was turned on by the teasing. My nipples tightened at the idea, straining against the satin of my bra. "I mean, that's the kind of thing that's better done discreetly."

"We have a room," Evan said. "If you wanted to take us upstairs, you should have just asked."

There was that plural again. *Us.* The notion they knew exactly what they were doing filled me with a new level of trepidation and excitement. "You started it," I said.

"It's true"—Evan turned me toward the door—"but we'd rather not finish it alone."

"We're still talking about the pictures, right?"

"For now." Trevor stepped next to me.

Hesitation raced back in. Being bold was one thing, but I'd known these guys for less than half an hour. And *known* was a generous term. I wanted to say *fuck it* and go along with them, but I couldn't silence my concerns enough to make that leap. "Who decides if it's about more?" I tried to keep my tone light, but a shadow crept in.

Evan shifted enough to look me in the eye. "You have the final say. I promise."

He seemed sincere. They both did. But could I trust my gut on this? "I just…" I wanted to give a clever answer. Something to keep the conversation going, instead of scaring them off. Words failed me. The idea was enticing, but I couldn't find a way past my doubts.

Evan studied me for a moment. "You said you were meeting people later. Right?"

"Yes."

"Text one of them. Give them our room number. Tell them to send management up if they don't hear from you in an hour." He paused and furrowed his brow. "Unless you're not interested."

The ache of my nipples hard and straining against my bra insisted I was, and my curiosity and sense of rebellion wanted a reason to say *yes*. I hesitated a moment longer, before sending Jackson a quick text. Then I turned my smile back on the guys and let the fun glide back into my response. "Behave, or someone comes knocking when our time is up."

Evan intertwined his fingers with mine, and Trevor placed a hand at the small of my back, both of them prompting me toward the elevator.

"I never promised we'd behave. Just that we wouldn't misbehave unless you wanted to," Evan said.

My heart hammered in my throat, and damp excitement grew between my thighs. I had no idea how I got myself into this, but I was going to enjoy it for all it was worth.

THREE

As we stepped into their hotel room, anticipation spiraled through my veins, but my newfound confidence evaporated. It was easy enough to fall into the joking and flirting when I didn't have time to stop and think, but I stood in the middle of a room, with two gorgeous men who seemed very interested in me, and I had no idea what to do next.

Evan placed a finger under my chin and forced my gaze to meet his. "Are you all right?" His voice still held a seductive tone, but it was laced with concern. Staring into the deep pools of brown that were his eyes sent a sense of comfort over me, but it wasn't enough to bring my thoughts back under control.

I nodded. Damn it, where had my voice gone? "I'm good. Great even."

"May I?"

I wasn't sure what he was asking. That didn't stop me from saying, "Yes."

"The thing is"—Evan settled his hands on my hips, gaze never leaving mine, and turned me so I stood between the two of them, back to Trevor and his camera—"it's all about the teasing and seduction." He glided his hands down my hips, toward the edge of my skirt. "Not about being obvious." He jerked his arms, and I turned my head in time to catch a glimpse of my skirt flipping up. Cool air brushed the back of my legs, and the camera flashed.

Excitement returned in a rush, bringing my smirk with it. "I think I see what you're saying."

"Show me." Trevor's command dragged icy heat down my spine.

I twisted so he faced my side, and pulled up my skirt, hand on my hip. He continued to snap shots, as I twisted and turned. A tiny voice in my head told me I looked ridiculous. I banished the doubt it insinuated. I hooked my thumbs in the elastic of my panties and tugged the waist down enough to expose skin.

Evan stepped behind me and covered my hands with his, halting me mid-pose. I caught my breath and leaned back into him. "Careful, Kitten." His chest vibrated against my back with each word. "Do you really want to take things to that level?"

Yes. My brain screamed with the answer. I wanted to hear him say it though. There were some assumptions I wasn't willing to make. "Depends on what that involves." My voice came out husky.

He nudged our hands and my clothing a smidge lower. "It probably starts with me stripping these out of the way. Are you willing to bare it all for the camera?"

A fresh wave of arousal spilled through me. I had to be soaked by now. "Only if we all enjoy it."

"Trust me, we will." Trevor pulled up a chair and dropped into it, viewfinder still pointed in our direction.

"Then yes." My agreement tasted wicked.

Evan dragged down my panties, leaving a trail of delicious friction behind. I stepped out, and he tossed the clothing aside. Still behind me, he flipped the front of my dress.

Trevor snapped another picture. "You shave." His appreciative gaze lingered below my waist. "You get hotter every minute."

"Wax," I said. Stubble drove me batty.

Evan stepped in front of me and looked me over. "God, I'd worship a pussy that gorgeous."

Was this a good idea? The lust spilling through me insisted yes, but habits and the fact this was all being captured on camera gave me pause.

Fuck it. If I was going to be someone else for a few days, I'd go all out. The moment for hesitation was gone. I was going to live this moment, whatever happened, and not let my inhibitions stop me. I dropped onto the edge of the bed, knees together. Enjoying the feeling of two pairs of eyes watching my every move, I trailed my fingers up my thighs, spreading my legs with each passing inch, until I had exposed myself again. "I like the sound of that."

He shook his head with a throaty chuckle. "You do realize the kind of worshiping I want to do is hands-on?"

I'd hoped, but the acknowledgment called to the need pulsing from my sex. God, was I really putting on this show for two complete strangers? And inviting one to participate? Even my dreams weren't this vivid. Apparently, my imagination needed to step up its game. The entire arrangement felt surreal, but I'd never been more turned on. From my rigid nipples to my swollen clit, my entire body ached for attention. I opened my legs another inch and glided my finger over my smooth, slick lower lips. I gasped at my own light touch and the moisture that coated my fingertips. "I definitely like the sound of that. Show me."

Trevor kept the camera trained on us. The outside attention heightened every nerve in my body. Evan knelt at my feet and kissed up the inside of my thigh. The scuff of stubble on my sensitive skin coerced a groan from me. I whimpered and squirmed when his hot breath caressed my wet mound, but instead of making contact, he kissed a path down my other leg. I was intensely aware of the clicks of the camera phone with each new shot. The fact Trevor still took pictures spiked my arousal.

Evan dragged his thumb up my slit. "You're so wet, and I've barely touched you. Showing off is a turn on?"

A bigger one than I'd thought possible. Every inch of me hummed like a live wire, singing with each new caress. "Only for the right audience."

"In that case, lucky us." He blew on my wet skin, and a pleasant shudder rolled over me. Seconds later, his tongue followed the path his thumb had drawn. When he wrapped his lips around my tender button, a moan tore from my throat. I leaned back, supporting my weight on my wrists, and closed my eyes. He traced dizzying patterns with his tongue, and my groans grew louder and more punctuated. He lingered on the area, sometimes pressing harder, then pulling back when I ground against his face. The teasing buildup already had me on edge, and the wax and wane of contact drew my climax closer to the surface.

"Fuck," Trevor muttered. I heard the distinct sound of a zipper sliding down.

Was he...? The notion he might be jerking off to the show made my head spin. Evan shoved two fingers inside me without warning, and sucked harder on my clit. Orgasm built inside, spilling through my veins, rolling over me, consuming me as I cried out. I pressed against Evan until his touch became too much, and then I pulled him up and crushed my mouth to his. The taste of musk and sex—of me—lingered on his lips.

He tangled his fingers in my hair and yanked. Shock surged inside, filling me with a need for more. Of him. Of this. Of all of it. He forced his tongue in my mouth, and it danced with mine. A frantic dance for dominance. A drive to be closer.

He pulled back with a ragged gasp, held my head, and looked me in the eye. "Though you may not believe this"—a gravelly current undercut his words— "we really did only want pictures. But Christ, you're hot. I need to be inside you."

I nodded over his shoulder. "You're sure Trevor doesn't mind watching?" I didn't have a problem with it.

Evan kissed up my neck, a series of hard sucks and hungry nibbles, until he reached my earlobe. He caught the flesh between his teeth and tugged lightly, before letting go. "I'm sure he'd rather join in."

His words rumbled over my skin, and my brain jolted to a stop. It wasn't as though the idea of multiple partners was a foreign one. Jackson was in a poly relationship. Except that was the big difference—he was committed to his partners. Besides, I was boring, shy Kathryn. This wasn't the kind of opportunity that presented itself to me. Except apparently, it was. The idea of being with two guys at once, the fact it was about to become more than a fantasy, brought back my arousal full force.

"Are you okay with that?" Evan asked.

Logically, reasonably, in everyday life, I shouldn't be. I couldn't talk myself out of wanting it though. The entire idea made my body hum for more. "Absolutely."

FOUR

It didn't take us long to shed our clothes. I wasn't sure which sight I appreciated more. Trevor's wiry frame and pale skin, with cords of muscle trailing through his forearms and a trail of dark hair running from his navel downward, or Evan's defined chest, six-pack abs, and—oh, my hell—those lats. One of them had condoms. I wasn't even sure who.

Evan sat on the edge of the bed and tugged me toward him. He laid a trail of kisses along my hips, over my stomach, and up my chest. Each feather-light touch tingled through me, culminating in a sharp need between my legs. My clit throbbed, wet and eager. I'd never been interested in continuing after I got off. Not by myself or with one of the few boyfriends I'd had. Right now, seeing them get off—and me at the same time—was an all-consuming thought.

Two fingers slid between my pussy lips from behind. Trevor. I groaned. He nipped at the soft skin where my shoulder met my neck, and stroked between my thighs. He pressed close, his chest meeting my back, and his groans rumbled through me.

Evan lay back on the bed and tugged me forward. "I want to watch you ride me. See your face this time, when you come."

I straddled him. He covered my hand and directed it back to

wrap around his cock. He grunted when I grasped his thick shaft. Trevor continued to stroke me, spreading my juices to my ass. I guided Evan toward my opening, pumping him slowly, rhythmically. Hovering above the head of his dick. My senses chirped and jumped in anticipation. Each new touch was another switch on my arousal. When Evan thrust his hips up, driving himself inside me and spreading me open wider than I ever had been, I cried out. The delicious burn spread through me, swelling and growing as he pumped.

Trevor shifted his attention toward my ass, slipping easily along my slit. A finger nudged my second opening, and a new shock of pleasure filled me when he pushed in.

Evan cupped my ass and squeezed so hard I was sure he'd leave a mark. The idea heightened my excitement. He glided his palms up my spine, pulling me toward him until my chest pressed into his. Crushing my hard nipples against his skin. Each time he slammed inside me, he hit a tender spot that made my lungs squeeze for air and my toes clench. "Have you ever been fucked in the ass before?" he asked, holding my gaze captive.

I'd never even been asked so bluntly before, but I still had enough sense to remember I was playing a part. Beyond that thought, the rest of me was lost in the new and incredible touches. I forced myself to nod. "Of course." My reply came out a dry rasp, and I licked my lips.

He raised his eyebrows, but if he doubted my answer, he didn't say so. He moved his palms back to my butt cheeks, gripping and spreading.

Trevor's finger slid out of me, but I barely had time to process the shift in sensations before something much larger nudged my back door.

"Relax." Evan slowed his rhythm.

I tried, but my first reaction was to clench against the intrusion. I forced myself to breathe, and when Trevor began entering me, I thought my head might burst in a shower of sparks and pleasure. He dug his fingers into my hips and inched in, rocking in time with Evan. The slow push in took a few moments, and stretched me in ways I'd couldn't have imagined, filling me up, pressing into new areas and flaring with bliss. His hips met my ass, and I knew he was buried inside.

The pace increased again, quickly becoming frantic. I didn't know where to focus. The sensations were all new, intense, and overwhelming. Evan cupped one of my breasts, and squeezed hard, in time with the pounding. He pinched the nipple. Rolled it between his fingers. Tweaked enough it hurt. Climax rolled through me again, building in my belly, merging with the delicious pain in my chest, and culminating between my legs, until my orgasm ripped a shout from my lungs. I lost myself in the moment, riding the waves as they crashed over and through me.

The feeling didn't ebb the way I expected. It receded for a moment, and then rushed back, full force. I heard a grunt or two. The men slammed harder against my frame, more punctuated. Fingers gripped my hips harder, Trevor's short nails digging into my flesh. Evan shuddered underneath me in a series of gasps and groans, before slowing.

The room spun. Or maybe it was the lack of oxygen and blood in my brain. I struggled to catch my breath, and clung to the edge of enjoyment bursting through me. Trevor slid out of me first, and I reluctantly rolled off Evan to collapse between them on the comforter.

The three of us lay sprawled in the middle of the king sized mattress. They looked as dazed as I felt. Evan tangled his fingers with mine, and Trevor rested his head on my thigh. The sounds of breathing returning to normal and the occasional happy sigh mingled with the climate control. My mind was numb. I liked that.

A mechanical whistle shrilled through the air. My heart leapt, trying to jump through my ribs, and the two bodies next to me jerked. I laughed and pressed one hand to my chest, feeling the pulse hammer against my palm. I reluctantly extracted my fingers from Evan's, to reach for my phone. "Sorry."

Trevor squeezed my leg. "At least your friends are looking out for you."

Sure enough, the message was from Jackson. *You okay?*

Had we really been up here for an hour? Wow. I sent back a quick, *I'm good, thanks.* >.> <.<. The emoticons at the end would let him know it was me sending the note. I set the phone next to me on the comforter.

Now what? The moment had been amazing, but I didn't have any illusions it was meant to last beyond now. Did we say our good-byes? Were we still playing the ARG as a team? Would we ignore each other once we left the room?

Evan traced the pads of my fingers with his thumb. "You've never done this before."

The kind tone, combined with the direct statement, sent pins prickling through me. Was he surprised? Disappointed? It didn't matter. I pushed out my casual bravado. "Of course I have. Haven't you?" I shouldn't have asked that. It bit into the pleasant fantasy and planted it in the middle of honest, blunt, non-playful reality.

Trevor's grip tightened on my thigh for the briefest of moments. "We, um…"

Evan paused in his attentions. "It's not like it's something we make a habit of. The whole pictures thing? That was brand new and fucking hot. But, yeah, we've shared before."

Shared. The word rubbed me the wrong way, and I couldn't pinpoint why. Here I thought *never done this before* referred to a casual hook-up, not the fact we'd just made a Kathryn Sandwich. I didn't know what to do with the revelation.

Part of me had known the pickup was too smooth. Too easy, and it wasn't as if I thought I was either guy's first, but I couldn't ignore my disappointment that this hadn't been a completely unique, spontaneous moment. I drowned the sentiment. No reason to blow things out of proportion. Their past experience didn't change the fact this moment had been amazing, and I'd acted on the whim, not caring at the time about the details. As I repeated the reassurance, most of the gnawing in my stomach faded.

My phone chirped again, slicing through questions I didn't want to face. Another note from Jackson. *You sure?*

I studied the simple message with a frown. Jackson was as

protective as any brother, but he'd never been a nag about it. Two words shouldn't concern me so much.

"Everything all right?" Evan righted himself and turned to face me.

God, he was gorgeous. And only for looking at, now on. I pulled my gaze from his defined chest before my eyes could drift lower, and directed it back at the device in my hand. "I think so." I replied to Jackson as well. *Unless you know something I don't, I'm fine.*

I didn't even have time to look up, before his response chimed through. *Then you're taking up modeling?* Huh? I stared at the cryptic words. What the hell? Seconds later I received a link, followed by, *Carter found these on some new stock photo site.*

A glance told me two pairs of eyes watched me with concern and curiosity. I gave a generic wave of my hand, not sure what it meant, and clicked Jackson's link. "What the...?" The faint words tumbled past my lips, and I trailed off. It was exactly what Jackson had said. The collage on the splash page had two pictures of me, taken that morning in the conference room downstairs. Several others on the site were from the convention too. I let myself linger on a touch of relief they were all from downstairs. Still...

I sent Jackson back an, *I don't know what this is. But it doesn't have my okay. Looking into it.*

Okay, his next message read. *Ping me if you need help.*

"Kitten?" The concern in Evan's voice dragged me back to the room.

Right. I wasn't alone. I wasn't sure what to say, so I handed him my phone. Trevor shifted his weight, to look over Evan's shoulder. "The fuck?" Evan said, as he handed the device back. "We just took those."

This wasn't good at all.

FIVE

I wasn't going to panic over it. I knew the pictures taken downstairs would be made public—that was the entire point. However, I hadn't signed any sort of release with this site, or given them my permission in any way. In addition, those images were only posted an hour ago, and as part of some silly convention game. What kind of stock-photo site had to scan a ridiculous hashtag, to steal images for resale?

None of it made sense. I stood, lost in thought. All my concerns about whether or not the encounter with Trevor and Evan had been a bad idea tumbled to the back of my mind.

"Kathryn?" Trevor's voice cut through a mental speculation with no real direction. "Talk to us?"

Correction—all my concerns about the shared moment between the three of us had vanished, except for one. "Those are your pictures." I found my top and bra draped over the back of a chair, and pulled both on. It wasn't an accusation, and I wasn't certain the images came from Trevor, but most of the other shots taken downstairs had someone posing next to me, or people in the background. Only Trevor and Evan's pics would be clean. Their pics from downstairs, anyway. My skin heated at the still-fresh images flooding my mind.

"They definitely look like mine." Trevor held up his phone and showed me a shot identical to the one on the newly-discovered site. Even though he'd made time to dig up a picture, both men still sat naked on the bed, watching me. I wasn't going to stare. More important things were going on than two naked human gods watching me have a meltdown. I fished my skirt from under the desk, but my panties were nowhere to be found. Fuck it. I was going to my room, anyway. I'd grab a new pair.

A new thought occurred to me, and as ridiculous as it was, I had to ask. If anyone got their hands of the pictures Trevor took up here… why didn't I think of that before he started snapping shots? "You weren't hacked, were you?" What if he'd pissed off a girlfriend they'd *shared*, and she had access to some account he synced his phone with, and oh God… I sank onto the edge of the bed. I'd been so stupid.

"I promise I wasn't." Trevor shifted until he sat next to me. "I don't sync the device, and not even Evan knows any of my login information. Your pictures are safe."

A paper-thin wisp of relief floated through me. "That's something." At least I had a valid reason to make a weak excuse and scoot my butt out of here. The thought of walking away for good echoed inside me, bouncing around and bruising my tentative grip on control. I had no idea why I was so reluctant to leave these two. I still knew nothing about them beyond that they were amazing in bed. Hardly the basis for a long term relationship of any kind.

Being spontaneous was one thing, but now I was irrational. Time to go. "Thank you for"—I waved my hand, not sure what to call it—"this. I need to go. Figure out how to contact whoever owns the site and get those pictures taken down."

"Kitten." Evan grabbed my wrist tightly enough to make me pause, but not so I couldn't break free if I wanted. "We're in this together."

His firm grip, the heat of his rough palm on my skin, re-summoned all my doubts and questions. Why? What did any of it have to do with them?

My question must have shown on my face. "They're my photos," Trevor said. "Also, as far as I can tell, there's no way to get a hold of anyone on this site. No form, no email, no phone. Not even a broken *Contact Us* link."

Wonderful. He had a point, about having a stake in this. He hadn't been violated the way I had, but it still wasn't right. "There are ways to look into domain ownership. Even locked and private information. My laptop is in my room. I can't do anything from here but stare at my phone."

"Then go grab your computer and meet us downstairs in half an hour." Evan let go of my hand. I tucked aside my sudden surge of longing. He stood, and it took the last of my willpower not to let my gaze drift over him and linger on his cock. I didn't quite succeed. I looked back up, to find a smile playing on his face. "We can all shower, get dressed—though don't feel obliged to change on our account"—he looked me over—"and find each other in the lobby."

He wasn't asking. I wanted to argue I could handle this alone and let them know what I found. The words struggled in the back of my mind, to force their way out. My mouth wasn't willing to surrender the chance to spend more time with them. "Half an hour. See you downstairs."

I had my hand on the door latch, when Trevor said, "Kathryn."

I whirled, to find him standing directly behind me. My breath caught at the close proximity. The sharp coolness of his body wash mingled with traces of sweat and sex, filling my head and making me wish this wasn't over. "What's up?" I was surprised I managed to keep my voice steady.

He planted a hand at the base of my neck and kissed me. I parted my lips, stunned by the abrupt gesture but enjoying every bit of it. Sinking into the hunger. His tongue accepted the opening and danced into my mouth. I pressed closer, into his bare form, wanting—needing —to feel his skin against mine. I dug my fingers into the sinewy strength of his arms. Clinging. Drowning. His rock hard cock dug into my hip.

This wasn't fair. He shouldn't spark something so primitive and needy in me. Unlike with Evan and the control he exuded, this was a give and take. An equal struggle to dive into each other but still keep our distance.

Trevor broke the kiss but didn't let go. "I had to know what that felt like." He rested his forehead against mine, his voice low, meant only for me. He stepped back. "See you downstairs."

My head was a no-man's land of chaos, as I headed toward the elevator. With every step I took, the cool air brushed my bare mound, kissing the dampness and reminding me of what I'd done. The pleasant ache in my backside was a unique token of the morning as well. Years of instinct and indoctrination from the world around me insisted I should be ashamed. I didn't have any regrets, though. Well, maybe that it was only a one-time thing, but that was more of an unrealistic longing, to be stowed away under the amazing memories.

I barely registered the people around me, as I rode up to my floor and spilled into the hallway with a handful of other costumed folks. Several of them were bent over their phones, chattering. It was none of my business. My own life had gotten infinitely more interesting.

Back in my room, I stripped off my cosplay and stepped into the shower. I kept things quick, to resist the temptation to dive into the memories one more time. To finish off what my body started when Trevor kissed me. I didn't need to rub myself raw.

I dried and dressed in cutoff shorts and a T-shirt. Suddenly the costumes I brought held too much meaning to be appealing. They carried both my desire to share them with the guys, and the irritation I felt at having my image stolen and posted online for the world to purchase.

I splashed cold water on my face, to force myself back to reality, shook away most traces of my euphoria from earlier, and headed back downstairs with my laptop bag slung over my shoulder. Now that I had dragged my head out of the clouds, I was more aware of the people around me. Several groups, most of them in costume, huddled around phones. I expected it to a point, but this felt wrong.

Most I passed were grumbling and cursing, and some seemed on the edge of hysteria.

I planted myself in front of a group of three people. I only acknowledged in passing thought that I never would have been so bold this morning. "What's going on?" I asked.

One girl in black-and-white face makeup, and a red-and-black corset with more cleavage showing than I had boobs, looked up. "You were in the ARG room this morning. Right? We took your picture."

I nodded. "Are you looking at the photo site?"

"Check the hashtag." She showed me her phone. "There's more than one. So far, people have found at least ten sites with their images on them."

The chaos in my skull merged with the bedlam and erupted into an anxiety that crawled through my nerves.

"Thanks." I was already walking toward the stairs, too impatient to wait for a car packed with people. One site was bad luck. More than ten, all in a few hours? The coincidence was beyond implausible. What the hell was going on? I wanted to get in front of my laptop and figure this out.

More whispers, grumbles, and very loud complaints reached me. Everyone involved was already doing everything I could do. Seeing who owned the domain, looking for contact information, finding Cease-and-Desist form letters online.

I paused midstride, as something occurred to me. Our pictures hadn't been stolen. This was the game. So what was the point? Chloe had mentioned software testing and security. Pieces clicked in my head. They wanted to see if people could find out who was behind this. I wasn't certain, but it seemed as good a lead as any.

I spun back to my room, to ditch my laptop. If everyone was busy online, I needed another approach. An angle nobody tried yet.

SIX

I kept half an eye on #RINARG, on my phone, and the rest of my attention on my surroundings as I wove through the lobby. The events online were the equivalent of a digital meltdown. People threatening to sue. Publicly crying about their families or coworkers seeing them in *that* costume. The most significant thing to me was the shared links about what had already been discovered. There was too much information to process while I walked. I paused and brushed my gaze over the faces around me. Evan and Trevor were nowhere to be found.

Something nudged my mind. A phrase just out of my grasp, but what was it? Words I'd heard earlier. *Twisting my head.* The thought fluttered on the edge of my consciousness.

"Hey, Kitten." Evan's breath caressed my cheek, and his arm settled against my back. "Miss us?"

Did I miss my random, impulsive fling? The happy flutter beneath my ribs at their presence said *yes*.

Trevor stepped around us and headed toward a nearby sofa. He didn't meet my gaze until he took a seat. "Changed your mind on the computer?" His tone was cool, and his smile didn't quite reach his eyes.

Some of my giddiness faded. I needed to remember what happened upstairs was not the same as what we were doing now, and not interpret Evan's overt friendliness as anything more than that. "I don't think I'm going to need it."

Evan nudged me forward, dropped onto the far end of the same sofa Trevor occupied, and tugged my hand, prompting me to sit between them. I offered zero resistance. Cool reception or otherwise, my skin still hummed with the memories of being in the middle a short while ago.

"I looked for contact info while he showered." Evan leaned back and draped an arm on the couch behind me. "There's nothing out there. What made you back off?"

They didn't see it. I let a sliver of satisfaction slide in. "It doesn't matter. It's part of the game." I related everything I'd overheard and managed to glean in the halls. "My guess is, within the next half hour or so, someone will find whatever they're meant to, online, and Rinslet will own up to it being a clue."

Evan scowled. "So we sit back and let someone else get there first? Then what's the point?"

"Nope. We get our information another way." I pulled up a mobile version of the website for Rinslet's latest game. They had a massively multi-player online role-playing game in public beta testing. Based on the list of social features offered, I was almost certain the stock photo sites were an indirect way of testing their security. "One of you puts on your smoothest sweet talking voice, calls support, and coerces your way into finding out whatever it is we're supposed to know, to get the next clue."

"I like it." Evan pulled his phone from his pocket. "Tell me what I need to say."

Trevor shook his head. "Hang on. It won't be that simple. It's a good idea, but it's not going to work the way you think."

I frowned at being shot down so quickly, without a discussion, and defensiveness leaked into my voice. "Why not?"

He held up a hand. "It might. I'm not saying it's a bad idea. The thing is odds are pretty high we'll get a guy on the phone, if we call."

Being the only women on a team of twenty five at the call center I worked at, I knew he was right. Still, I wasn't sure why it mattered. "And?"

"And silver-tongued serpent or not, that seriously decreases the odds of Evan sweet talking his way into information."

"Oh." I sank back into the cushions with a sigh. "Never mind."

"It's still a good idea." Trevor shifted so he faced me, and his knees brushed mine. "I'm thinking someone else needs to be the executioner."

Evan squeezed my shoulder. "You've got my vote. It's your idea, so you already know what to say. Right?"

My gut flopped in on itself. "I don't think I can."

"Why not?" Evan asked, no accusation in his voice. "You've got all the right skills."

I had a lot of bluffing and bullshit. But if I backed out now, they'd know I was faking this whole smooth-and-confident thing. I swallowed my nervousness. "All right. I'll call."

"You'll be brilliant," Evan whispered.

As I dialed the support number on the beta-testing website, I wished I had his confidence. Each ring in my ear was like another chime on my death march. The idea sounded so much more brilliant when someone else had to pull it off.

"Thank you for calling Rinslet Beta Support. My name is Grant. How can I help you?" The voice on the other end of the line spoke so quickly, words all running together, it took me a second to process what he'd said.

I shook off the confusion, dragged up self-assured me, and prayed whatever came out of my mouth wouldn't be stupid. "Hey, Grant." Wow, did I really sound this breathy on the phone? I needed to roll with it, not overthink it. "I'm hoping you can help me. I'm one of the testers for the new game, and"—I gave a tiny sigh—"it's giving me some trouble."

A long pause grew between us, and for a moment I was worried he'd hung up. "Sure." His reply came sharply and abruptly, startling me. "I just need some basic information. What's your character name?"

"I... What?" I knew exactly what he was asking, but I figured pretending I thought I was in the right place would help my cause. "I don't think we're talking about the same game. This is Rinslet Testing Support, right?"

Evan snickered, and I glared at him, willing him to be silent.

"Of course," Grant said. "But the only game we have in testing right now is *The Hoarde Online.*"

"Oh, my God." It turned out, if I let the words roll, they came pretty easily. "I love *The Hoarde*. I mean..." I trailed off. I realized I was twirling a strand of hair around my finger, even though he couldn't see me. Trevor closed his hand over mine and shook his head with a smile. I rolled my eyes and turned my attention to the phone call. "Don't think I'm pervy or anything, but Darla, in number three... that part of the game where she's proving to her boyfriend she can keep up?"

"Yeah?" Grant said.

"So hot. I mean, she's gorgeous. Is it okay if I say that?"

Yes, Evan mouthed at me, looking like it was taking all his restraint not to laugh.

"Best. Scene. Ever." Grant's enthusiasm was almost tangible.

"Right?" I was really getting into this. It was kind of fun, to be honest. "Chloe Nielson is here. She was the head writer on that, wasn't she? Total girl-crush on her."

"Uh..." Grant trailed off. "Here, where?"

"She runs the game I'm helping test. They told you about that, right? I mean, do I need to talk to someone else? I like talking to you, Grant. I'm really hoping you can help me."

"No, of course I can. Whatever you need. What's going on?"

"It's just..." I chewed on my bottom lip. Trevor ran a finger along the flesh and pulled it away from my teeth, his brows raised. I stuck my tongue out at him. "I had this email address—to get a hold of her, you know? And I swore I put it in my phone, and now I can't find it anywhere. Can you give it to me?"

"Of course." Grant rattled off Chloe's contact information.

I traded a few more quips with him about *The Hoarde*, and gave him a friendly *thank you* before hanging up.

"God, you are fantastic, Kitten." Evan threw his head back with a barking laugh. "Absolutely brilliant."

"I second that," Trevor said.

I was already typing an email out to Chloe, including the guys' user names in the message and letting her know we could issue a formal Cease-and-Desist to Rinslet to take the photo sites down, but we were hoping it wasn't necessary. As an afterthought, I added *PS — Grant says hi.*

Within moments, I had a reply, congratulating us on being the first to crack the clues, telling me the sites would all be gone within minutes, and implying they hadn't even thought to check security on the Tech Support side of things. She wrapped it up by letting me know they were giving everyone else new clues, and the next phase of the game would start in the morning.

"Well?" Two pairs of eyes watched, expectantly.

I read Chloe's email out loud. "As of now, we're in the lead."

"Fuck, yeah!"

I was surrounded by cheers, high fives and hugs. I sank into it all, lingering on the happiness. This was so much fun. It was a shame it wouldn't last once the con was over. There was no way I could keep this up twenty-four-seven. I might as well enjoy it now.

SEVEN

Evan and Trevor didn't seem to be in a hurry to get anywhere else. The three of us hung out, hit up various panels, and wandered through the Dealers' Room more times than I could count. I'd never had so much fun doing random things. Innuendo and jokes flowed between us. It seemed like no topic was off limits, and that included quantum theory and whether or not Hentai—animated Japanese porn—was a legitimate art form.

The clock crept toward five, and then the afternoon blasted into evening. None of us mentioned going our separate ways, and with no real lags in conversation, I wasn't going to be the one to cut things short. We took a break from the crowds, to stroll a few blocks and grab dinner at a tiny place Trevor swore had the best Tiramisu in existence. I had to agree, and it wasn't only because it was too fun taking turns feeding each other. I tried to ignore the fading light outside, and that it meant this day would end sooner rather than later.

My phone buzzed with a text from Jackson. *Never heard back. You're good?*

I frowned at the message, guilt marring my good mood. *I'm sorry.*

I should have let you know. It was just a game, apparently. Explain more when you get here.

His reply came through a moment later. *About that… Zoe's working late. We don't want to go without her. See you there tomorrow?*

Totally. I couldn't ignore my ambivalence. On the one hand, I'd been looking forward to hanging out with Jackson, his boyfriend Carter, and their girlfriend Zoe. On the other, if they weren't here, I didn't have to choose who to spend time with.

Evan covered my hand with his. That seemed to be his default—a hint of contact here, a light touch there. I didn't mind. "Every-thing okay?" he asked.

"It's all good." I grabbed my smile. Might as well focus on the positive. "My friends can't make it until tomorrow."

"So no one's going to notice if we kidnap you?" he asked with a teasing grin.

I painted on a wide-eyed look of shock. "Oh no, mister. Are you going to steal me away and tie me up and do naughty things to me?" Actually, I liked the sound of that.

He ducked in and brushed my earlobe with his lips. "Only if you beg." His voice was low and husky.

My laughter died in my throat when I met Trevor's narrow-eyed gaze. His scowl vanished in an instant, expression going blank. Had I done something wrong? I was taking things too far, and he was tired of me. Nothing else made sense. Not anything else I was willing to believe. It definitely wasn't jealousy. Evan was friendly, but I had no illusions this meant more to either of them than a bit of fun and distraction.

Evan sank back into his seat, breaking all contact with me. "The truth this time. This is a first for you."

At least now I understood what he was talking about. I could deny it again, but they already suspected otherwise. That, and temporary relationship or not, I didn't want to keep building secrets on lies. "Being picked up by two gorgeous guys? Taken back to their room. Ravaged? This is a first."

"You don't seem to have a problem with it," Trevor said.

"Should I?" Besides the complete unlikeliness of it happening, the entire thing had been amazing. It still was.

Evan studied me. "Some people do."

"Not the people who say yes, I hope." I winced as the words slipped out. I didn't want the reminder this wasn't special.

Trevor drummed his fingers on the table. "Actually... Those people. Yes. I mean, it's all consensual and they enjoy it as far as I can tell, until it comes time to admit to anyone else what they've done."

"That sucks." I couldn't think of a better way to phrase it. "Why go participate if you're not cool with it?"

Trevor turned away, fiddling with his straw.

Evan clenched his jaw and paused for a moment before responding. "Fantasy fulfillment. Right? No one actually has three person relationships."

"Sure they do."

Two heads snapped in my direction, eyes wide. "Not in real life," Trevor said.

"Yes, in real life." For a couple of guys who shared women for fun, they were a little closed-minded. "My brother has a boyfriend and a girlfriend."

Trevor shook his head and gave a snort. "And they know about each other?"

"They all live together. Happily." Jackson didn't mind discussing his relationship, but I didn't like the questions with underlying hints of judgement. Especially given how Evan and Trevor spent their morning. As in, fucking me.

"Really?" Evan's tone held no disbelief. His expression was open, and his tone curious.

Trevor frowned. "That's three people out of millions. I'm not saying I have a problem with it, but their experience doesn't make it status quo, or even likely anywhere else."

"Anyway." Evan's voice was clipped—a sharp contrast to seconds ago. "What's next?"

Trevor shrugged. "Whatever."

A chill from the air conditioner sped down my spine. Or I was pretty sure that's what caused me to shiver. "Viewing room?" I tried to keep my tone light, wanting to go back to the fun we'd been having before the conversation turned serious.

They exchanged a look I couldn't interpret, with Trevor's lips drawn into a thin line, and creases marring Evan's forehead.

A buzz broke the bizarre staring match, and Trevor grabbed his phone from his pocket. "Fuck." He scowled at the device.

"Work?" Evan asked.

And like that, the tension vanished. Or maybe it had never been there, and I was paranoid.

Trevor nodded, scrolling through something on screen. "Servers crashed. Night guy can't get them back online. May have to drive to the data center."

The words had meaning to me, but only barely. Their biggest significance was the reminder we all had lives outside this pocket of reality we'd built around ourselves.

He pushed away from the table and stood, scowl stamped on his face. "This might take a while. I'm sorry."

"Hey." Evan nodded at something behind Trevor.

"Sure." Trevor pressed his phone to his ear, and seconds later, stepped outside.

I felt like I missed something significant. "What was that about?"

"If he has to drive out to where the machines are, he'll be a couple of hours. He'll meet us when he's done." Evan offered me his hand. "That is, unless you want to call it a night."

"Not without you." The words were bolder than I expected from myself, but they tasted right. I placed my palm in his and stood. What would it be like to have the kind of connection with someone, that an entire conversation could be conveyed in a couple of words and a tilt of the head? Evan didn't let go of my hand right away, but when we stepped outside, his fingers drifted from mine. We meandered down the streets.

"Where are you from?" he asked. "What lucky city claims you, when the weekend is over?"

The way he phased the question filled me with a pleasant glow. Then again, most of what Evan said to me sounded both flattering and sincere. "I'll be heading back to a town a whole ten or fifteen minutes away. I'm local."

"Really?" If it was possible for a single word to embody the term *pleasantly surprised*, he'd pulled it off perfectly. "Us too."

My pulse leaped in my veins. That meant seeing them after the weekend was a possibility. I shelved the thought quickly, but not before disappointment set in with the reminder this wasn't what we had. "So getting a room makes it easier to pick up..." My question died in my throat. I didn't want to hear his answer. Well, the morbid part of me did, but the rest of me already knew I was just a random girl in the right place.

Evan glanced at me, expression unreadable. "No." His refusal sounded as sincere as everything else he'd said. "It was so... uh..." He looked away. "Because it's more convenient than heading home at night. You know?"

"I do know. Me too." So why did it feel like the one thing he'd said today that wasn't one-hundred-percent honest?

Silence descended over us. I turned my attention to my feet. Small talk had never been my forte.

"Is Trevor in IT?" I blurted out the first question that popped into my mind. When I didn't get a response, I glanced sideways, to see Evan studying me.

He smiled and looked away, shoving his hands in his pockets. "He is. Director for a little start-up that makes web applications."

"That's cool." Way to be witty, me. This hadn't exactly opened the floodgate of conversation I hoped for. Except, now that I'd broached the subject, I wanted to know more about both these men whose lives I'd dropped into for a day. "What do you do?"

He relaxed his shoulders and seemed to walk straighter. "I'm a Materials' Process and Physics Technical Analyst, at Boeing."

My mind ground to a stop, stuttering on the words. I got the basics of what Trevor did—I was telephone support for networking hardware. Whatever Evan just said had no bearing in my world. I'd expected him to say Sales, or something along those lines. That was what I got for making assumptions. "I... What?"

His chuckle had the same lighthearted feeling as earlier. At least he was over the weird tension. "I'm a chemical engineer, and I work with the compounds they use for planes."

Oh. "That sounds infinitely more genius-level than... Well, anything, really."

"It's not." He settled a hand at the small of my back, to point me toward the intersection. His touch lingered, and warmth from his palm spread over my skin. "It's just a different way of looking at the world."

"Standing on my head is a different way of looking at the world." I realized he'd been the one leading the conversation about quantum physics, earlier. Something told me he was a lot smarter than he let on. It wasn't that he acted stupid; it was that never once during the entire day had he talked down to anyone.

"It's true. It is." He glided his hand along my back and hooked it on my hip, pulling me closer. The gesture felt natural, and I leaned into him. We slowed our pace to make it easier to walk that way. "But the job is what I have a knack for. It's cool, but it doesn't make me special. What do you do?"

Things way too boring and trite, compared to a guy who designed stuff for planes. "Tech support." My answer came out flat.

"You don't like it?"

"It's not bad."

"But it's not great. What would you rather be doing?"

My instinct was to keep my answers short. To redirect the conversation back to him. Except he sounded genuinely interested. "Teaching."

"As in, school? High-school kids or something?"

Embarrassment flooded me. "Aikido."

"Really?" The single word exuded curiosity. "That's really cool. You must be amazing, to be able to teach."

"I'm a black-belt. I think I'm pretty good." My sensei said I had a natural talent for it, but saying so felt like bragging.

We reached the hotel, stepped out of the flow of traffic, and paused in the lobby. I wasn't ready for this night to end. Evan faced me but never broke contact. Admiration shone on his face. "That's wicked. I bet you're better than you let on. Why don't you do that, then? Are the jobs hard to get?"

I didn't do *that*, because I was too shy to stand in front of a class and teach. I'd thought I could do it, but I flopped fantastically during my interview audition. Completely froze, in front of a group of new students. I couldn't admit that to Evan, though. "I'm not good enough to ne an instructor."

He traced his fingers lightly down my arm. "You're being modest."

"There's no way you can know that." I desperately wanted the conversation to focus on anything but me. I didn't mind the attention—I couldn't think of the last time anyone was so interested in hearing about my life, and it made me feel wonderfully gooey inside. But if we talked about it much longer, I had a feeling I'd have to keep making things up, to hold his interest, and temporary relationship or not, I didn't like the idea of deceiving him. "Did you have to go to school for your job? I mean, of course you did."

"Yup." His mouth twisted, and he studied me. "Five years, Master's of Science. I did a little sparring in Basic, but nothing as intensive as aikido."

And now we were back on me. "Basic. As in… You were in the army."

"Four years. It's how I paid for college. And learned to work on and fly helicopters. Would you show me some of what you know?"

The request knocked me off guard. "What? Like, now?"

"Sure." He tugged my fingers. "Hotel's got a workout room with yoga mats. Show me a couple of throws or tumbles?"

He was a foot taller than me and had to be at least fifty pounds heavier, and he wanted me to show him some throws? "I'm not really dressed for it."

"Nothing intensive." He pulled me toward the exercise room. "Unless you really don't want to."

Did I? The answer rushed to me more quickly than I expected, almost bowling over my thoughts. "I'd definitely like to."

The room was empty. At least that was something. I set my shoes by the edge of the pads, and he mimicked my actions. My heart hammered in my chest with both fear and excitement. I wanted to impress him, but I also didn't want anyone to get hurt.

I moved to the center of one of the workout spot, and he hovered at the edge, watching. I grabbed his hand and pulled him closer, then spun so he was behind me. He wrapped his arm around my neck and pressed into my back, and a shock of familiarity raced through me. "I like this kind of demonstration," he purred, lips touching the back of my neck.

It would be easy to say *forget it*. Sink into his touch. The temptation surged inside, and I pushed it back. Easy, but somehow also not right, with only the two of us here. "Relax your posture," I said.

"Yes, Sensei." His tone shifted to business in an instant.

I situated my hands on his arms. "This is a little more advanced than what we teach beginners, but you said you've done some sparring. Do you know how to roll?"

"As in, tuck myself into a ball and tumble, so I don't get hurt? I've got some idea."

"Good." I resisted the urge to press back into him and drown in his touch. "I'm going to go slowly. When I toss you forward, fall into the momentum."

"You're going to toss me?" Disbelief crept into his question.

"Yup." Without warning, I shifted my weight, planted my feet, and altered my stance to turn my own body into a fulcrum. I felt him falter behind me, and I used his weight and uncertainty to bring him over my shoulder.

He hit the mat with an *oof* but rolled into the gesture.

I rested my toes on his chest. "Point for me."

He brushed my leg aside and climbed to his feet. "That was fantastic. Never saw it coming. I have to know how you did it. I mean, I get the physics, but show me again."

We spent the next half hour repeating the move, with him trying it several times until he was happy. And then I sped it up to full pace. I had him rush me from behind, and planted him on the floor. I straddled him, hands on his wrists, to hold them above his head, both of us laughing.

"You were wrong, you know." His voice dropped an octave,

brown eyes searching my face. "You're a fantastic instructor. If someone told you otherwise, you need to find a new dojo."

"Thanks." I flushed at the compliment and the closeness of his body. It would be so easy to lean in and steal a kiss. So tempting… I crammed the thought aside, stood, and offered him a hand up.

He didn't let go of my hand when he was on his feet. "Do you have anywhere to be?" he asked.

"Not really. They're running a Kurosawa marathon all night on the hotel convention channel. That was my only plan."

"So come watch in our room." He squeezed my hand.

As we made our way upstairs, I wondered what the rules were about staying friends with a fling after it was over. That was probably a stupid idea, but as I glanced at Evan, I couldn't help entertaining the thought.

EIGHT

The door creaked open, and Trevor stepped into the room. When his gaze landed on us　me half-sitting, half-lying on Evan, both of us propped up against the headboard—a shadow passed over his face. He shook his head, dropped his phone on the nightstand, and sank onto the edge of the bed. His attention stayed on the TV when he asked, "Did I miss the fun?" It sounded as if he was trying to be upbeat, but his words fell flat.

I'd enjoyed my time with Evan, but Trevor wasn't talking about that. Honestly, while getting physical had been a background thought, it never became more during the evening. I'd been focused on other things.

"We wouldn't start anything without you," Evan sat, disentangling himself from me in the process.

I scooted a little further away, an uneasy pit forming in my gut. I almost felt guilty, as if I'd been caught doing something I shouldn't. The thought didn't make any sense, and I dismissed it. "Is everything better at work?"

"For now." Trevor finally looked at us again.

"You fixed it with your massive, impressive brain?" I drawled out each word with teasing innuendo.

The shadows melted from his expression and were replaced with hesitant amusement. "I don't know if I'd call it impressive."

"You're being modest." I winked.

"The woman's got good taste in"—Evan cleared his throat—"brains."

"She's not a zombie." Trevor's shoulders relaxed.

"I might be. Or maybe I just have a solid appreciation for a nice organ."

Trevor leaned back and planted his palms on the mattress behind him. "I'm more than a sexy brain."

Evan scooted closer to me. "At the risk of shattering all this innuendo, *God*, I'd love to watch you suck his cock, Kitten."

Arousal rushed through me at the direct request, flooding my skin and drawing my nipples to hard nubs. That escalated quickly. Then again, I didn't have any illusions about why I was in their room. I looked at Trevor and licked my bottom lip.

He shifted his hips. "You won't get an argument from me."

Gaze never leaving Trevor's, I slid from the bed and crawled the short distance to where he sat. Still on my knees, I glided my hand up the inside of his thigh. Desire unfurled in my belly, and Trevor groaned when I caressed his bulge. I stroked him through his jeans. His lips parted, and he closed his eyes. With each new touch, I was intensely aware we weren't alone. Evan's breathing grew heavy behind me, making the dampness between my legs spread. I moved higher and undid Trevor's jeans.

I freed his cock, and it jerked against my hand when I wrapped my fingers around the smooth skin. The air around me hummed with anticipation. Every time I shifted my weight, the seam of my shorts rubbed against my swollen clit. I flicked my tongue over the bulbous head. Trevor sucked in a sharp breath through his teeth. I pumped while I licked tight circles along his shaft. When I took him in my mouth, I swore my whimper matched his gasp. I had to keep my hand in place, to prevent him from thrusting down my throat.

He thrust his hips toward my face. I squeezed my legs together, as the throbbing between my thighs intensified. The little movements were enough to tease me, sending satin over my nipples and denim pressing into my sex, but I wanted relief for the intense sensations.

Trevor tangled his fingers in my hair, holding my head in place. I looked up again, to find him watching me, pale eyes wide. His breath came in jagged pants, chest heaving each time I slid my lips along his cock.

A hand—Evan's; that would make sense—palmed my ass, then pushed between my legs. He pressed my clothing into my slit. Massaging my ache. I groaned against Trevor, the vibrations running into my touch. Trevor jerked against me, breathing growing shallow. Evan massaged harder, stroking me and drawing out my pleasure. Every gasp, grunt, and sigh bounced in my mind, blurring my thoughts.

"I want to watch him come in your mouth," Evan said.

"No. Not like this." Trevor spoke as if forcing the words through gravel. He jerked from my grasp and yanked me to my feet. Before I could push out a question, or even figure out what I should say, he crushed his mouth to mine, desperate and hungry. He only broke away long enough to tear my shirt over my head and fling it aside. Desperation welled inside, consuming me. I couldn't get close enough. I sought purchase, digging my fingers into his solid arms.

Evan grabbed my hips, and then scraped his fingers forward to pop the button on my cutoffs, and drag down my zipper. Trevor deepened the kiss. He massaged my breast through my bra, pinching and kneading. Pulling groans from me. Too many sensations demanded my focus, and I wanted to absorb every one. I wrapped my fingers around Trevor's cock again, stroking in time to the bump and grind between the three of us.

The sharp scent of fresh soap mingled with the musk of cologne and sex. Trevor kissed down my neck, sucking the skin, nipping with his teeth, drawing the sting of pleasure to the surface. Evan dipped under my panties and dove for my folds. I mewled when he found my clit, struggling to find my breath as he circled the swollen nub.

My legs wobbled, but two sturdy bodies kept me upright. Trevor increased the attention to my nipples, thrusting his hips in time with my hand. Evan's dick pressed into my ass, insistent even through our clothes. I ground against his fingers. Waves rolled through me, building and battling for release. Orgasm crashed over me, and I cried out, riding every feeling.

Before my climax could ebb, Evan yanked my shorts to the ground.

"I need to fuck you." Trevor's voice was strained, and his eyes were wide, making him look as unwoven as I felt. He jerked his shirt over his head, then shed his jeans and kicked them aside.

"God, yes. Please." I wasn't in the mood for that kind of drawn-out teasing. His bare skin against mine was heat and ice, soothing my desire and stoking the flames.

He grasped my hips, spun us both, and nudged me onto the bed. He fell on top of me, hands on either side of my head.

"Condom," I managed, hating the necessity.

Trevor gave a shaky laugh. "You're going to kill me."

Evan handed him a foil package.

Trevor fumbled, before extracting the rubber and rolling it on. He searched my face one last time, and then thrust inside me. I arched my back at the harsh penetration, almost coming again when he plunged deep.

Evan stood next to the bed, dick in his hand, stroking fast. I tilted my head to the side and licked the head. Trevor pushed my knees forward, slamming against my G-spot. I gripped the sheets in my fists, needing something to grab, to keep from drowning in the moment.

"Oh, God." Evan increased his pace, and a stream of white—warm and sticky—spurted across my chest and face.

Trevor's grunts became more punctuated. Staccato bursts of enjoyment. He dropped one of my legs and pressed his thumb to my clit. With him fingering me, I came again, grinding against his pelvis, riding out the torrent flooding me. My pussy spasmed and clenched around his cock.

He gasped and shuddered. I knew it was impossible even if he weren't wearing a condom, but I swore I felt him spill inside me. He slowed, and then stopped.

Silence blanketed the room but didn't mute the energy still

buzzing in the air. Adrenaline still rushed through me, but my waning pleasure kissed away some of the excess. I wasn't sure how we'd gone so quickly from playful teasing to frantic fucking. My mind wasn't in the right place to puzzle it out, too happy to drift along on euphoric clouds.

No way would any con experience ever top this one. It didn't matter what happened after tonight. I needed to believe that.

NINE

A barely-there noise scraped into my drifting consciousness and dragged me awake. Where was I? Something weighed on my hip. Evan's arm. Right. I'd fallen asleep in their room. My gaze fell on the other bed. Blankets tossed aside. Sheets twisted. Pillows in disarray. Trevor hadn't slept next to us. I don't know if that made me sadder, or if it was the fact he wasn't there now.

It was true I'd known them for less than a day, but Evan seemed to wear most of his feelings near the surface. Trevor was harder for me to read, though. I wasn't sure why that gnawed at me. Why it mattered at all. Once the con was over, we'd all go back to real life, most likely never to stumble on each other again in this city packed full of people.

Knowing that didn't silence my nagging curiosity. I disentangled myself from Evan, careful not to wake him, and swung my legs over the edge of the bed. It wasn't hard to figure out where Trevor was. The only sources of light in the room came from under the door to the hallway and from the curtain leading out the balcony. Trevor stood outside, attention directed at the city, jeans hanging low on his hips and nothing covering his torso.

I scanned the room for my discarded clothing, and finally

glimpsed a T-shirt the same color as mine. It draped halfway down my thighs when I pulled it on, and I looked down. Apparently, this was Trevor's. Would he mind? Again, it was so difficult to tell with him. There were moments when we clicked and everything we did felt intimate—even swapping random movie quotes. Other times I swore he built a wall of ice between us. I didn't want to take the shirt off. It was selfish, but being wrapped in something smelling so distinctly of him settled my rambling thoughts.

I stepped outside and closed the door behind me. He didn't look back at the soft swish of glass sliding in its frame. His knuckles paled as he gripped the safety rail in front of him, but he didn't speak.

Maybe I shouldn't be out here. I didn't know what to say. Breaking the stillness felt like a violation.

"Have you ever been to L.A.?" His low voice merged with the calm instead of shattering it.

"Once." I stepped next to him, both to see what he was looking at and to hear him better. "Anime Expo, a few years ago."

He gave a short laugh. "Us too. First time we did this. She didn't stick around after. None of us were interested."

A raw ache grew in my throat. Was that a hint? Snippets of the day raced through my mind, from their insistence we still meet up to talk about what turned out to be the ARG, to dinner, to the second invitation back to their room. I might not be the boldest person, but I wasn't completely oblivious about the world around me. Despite Trevor's flashes of hot and cold, I didn't think this was his way of telling me to leave. I wasn't sure how to respond.

"It was his idea." Trevor raked his fingers through his hair. "Not that I took much convincing. I'm a guy. I don't mind kink, I love sex, and the environment was right. People live different lives at cons. Step outside their shells. Let their guard down."

I knew this all too well.

Trevor turned to face me, and a smile cracked his somber expression. His gaze traveled over me. "Nice shirt." An edge lined his voice.

"It was dark. It's what I grabbed. I hope that's okay."

"It's fine. Better than fine. You look incredible."

Heat flooded my skin. "Thanks."

He stepped behind me, fixed his hands on my hips, and pointed me toward the city. "Do you see that?"

I looked out over the view. A million tiny lights, like stars on the ground, twinkling until they reached the mountains and faded into blackness. Something told me he was looking for a more specific answer than that. "See what?" I asked.

"In L.A. it didn't matter if it was two in the morning. There was always traffic. The roads were never empty. We're smack dab in the middle of downtown Salt Lake City, and you can only see maybe ten cars from here. It's quiet, it's unassuming, and it's calm. But people don't want to live here. They want to live in Hollywood. Places like this are boring."

"I think it's pretty. I love the way the valley looks at night."

He slid his palms forward, until his fingers interlocked and rested on my stomach. I leaned back into him, and he set his chin on the top of my head. A tiny voice told me this was too intimate for the relationship we had. I ignored it. Everything about this moment was right for now.

"Me too." His chest rose and fell against my spine when he sighed. "I always thought it looked like the sky, but upside down."

I sank further into his embrace, a new kind of warmth filling me when his words synced up so well with my thoughts. "When I was little, one Fourth of July we drove up to the very top streets in The Aves, to watch the fireworks." The moment from my past sparked in my mind, happy and bright, tinged with a sprinkle of bittersweet because it was one of the few holidays Dad was able to take off and spend with us. "When it was all over, we stayed up there for a while. My dad didn't want to deal with traffic." I had no idea why I was sharing the memory. It was something I never talked about, even with Jackson. An idea I'd tucked away long ago. Telling Trevor felt right. The relaxed arms holding me, the way his breathing matched mine, and the stillness of the night drew the words out. "I remember looking out over it all and wondering, if I grew up to be an astronaut, would the sky look like that when I was actually a part of it?"

"I did something similar when I was little"—his lips moved against my hair, his voice low and soothing—"except I was going to be an X-Wing pilot."

A tiny laughed slipped past my lips. "I'm being serious."

"So am I." His chuckle destroyed any attempt at indignation. "There was no way Luke Skywalker was a better Jedi than me."

I rested my hands on his. "I wouldn't fly an X-Wing. I'd want a Bebop."

"I think that's the ship's name. Not what kind it is. But I won't argue the technicalities of a cartoon. You'd be a space cowboy, huh? Fae?"

I didn't want to be the sexy hustler in the skimpy yellow leather from *Cowboy Bebop*. I wanted to be the smart hacker girl everyone underestimated. "Ed." I adored that he knew what I was talking about without explanation and at the same time hadn't gone hard-core fanboy about my possible misrepresentation of the show. In fact, nothing about the moment left me wanting.

"Brilliant, lost, independent hacker girl, who doesn't care what anyone thinks of her. I can see that. Does that mean you need to be found?"

"Depends on who's looking for me."

The conversation slipped from one topic to the next. A shared stream of consciousness with seemingly no end in sight. I didn't know how many hours passed, but light was pushing the dark from the sky when I yawned for the third time in as many minutes.

"We should sleep." He sounded disappointed.

Or I was projecting. Both, probably. "I suppose."

He let go of me enough to lead us inside. He studied me again, brows pinched and an unreadable emotion darkening his eyes. With a shake of his head, he dropped my hand. The loss of contact was an icy shock to my system. I tangled my fingers in his before he could fall into his bed. "Don't," I whispered, not wanting to wake up Evan.

Trevor raised his brows, and a sad smile flashed over his face before vanishing. "Why not?" His question barely reached me.

I pressed closer. "Because then I have to choose." The quiet words echoed in my head as loudly as a scream, carrying more meaning than I intended. Far more significance than I wanted them to.

He planted his hands at the small of my back, dipped his head, and brushed his lips over my cheek. "Then choose me."

Three simple words. We were only talking about where to sleep for a single night. I looked up at him. "Please?" I wasn't even sure what I was asking, but this didn't make it any less important he understand.

"Only for you." Using his entire frame, he pushed me back a step, toward Evan's bed. I couldn't help my smile as I slid between the sheets, next to a sleeping Evan. Trevor joined me and drew me close, my back to his chest and his head resting against mine.

A flood of warmth and acceptance blanketed me, singing in my joints and dancing under my skin. I'd never connected with anyone the way I did with Trevor. And while it was completely different with Evan, the bond with him felt just as strong. I was being sucked in by best friends, who were only looking for a random hookup at a convention. Who, as time wore on, made it very clear this was the only time they shared. I needed to lock away my reactions soon, or at the end of the weekend I would be moping over something I had no right to miss.

Evan stirred but didn't open his eyes. He reached out and covered my hand with his.

Trevor slid his palm under my shirt and settled it on my bare hip. "Goodnight, my amazing Kathryn." His whispered words sank into my thoughts.

If I didn't get a handle on this now, my psyche was going to be fucked. I refused to give credence to the ache in my chest, the dull throb telling me my heart wouldn't fare so well either.

TEN

"That's not what I'm saying." The muffled shout jarred me awake.

I jolted upright, as my surroundings slammed into focus. I sat in an empty bed, and Evan and Trevor stood on the balcony. My fuzzy thoughts told me that was probably Evan yelling.

"It sounds like it to me." Trevor's voice was just as loud.

I blinked bleary-eyed at the digital clock next to me. Seven in the morning. On a Saturday. The hotel guests had to be loving this. An invisible fist squeezed my chest, as I studied their faces through the glass, both twisted with fury.

Evan clenched his fists. "Because you're not fucking listening."

"Or you're talking over my head."

"I'm done here, until you pull your head out of your ass." Evan spun away and flung the door open. He paused, one foot in the room, when he saw me. He clenched his jaw, then shook his head and strode past, floor shaking with each step. Seconds later, the door slammed shut behind him.

Concern flooded me. I was on my feet in an instant, not caring I still only wore a shirt. I blocked Trevor's path when he came back inside. "What's going on?"

Trevor stepped around me and grabbed a new T-shirt from a duffel bag on the floor, never looking directly at me. "Don't worry about it."

The casual brush-off stung. "Don't do that. I obviously am worried about it." It was easier than admitting the shrug-off left an empty pit inside me.

He met my gaze. "I have to leave the con early. Whatever happened last night at work isn't fixed after all." His jaw was clenched, and he wouldn't make eye contact.

"So that makes the two of you shout at the top of your lungs, first thing in the morning?"

Trevor's nostrils flared, and the corners of his eyes tugged down. "Don't push this, Kathryn. It is what it is, and having a long, drawn-out discussion isn't going to change that."

Whatever happened between us last night, the shared moments on the balcony seemed to be non-existent now. The realization added a new sting to his dismissal, but I couldn't help bargaining anyway. Even though I knew his going back to work wasn't at the root of what had happened, it was all I had. "Can you fix it and come back? Get someone else to work on it remotely?"

God, I was pathetic. He already told me to let it go, and it wasn't as though any relationship with either of them was going to last past this weekend. Why did I push so hard?

"No. That won't fix anything." He tossed his clothes in his bag. "Keep the shirt. You wear it better than I do. I'm sorry I can't help you finish the game."

"I don't care about the fucking game!" My retort burst out louder than I expected, and I bit the inside of my cheek. "I care about…" I couldn't force the word out, even though it was right on the tip of my tongue. All I had to say was *you*. Except something told me it wouldn't make this better.

"Yeah. Me too. That's the problem."

My heart felt like it might crumple in on itself, and I couldn't find a response.

He shook his head and hooked his bag over his shoulder. "We all knew what this was." The fight was gone from his voice, as was all emotion. "I enjoyed every minute of it, but the weekend is over for me. If you run into Evan, whatever you say to him is between the two of you."

He felt the same way I did. Defiance burst forward. I couldn't let him leave like this. I wished Evan were here too, but I had to start somewhere. "Trevor, I don't want—"

"Stop." He spoke through gritted teeth. "Whatever you're going to say, don't. It's been twenty-four hours. We don't know each other, and in a few days, you'll be glad you kept this to yourself."

He was wrong. Keeping my mouth shut wasn't the answer. Except, his certainty knocked mine off-kilter. They didn't know me. I wasn't some bold, outgoing, fun person. I wore a mask, to make the day more enjoyable. What if they did the same—either or both of them? Even if they didn't, and if did actually had any fraction of the same feelings I did, it wasn't for the real me. My protests died, choked off in my tight throat.

He turned away. "I have to go."

CHLOE EMAILED me with the next clue while I was showering, and I tried to ignore the unreasonable ache inside when I sent her a quick note saying, *Sorry, have to bow out.* Trevor's shirt taunted me from the bathroom counter, where I'd tossed it. I hovered my fingers over it, tempted to put it back on, but I'd managed to mostly replace the scent of his cologne with body wash. I couldn't dive back into that unrealistic memory. That didn't stop me from tucking the shirt into my luggage.

I wandered the convention, unsure where I was going or what I wanted to do. As the top of each hour rolled around, I hovered near a panel, sometimes drifting into the room and then deciding I wasn't in the mood after all. Logic and reason sided with Trevor's words, asking why I let this get to me.

"Hey, Sis." Jackson startled me, as he fell into step beside me and draped an arm over my shoulders. "Did we miss anything interesting?"

Yup. Me being impulsive and doing things I knew better than to do. It wasn't that I regretted the time spent with Evan and Trevor, just that I'd started to believe it meant more than it did. "Not really," I said.

Carter held up a bag. "We brought lunch."

The smell of Chinese food wafted toward me, and my stomach growled in response, reminding me I'd skipped breakfast and it was almost two.

"Sorry we took so long." Zoe stood on my other side. Being surrounded by friends helped push my wallowing to the back of my mind, and dragged me to the surface. "Traffic, errands... Blah, blah, blah."

"You're not answering your phone." Concern leaked into Jackson's voice. "We almost ate without you." He spun me to face him, his brow furrowed. "Are you sure you're okay?"

I forced a smile onto my face and nodded toward the elevators. "Fine. Why do you keep asking me that?" I knew my laugh sounded forced. Jackson would see right through it. With any luck, he'd let it slide, though. What I needed right now was to pretend to be happy, to get over the fact I was no longer pretending to be fun. "Come up to my room. I'm starved."

Jackson studied me. "You've been so engrossed in this thing"—he nodded at our surroundings—"you forgot to eat *and* ignored your phone? Guess you are fine."

"See?" I half dragged him toward the elevators, and his partners followed. They kept up a steady stream of chatter, and I chimed in when appropriate. We settled into my room—at least I was getting some use out of the place—and spread the food out on the desk. The longer they talked, the more I managed to pull myself into some semblance of normalcy. My mood lifted, and I was able to silence the chanting voice in the back of my mind insisting I missed the guys.

I watched Jackson, Carter, and Zoe while we ate and bantered. The way they interacted with each other looked so natural. No one scowled when the other two shared a touch. They all looked equally comfortable with little things like a hand-squeeze, a kiss on the cheek, or even a pat on the ass. A tinge of envy wormed through me, not because Jackson had a gorgeous boyfriend—that was always the cause for it in the past—but because they all looked like they wanted to be with each other.

I wasn't greedy. I'd take this from just one person. My chest squeezed in protest, and I ignored it. I never should have let myself project this desire on two strangers, especially convincing myself I clicked with them. My heart hammered harder, almost painfully, against my ribs. Stupid emotions.

"Can I ask you something?" I wasn't sure who I was talking to, or even why I blurted out the question.

"Always," Jackson said.

"Do you guys ever worry about...?" I clamped my jaw shut when I realized what I was about to say? Why would I do that? I already knew the answer. "Never mind."

"About what?" Zoe asked.

I was happy when Jackson started dating her. She gave him a calm center he hadn't had before. Grounded him, without restricting him. He said she helped him become more... *him*. I never understood what he meant, but maybe I got it more than I admitted. "About what people say. Not about the three of you together. Well, not quite." I wasn't asking this the right way. The words were botched before I even said them. They were all so unique, and didn't seem to care if people saw it, when I felt as if the world watched and judged me the entire time I put myself out there yesterday.

"Are you going to tell me what's going on?" Jackson asked.

"Probably not. Not today, anyway." I wanted to talk about it, but I needed to sort through it first. It had to make more sense to me, before I got someone else's input.

He shrugged. "The thing is people always talk, no matter what you do. They don't limit their whispers to the outgoing girls in their cosplay, or the group of three who can't keep their hands off each other. You can stay single, and they'll gossip. Date a rich guy, a poor guy, a girl, an older man, a younger man—*they'll* have an opinion. Even if you keep your head down and never talk to anyone you think doesn't want to be talked to, someone will have something to say about it." He almost stared right through me, his gaze peering into my soul. "The people who talk will always find something to talk about. That's why you have to ask yourself what you want, instead of what you don't want them to say."

He made it sound so simple. Jackson had told me things like that before, but they never really made sense. They almost did now. Except he still didn't tell me what to do about Evan and Trevor. Let them go—like a normal, sane person would do after twenty-four hours of insane fun and meaningless sex—or listen to the part of me whispering maybe it wasn't so meaningless.

I pushed the rest of my food aside, as my mouthful of orange chicken turned to sawdust. Why couldn't I let this go?

ELEVEN

My mood lifted the longer I hung out with my friends. We stayed up way too late, ate too much junk food, watched too many cartoons, and drank more alcohol than I normally consumed in a month. I finally invited them to crash in my hotel room, rather than send them home in a cab.

The next morning, while the pile of three slept soundly on the second bed, I dressed quietly, and made my way downstairs. I'd go pick up breakfast or something. It was the last day of the con; we should make sure we had fun. The problem was, alone with my thoughts and sober, I had time to remember the day before. Longing surged back, and I grabbed my phone. Too bad I didn't have an email address or phone number for Trevor and Evan, but I had their user names.

I shouldn't do this. Trevor's words about regretting speaking up echoed in my head, but I didn't think he believed them any more than I trusted myself. If I didn't do this, I'd never stop wondering what could have been. It wasn't as if I expected either of them to fall down on one knee and confess their undying love, but I did want to spend more time with both of them and see what came next.

I dashed off a quick private message, copying Evan and Trevor on the same note. *I'd like to see you again.*

I didn't want them to believe I was trying to pull them apart. The thought seemed to spring from nowhere—a truth I hadn't recognized yet. It was unreasonable to expect an answer right away, or even at all, but that didn't stop sadness from sinking in when my phone stayed silent. I jumped when it chimed in my hand, then laughed at my own reaction. The text was from Jackson, and my disappointment grew. *Making plans for the day. You anywhere interesting?*

Grabbing breakfast. Back soon, I replied.

I should do that. The hotel had a coffee shop with bagels and muffins. I'd snag us some food there, and head back upstairs. My feet stuck to the floor, legs refusing to move, when I realized Evan stood a few feet away, at the checkout desk. In the second it took him to turn in my direction, a billion options presented themselves to me, boiling down to a smile and acting as if seeing him was nothing, ignoring him and walking away, or telling him at least a little of what was on my mind. The last option terrified me, but it was the only one I could choose.

"Kitten." The nickname sliced into my soul, sharper than any blade. His smile didn't quite form. "I'm sorry I didn't answer your message. I wasn't sure it was a good idea."

"Leaving already?" That was weak. And really obvious. The gears of my mind refused to turn, though.

"Should have left yesterday." He stepped closer, moving out of people's way. His familiar scent, sharp and clean, threatened my grasp on composure. How could I have such a strong reaction to someone I barely knew? He raised a hand, as if to reach for me, then let it drop limply back by his side. "I don't know what Trevor told you."

"Nothing. Not really. That he had to leave early for work, and goodbye."

Evan's laugh was clipped. "Sounds like him. You deserve a little more." His shoulders rose and fell when he sucked in a deep breath and then exhaled. "Look, I know we told you we've done this before, but you were different."

I tried not to read too much into the words, but they already buoyed hope inside. "I feel the same about both of you. I mean that you're different. You already know this was new for me."

His expression wilted. "That's part of the problem. We know this doesn't go past this hotel." He furrowed his brow. "It won't. It can't."

And like that, my mood shattered. I swallowed hard, but couldn't rid myself of the lump in my throat. "Of course."

"The thing is"—he clenched and unclenched his fist—"if you tell yourself it's because this was never meant to be more, if you believe our original intentions are the only reason it's ending, you're doing yourself and the memory a disservice. If you'd prefer, it's not you. It's us. Trevor has been my best friend forever. So long, I barely remember how we met. I like you. I can't speak for him, but it's a fair bet he feels the same. And maybe one of us would click with you, and maybe the other would be happy being a third wheel, or maybe we'd date and it wouldn't work out, and all this over-analyzing would be for nothing. Lots of maybes."

I struggled to process his words without letting my frustration show. My voice wouldn't work, and unshed tears stung my eyes.

"The only *not-maybe*, the only sure thing, is I can't lose Trevor. I'm sorry, Kitten. That's what it comes down to."

They fought over me. It made sense the moment I thought it. I'd known it in the back of my mind, but the same part of me that locked the realization away still denied it was possible, despite the proof I just heard. I forced myself to sound something other than completely bummed out. "I get it. It's okay." It wasn't. Not really. But I didn't want to come between them. "See you around." I stepped back. "Or not. You know. Whatever." I spun and ducked my head, ignoring anything else Evan had to say. I kept my pace normal as I walked back toward the elevator, despite the prickle in my throat and the burn in my eyes. Why did this hurt so much?

225

I WAS NEVER one of those people who hated Mondays. Work paid the bills, and I didn't mind my job. But two weeks after the convention, my third Monday back in the office, I sat at my desk, staring at my call stats and waiting for the next person to ring through. I wanted to be anywhere else. Or maybe I simply wanted to be at the one place I couldn't. I refused to let myself think their names.

At least I was second-tier support, so I only had to answer questions from other technicians. And we supported networking hardware for large corporations, so most of the people calling in were experienced and professional. I might not be as patient as needed with end-users. I'd already snapped at one tech, when he asked me the same question he called with every other day.

My phone rang, and I forced the cheer into my voice. "Help desk. This is Kathryn. What's up?" We were supposed to use a more formal greeting but had a little leeway for internal people.

"I have a customer asking for a supervisor."

Escalation. *Yay.* My gut twisted in on itself. We were the next line of support when someone was pissed off and wanted to talk to someone in charge. I guess it kept management free to do their other work. I didn't like talking to pissed-off customers, and they didn't make it to my line unless they were just that. I always cowered and caved the moment they started to yell. "What's the issue?"

"He won't tell me. He demanded a supervisor the moment I picked up, and that's all he'll say."

Ooh, he was extra angry. Even better. I stashed the sarcastic thoughts, swallowed my pending anxiety, and said, "Pass him through." The line clicked, indicating I'd been connected to the caller. "This is Kathryn. I understand you're having an issue. How can I help you today?"

"Hello?"

I refused to roll my eyes. It would crack the shell I had to wrap myself in, to deal with these calls. If I were more like the woman I'd pretended to be at the convention, maybe I'd handle them better. As it was, I already knew I'd bend, break, and acquiesce before the call was over. I always did. "Yes, sir. Hello. How can I help you?"

"I asked to be passed to a supervisor, not a secretary. Let me talk to someone in management."

I clenched my jaw. I could do this. It wouldn't be a problem. I'd take care of things and then go on break, to unwind. "I'm a supervisor. What seems to be the issue?"

"You're not listening, missy." Condescension oozed from his words. "I want to talk to someone who has the authority to help me, not the gal who answers their phones. Get me someone competent on the line, or I'll have my lawyer contact you."

A growl rose in my chest. I breathed through my nose, focusing on staying calm. "I assure you, I'm able to resolve any issue you're having. Is this a router problem? If you'll give me your company name, I can pull up your hardware information."

"Listen, little lady. I'm trying to be polite, but you're testing my patience. If you don't transfer me now to someone who can help, instead of prattling on in what I'm sure someone thought was a soothing voice, I'm going to start yelling."

Something inside me snapped so cleanly, I swore I felt the rush through me. "Do you have children, sir? A daughter perhaps."

"Not that it's any of your business, but yes. Are you going to transfer me or not?"

My messenger window on my computer chimed with a note from my boss. I ignored it. "What would you do if someone talked to her this way?" I asked. I'd never acted like this at work. It was always suck it up, listen to the shouting, and then apologize until the customer was happy.

"They wouldn't, because my daughter isn't an impertinent bitch."

My blood pressure soared. I muted my computer to keep it from chiming. I was in so much trouble, and I wasn't sure I cared. What happened to me? "Perhaps if she had a father who wasn't a sexist asshole, she'd be a more useful member of society." That wasn't fair; I didn't even know the poor girl. I did pity her, though.

"Listen, you stupid cunt. Do you have any idea who I am?"

My anxiety was gone, replaced with fury. "I don't. Do you know why? Because you haven't given me your fu—"

"I'm sorry about that, sir." A new voice cut into the line, talking over me. Seconds later, my line disconnected. I clenched my teeth, seething with fury.

"Greggers." My barked last name filled the call-center floor. I spun in my chair, to see my boss, Brad, standing in his office door, face red. "In here. Now."

I flung my headset aside and stalked toward him. If every eye in the room hadn't been on me before, they were now. Good. Let them stare and whisper.

Brad shut the door the moment I was inside. "Sit down." His words were clipped. He didn't do the same, standing near his desk instead. "What the hell was that? Quality assurance was on that call, you know."

"Too bad." I shouldn't snap at Brad, but the guy on the phone had me that furious. "If they'd given me thirty more seconds, I would have told that asshole where to stick it."

Brad raised his eyebrows and pursed his lips. "This isn't like you."

"Do you blame me?"

"I can't let you talk like that to customers."

"That's not what I asked." My rage was ebbing, but I still didn't feel I was in the wrong.

He gave a snorting laugh. "I don't blame you, but I still have to write you up."

"Not fire me?" I needed my job. At least until someone came up with a way for me to do anything I wanted without having to pay bills.

"You're good at what you do. Take the rest of the day off. When you come back tomorrow, don't let it happen again."

Except part of me wanted to let it happen again. It felt good to tell that guy what I thought. Even more, I'd rather not come back at all. I wanted to be doing something else. With someone else. Or rather, two someone elses. I couldn't afford to think like that, and I couldn't take any more time to straighten out my head. Real life wouldn't wait while I did.

TWELVE

Most of a day off work, completely unplanned. I should be thrilled, regardless of the circumstances. Instead, I found myself sitting in my apartment, staring at the TV without really processing what was on. Now I'd stepped away from the situation at work, I could look at it objectively. What had I been thinking? Yelling at a customer, making things personal...

Except he'd started it. As childish as that sounded in my own mind, it was the best description of the situation. I shouldn't have to roll over and play nice, just because some douche nozzle had wife issues. I expected a surge of nausea at the self-justification. A physical reminder I wasn't allowed to think that way. A ghost of the discomfort was there—an itch that had no source. On the other hand, I felt good about not taking the verbal abuse and speaking up when I needed to.

The con weekend had flipped a switch in my head. Not that I was willing to make myself the life of every party now, but something inside me had changed. Some of my trepidation was gone. The realization brought a sudden wash of sadness with it. A nudge I'd lost something too. Two men I wasn't meant to have.

They'd wanted to end things then and there, but I couldn't let it go. With any luck, now that they'd had time to chill out—that we all had—they'd be more receptive to talking. Who was I kidding? This wasn't a rational decision on my part, the same way yelling at the customer had been completely impulsive. I wanted to see Trevor and Evan again, and I wasn't going to sit around and hope they read my mind from wherever they were.

I sent them a quick DM, copying both of them like I had before. *Thinking of you.* There. Basic enough. Impulse snaked through me, and as an afterthought I also included my phone number.

I didn't have a chance to sink back into the couch before my phone rang. The number on the screen wasn't familiar, and I pressed *Answer* with more enthusiasm than I should have. "Hello?" What I meant to be a cheerful, upbeat greeting came out as tentative.

"Kitten."

A huge weight lifted from me, and I grinned at the empty room. "You called." Not the most brilliant thing I could have said, but I'd done worse.

"I was thinking of you too." Evan's voice calmed the chaos in my head. "I don't like the way we left things at the con."

That made two of us. "Can we meet somewhere? Nothing formal. Coffee or something, all three of us? Take a step back, get to know each other... Just hang out."

His sigh echoed over the line. "I can try, but I have a feeling it'll only be you and me. I'm working late tonight. Tomorrow?"

Was he bummed because Trevor couldn't be there? I had to admit, I didn't like it either, but I still wanted to see Evan. "I have an Aikido class. What if we do it Saturday? I've got all day, and we can figure things out as we go." Did I sound needy? I was okay with that.

"Sounds fantastic." A hesitant note lined his voice.

It wasn't much, but I knew I'd heard it. "I said something wrong."

"No." The cheer was gone from his voice, replaced with something sad. "You said exactly the right thing. In a lot of ways, you remind me of Trevor."

"I'm— Um…" I had no idea how to respond to that. "Thanks?"

He let out a light chuckle. "It's a good thing; I promise. It's just a little bittersweet. He's not talking to me right now."

"Why not?" I asked. A pause carried over the line, and realization clicked in my head. It was because of me. "I'm sorry."

"It's not your fault. I mean that sincerely. I'm not brushing you off." He clucked, as if tossing a thought back and forth. "Anyway. Saturday is perfect."

We figured out a spot we both knew, to meet at, and said our goodbyes. I wanted to say more, but I'd rather it be face to face. I didn't like the idea of having to wait so long to see Evan, but the situation was certainly better than before I messaged him. Maybe it would give me enough time to figure out what I really wanted, instead of getting by on instinct.

I felt like I could breathe again, and still had an entire afternoon free. Nervous energy hummed through me, looking for an outlet. The dojo I worked out at had open classes during the day, where anyone was welcome to participate. It sounded like the perfect solution.

Two and a half hours later, every inch of me ached, and I was in desperate need of a shower, but my mind was clear. I grabbed my phone from my duffel bag, and the flashing light caught my eye. Probably a random email or something. My heart jammed in my throat when I saw the series of text messages, one every thirty minutes or so.

It's Trevor. I got your note.

I'm sure you're busy. Just wanted to say hi.

I don't know why I'm still bugging you.

Probably because I'm thinking of you, too.

I had to stop the giddiness from making my hand shake before I could send back a reply. *I missed you.*

Have dinner with me tomorrow. His answer came seconds later, and I couldn't help but smile.

I have an Aikido class.

Oh.

He didn't give me much to go on, but I wasn't ready for the

conversation to be over. I typed back, *Have coffee with us Saturday.*

Us? His message said. *So you're talking to Evan.*

It should have been obvious I reached out to both of them. *He called me back. Was I going to ignore him?*

Busy Saturday. Sorry.

Hurt welled inside. *Fine. Be that way.* It was a childish answer, but he wasn't acting any better.

Wait. If a single word, via text message no less, could convey torrents of meaning, his had. At least I wanted to think that was the case. *I really am busy*, his next message read.

I hovered my fingers over the screen before I typed, *Friday? Just us?*

Seeing them separately wasn't the way to do this, but maybe I could nudge them toward common ground.

I'll be there, he replied.

I needed this to not be a massive mistake.

I headed home, tossing a million ideas around in my head about how to distract myself while I waited for time to pass.

It took about thirty seconds to make sure I updated my phone and associated Evan and Trevor's names with their numbers. Another two minutes, maybe, to put reminders in my calendar for our dates. Not that I needed anything more than my buzzing thoughts to remind me, but it was something to do.

And then I sank onto the couch and stared at the wall. I should watch a movie or something. Or maybe I wanted to go out to eat. This was weird—I never wanted to go out alone. For once, though, I didn't care if people whispered and talked about the girl sitting at a corner table, dining by herself.

I walked back into my apartment around nine. Dinner had been nice, but I wasn't able to stretch it out long enough. Should I watch a movie? Fall asleep early? I wasn't tired.

My phone rang, and I jumped. I laughed at the empty apartment and my own skittishness. A smile threatened to split my face when I saw Evan's name on the screen.

"Hey." Giddiness fluttered in my chest. "I thought you were working."

"I just got off."

"And you didn't let me watch." *Oops, maybe I shouldn't have said that.*

His laugh relaxed me. "You're going to kill me with lines like that." He sounded like he looked forward to it.

I sat down, and pulled a throw pillow onto my lap. "I could apologize if that helps."

"Definitely don't do that. I like knowing you meant it. Besides, I was thinking it, so I would be disappointed if you didn't say anything."

I wanted to take the flirting further. Fall into the teasing. The excitement racing over my skin made me curious to see how far we could go over the phone. Except, something about getting too sexy with just Evan felt like cheating. It wasn't a rational thought, but that didn't make it any easier for me to feel otherwise. "What's up?" That sounded casual, right?

"Honestly? I just wanted to talk."

"And you called me? I'm flattered." I tried to sound flippant, but the sentiment had me glowing.

"You should be. I didn't want to talk to anyone else…"

Except Trevor. I almost heard the words buried in his unfinished sentence, and I didn't know how to respond.

"I wanted to hear your voice." Evan's tone firmed and took on the confidence I expected from him.

I lost track of time as we fell into conversation, touching on everything from what movies we were waiting for to places we'd love to visit, to how we felt about karma.

When I yawned for the fourth time in as many minutes, he said, "You need your sleep, Kitten."

Was it really almost two? I didn't want to hang up, but we both had work in the morning, and mine promised to be horrible even without exhaustion looming over me. "Sleep is for the weak."

"Then that's me." His voice took on a somber tone. "I'll see you this weekend."

We said reluctant goodbyes, and I barely remembered to strip out of my clothes before collapsing in bed.

THIRTEEN

Waking up Tuesday morning was like grating my soul over a gravel pit. I forced myself to follow my routine. Go to work. Ignore the stares. Not yell at obnoxious customers. Head to the dojo.

I was dragging by the time I made it home that night. I needed to unwind after my workout, and a shower helped, but experience told me my muscles would hate me in the morning if I didn't sit up for at least a little while.

I settled on the couch and grabbed the remote. My phone buzzed with a new text. A second wind of energy rushed through me when I saw a message from Trevor.

What're you up to? he asked.

Deciding what to watch.

Oh :(

His frowny face drew a similar expression from me. How was I supposed to interpret it? *I should be staring at the wall instead?* I hoped he'd get the teasing in my response.

No. I just wanted to catch you after class and before your shower.

I adored that he'd messaged me, but unlike with to Evan, over the phone, I struggled to infer the tone of the conversation based on typed words. *Because....?*

To give you something to fantasize about, while you rinsed off.

Oh. Heat flooded my skin, and any doubt about his tone evaporated. *You're assuming I wasn't already thinking about it.* If I hadn't been before, I was now. Slipping and sliding together in the shower. My pulse raced at the vivid images.

His reply made my phone vibrate in my hand. *Me stepping up behind you? Wrapping my arms around your waist. Both of us soapy and wet...*

Fuck. That whole *this feels like cheating* thing was back, looming at the forefront of my thoughts. I didn't know what to say.

Except in your version, there are more than two of us.

I almost heard his disappointment. *I'd apologize, but I'm not sorry,* I sent back. No reason to keep avoiding this. I knew what I wanted. The revelation startled me. I really did know what I wanted, and it was both of them. Without a doubt. *It's not the same if you're not both there.*

Nothing. Several minutes passed without a reply. Had my message gone through? Had I pissed him off? I fumbled with a follow-up text, fluctuating between teasing and serious.

His response buzzed in first. *So, what are we watching?*

I didn't want to leave things like that, brushing over my comment as if it never existed, but this wasn't the medium to have the conversation in. I'd see him face to face on Friday.

I should send back a series name. We'd be ridiculous and watch the same thing at the same time.

Damn it, I couldn't leave things this way. *I'm serious.*

Would things have been different if we met without Evan? Trevor's question burrowed deep into my thoughts. Shock hit me first. I shouldn't be surprised he asked, but it still felt like icy water racing down my spine. The longer the words lingered in my head, the more they hurt. *Would you really take that from me? From us?*

If you already know he's what you want, why are we talking? You've made up your mind. Why lead me on?

I clenched my jaw at the accusation, especially since I'd just told him this wasn't what I wanted. *You're misinterpreting my words. Fuck that. You're just being an ass.*

Spell it out for me, so I don't have to guess.

Were we really fighting via text message? One of the guys I wasn't actually dating, who I was never supposed to see again after two weeks ago? It was ludicrous and infuriating, and it felt right. *I already spelled it out. More than once. Don't make me choose.*

I'm sorry. I'm being cruel.

Damn straight. Instead of sending back my gut response, I typed, *I don't know what else to do but be honest with you. I don't want this to be you versus Evan. I don't know why you think it has to be.*

Because that's how relationships work. Two people hook up, form a bond, and see how far they want to take things...

No, I typed. *That's how most relationships work. If we want something different, we can make up our own rules.*

Just because you know someone who made it happen, doesn't mean it's that easy or that everyone can do it.

He was being stubborn. I growled at the empty room and forced myself to think rationally. *I'm not saying everyone can do it. I'm suggesting in our case...*

Big difference here, Kathryn. Your brother likes guys and girls. I've only got the one preference. It's not like I can just flip a switch because you think it sounds like a good idea.

I didn't have an argument for that. *I know. I was just hoping...* What? Trevor was right.

Hoping it would be different with Evan? He's still got the wrong body parts.

But he's your best friend. Wow, that was weak. I hated to admit defeat, but I couldn't force either of them into this if they didn't want it.

Just because I hang out with the guy doesn't mean I want him sucking me off.

You're right. I'm sorry.

Me too.

Was the conversation over? Did he expect me to say something else? He hadn't given me a lot to go on. Several minutes passed without another response. Maybe I ruined any chance we had at finding common ground. Not that there ever had a chance, based on our exchange.

A note buzzed through. *What are we watching?*

I should tell him nothing, and that I needed to go, but I wasn't ready to end things like that. *Something classic. High action. And really corny.*

Captain Harlock?

Maybe if we couldn't have a romantic relationship, we could have a friendship. I sent back, *Sounds great.*

We spent the next couple hours exchanging quips about how good or bad or just plain funny the movie was.

FOURTEEN

W ednesday came and went without contact from Evan or Trevor, and I couldn't ignore my disappointment, even if it was unreasonable. On Thursday, I decided it was ridiculous to wait for them, and sent them both a *good morning :)* Trevor replied with a similar message, but it hurt when I didn't hear from Evan.

Thursday afternoon, I finished up Aikido class, shouldered my duffel bag, and hovered at the edge of the floor mats, watching the next class. They guy teaching was a classmate of mine. He'd been doing this for years, like I had, and now he stood up there, in front of a group of pre-teens, taking them through their forms.

I wanted to be doing that. Why wasn't I? I had no right wishing Evan and Trevor would step up and recognize how they felt, if I wasn't willing to do the same. I was happy to admit how I felt about them, but I was still holding back when it came to work. I set my bag aside and padded to the main office.

My sensei—the guy who owned the dojo—looked up from his computer. "What's up?"

I twisted my fingers in on themselves, grabbed my will to do this from deep inside, and stood straighter. "I'd like another chance teaching."

He shook his head and turned back to whatever he was working on. "I'm sorry, Kathryn. You're very talented. It's obvious you love doing this, and you've learned a lot over the years. But you don't have the kind of presence a teacher needs."

The words stung even more the second time around, and left my skin prickling. I shoved it aside and forced the confidence into my voice. "I don't agree. I think I can do this."

Now I had his full attention. His brows were half raised, his eyes wide. A combination of surprise and... hope? "You did poorly during your practical test," he said.

That was the part where I had to actually teach a class. "I know. It was a poor performance. I really think I can do better. Let me assist someone else, to prove it. Then if I do better, let me take on classes of my own?"

He drummed his fingers on his keyboard, not compressing any keys, and then stood. "All right. One more chance. Do this, and I'll let you start teaching classes. Follow me."

I fell into step behind him but almost stopped moving when he stepped up in front of the current class. He halted them and bowed. A dozen heads returned the polite gesture. "We have a special treat today," he told them. "One of our black belts, Kathryn, is going to face off with your sensei. It will give you an idea of what you'll be able to do if you keep at this."

All those faces turned in my direction, and a hot flush spread over my face. I gritted my teeth, locked my hesitation aside and stepped to the front of the class. I could do this; that was the point. What Jackson had told me bounced in my head. It didn't matter how many people watched. Those who were going to talk would do so, no matter what. Besides, these kids were living life, like the rest of us.

I bowed to my counterpart, and we both fell into defensive stances. A twitch from his foot, and the spar began.

For the next five minutes, to the tune of gasps, claps, and *oohs*, we grappled, tumbled, and danced. The demonstration ended with me dropping him to the mat and pinning him until he tapped out. I helped him to his feet, we faced the class, and gave one more bow.

Seconds later, the kids surrounded us, asking questions and talking over each other. They looked at me in awe, instead of disgust or amusement.

Sensei stood at the far end of the mats. He gave me a small smile. "One week. You help with classes. Then we'll see. Email me your schedule, and I'll fit you in."

I wanted to squeal and clap and give him a thank-you hug, but I restrained myself. Instead I simply bowed. "You'll have my schedule tonight. Thank you."

My mood increased another notch when I pulled my phone out on the way to my car. One missed call, from Evan. I dialed my voicemail and dropped into my vehicle.

"Hey, Kitten." His voice was more soothing that I thought possible. "I've been in meetings with contractors on the East Coast since early this morning, and just got your note. If you're free, call me."

I wanted to get him on the line right away, but I also wanted to be somewhere I wouldn't have to hang up anytime soon. Traffic seemed to flow like molasses as I drove home. By the time I unlocked my apartment door and pushed inside, every inch of me was tense. I tossed my duffle bag aside, already bringing up Evan's number.

"I think I'm addicted to your voice," he said as a greeting. "I'd much rather hear you say *good morning* than see a text. Not that I'm complaining."

Even though it had been almost two days, the conversation with Trevor was still fresh in my mind. Not that I'd re-read the messages or anything, trying to figure if I could have said something different. Well, not more than a few times. Would flirting with Evan end in the same disaster? I couldn't be rude. "How about a *good evening*, instead?"

"It's a start." His smile was audible. "At least one of you is still talking to me."

That answered the question of whether or not bringing up Trevor was off the table. "I'm sorry you haven't heard from him." Was this my segue to ask if Evan was interested in a more-than-two-person relationship? I didn't have any right. Trevor made himself clear, so even if Evan was interested in the same thing as I was, it wasn't going to happen.

"Can I tell you something?" Evan asked. His voice was so quiet, I had to strain to hear him.

A million possibilities raced through my head. Among them, the selfish option that he'd spend more time with me regardless. But I'd struggle with only being with one of them. I needed to stop guessing, before I drove myself insane. "Of course."

"For the longest time, I thought I was gay."

Wow, that came out of nowhere. And here I thought *I* was about to dump an intense conversation on us. "Past tense?"

"Trevor doesn't know. It's the one thing I never told him, growing up. Because"—Evan sighed—"he was the reason I thought that, and there was no way I'd tell my best friend I was interested in him *like that*."

The air rushed from my lungs, as if a vice squeezed them tight. That was nowhere on my list of guesses. Should I feel bad that it was a relief to hear it? "What did you do?"

"When we hit high school, I got so much tail, it distracted me. Football team, student council... It was easy. I threw myself into being with girls, and it wasn't bad. If I pretended hard enough, Trevor was just another guy. I don't know why I'm dumping this on you. Like I said, you remind me of him, but you're different."

"It's okay. I don't mind." I was intensely curious, but it was only my business if he felt like sharing. It didn't feel right to push.

"Thanks." A hint of relief lifted his voice. "So I enlisted, thought I'd put it all behind me, and when my bunkmate hit on me, I wasn't into it. There weren't any other guys catching my attention. I came back, and there Trevor was. My best friend and the only guy I dreamed about at night."

"I don't blame you for dreaming about him." I tried to keep my tone light and teasing, but still sympathetic.

"Because you've got good taste." More of the tension faded from his voice. "The first time we picked up a girl together, it was my idea. I needed an excuse, and that felt more subtle than, *I think you're hot, but I need to suck you off to find out if it means anything*. It turned out we both liked the experience, though he didn't enjoy it for the same reasons I did. So now you know my secret. I pick up women with my best friend, as an excuse to be with him. And then you came along and—"

My heart sank. "Got in the way."

"No." He spoke quickly. "Completely the opposite. You fit too well, but he and I don't have *that*."

"Maybe you could." It was selfish of me to encourage Evan, knowing how Trevor felt, but I couldn't take it back.

"Not going to happen," he said. "I've hinted at it, asked him indirectly, and he's not interested."

"What if the question simply needs to be asked differently?"

"No."

I hadn't expected the abrupt retort. "Okay. Forget it."

"It's not that. I meant it when I said I can't lose him. Dancing around the subject is better than the last few weeks of not talking to him have been."

"I'm having dinner with him tomorrow night." I shouldn't have said that.

"He gets you first?"

Defensiveness raced through me. "It's not like that."

"I know. I didn't mean it to be."

I twisted my ponytail around my finger. "Meet up with us. Talk it out. Not necessarily *that*, but make things right with him." I was negotiating for them, as much as for me. An empty ache grew inside when Evan sighed again. I wanted to see him happy, with or without me.

"I see what you're trying to do, and I appreciate it"—his voice was low and sad—"but this has to stay between you and me. Always. Promise me."

"Of course." I could do nothing else, given the intensity in his plea.

"It's not right that I have to make this choice. In a perfect world, I'd know he felt the same, we'd get to know you better, and… This isn't that world. He's only interested in me as a friend, and neither of us is mature enough to see you with the other. God, Kitten, it kills me things happened this way."

"Me too." Killed me. Devoured me. Tore me apart. "But think about it. Please? I'll send you the address."

"You're meeting at the Italian place on Fourth and Thirteenth, at eight."

I stared my phone for a minute. "Did he...?"

"I assumed he set the time and place. Lucky guess on my part." Evan's words were tinged with sadness. "I'll think about it. If I'm not there though, please don't take it personally."

"How else am I supposed to take it?"

"Good point." His laugh was strained.

We chatted for a while longer, but the levity that was there during the con and on Tuesday was missing. A heavy cloud hung over the conversation, nagging that this wasn't going the way either of us wanted.

When we hung up, I sent Trevor a text. I didn't think anything would come of it, but that didn't stop me from hoping.

I invited Evan to join us tomorrow night.

I couldn't wait for a reply. I sent one message after another. *I don't know if he'll show.*

And if you don't either, I'll understand.

It'll hurt, but I'll understand.

But you can't let this ruin your friendship. The two of you deserve more than that. So let him make things better between you. I had no intention of breaking my promise to Evan. I was willing to take a lot more of a stand than I used to, when it came to anything, but I couldn't try to open Trevor's eyes when this wasn't my secret to share.

I could push and prod for them to work things out, though.

———

I sat in the restaurant parking lot, staring at my steering wheel and listening to my mind ramble on. I wanted to walk in there and tell Trevor how it was. Nudge him until he admitted he felt the same way about Evan and me that we did about him. Except that wasn't my right. I'd already told him how I felt, but the rest was out of my hands.

The clock ticked up on meeting time, and I stashed my internal argument. Maybe it was time to play things by ear. I found Trevor on the sidewalk, right outside the front door, his hands jammed in his pockets. He grinned when he saw me, and my heart danced happily against my ribs. I reached out for a tentative hug. He squeezed me tight, and I sank into the embrace. I hadn't realized how much I missed this the last couple of weeks. Part of me wanted more. A kiss, long and passionate.

"I missed you," he murmured against my hair. "And I'm sorry for how I left things the other night." His apology sank into me, soothing an anxiety I hadn't been able to quell.

"I thought you might not show, because of the messages I sent last night." I didn't want to bring them up, but sweeping them under the rug wouldn't help anyone.

"I almost didn't." He pulled back enough to study my face. "I... uh... made a call, after you texted me. What you said on Tuesday made me think about things I've been trying really hard not to think about. I don't know if I can do what you're asking, but you're right. I don't want to lose my best friend."

A hand settled on the small of my back. I assumed not Trevor's, since he still grasped my hips.

"Hey, Kitten." Evan's familiar voice lifted my spirits further. I leaned back into his touch, careful not to break contact with Trevor.

"We talked a lot," Trevor said.

This had to be good news, or they wouldn't both be here. "And...?"

"But not about *everything*," Evan added.

Trevor furrowed his brow. "Apparently there are some things he can't say without you here. You're his translator?"

"I don't think that's quite right." Then again, I didn't know for certain. Evan seemed to hold a few missing pieces to this conversation. I reluctantly extracted myself from his touch and turned to face him. "I can't translate, unless I know what I'm saying."

"Let's go inside." Evan nudged me. "We'll sit. We'll talk."

Trevor trailed his hand down my arm and tangled his fingers with mine. "Come on."

Whatever they'd hashed out, apparently the jealousy had faded. Neither one of them seemed to have a problem with the other touching me. I wasn't complaining, but I wondered what I'd missed.

I stepped away and leaned against the wall, so I could see them both. "I won't be tag-teamed." I winced as soon as the words were out of my mouth. Maybe not the best phrasing.

Evan lowered his mouth to my ear, his voice quiet. "I thought this was part of the point."

Trevor shook his head, but he didn't look irritated. "Inside. We'll talk. Or someone will." He shot Evan a pointed glare.

"Fine." Evan held his hands up in surrender, but he was smiling.

Moments later, we were seated at a in the back of the restaurant. Evan and Trevor knew the host, so despite the Friday night crowd, we had a premium, almost private spot. I hesitated next to the booth. Who sat next to whom?

Each guy slid into a separate side, making my decision even more difficult. Trevor grabbed my hand and tugged, and Evan didn't look even a little bit hurt by the gesture. This was too easy.

I locked my gaze on Evan. "What did you tell him?"

Evan stared back without hesitation. "I told him I'd back down if you both wanted me to, but he had to hear me out, and you had to be okay with it."

I pursed my lips and looked between the two. "I think I've made myself clear."

Trevor squeezed my knee. I wanted to be irritated with him—with both of them—for spoon-feeding me this information, but the gesture was reassuring. He opened and closed his mouth a few times, before finally speaking. "I told him I wasn't going to choose between him and you."

Great. Now we were back to the part where Kathryn stepped aside, so two great guys could stay friends. I didn't begrudge them the decision, but I would miss them. A lump grew in my throat, and I tried to swallow past it. "And?"

"And he got really stubborn and just kept repeating I had to hear him out and you had to be there."

I looked back at Evan. "Are you enjoying this?"

His smugness faltered. "Not as much as you might think. I'm kind of terrified, honestly. I know what I said before, but maybe you could—"

"No." I kept my voice kind. As much as I wanted this out in the open, it wasn't my place to do the revealing.

Evan waved down the waiter and ordered three beers. He shifted in his seat, and then again, before he finally looked at Trevor. "I love you." The words ran together in a single syllable.

I almost didn't want to look at Trevor, but I had to know. His expression was blank, except for his wide eyes. I swore I heard a clock somewhere, ticking away the seconds as silence stretched across the table.

"You mean her, right?" Trevor's question came out strained.

Evan frowned. "Soon, probably. Though, no offense Kitten, we're not there yet. I mean you, Trevor. My best friend. The guy who's always been there. The only man I've ever dreamed about, and they're some intense fucking dreams."

"I can't—" Trevor nudged me.

I slid out of his way, and he brushed past me without another word, to vanish out the front door seconds later.

"That went well." Evan grabbed one of the beers the waiter set on the table and drained half the bottle in a single swallow.

"Give him a little time to process?" I wasn't sure what I was saying. They knew each other better than I did. Now even more than before.

Evan scrubbed his face. "What if time doesn't fix it?"

I gave him what I hoped was a reassuring smile. "It's been thirty seconds. Too soon to tell. Besides, you both showed up tonight, and I think that counts for something."

"I was so glad he called me." Evan slammed the bottle into the table. "I have to go talk to him." He fished a twenty from his wallet and tossed it next to the drinks. He stood and held out his hand.

"You want me to come with you?"

"You're in this with us. I would never say you caused it—don't think that—but meeting you was the catalyst." He pulled me to my feet. "You'd rather I do it without you?"

I fell into step beside him. "No. I just didn't want to assume."

He muttered a quick apology to the host, said something came up, and held the front door open for me.

We found Trevor on the side of the building, back to the wall and one foot propped up. His gaze was directed at the night sky, and he didn't move when we shuffled up next to him. "Give a guy some warning, why don't you?" His voice was quiet.

"I don't have any practice with this kind of thing," Evan said dryly. "Was I supposed to lead with, *I have this friend who likes you...?*"

Trevor pushed from the wall and finally looked at Evan. "It might have helped. Do you want a do-over?"

"Not really. It won't change anything."

Trevor raked shaky fingers through his hair. "In that case, me too."

I almost asked when he meant, but my brain caught up before the question spilled out. He was talking about loving Evan. Hope sparked inside me. I couldn't find the strength to suppress it, but I didn't dare speak and ruin the moment.

"I told you I've been thinking a lot over the past couple of weeks"—Trevor took another step toward Evan, gravel lining his voice—"and not just about Kathryn, though God damn if that woman isn't addictive." He kept his gaze on Evan, but his words sent another flutter through me. "She's not the reason I couldn't call you. I'd be pissed if the two of you hooked up without me, though."

Evan opened his mouth, and Trevor held up a warning finger. "I'm not done." His gaze never left Evan. "It was really easy to ignore how I felt, once you enlisted, but then you came back. Don't get me wrong; I've never been more grateful for something. Then you had to suggest we pick up a girl together. And fuck if I wasn't willing to do it again and again, just to be with you. Not that I could admit to myself that's why I did it. It didn't matter how many times I woke up in the middle of the night, cock hard as a rock, your image burned in my dreams, driving me to beat off until

I was raw. I still wasn't interested in you. That's what I told myself."

The intensity in Trevor's confession stole my breath and sent my imagination running rampant. It filled me with a rainbow of conflicting and complimentary emotions. I didn't know if I was relieved, worried I was about to lose them both, or happy to see them finally admitting the truth.

Trevor stopped with his shoes nudging Evan's. While a mixture of hope and concern peppered Evan's face, Trevor didn't reflect any emotion. His voice was heavy. "And then she came along, and the two of you were good together. Incredible, even. And something pinged in the back of my mind that I was about to lose her. Which made no sense, because I didn't have her. When you stormed out of our hotel room that morning because she was wearing my shirt, I was terrified. More scared than I'd been since they deployed you to a fucking war zone. Because I have to have you in my life."

Trevor tangled his fingers in Evan's hair and kissed him hard, mouths crushing together, moans mingling. If being pressed between the two of them was hot, this was scorching. A bitter copper taste hit my tongue, and I realized I was biting my lip.

"So are we good?" Evan was breathless when they broke apart.

"I fucking hope so." Trevor finally looked at me. "You're really tough on a guy's psyche. You know that? Making me think, and admit I have feelings, and all that bullshit?"

I laughed, as much to let the tension out as anything. "I didn't mean to."

"That's part of what makes you so amazing." He wove his fingers with mine, other hand still settled on the back of Evan's neck. "You're just making it up as you go along."

I couldn't hide my grin. "So do we all want the same thing? No having to choose. No pitting you against each other?"

"I'm in." Trevor squeezed my hand.

Evan spun me to face him and brushed his lips over mine. "Me too." He kissed me again, more deeply this time. He slid his tongue into my mouth and it danced around mine. Heat and hunger made my blood roar, and my need grew, drawing my nipples to hard nubs and pooling wet between my thighs.

Trevor tightened his grip on my hand and sucked in a deep breath through his teeth. His response heightened my arousal. "I'm thinking it's a good thing we brought this outside." His voice was strained.

FIFTEEN

"My place is about five minutes away." Evan nodded toward the main road. "We could talk about this in a more intimate setting."

The way he said *intimate* sent a pleasant shiver through me. "Yes, please," I said.

"Wait." Trevor tugged me back. "Is it really this easy?"

Disappointment set in at the hesitation, but it didn't ease my arousal. "You call two weeks—or several years in your cases—of soul searching and denial *easy*?"

Trevor studied my face, as if he might find some deep, mysterious answer hidden there. "Why did you push this? You and I click. It's like we operate on the same wavelength sometimes. We're incredible together."

His words both warmed and worried me. I thought he wanted both of us. Except I was too focused on what Trevor said and not on how he said it. This wasn't accusation or regret. His tone was curious.

And he deserved an answer, rather than me making broad statements like, *Now we all belong to each other, 'kay?*

Two gazes lingered on me, heavy with expectation. "Kathryn?"

Playing things by ear. Right. I needed to dive in and hope I didn't say something stupid. "It's true; we do. But I click with Evan too. You just said so. I don't need to justify it. You see as well as I do that the three of us work."

Trevor's mouth twitched in an unformed smile. "So how does this go? Do we always all have to be around?"

I raised my brows. "First of all, I'm talking about more than just sex. It's not like all three of us are always going to be in the same place at the same time. Beyond that, do we have to label it? Sometimes it's going to be all three of us, and sometimes someone will be busy or not in the mood, and I figure it's all okay as long as there are no secrets. We still need to get to know each other and get comfortable with our dynamic. No reason to put a fence around it before we even know what *it* is."

"So"—Evan dragged the word out—"if Trevor and I were to hook up when you weren't around, you'd be okay with it, as long as someone told you about it after, in vivid, lurid, filthy detail?"

A visual rolled through my thoughts. The two of them stripped down, kissing, hands roaming each other's hard, bare bodies. I squeezed my legs together, to suppress the throb, and chewed my bottom lip. "I'd rather someone took pictures. But I guess if the photographer's busy, a verbal play-by-play would be all right."

Evan prompted me toward the parking lot again, but locked his gaze on Trevor. "*Now* we're going back to my place."

THE DRIVE to Evan's house might have been the longest five minutes of my life. I was squirming by the time he led us inside.

Before the door was all the way closed, Trevor twisted his fingers in my hair and held my head captive. "God, I missed you," he growled before crushing his mouth to mine.

I whimpered at the intensity, the weight of his kiss driving into me.

I dug my fingers into his chest, needing something—anything—to hold onto, and slid my body against his. The faint scent of his body wash, cool and sharp, filled my thoughts and dialed up my pulse another notch.

Evan brushed my hair off the back of my neck, and a second set of lips traced over my skin.. I whimpered against Trevor's mouth. Trevor dropped his other hand to my waist and pushed under my T-shirt. The heat of his palm on my stomach was like a million sparks of energy, flaring across my skin. Evan nipped my earlobe with his teeth and then trailed his tongue down my neck. His erection dug into my ass, hard and insistent. God, I loved being caught between these two. I never imagined it could be like this.

Evan sucked on my sensitive skin. Biting. Flicking his tongue over the flesh. Marking me. Trevor glided his hand higher until he cupped my breast. He kneaded, pressure and focus increasing until he pinched my nipple through the fabric. He rolled the hard nub, sending a delicious spike of pain and pleasure through me. I needed to be closer. To feel more. I grabbed the hem of Trevor's shirt. He broke the contact long enough to yank the Tee over his head and toss it aside.

Evan continued his attentions along my shoulder, hands on my hips and fingers gripping tight. His every groan vibrated through his chest and my back. I worked my pelvis in rhythm, grinding against the shaft digging into me.

I traced Trevor's slender torso, following the lines and definition. I dragged a thumb over his nipple. He sucked in a sharp breath when I drew tight circles around the button. He looked me over, lust darkening his gaze. "You've got too many clothes on."

"I agree." Evan stripped my shirt off in a single, fluid gesture. I barely registered lifting my arms long enough for him to do so. Trevor shoved my bra up, building friction and scraping skin in need of more attention. He lowered his mouth and flicked his tongue over my swollen nipple. I gasped at the light gesture and the shock of cool, when he blew on the skin.

The tension on my shoulders vanished when Evan unsnapped my bra and drew it away. Trevor took my nipple in his mouth, and sucked. He massaged my other breast, pinching and tugging in time with his mouth. I shifted my weight. My lower lips slid easily, already wet in anticipation. Evan grabbed my hips again and pulled me back into his cock. The hard shaft teased me through denim, and he grunted every time I pressed back.

I scraped a nail down Trevor's chest, past the waistband of his jeans and to the thick bulge waiting for attention. He jerked against my touch and sucked my nipple harder. There were too many sensations, and at the same time not enough contact. Their scents mingled and filled my head, and their voices were the most erotic song I'd ever heard.

I stroked Trevor through his pants, pumping my hips with each new touch, bite, or squeeze from either man.

"I bet you're soaked, Kitten." Evan's voice had dropped an octave.

"You'll never know unless you check." It took more focus than I wanted, to keep the teasing in my voice amid the rainbow of sensations driving over me.

Evan sought out my button and zipper. Seconds later, he dragged the remainder of my clothing down my legs. Searing heat built over my skin, and the air kissed my wet mound. His fingers pushed between my legs from behind, parting my folds.

"This is amazing." I forced the words out between gasps and locked my gaze on Trevor. "But I want something else."

He smirked and pulled his mouth from my breast, hand still kneading. Evan's touch danced along my slit, light enough to tease, never making contact with my clit or dipping inside me.

Trevor studied my face, green eyes wide and curious. "Anything you want."

"You." I nudged his shoulders, guiding him back toward the sofa. "I want to taste you." I fumbled with his belt and jeans for only a moment, before undoing both and pushing those plus his boxer briefs to the ground.

He landed on the couch with a quiet grunt, his cock at full mast, begging for attention.

I knelt next to him, wrapped my hand around the base, and

stroked. "This time, let me finish you?" I held his gaze, my voice gravelly with desire.

"Fuck, yes." Evan's words melded with the moment.

Trevor traced a finger over my bottom lip, pulling it into a pout before letting go. His smile grew. "How am I going to say *no* to a request like that?"

SIXTEEN

I dipped my head but kept my gaze on Trevor's, as I flicked my tongue over the tip of his cock. He groaned and dug his fingers into my shoulder. The sharp pressure spurred me on. I took his entire length in my mouth. Evan dipped between my pussy lips again, still tracing over skin and teasing. My head swam from so much sensory input, feeling light, as if it might float away at any minute. The room buzzed with gasps and groans. I knew exactly which belonged to whom, but they still mingled in an intoxicating melody.

I stroked Trevor's shaft while I sucked, speeding up according to the sounds he made. Evan slid a finger inside me, and I groaned in delight. My clit ached for attention, throbbing more each second I ministered to Trevor. I shifted my hand to cup his balls, which were already tight. He rested a hand at the back of my neck, holding me in place and guiding the pace. I was trapped between the two of them, hovering near the height of pleasure, held in place by hands and unseen bonds. My heart screamed in excitement.

Trevor's hand tightened, and his breathing grew punctuated. "God, Kathryn, I'm gonna come."

His words almost had the same effect on me, especially with

Evan's finger gliding in and out of me at a slow, steady pace. I sucked Trevor hungrily, bobbing against him. He rose off the couch with a loud moan, and warm, salty fluid hit the back of my throat. I continued to lick and stroke until he shuddered away from my touch.

As I pulled back, my satisfied grin vanished in a moan when Evan shoved more fingers inside me, enough to stretch me out. Trevor grasped my face, and pulled me up to kiss me, tasting himself on my lips, thrusting his tongue into my mouth, and swallowing my cries.

I was vaguely aware of the sound of a zipper behind me. Evan pumped his hand against my opening.

Trevor dipped his head next to my ear. "I wanna see you come. Hard." His lips moved against my skin, his words as much touch as whisper. "I wanna see Evan bury his thick dick inside you, all the way to the hilt, and I want to hear you scream in pleasure."

It took the last of my resources to summon a response. "That's a long list."

Trevor nibbled on my ear. "And you're not complaining." He slid two fingers down my breastbone, over my stomach, and between my legs, and found my clit with little searching.

The new touch, abrading my already swollen sex, mingled with the sensation of the fingers hooked inside me and hitting just the right spot. Orgasm shredded through me, flooding my limbs and leaving me wobbly. My body jerked from Trevor's touch when my clit protested at the over-stimulation, but he kept up the pressure. Evan pulled his fingers out of me, but seconds later a blunt head nudged my opening.

Evan drove his cock deep inside me and grabbed my hips tight, slamming his pelvis against my butt. "You're so tight, Kitten." It sounded as if he spoke through clenched teeth.

I couldn't muster a response. The two contrasting and complimentary touches had me hovering near climax again, but my body refused to yield. Evan tightened his grip, and his breathing grew shallow. The short strokes from behind and gasps for air made me think he was as close as I was.

With his free hand, Trevor sought out my nipple again. He resumed the attention he'd given it moments ago, but this time the rough pinch met already tender skin. The new spark sent me over the edge. I screamed when I came. Stars danced in my vision, as arcs of pleasure and release spilled through me. My pussy clenched around Evan's dick. Spasming. Gripping.

Trevor eased back in time with my slowing gasps.

Evan let out a series of short grunts followed by a long groan, and I knew he'd finished as well.

Euphoria sank in, as the room spun to a stop and my surroundings blurred back into focus. My head still buzzed from the overload, and a giddy laugh escaped my throat. My legs wobbled, and from Evan's faltering grip behind me, I wondered if he felt the same. Trevor helped me shift and drew me into his lap. Evan dropped onto the couch next to us. He pulled my legs over his and leaned his head on Trevor's shoulder.

The only sound in the room was breathing returning to normal. A few short weeks ago, I'd never have guessed this could be me. But now, wrapped into a pleasant tangle with two wonderful men, I couldn't imagine things happening any other way. Trevor rested his head on Evan's and traced tiny circles over my shoulder blade. Evan covered my shins with his palms.

Yup. This was absolutely perfect.

THREE MONTHS later

I glanced one last time at the king-size bed in my hotel room, grateful someone else was paid to make the bed this weekend, and let the door swing shut behind me. I strode toward the elevator, skirt swishing around my legs. Back in L.A., for the first time in years. Attending one of the conventions that started my love of these things was exciting. Especially when I was with the two men who inspired so many other new things in me.

I squished into the waiting car, not minding that it was already too full of people. The last few months were an amazing ride of discovery. Getting to know Trevor and Evan better. Falling into my teaching role at the dojo. Handing in my resignation at the call center.

For the first several weeks, Trevor made it a habit to point out things still might not work. We didn't all know each other. The thrill would wear off. Life would intrude. He hadn't brought up any doubts in a while. When I'd asked him about it, he said he'd decided there was no reason to worry.

I didn't know what the odds were my brother and I would both end up in poly relationships, but Jackson was as supportive of the entire thing as he always was—after a few threatening glares and muttered warnings about my guys not breaking his little sister's heart.

The elevator slowed to a stop on the main floor, and people spilled out. I stepped out of the flow of traffic and positioned myself near a blank slice of wall. Where to look for Evan and Trevor first? They both ducked out early this morning, wanting to attend panels that didn't hold the same appeal to me as sleeping in.

A finger trailed down my spine, leaving a delicious tingle in its wake and ending with a palm cupping my ass. "A cute little kitten like you shouldn't be wandering a place like this alone."

I leaned back into Evan with a smile, inhaling his familiar, crisp scent. "I'm not alone if you're here."

"Hmm..." He trailed his lips along the back of my neck. "I don't have an argument for that."

Amusement bubbled inside. This was going to be an awesome weekend. "Were *you* alone?"

"Nope." Trevor stepped up in front of me. I had no idea if he'd magically materialized, or the crowds had parted to let him through. He handed me a cup of coffee. "I thought you'd want this."

I took a long sip of the drink, not caring it scalded going down. "My hero."

Trevor kissed me on the cheek. "Only for you." He paused, raised his brows, and nodded at Evan. "And him, I guess. But I don't fetch coffee for anyone else."

Evan gave my butt a light squeeze. "You know, half the guys here watched you waltz off that elevator."

Months ago, I would have been mortified to hear that. The impulse to be embarrassed was still there, but it was overridden by a hint of pride. "More of them would stare if they knew what I'm—sorry, what I'm not—wearing under my skirt."

Evan inched my skirt up, until his fingers brushed bare skin. A tremor ran through me. It didn't matter how much we experimented or what kind of things we got up to, either one of them still made me wet with a single touch.

"No distracting him." Despite Trevor's words, his gaze drifted below my waist. "For at least a couple of minutes. We were talking this morning, and Evan wants to ask you something."

"The answer's yes, if you can find us a restroom with locking doors down here." I kept my tone light and teasing, imagination already skipping ahead to me being pushed up to the edge of the sink, skirt hiked over my hips—

"Not that." Evan cut into my thoughts. "Well maybe that, but this first." He spun me to face him. "I don't like that the two of you have to go home at night." He furrowed his brow and studied my face, as if searching for a clue. "I want you to both move in with me. I mean, it doesn't have to be my place, but my house is bigger…"

A grin threatened to split my face. "You already asked Trevor, and he said yes?" I wasn't worried they'd talked about it without me, as long as they included me now.

"Not until you give me your answer." Evan said.

My smile grew wider. "He did say yes, or you wouldn't be asking me like this. And I'm saying yes, too."

Evan brushed his lips over mine, then cradled my face in his palms and deepened the kiss. I felt Trevor behind me, hand on my hip, breath on my neck. I gasped, still riding the rush of the moment, when Evan broke away.

"I didn't think you'd say no"—Evan gave me a sheepish smile—"but I was still a little worried."

"I'm definitely saying yes." I threw my arms around his neck. He squeezed me tight, Trevor's palm still on me.

I lingered in the shared embrace a little longer, savoring the moment and everything that led up to this point. We might hit a few bumps along the way, as our relationship grew and shifted, but we could work our way through any of it. Both of them—all three of us—we were a perfect discovery.

———

ROLL AGAINST BETRAYAL

ONE

Sydney fumbled with a wire shelf for her booth display. This was normally a two-person job, but if she could just twist her arm in one direction and snap the securing clip in by reaching around and under...

Her phone chimed with a new text, startling her, and her grip slipped. She maneuvered herself into the right position again and let out a pleased yelp when the fixture snapped into place.

She grabbed her phone. The message was from Kim.

I can't make it this weekend. Family stuff. Super sorry.

Sydney snarled at the text. Because of course, when she hired Kim to help her at the convention and asked, *Are you sure you don't have any issues with this being over the Labor Day weekend,* she'd taken Kim's *I'll be fine* at face value.

All wasn't lost yet. Unlike the last several cons Sydney exhibited at, this one was in her hometown. She had to have at least one friend who could hop in to help her out.

She sent out a series of texts and emails, and returned to setting up the framework for her booth while she waited. As one reply after another rolled in, her frustration grew. Everyone was either working tomorrow or already out of town. One person said they might be able to pop in for a few hours on Sunday, but they weren't sure.

Sydney had the rest of today to get the booth set up, and she could do that on her own. It would take more than twice as long, but she'd manage. Surviving a three-day con without help, though? That was going to suck.

Just thinking about it made her want to double up on the coffee. Which was a good idea. She needed a break anyway.

She padded through the brightly-lit convention center, her sneakers scuffing softly on the concrete floor. Most of the concessions weren't open yet, since the event hadn't started. The one coffee shop that was had a line that grew out the door and wrapped around a couple of pillars.

It was a good excuse for her to take a longer break.

Most of the people in line were on their phones, but she was caught up on her email for now, and wound too tightly to scroll through social media.

A squeal echoed through the halls, and a couple of cosplayers in their mid-twenties ran past. One wielded an ax as big as she was, while she chased her friend.

The people around Sydney were dressed more like she was—jeans, T-shirts, and sneakers. The *I expect to get dirty* uniform of the veteran vendor. Snippets of conversation drifted toward her: speculation about whether the show would clear one-hundred-thousand attendees, people wondering if they'd brought enough figurines, and exclamations of disgust and awe about how much celebrity autographs were going for this year.

Sydney loved the energy that hummed through the room. Her game, *Changelings and Caverns*, started as a way for her and her friends to spend weekends being geeky but in a new way. Like any of their favorites, the setup involved figurines, a board game, and a lot of roleplaying.

Sydney tweaked and modified the rules until it morphed from a knock-off to its own unique experience. Then she'd gone out on a limb and had a few hundred copies of the game manufactured.

What started as a labor of love had turned into a revenue

stream for her. She was still thrilled every time someone bought a copy of C&C. Attending fantasy cons and comic cons all over the country, to get the word out, was an added bonus.

She also liked seeing new places and people. For instance, the sexy guy who just moved into view a few people back in line. His dark hair was trimmed short, and the faint scruff of beard was kind of sexy. Like really sexy.

As in, she should probably stop staring. Or take one of those sneaky pictures. She could send it to Kathryn and share the love. Remind her best friend how much she was missing out on, despite being at the lake with her two boyfriends.

Yup. Two. And Sydney had a hard time keeping one. Go figure.

She tried to be subtle about angling her phone up, making it look like she was just checking something at a really high angle. She clicked the button to take the pic, and the flash went off.

Fuck. He looked up and met her gaze for a blink, before she ducked her head and dropped her phone into her purse.

Fortunately, the line chose that moment to inch forward, taking him out of her line of sight.

Despite almost getting caught, she was tempted to glance over her shoulder for another look. Instead, she ordered her iced coffee —extra espresso and sugar—and moved to the other side of the counter, to wait.

The staff was working quickly, and drinks came up for the people ahead of her in rapid succession.

"Excuse me," a sexy voice said. "May I borrow your phone?"

Was he talking to her? She looked up, and her pulse kicked up at the sight of Sexy Guy, who was apparently the owner of Sexy Voice. He watched her, the corners of his dark brown eyes crinkled in amusement.

"Is yours broken?" She mentally facepalmed. *Real smooth, Syd.*

"Nah." It came out like *naw*, with just a hint of a drawl. "But I don't need pictures of myself. Seems like you do."

She was glad she wasn't a blusher, because with the heat racing under her skin, she'd be bright red. "I wasn't..." She couldn't force the denial out.

"My mistake. I'm Dylan, by the way."

"Sydney."

"Pleasure to meet you." He shook her hand. His grip was warm and firm and sent delicious images dancing through her head. Fantasies of what else he could do with those hands.

"Same." She forced herself to speak. No other words came, though. She wasn't so great at small talk with strangers. He was going to think she was a dolt.

"What are you selling?" he asked.

The question didn't attach to a point of reference, and she stared back blankly. "Excuse me?"

"Your booth." He nodded at her badge. "What are you selling?"

"Oh. Board games. You?" Crap. That was her opening to give him the snappy elevator pitch about her game and impress him when she said she was the creator.

He thumbed his lanyard to spin his badge around. It had the huge *Volunteer* stripe down the side. "Myself, I suppose." Was he flirting?

"Right. Of course." Why couldn't she carry on her half of this conversation? "What are you volunteering, besides time? I mean... I promise I usually make more sense. Do you get to meet anyone famous?"

Every time he smiled or laughed, the corners of his eyes crinkled. It was cute plus sexy, and that was a lethal combination. "That remains to be seen. Are you famous?"

I'm hoping to be. The words stuck in her throat.

"Iced coffee. Extra sugar and shot. For Cindy." The barista called.

Sydney gave Dylan a regretful smile. "That's me. It was great meeting you. Enjoy the con."

She grabbed her drink, and as she strolled away, her mind treated her to an instant replay of every moment in the conversation when she could have been wittier. Handing over her phone to a stranger seemed like a dumb move, but if he'd taken a picture, she could have asked him to include his number along with it. Or asked how much he charged, if he was the product. Or anything more interesting than, *Do you get to meet anyone famous?*

Fantasizing about Dylan would keep her company tonight, but for now, she needed to finish setting up her booth.

DYLAN WAS INTRIGUED by the woman with the red and blue Harley Quinn pigtails and the shirt that said GEE*K IS S*EXY. The way her hips filled out her jeans and her breasts stretched the letters on her Tee was sexy. If he could get her over the nervousness, the conversation might be even better.

It might not be, but the only way to find out was to keep her talking.

Too bad she was gone.

He snagged his iced tea when it was ready. As long as he was here, he should roam the vendor hall floor. He'd scored the volunteer badge by writing up the legalese for the convention   policies on harassment, cosplay, weapons and the like—and it gave him permission to wander anywhere not marked *Private*.

An unforeseen and fantastic side-effect of passing the bar a few weeks ago.

He'd wanted to be a lawyer since he was a kid. His friends played fireman and astronaut, and he acted as an arbitrator when they fought. Kind of boring-sounding when he looked back on it, but he enjoyed it. When his grandmother died, several years back, she'd left most of her savings to him. It wasn't enough to make him wealthy, but she'd asked he use it to pursue his dream, and he had.

Her money took him through pre-grad. Working for the biggest corporate-contracts law firm in the city had covered the rest.

Dylan headed into the main convention hall. He'd never seen it this way before. This wasn't his first convention, but he'd only been an attendee in the past.

The various booths sat in different stages of completion, and it was neat to see. Some spots, the vendors had finished assembling and setting up already. Others, people scurried around with boxes and dollies, setting up. Most of the booths were still curtains and cards with company names that would be occupied by later today.

He turned down another aisle and approached a larger booth, filled out with wire displays, similar to what many vendor tables would look like in twenty-four hours.

And there was Sydney. The view was just as fantastic from behind, and he trailed his gaze along her curves as she reached up to place an uncooperative box on a higher shelf.

He hurried to her side and grabbed the lagging end. "Let me help."

Working together, it was a simple task to secure the limited edition Sephiroth motorcycle.

"Thanks." Her shy smile returned when she looked at him.

He tried to help with the awkwardness by glancing around the booth. "Are you here alone?"

"I don't have a boyfriend." She covered her face. "Oh God." Her hands muffled her voice. "I'm such an idiot."

He tugged her wrist, so he could see her again. When he was younger, he got in trouble for not thinking before he spoke. Since then, he'd learned to make it work for him. For the most part, what came out of his mouth was best left unfiltered. "Nah. You saved me a question. Let's get this out of the way up front, and maybe it will help. Yes, I'm flirting."

Shock spread across her face. That meant she wasn't hiding anymore. She glanced over her shoulder, then back at him. "Me?"

"Yes. Now that we've covered that, are you working the booth alone? Do you need more help?"

"With my flirting, apparently." Her laugh was hesitant but melodic. "And help would be wonderful. My assistant bailed for the weekend, and I thought I could handle things, but if you're offering, I'm accepting."

"Point me in a direction, boss."

She gestured to a middle section. "Boxes are stacked by order they go up. Make things look nice and neat on the shelves."

Simple enough.

He went to work. After a couple of minutes, he glanced over his shoulder, to find Sydney watching him.

"Enjoying the show?" he teased.

"Yes, but no. But yes. I... You didn't ask any questions."

"About the work? Seems pretty straightforward."

She smiled and turned to her own section.

He tried to start a conversation a few times, but the tearing of tape and boxes and the clatter of shelves kept cutting him off. That was a shame.

He finished his tasks and found her arranging the front table with several boxes of *Changelings and Caverns*. "Is the game that good?" he asked. "I mean, good enough that it dominates your display."

"It's a fantastic game. And I'm not just saying that because my company makes it."

He was glad to hear it. She probably didn't care what her boss did with the intellectual property, but Monday morning, Dylan was meeting the guy to negotiate a more robust publishing and distribution deal with one of his clients. This would be a good chance to get to know the product better.

A short while later, they wrapped up. She stepped into the aisle and surveyed the entire booth. "It looks fantastic. Thank you. I would have been here all day if you hadn't come along."

"Glad I could help."

She wiped her sleeve across her forehead and grimaced. "I'm all gross. I need a shower. You could help with that, too." Her scowl deepened. "That was over the top, wasn't it? I was joking."

"You're putting too much thought into it." He was glad to see her more comfortable around him. He was enjoying her company, despite not having exchanged many words with her.

"Is that a tip from a professional flirter?" she asked.

He grinned. "First lesson is free, and after that... Yeah, never mind. I have no idea where that's going."

Her laugh came more easily this time. "So even the smooth and suave Dylan fumbles sometimes."

ALLYSON LINDT

"All the time." He didn't have an issue admitting that. "You said your assistant bailed for the entire weekend?"

"Yes."

"Do you want me to stop by for a couple of hours tomorrow and help you out?" He was here to enjoy the con, and if things went well with Sydney, he could add hot, naked, orgasmy enjoyment to the list. Or at the very least, a geek-reference-filled afternoon of fun.

"I can't ask you—"

"Let me stop you there." He held up his hand. "You didn't ask, I offered." He thumbed his badge out. "Volunteer, remember? Would you like my help? *Yes* or *no*."

Her smile was back. "That would be fantastic."

"Great. I'll see you tomorrow." He leaned close. "Enjoy the shower."

She shook her head and stepped away. "Nope. That's definitely too much. It says *needy*, and that's not how you strike me."

"Touché." He gave her an exaggerated bow. "Until then."

Dylan was grinning as he strolled out to the underground parking lot.

His phone rang. It was his roommate, Josh.

"Hallo," Dylan answered.

"How quickly can you get online? We had a senior partner fuck up a contract, and I need to know what you remember."

Dylan groaned. He didn't need to ask which partner. "I'll be home in half an hour."

TWO

I f Josh ever found a magic lamp, he was pretty sure he'd wish for an always-full mug of coffee.

On mornings like this, he'd make copious use of it.

He stifled a yawn and inched forward with the rest of the line in the espresso bar. After staying up until nearly three with Dylan, ensuring the corrupted contract literally had every *i* dotted and every *T* crossed, Josh needed something stronger than what the pot at home offered.

Dylan—lucky bastard—had the week off. So he was in the hotel room he'd reserved for the con, and was probably sleeping his day away. He and Josh had been roommates the beginning of law school. They'd both graduated since, but paying student loans on a junior lawyer salary meant splitting the rent still made sense.

As the queue crawled forward another person, Josh checked the time on his phone. The law firm where he and Dylan worked was a few floors up in this building, and Josh had plenty of time before he had to be up there, but he wanted to get to his desk before anyone else came in. He had research to do.

It didn't matter that Josh's last name was on the firm marquee—

271

his grandfather founded the group, and his mother was one of the current senior partners—he wasn't afforded any leeway.

Unlike the asshole partner who caused so much work for them last night, and would slide under the radar because he was fucking Josh's mother.

"Next," the girl at the register called.

He stepped forward with a smile. "Hey, Luci. Mocha Red Eye. As big as it gets."

"TGIF?" She marked his drink order on a cup, then handed it to the barista.

"So very much. But Comic Con this weekend."

She laughed. "Do you do the whole dress-up thing?"

"No. I like to let the world revel in my natural awesomeness."

"That's very noble of you. Catch you Monday?"

"Of course." He stepped aside, so the next person could order.

He'd miss the rituals here. The people. The coffee. But he couldn't wait to get out of this place. Law might be the family tradition, and he liked practicing, but this firm wasn't for him. He did his job because it was his job. His other plans were why he'd gotten to the office early, though.

"Extra-large Mocha Red Eye," the barista called. He was a new guy Josh hadn't met yet.

Josh would know his name in a week or so. He grabbed his drink and headed for the elevator. A few minutes later, he settled in at his desk. Half the lights in the place were out, and no one else had arrived yet.

It was time for research. The firm represented a large game distributor, who specialized in tabletop and roleplaying games. The distributor wanted to acquire rights from the local company that had created *Changelings and Caverns*. Josh had maneuvered his way into working with the client. His goal was to meet some people, make some connections, and move into a new role, in a very different industry.

Part of that good impression would be learning everything he could about them, in order to represent them properly.

He used to make up games like C&C with his ex-girlfriend, and he'd loved it. She was the creative one; he was more about helping her grow her ideas. He wanted to do more of that. Help someone with a talent like hers expand their products and reach more customers.

He tumbled down the research rabbit hole, not emerging until the chatter grew around him. The office was bright now. Most desks occupied. Phones ringing. People shouting information at each other.

The rest of his reading would wait until later. He dove into work, pulling files, doing legal research, typing up documents to file with the courts—whatever anyone needed.

His phone rang, and *Laurie Hunter* flashed on the display. His mother. "Hello, Ms. Hunter," he answered. He never called her *Mother* at the office. It was almost TV-show cliché.

"I need to shift your priorities, Josh." Her tone was cool and professional. "We're working on new boilerplate language for Automan Life, and I want you to shadow the lead attorney. To learn, and also to double-check their work."

"What am I handing off in return?" The moment he asked, he knew the answer.

"The Polar Bear negotiation. Dylan will step into that spot instead. You can fill him in, but I need you on Automan. I trust you to do this."

Josh liked her confidence in him but didn't care for the news. "I can do both."

"No. I'm sorry. I need you focused on Automan. I know you were looking forward to working on the other, but you're going to be stretched thin as it is. In fact, I need you to take Saturday to come up to speed. Your meeting with them is Monday."

Well, fuck.

"But I was going into Tosche Station, to pick up some power converters!"

"You can waste time with your friends when your chores are done."

The lines from Star Wars echoed in his head, but he resisted the urge to launch into them to make a point. So much for catching Comic Con with Dylan.

He sent his roommate a text. *Working this weekend. If you hook up, don't be stingy with the details.*

The new contract information was already waiting for Josh in his email. He clicked into it and dove in.

SYDNEY WAS BRACED for a long day of solo-play. Hanging with Dylan yesterday was fun, but she didn't expect him to be back.

That was all right. His flirting was enough for her to feed her fantasies last night and expand it into a vivid scene. One where they did end up in the shower, slipping and sliding against each other, water cascading around them as he knelt at her feet and licked her to orgasm, then bent her over—

A throb pulsed between her legs, and she squeezed her thighs together. Thoughts like that needed to wait until she wasn't about to be set upon by crowds of people.

"Where do you want me boss?" Dylan asked.

She started when she realized he was behind her, and not in her head still. "Hey." Great. Now she'd forgotten how to speak again.

"You look surprised to see me."

Sydney shrugged. "It's nothing personal. Most people wouldn't come back, and I don't know you well enough to bank on anything else."

"Let's change that." He stepped into her booth. "First, tell me what I need to do."

She could do that. She gave him a rundown of pricing. She'd handle the money. "No offense," she said.

"None taken. I understand earning trust, and this is someone's livelihood."

People were starting to wander the aisles. Not a lot—the doors opened an hour early for gold-pass members—but enough that Sydney felt like she should focus on them instead of the hottie standing next to her, arm brushing hers every couple of minutes.

A group of three walked by, their gaze drifting to the table.

"Do you like games?" Sydney called.

They broke eye contact and hurried away quickly.

There would be a bit of that this weekend, but it was disheartening to start Day One off that way.

A pack of five girls in their late teens wandered past. "You ladies like to have fun?" Dylan called.

They exchanged looks and giggles. "Yes," one said.

"We've got an assortment." He nodded to the shelves behind him.

"No thanks," another replied. They walked away, glancing back until they rounded the corner.

And then someone said *yes*. Before they finished their transaction, another person was waiting to buy a game.

It didn't take long before Sydney and Dylan had their hands full, bagging purchases, making change, and answering questions.

When there was a lull in the crowds, as new panels started, Sydney sank into her seat. She was grinning, despite her aching feet.

"This is insane." Dylan shifted his weight. "Do you do this a lot?"

"Every weekend there's a big enough convention."

He shook his head. "I don't know if I'd love that or hate it, but I wouldn't mind giving it a try."

"What's your favorite flavor? Fandom, I mean?"

He furrowed his brow. "I have to pick? All of the above." He gestured to the room.

That was so vague. Sydney wanted to keep chatting, but someone else was looking at her C&C. "Do you like games?" she asked.

The woman, who was dressed in an intricate Poison Ivy costume that left little to the imagination, skipped forward. "Love them. You?" Her voice was low and sultry, as she spoke in-character.

"Yeah. Absolutely." Sydney grinned. "What's your favorite kind?"

Ivy licked her lips. "Anything with vines or tentacles." Wow. She did the whole roleplaying thing beautifully.

"Sounds kinky." Dylan chimed in.

"It is, handsome. The kinkier the better. You two like to party?"

Not really. The answer died on Sydney's lips when Dylan said, "Depends on the party."

Ivy handed him a flier. "Upstairs, after everything shuts down tonight. They'll ID you, and there's a cover charge."

"We'll see if we can make it." Dylan took the leaflet.

Ivy strolled away, hips swaying.

Sydney glanced over Dylan's shoulder. The invitation was photocopied black text on green paper. It looked like a generic invitation, covered with cosplay clip art, including a maid costume, handcuffs, and a whip.

Dylan glanced at her. "Could be fun. Want to be my date?"

There was no way she was turning that down. "Sure."

Something brushed her leg, and she swatted at it without thinking. A second brush, this one harder, pressed in on her leg, and she looked down to see her cashbox gone.

A short, thin guy crawled out from the other side of the table and ran into the crowds.

"*Fuck,*" she shouted. "That kid just stole my cash box."

THREE

"I'll be back," Dylan yelled over his shoulder. He was already chasing the cash box thief.

The aisles were crowded, making it difficult to move. The kid was at least a foot shorter than Dylan and wove through people's legs, knocking several off balance.

The thief was pulling ahead, and frustration spilled through Dylan, mingling with adrenaline. He shouted "*Move,*" and earned a couple of dirty looks and several laughs for the command.

And then he spotted an opening between booths, thanks to a group of people in costumes, getting their pictures taken. He darted between tables, behind the curtains that divided one aisle from the next.

Debris spilled into his path, but he hopped over it and emerged on the other side, ahead of the kid.

He grabbed the thief by the arm. "Give back the box.'

"*Get your hands off me, you freaking pedo-bear,*" the kid screamed.

Sure. *Now* people turned to look.

Dylan wasn't taking this bullshit. "Give me back the cash, you little thief."

"Is there something wrong?" A volunteer approached.

Dylan recognized one of the security guys, not only from the shirt that said *Security* on the back, but they met during orientation yesterday.

"Jesse, hey." Dylan tightened his grip when the thief struggled and tried to jerk away. "He stole the cash box from one of the vendor booths."

"I found it on the floor." The kid hugged his prize tighter. He couldn't be more than twelve or thirteen.

Jesse extracted the box from him and handed it to Dylan. "You'll make sure it gets back safe?" Jesse asked.

Dylan nodded.

Jesse escorted the kid toward the exit.

With the show over, everyone turned back to what they'd been doing. Dylan's pulse still raced through his veins, and in a few minutes, the adrenaline would start to sit heavy in his gut.

He made his way back to Sydney's booth. He would have chased the thief anyway, but her smile when she saw him was the perfect reward.

Dylan handed her the retrieved box. "I'm pretty sure he didn't have time to open it."

"Thank you, thank you." She turned it over in her hands. "Nope. Lock is still intact. Did I say *thank you*? I can't believe you did this for me."

He gave a deep bow and tipped an invisible hat. "'Twas my pleasure, m'lady."

"Hey, man. That was awesome, what you just did," said a male voice.

Dylan turned to see a couple of guys waiting to shake his hand. He obliged. "Thanks. I hate it when anyone thinks they can get away with that shit."

"Totally." The second guy picked up one of the C&C boxes. "I've heard about this. Is it any good?"

"It's the best." Dylan had spent a little time last night researching, and it looked like a lot of fun.

"I'll take it." The guy handed over money.

For the next bit, people who heard what Dylan had done

trickled in. The constant traffic drew additional attention, and they sold several copies of the game.

As the crowds thinned again, Dylan finally had a chance to breathe. He looked at Sydney, who was flushed but smiling. "I don't know how you do this all the time," he said.

"I love it. But it's also not usually this busy. You're my lucky charm. Either that, or I've used up all my good karma for the next year by meeting you."

"Something tells me you have more in reserve." He had a hard time imagining there were many red marks in her ledger.

"You shameless flatterer." Her shyness looked exaggerated.

He liked seeing her relaxed—the way she moved, her smiles, those gorgeous, full curves. "I'm being sincere."

"Excuse me. When you two are done hanging off each other?" an irritated woman interrupted.

Sydney clenched her jaw.

"I've got this," Dylan said softly enough only she would hear. He faced the woman. "May I help you?"

"Are you the asshole who tackled and assaulted my boy earlier?"

Great. He was dealing with the brat's mother, apparently. His defensiveness cranked several notches. "Since I didn't tackle or assault anyone, no. Was it your kid who stole my boss's cash box?" He wanted to toss back the insults, but if he was being approached this way, he wasn't giving her any legal footing.

"He found a box on the floor and picked it up. He didn't know what was in it. Next thing he knew, some maniac was chasing him and threatening him."

"Witnesses say differently." Irritation flipped a *play it cool* switch in Dylan's head. He would freeze this woman out one way or another.

"Are you calling me a liar?"

Dylan shook his head. "No. I'm calling your son a liar."

"Absolutely ridiculous. Slanderous, in fact. I'm going to sue you until you can't spin without running into a wage garnishment."

She'd gone there. Dylan hid his smugness. "That doesn't even make sense. But you do that." He pulled his wallet from his pocket and plucked a business card out. "You can reach out to my employer directly. They'll represent me."

She paled when she looked at the card. "You don't work there."

"Then you humiliate me by sending any legal papers there. Give it a try and see. I'll be waiting to be served at that address."

"Fine." She jammed the card in her purse and stalked away.

Who needed coffee, when there was this much excitement in the day? Dylan's heart hammered against his ribs at the confrontation. Or rather, the lack of a resolution.

He wanted to demand she come back so he could finish the conversation. Logic her into a corner she couldn't outrage herself out of.

She'd been bluffing with the lawsuit comment, so he'd never see her again. That was the most disappointing thing of all. That kid would keep pulling the same bullshit until his mother wised up or someone else stepped in.

SYDNEY WAS grateful Dylan dealt with the irate woman. Confrontation wasn't her forte.

When Dylan handed over a business card, Sydney's gut twisted in on itself a second time. The *Hunter & Associates* logo was one she'd never forget. Her ex's mother had drilled that family legacy into Sydney's head repeatedly.

"You work for Hunter & Associates?" She made sure to keep her voice steady. This wasn't worth overreacting to.

He nodded. "Just moved from paralegal to attorney."

"Congratulations. Do you like your job?"

He shrugged. "It's pretty decent. They gave me the weekend off, to hang out here, and I can't complain about that."

"I guess not." She smiled. Sydney wouldn't say anything negative about the firm. She had her issues with *Ms. Hunter*, but if Dylan was happy there, she wouldn't drag him down with her bias.

She needed to shake off some of this excess energy. "I'm going to take a break. Are you okay to watch the booth for a few minutes?"

"You trust me here with all of this?" He gestured. "Alone?"

Maybe that was naive of her, but she did. "You had a chance to rip me off and didn't. Plus, I know where you work," she teased.

"Take a break. I'll hold down the fort, boss."

Walking away was its own kind of stress. She left assistants with the booth at every show, but she didn't know this guy, and it was too easy to like him.

As she wove through con-goers, her thoughts cleared and calm returned. She didn't want to leave Dylan alone for long, but she paused at a few booths, to appreciate the unique art and designs.

The brief stroll was enough to refresh her. She paused at a food stall on her way back. When the woman asked her what she wanted to drink, she stalled on an answer. What did Dylan like, besides coffee? She got two Mt. Dews and hoped for the best.

As Sydney approached her booth, her footsteps slowed. Dylan was talking to a woman in yellow vinyl hot pants and a matching sleeveless top with a red shirt thrown over it. The character was Faye from Cowboy Bebop, and the woman made the outfit look better than Poison Ivy had earlier.

Faye laughed at something and rested a hand on Dylan's arm. He was grinning, eyes bright and posture casual. They stood close, and whatever they were talking about, the conversation flowed easily.

Sydney swallowed the rush of jealousy. What did she expect from the bold, flirty, gorgeous guy who was too good to be true?

She pasted on a smile, hoped it didn't look too fake, and joined them.

FOUR

Dylan's smile when he saw Sydney warmed her.

It's not the same smile he's giving Ms. Gorgeous.

Right.

"I promise I wasn't slacking." Teasing lined Dylan's voice when she drew within earshot.

Sydney made her mask-smile even wider. Was she overcorrecting? She probably looked like she was grimacing. "No worries. I'm not a total slave-driver." She forced a chuckle.

"No? Shame, he might like that." Ms. Gorgeous nodded at Dylan.

He rolled his eyes but looked amused. "Tori, this is my temporary boss, Sydney. Syd, this is my cousin. She's heading up the cosplay parts of the con. Got me the volunteer gig."

Cousin. Of course. *Could I be anymore cliché?* But Sydney couldn't ignore the relief that flowed through her. "Nice to meet you."

"Same." Tori trailed her gaze over Sydney. "He's right. You're cute, in that sexy-vixen kind of way. Do you cosplay?"

He told someone that about her? "Not really." She didn't care if other people ignored body-type for a costume, but she'd never been comfortable squeezing into spandex bodysuits or short skirts.

282

"You should. I'll hook you up sometime. And I'm sorry to meet and run, but I'm supposed to be in a panel soon. Nice meeting you," she said to Sydney. "I'll call you later," she called over her shoulder to Dylan as she walked away.

Less than a day into the actual con, and this was already one of the more random shows Sydney'd ever been to. She was good with that, as long as more of the random leaned toward *complimentary friends and family* and farther from *cash box thieves and their overprotective mothers*.

The rest of the day was uneventful, beyond the fact that Dylan was an incredible salesman. Sydney didn't know the last time she'd had such a good first day. She was looking forward to heading up to her hotel room—she always got a room, even for local shows, because it was less stressful than commuting—and curling up with a book, and maybe some fantasies about Dylan.

He held up the flier Poison Ivy gave them earlier. "You up for a party?"

She'd forgotten about that. Her instinct was to say *no*. She definitely wasn't a party person. That it was him asking made her hesitate. "Sure. I could do that for a little while." Except not like this. She was dusty and sweaty. "If there's time for me to clean up first."

Maybe she shouldn't have said that. He had to be local if he worked for Hunter & Associates. Would he get bored, waiting for her? Decide it was easier to go home?

Why couldn't she shut her brain up?

"I doubt anyone is going to care if we're not there right when things start." Dylan's reply saved her from her thoughts. "Meet me back in the lobby in an hour? Is that enough time?"

It was probably too much. Her head would think her into a million different scenarios between now and then. "Thirty minutes?"

"Even better. Until then." He grasped her fingertips and kissed the back of her knuckles.

Heat flooded under her skin until she thought she might combust. "Until then." Her reply came out as a squeak.

The next half hour crawled at a snail's pace and moved at lightning speed simultaneously. Sydney took the quickest deep-scrub shower in history. *Everything* had to be scrubbed and pristine and flowery-smelling.

Her hair would have to stay pulled up, though. Washing and drying it took eons.

She stood in front of her luggage, shaking her head at every piece of clothing she'd brought. Why did she have to be such a practical packer? It was all jeans and T-shirts. Not even notable ones. All of it meant to be comfortable for a day of standing around and working.

At least she'd brought cute panties. Not that it would matter, but her imagination had already jumped ahead several hours. On the teensy, tiny chance he wanted to stick around for the night, she'd be happy she had the cotton bikini briefs with the subtle Wonder Woman logo on the left hip.

Or was that stupid? Did she wish she'd brought lace?

"Shut up, brain," she said aloud, to kick herself out of her head.

When she was finally ready, there were eight minutes left of her thirty. She sat on the edge of the bed. How long did the elevator ride down take? If she left now, would she be too early? She didn't want to keep him waiting, but she didn't want to appear over-anxious.

Why not?

Good question. Was it such a big deal if he thought she was eager?

She was looking for reasons to procrastinate. She grabbed her wristlet and headed downstairs.

Dylan was already in the lobby, and he flashed her a drop-dead sexy smile when she caught his eye. "You ready to see what all the excitement is about?" he asked.

"Now's as good a time as any."

He produced the flier from Poison Ivy, noted the room number, and a moment later, they were knocking on the door to the second-floor suite.

"Hey. You made it." Ivy opened the door enough to see them. The room behind her was dark. "Before I let you in, you have to promise you're both over the age of eighteen and that you're not easily offended."

Odd disclaimer.

Dylan glanced at Sydney, and she shrugged. "I promise," she said.

"Me too. Adult. Not easily offended."

Ivy's smile grew, and she let them in. The suite connected to another, and the entry between was open. Faint flickers came from the other rooms. "Contemporary and school girls behind me, occult and fantasy in the other living room, and tentacles in the second bedroom. Take your pick. It's like Las Vegas—what happens here, stays here. Enjoy." She winked.

Tentacles?

"What's your poison?" Dylan whispered, his breath hot against Sydney's cheek.

"Occult and fantasy?"

He rested a hand at the small of her back and steered her toward the adjoining room.

The TV on the far wall was playing anime. A flush covered the priestess' cheeks, and a pixelated penis was thrust into her mouth.

Correction, they were playing hentai—anime porn.

In the room, a couple sat on the couch, and another in the chair next to them. A girl was reclined in the corner on a beanbag. They were all in various states of undress, groping themselves and each other while the video played.

Heat spilled through Sydney's veins.

"Pick a room or leave." An irritated woman's voice came from behind.

Dylan pressed his frame into Sydney's back, nudging her out of the doorway. His hard length pressed into her ass.

He was turned on by this? Then again, the throb and growing dampness between her thighs confirmed she was too. Not because of the cartoon. Rather, the people in the room, exploring each other, not caring who watched, had her pulse hammering in her ears and her nipples straining against her bra.

Dylan brushed the edge of her ear with his lips. "Do you want to stay?" His question was so soft, she barely heard it.

Yes. *Fuck* yes. Arousal and curiosity kept her feet to the floor. Propriety and everything else she'd ever experienced told her this wasn't where she wanted to be. Would he stay without her if she said *no*? Make himself comfortable with the solo girl with the blue hair, whose gaze kept flicking to them as she pushed her shirt up to tease her breasts through her bra?

"Do you?" Sydney asked.

He slid his hands to her hips, then forward along her pelvis. "I'm thinking about it. But not alone."

"Maybe for a little while."

"Is that a *yes*?"

She nodded.

He leaned against the wall, tugging her with him, her back pressed to his chest, and he wrapped his arms around her waist.

"Kind of hot, isn't it?" His voice was still low, not meant to reach beyond her.

Cartoons fucking? Not her thing. Though she was a teensy bit captivated by the priestess, who seemed to be enjoying sucking on one pixelated man while another penetrated her from behind.

"The potential audience, that is." Did his voice just drop an octave?

She didn't have an extensive sex life of experience to draw on, but she had her fantasies. One she'd only ever told Josh about, and loved to fall into alone, was being on display—knowing someone was getting off watching her do the same.

"Yes." Her reply came out a dry squeak, and she licked her lips.

Blue was watching them rather than the TV, her eyes wide and her bottom lip caught between her teeth. She worked one breast free from her bra and teased a thumb along her nipple.

Sydney's imagination was running rampant with fantasies of Dylan, stripping her down in front of the private group. Teasing her until she begged to come. Of him, freeing the erection that teased her back and letting her wrap her lips around it.

There was no way she could do any of that. It was called *fantasy* for a reason.

The need thrumming under her skin and the subtle sway of his hips nudging her insisted she take the opportunity if she had it

Dylan traced his mouth up the side of her neck, not making contact but leaving a trail of temptation in his wake. He nipped her ear with his teeth, and her desire spiked. "*God*, I want to find out how wet you are," he murmured.

Fear stole her voice, and need hammered at her skull. The atmosphere in the room erased a layer of her inhibition. If she said *no* and walked away, how badly would she regret it?

Maybe she wouldn't. She could always play out the *what if* in her head, on her own time.

But she wanted to find out for real. She undid the button on her jeans and pulled down the zipper, intently aware of Blue's eyes on their every move.

Sydney covered Dylan's hand, eliciting a groan, and guided it under her panties.

"*Fuck*, Syd." He pressed his lips into her shoulder and moved his hand lower.

Blue watched them, lips slightly parted, and mimicked Dylan's motions, dropping her own hand into her pants.

Sydney gasped when Dylan dipped between her legs. The couple in the chair turned in their direction, and her heart leaped into her throat.

They wore soft smiles.

Holy fuck, she was really doing this. Not that anything was visible, but—

Dylan brushed her clit. "You're soaked. You like being a show?"

"Yes." So much better than in her head.

He teased her swollen button, caressing it until she thrust against his hand, then easing off. The heat of their audience's stares burned through her.

A new wave of boldness surged inside. She hooked her thumbs on the waistband of her clothes, and pushed her jeans and panties down, just enough to put her pussy on display.

"Fucking hell." Dylan bit her shoulder. He stroked her clit faster, and she closed her eyes, falling into the sensation.

He hit the right angle, and climax sparked inside. She bit the inside of her cheek, to keep quiet, but a moan slipped out anyway.

Dylan pushed her past orgasm, rubbing as she pushed into his touch. He eased off as the thrust of her hips slowed.

Her eyes fluttered open.

They still had a captive audience.

"I want to feel your lips around my cock," Dylan said.

The heady buzz of coming lingered in her head. She'd let him strip her naked and fuck her bent over the back of the couch right now, if he asked. She spun to face him, showing her bare ass to the room.

A loud hammering on the outside door screamed through the room, and her hammering heart threatened to burst through her ribs.

"This is the hotel manager," a man called. "Can you open up, please?"

FIVE

Dylan had never seen a group of people yank their clothes on so fast. Not that he spent much time around large groups of naked people.

"We've had some complaints about activities in these rooms." The hotel manager's voice drifted in.

"I... We're not doing anything wrong." Ivy's earlier confidence was gone.

Dylan felt bad for her. Being sexy and flirting with other con-goers was one thing. Facing down an authority figure was an entirely different beast.

It was going to be tough for Dylan to think through his hard-on, but it was going limp anyway. Talk about a mood-killer. He needed to step in.

"You can't be doing... certain activities... in here," the manager said.

Dylan looked at Sydney. Her bottom lip was caught between her teeth. "Should we go?" she mouthed.

"Soon." He couldn't listen to this. He joined Ivy. "Is there an issue?" Dylan asked.

The hotel manager paled and took a step back. "We've had complaints."

"Plural? That sounds serious." Dylan kept his tone even and cool. "What kind of complaints?"

"Well… that is, someone said there were… things going on. Look at the way she's dressed." The manager nodded at Ivy.

She wrapped her arms around herself and ducked her head.

Dylan hated that someone had tattled. "Her clothing isn't in question. This is a private room. The young lady is current on her account, isn't she?"

"I…"

"Yes or no?"

"Yes." Some of the confidence returned to Ivy's voice.

"And there's no damage being done to the room. We're not making excessive noise," Dylan said.

The manager worked his jaw up and down. "But there are things happening."

"*Things.*" Dylan let disdain leak into the word. "Consenting adults, watching movies and enjoying each other's company? Those types of things? Tell you what. How about you give the police a call? Ask them to remove us from the premises. Make sure to tell them to bring multiple cars, so they can transport everyone. I'm sure no one will wonder about the paying guests, being escorted from the grounds because you don't like the same kind of movies we do. And I'm certain Corporate won't mind the multiple phone calls tomorrow, from our attorneys, as we seek damages for mental pain and anguish."

The manager clenched his jaw. His face matched his red vest. "If I get so much as a hint of a complaint about noise or damages, I'm coming down hard on you."

Dylan swallowed a response to the innuendo.

"I understand," Ivy said. "Is there anything else?"

"No."

Ivy gave the manager a sweet smile and closed the door on him. She whirled to face Dylan and threw her arms around him. "Thank you." She pressed her lips against his neck.

He politely but quickly extracted himself from the embrace. "I'm here with someone."

"Oh." Ivy's face fell.

Dylan turned to Sydney, who watched with an unreadable expression. He wrapped an arm around her waist. "Thanks for the evening," he said to Ivy. "It was... exhilarating. But we're going to go finish someplace more quiet."

Sydney leaned into him as they walked from the room. They passed an empty alcove in the hallway, where the ice machine was tucked away, and he pulled her in. Pressing her to the wall, he trailed his lips along the edge of her ear. "That was wicked fun."

She sighed. Her curves molded to his body, teasing and tantalizing. "Turns out I don't mind sharing my knight in shining armor, under the right circumstances."

"I don't have anyone extra in my hotel room, but if you want to pick up where we left off..." He let the implied offer hang between them. *Fuck*, he hoped for a *yes*. Even this basic contact had him hard again. Images of her full lips wrapped around his cock danced in his thoughts. Fantasy mingled with the reality of what she'd let him do —literally gotten off on—in front of the small audience.

"The gold-pass people are allowed on the vendor floor at eight. I have to be up early."

That sounded like a *no*. "Should I walk you back to your room and leave you for the night?"

"*No.*" She winced as the sharp word slipped out. "I'd love to join you. I'm just letting you know I have to be up early."

"That's fine." He grabbed her earlobe between his teeth and tugged. "I wasn't going to let you sleep, anyway." He tilted her chin up with his finger and crushed his mouth to hers. He glided his tongue along the seam of her lips, until she parted them and let him in. Heat roared through him, pulsing under his skin and wanting to be closer.

It took immense effort to break away. "We should go," Dylan said. "I don't think Mr. Hotel Manager will be so willing to walk away if he finds us out here."

"Probably not."

291

He slipped a hand in her back pocket on the walk to the elevator. When a car stopped, there were three people inside. He led Sydney to the back corner and slid a hand under her shirt, to rest on her stomach. She leaned more of her weight against him.

The group wasn't paying attention to them, but if anyone turned around, they'd get a hint of a show. Dylan slid his hand higher, to tease Sydney's nipple through her bra.

She ground her ass against him, and his dick whimpered for release.

The lift stopped, and the other people got out. As the doors slid shut again, Dylan tugged down Sydney's bra, to cup her bare breast.

"Aren't there cameras in these things?" Despite her question, she leaned into his touch.

"Probably. Do you want me to stop?"

Her, "*No*," was breathless.

When they reached his floor, he helped her straighten her clothes and led her to his room. He didn't know what it was about her that made the reckless behavior so tempting.

It was probably because *she* was so tempting. Fun. Desirable...

The instant the door closed behind them, he cupped her face and kissed her hard. They should move further into the room. He was enjoying her soft gasps and the way her hip ground against his erection too much to break away. Even for a heartbeat.

"You said something about picking up where we left off?" Sydney's tone was soft, but desire lit up her eyes.

Did he? All the blood had rushed from his head. "That sounds familiar."

She watched him through her eyelashes, holding his gaze as she knelt in front of him. Her wide-eyed, eager innocence pulsed through his veins and hammered in his ears. She dragged down his zipper and licked her lips.

Fuck. Was that a conscious reaction? Her fingers were hot against his cock when she worked him free, and he groaned.

Dylan couldn't take his eyes off her. She flicked out her tongue —a light, playful lick—and he jerked. When she took him in her mouth, he almost came.

She continued to watch him as she swallowed his length. A lock of hair fell over her eyes, and he brushed it aside. He wanted to see those captivating eyes.

He rocked his hips against her face, moaning louder as she sucked and licked along his shaft. She stroked his balls, and they tightened at her touch. He was so close to climax, but he wanted more. It was a good thing he'd stopped at the hotel drugstore for condoms before she came downstairs.

Dylan pulled away from her with immense reluctance and was greeted with a pout.

"Is something wrong?" Teasing lined her question.

He grasped her hand and tugged her to her feet. "Everything—this entire night—is incredible. But I need to fuck you." He led her to the bed.

The instant he let go of her arm, she wrapped it across her chest, half covering herself, and ducked her head. He reached for the light switch, and she stopped him.

"You don't need to turn that on." Shyness replaced her playfulness.

"I don't have to, but I'd like to." He gently pulled her arm down. "I want to see you. *All* of you. Reality tends to be much better than fantasy."

She caught her bottom lip between her teeth. "You've been fantasizing about me?"

"Since I saw you in the coffee shop." He hovered his mouth millimeters from hers.

Her gasp was more of a suggestion than a sound. She closed the distance between them, giving him the softest kiss. "Me too." Her breath was hot against his mouth.

"Lights on?"

She hesitated, then nodded.

Dylan flipped the switch. He laid a series of light kisses along her mouth, and down to her jaw and her neck, while he glided his hands under her shirt and up her side. He yanked her top off, and she hugged herself.

He lowered her hands and dragged his gaze over her body. "I

like what I see. So fucking gorgeous." He kissed along the top of her breasts, teasing her nipples through her bra. "Everything else off, too," he said.

Sensuality laced her movements, as she stripped down to nothing. "I can't be the only one who's naked."

"That sounds fair." Dylan made quick work of discarding his clothes. "Lie on the bed."

He rolled on a condom, nudged her legs apart, and knelt between her thighs. "Fucking stunning." He lowered his head and drew one nipple into his mouth. When he wrapped his tongue around the swollen bud, she squirmed. When he scraped his teeth over the sensitive skin, she pressed into his mouth and his leg.

He wanted to spend all night exploring her, but he was ready to burst. Drawn-out play could happen next. He fisted his shaft and hovered at her opening before thrusting inside.

Sydney's sigh and the arch of her back added another layer to his need. Her pussy was tight and slick, gripping him and drawing him in. Her face was screwed up with pleasure.

He'd missed seeing that in the hentai room, and was glad to get a glimpse now. "Finger yourself." He wanted to watch her get off, and it was already taking more focus than he had, to keep from coming.

She slipped her hands between her legs. When her inhibitions faded, it was clear she liked putting on a show.

Dylan was good with watching or participating.

With each stroke, she dipped low enough to brush his shaft, until her motions grew shorter. Her gasps mingled with his grunts.

The flutter of her eyelids was enthralling, but the way she clenched his cock when she came was better.

Her hand fell away to grip the sheets. Her screams said she was still lost in climax.

Pressure built inside, narrowing his focus until he and she were the only things that existed.

Orgasm tore through him. Stars sparked behind his eyelids, as he slammed against her. He pounded until he was spent, and even then, was reluctant to slow.

He finally stopped and pressed his forehead to her chest.

The sounds of heavy breathing mingled with the whirring of the air conditioner.

Dylan kissed up her breastbone, to her mouth. "Incredible," he murmured against her lips.

Her giggle was soft. "You really are."

He stripped off and disposed of the condom, then fell into bed and pulled her back into him. His mind skipped along the next couple of hours. Maybe a shower to clean up, and using that time to explore her curves and find out what other buttons she had.

Dylan didn't know why she had this impact on him. He wasn't a stranger to a random hookup, and he didn't have the kind of skeletons in his closet that made him cringe away from a longer relationship.

But he barely knew Sydney.

She was fun. Sexy. Witty. Different.

Maybe he did know why he was drawn to her.

"When do you have to be up?" he asked.

"Seven-ish? I need an hour to get ready, get downstairs, and make sure the booth is set up."

"Stay here tonight."

She snuggled back into him and pulled his arm more tightly around her. "You got it, boss."

He liked that. They chatted, but the drowsiness in her voice was obvious.

Dylan wasn't aware he'd fallen asleep, until the jarring of the mattress dragged him back to consciousness.

"Fuck, shit, God damn it." Sydney's muttered curses pulled him further awake. She was yanking on her clothes, like she couldn't wait to get out of here.

"Syd? What's wrong?"

She didn't look at him as she slipped on her shoes. "I need to go. I can't believe— *Fuck.* I have to go."

SIX

When Josh finished law school, he'd hoped to serious cut back on weekend research.

Some things would never change, though. He'd spent his Saturday morning balancing the contract he'd been pulled from and learning about the one he was assigned to instead.

As he headed out for a late lunch, he was satisfied with the progress he'd made on both.

He was caught up enough to take Sunday off, and there was a spare key for the hotel room he and Dylan got for the con, waiting for him.

Josh had the windows rolled down on his Honda, as he followed traffic out of downtown. The sun was shining, the weather was mild, and he was going to enjoy the fuck out of the next thirty-six or so hours of his life.

He'd sent Dylan a couple of texts, to let him know he was on his way. There was no answer, but that wasn't a big deal. Dylan would get to them when he had time.

They'd take in the con, and at the same time, they could brain-storm how to get Josh in front of the game publisher.

Josh hit an open stretch of road and smiled at the breeze floating through the car. He turned up the radio.

In law school, he and Dylan had played a couple sometimes. Sometimes for the shock value or to prove a point. Other times because a couple made a better impression at a social event. Both of them were bi, and comfortable with the masquerade of being together, so it wasn't a big deal.

JOSH WAS TEMPTED to do the same thing now. If he were Dylan's boyfriend, it would be an excuse for them to both be at dinners with the client.

There was a huge issue there. Everyone at work knew better, and that complicated things.

The screech of tires drowned out the music. Metal and glass shattered.

Josh's skull slammed into the headrest, and his airbag pressed him tighter into his seat.

His ear were ringing. What happened?

The way his car had spun, and the shape of the passenger side —curved around a pickup truck—said he'd been broadsided. They were in the middle of an intersection.

He gingerly rolled his neck as the airbag deflated. Was he supposed to stay seated if he had a concussion? What about for whiplash?

Not really something they taught in law school.

He stretched his limbs as he climbed from the car. *Phone.* He needed that. It was still in its cradle, attached to the dashboard.

Good fixture.

He dialed 911 and stumbled toward the truck.

The other driver wore a scowl as he stepped onto the pavement. The instant he saw Josh, he started shouting. "You asshole fucking prick. Where the fuck were you going? You shouldn't have been in that intersection, you cunt."

Great. This was what Josh wanted to deal with. It added to the throbbing pain in his skull. He spared the man a glance. "Just a moment, please. I'm on the phone."

"Emergency services. What's your emergency?" a woman asked over the line.

"I'd like to report an accident at the intersection of 3900 South and Main Street. Two cars. At least two adults—"

"I'm talking to you, you pussy twat." The guy slapped Josh's hand aside, knocking the phone away.

"And I'll talk to you once I know someone has been dispatched to deal with this." Josh was so tempted to deck this asshole. He didn't want to bruise his knuckles, though. His skull screamed with every new sound, and his ears chimed like an elementary school bell at recess.

"Why the fuck weren't you watching where you were going?" At least the guy had a limited cursing vocabulary. When he stepped closer to Josh, alcohol rolled off his breath and clothes.

Awesome. Not.

Josh was going to ignore him. He crouched to pick up his phone, and the guy kicked it away.

Josh rolled his eyes. He breathed deep and pushed calm through his veins, then stood. "You ran a red light. You struck the side of my car."

"F'ckin asshole."

"Yeah. That's me." Josh kept his posture loose and his voice calm. Inside, every inch of him was prepared for the inevitable escalation of this conflict.

"Smartass." The guy swung.

Josh stepped out of arm's reach. It was a sloppy punch, and the guy's momentum propelled him a few steps past Josh.

Josh didn't want to do this. It wouldn't diffuse anything. But calm resolution didn't seem like an option anyway.

The guy let loose a rambling string of gibberish scattered with foul language, and charged Josh.

Josh sidestepped again, grabbed the guy's arm, and twisted it behind his back. Apparently he did have an everyday use for that black belt in Aikido.

The guy jerked against Josh's grip, and Josh let go. He didn't want to break his arm or make him even madder by pinning him down. Someone might actually get hurt.

THE GUY LUNGED A THIRD TIME.

Sirens chirped, and a police car pulled into sight.

It distracted Josh, and the guy clipped him on the cheek.

"Fuck." That hurt.

"What's going on?" The officer's tone was friendly as he stepped from his car, but his hand hovered near his holster.

Josh held his hands up, shoulder level and palms out. "Good question."

"Let's just move away from each other while we get things sorted, shall we?" The office stepped between them.

Josh complied, and was half-surprised when the pickup driver did the same.

Over the next few minutes, a firetruck ambulance arrived, as well as a couple more cop cars.

An officer and an EMT led Josh in one direction and Pickup Guy in another. The EMT checked Josh for surface injuries, while the officer asked for his version of the story. He'd been driving, the light was green, and someone plowed into him in the intersection.

Pickup Guy told a very different tale. It was easy to hear most of it, due to his volume.

The tow trucks showed up during the conversation. Josh would never drive that Honda again. Thank God for gap insurance, or he'd be paying off a totaled piece of junk for another couple years.

"You look fine on the surface," the EMT said. "You'll want to visit the hospital and get checked out more completely."

"Definitely." If anything was wrong, Josh wasn't letting it wait.

He got the case information from the officer, then called a friend, David, for a ride to the hospital.

At least the day couldn't get much worse.

Sydney's pulse raced a million miles a minute. She couldn't believe she'd slept in. She *never* did that. It had been years since she needed an alarm clock, because her brain woke her up first thing in the morning.

But Dylan was so comfortable and sweet and really fucking incredible last night, her over-active brain had shut off for a few hours.

Now he was sitting on the edge of the bed, staring at her with concern in his eyes.

Pity?

No. She wasn't doing that to herself.

"Syd." His voice was kind. "It's okay. Freaking out won't get you down to the vendor floor any faster."

That was disturbingly rational. "But I need to get showered and changed..." Could she skip all that and just go downstairs? Sweating all day after not washing off a night of sex? Gross.

"So do it." How was he so calm? Because it wasn't his business on the line.

Neither was hers, technically. She could still be downstairs by eight-thirty. She might miss a person or two, but it wasn't the end of the world.

Damn it. Now she was being reasonable, like him.

"How's this?" Dylan said. "Go get ready. I'll do the same, and we'll meet downstairs in fifteen minutes."

"All right." She needed to learn how to do that not-freaking-out thing. "Thank you."

She turned away, but he caught her wrist. He pulled her back to him, wrapped an arm around her waist, and kissed her hard. "I'll see you soon. Promise."

Heat flooded her cheeks, and she couldn't fight her dopey grin. "Okay."

She headed back to her room, her mind working on overtime. She couldn't believe last night happened. Was this a done-and-gone kind of thing? He was sticking around to help her with her booth. He had yet to mislead her, as far as she knew.

If she was going to spend more time with him, she should trust him at least a little at some point. Hell, she'd let him get her off while a room full of strangers watched.

Sydney reached her room and started getting ready.

Last night felt genuine—his words, his actions…

There had been a tiny voice in the back of her head since she met Dylan, that insisted he was making fun of her. Having a silent laugh at the expense of the chubby geek chick. She knew that voice, because it was always there. Most of the time she could ignore it, but when things were going too good, or too badly, it made itself known.

If Dylan's interest in her was a joke, he was an Oscar-quality actor. And if not, she was hooked on him.

Who was she kidding? She was hooked either way.

Would they see each other after the con? Could whatever this was become more? She was willing to push aside some shyness and ask, for a chance like this.

She showered and dressed in record time. One nice thing about running late—it cut out the opportunity to overthink her wardrobe.

She arrived at the vendor hall about the same time as Dylan.

His smile sent delicious tingles racing over her. "Shall we?" he asked.

"Let's."

He wrapped an arm around her waist, as if it were the most natural thing in the world.

What was she doing? She didn't care. This was fun. Delicious. Exciting.

They cut through the people, to get to her booth. A few con-goers were already hanging out, waiting to buy. The vendor next door had kept an eye on the place for her.

Sydney thanked the woman profusely and insisted lunch was on her.

Now, though? It was time to get to work.

The day passed quickly. Because it was Saturday, there was a whole new crowd who'd been working when the con started. It didn't leave a lot of time for chatting, but sales were fantastic.

She found herself reaching for Dylan's hand during lulls, and he always squeezed back with a reassuring smile.

A billion hours later—or ten—the vendor hall closed its doors to attendees.

Dylan slid up behind her and tugged her close. "What are your plans for the night?" His voice vibrated through her back.

Sydney could guess where the conversation was leading. Part of her wanted to opt in for a Round Two of last night. The rest of her was exhausted. "Honestly? Saturday nights are usually *soak my feet, take it easy, and tell myself I only have one more day* kind of nights."

"Don't you love conventions?" Dylan asked.

"So much. But they're draining. I usually need a day or two to sleep and recover after each one."

"After helping you once, I can see why. Are you interested in unwinding with me?"

"Yes." This was her best chance to find out what she needed to know. If she didn't find out now, it would gnaw at her. "But I have to ask you something first."

"Anything."

Of course that was his answer. Because she was trapped in a fairy tale, he was the perfect prince, and she never wanted to wake-up. "Is this going somewhere? You and me?" she asked. "I mean, I'm not asking for long-term commitment, and we don't have to put a definition on it—though if that happened in the future... Rather, is there a future? Do we see each other again after tomorrow? Or is this a one-weekend deal?"

"God, I hope not."

She twisted free from his arms to face him, and studied him with disbelief. Which question was that an answer to?

Dylan laughed. "I'll be more specific. I'd like to see you again. I'm really enjoying spending time with you."

"Yeah?" It was what she'd hoped for, but hearing the words still made her heart flutter.

"Yeah." Dylan nodded. "I don't know what to do, besides be me, to show you I'm sincere. Come up to my room. We'll set alarms on both of our phones and on the hotel clock, and schedule a wake-up call, so we don't oversleep. And if our night is chilling out and nothing more, I'm fine with that."

It was like someone made him in a computer. "Sounds perfect."

They rode the elevator up, and walked to his room.

Dylan unlocked the door and let them in.

Sydney's heart leaped into her throat when she saw someone else was already in there.

Not just someone.

Josh?

"Josh. Hey. Didn't think you'd make it." Dylan sounded like seeing her ex in his room was the most normal thing in the world.

Josh looked past him, to her. "Sydney?"

She worked her jaw up and down, trying to force something, anything from her throat.

What the fuck was her ex-boyfriend doing in her new not-quite-boyfriend's hotel room, and why didn't Dylan look surprised?

SEVEN

J osh struggled to take his eyes off Sydney. Partly because she was one of the last people he expected to see again, but also because she was more stunning than he remembered—perfect curves, and that hint of hesitation in the way she bit her bottom lip.

"Is this why you ignored my texts?" he asked Dylan. He needed something to distract him from the disquieting spike of jealousy.

She was his ex. He didn't have a right to feel jealous.

Sydney met his gaze. "He's helping me with my booth."

Those gorgeous blue eyes weren't any less distracting.

Dylan smirked. "Plus some after-hours extra-curricular activities." He leaned closer to Josh. "I mean sex," he said in a stage whisper.

Sydney ducked her head.

At least there was a little fun to go along with his twinge of envy.

"So… you two know each other." Sydney said it as a statement, rather than a question. "Of course you do. You both work for *Ms. Hunter.*"

"I think that's my line." Josh ignored the whisper of venom. Sydney had never gotten along with his mother. "How have you been, Tink?"

"Good."

Dylan held up his hands. "*Tink?* Like, *The* Tink? The girlfriend?"

"Ex," Sydney said.

Josh hated how quickly the correction came, but he didn't blame her.

She took several steps back toward the door. "The room is more occupied that I expected. I should…"

Would she finish the thought? Josh wasn't stupid or blind. He'd seen the way she was looking at Dylan when they walked in. Once upon a time, Josh would have seized this opportunity. A chance to draw Sydney into one of their fantasies, of sharing her. They'd never found a situation she was comfortable with.

Tonight he was the uncomfortable part of that equation.

"I'll leave you two to catch up." Sydney grabbed the door handle.

Dylan strode toward her and loosely grasped her hand. "Don't go."

"It's okay." Her tone was the flat one that meant she was hiding how she really felt. "We were just going to watch movies, anyway. Are you still available tomorrow?"

Dylan stepped closer to her, and Josh clenched his jaw.

"This doesn't change anything. I can keep you company in your room as well as in mine." Dylan's voice was soft.

She shook her head. "I really am exhausted. It's not a big deal. I'll get some sleep and catch up tomorrow."

"If you're sure." Dylan trailed a finger down her arm. "He's my roommate. I see him almost every day. He can wait."

Great. That made Josh feel special.

"It's all right. Stay here. I promise it's not a big deal," Sydney said.

"I'll see you downstairs, tomorrow morning. And everything else we talked about still stands." Dylan pressed his lips to hers, lingering long enough to draw a moan.

When they broke apart, Sydney glanced at Josh. "Catch you around." And then she was gone.

That was super awkward. "Didn't mean to cockblock."

Dylan sat on the edge of one of the beds. "Funny how you say that now, but I didn't hear you offer to leave."

So much for bros before—

That wasn't right.

Dicks before—

Josh didn't like the sound of that one either. "I didn't consider it. My bad."

"As long as you're not going to suggest I stop dating her." Dylan unlaced his shoes, toed them off, and set them aside.

"*Dating?* You've only known her a few days. And no, I'm not going to suggest that."

"Good. Because otherwise, I'd have to say *no* to you, and that might strain our friendship." Tension ran through Dylan's teasing.

Josh needed to back off. He should have anyway. This didn't involve him, and his breakup with Sydney wasn't her fault. Nothing to warn Dylan away from.

Josh was the one who fucked that up.

"That's really Tink?" Dylan's animosity had vanished. "You were right about those hints of naughty she's hiding from the world."

And just like that, the jealousy surged back. Josh had a couple of choices—he could go back to playing the bro card, with, *I used to date her; you can't,* or he could grow up and move on, the way he should have already done.

He didn't care for either solution.

DYLAN HEADED to Sydney's booth in the morning with Josh by his side. He'd explained to Josh that he was helping out with Sydney's work all weekend, and they could catch up after the con.

Josh wanted to see the booth and promised to keep his attitude to himself.

Dylan wasn't used to being at odds with Josh. They'd only known each other for a few years, but they got along great. Hell, they'd even explored the *friends with benefits* part of a relationship on several occasions.

When Dylan found out who Sydney was though, a sharp current of possessiveness coiled inside. He didn't know what he had with her, but he wasn't ready to give it up.

They reached Sydney's booth, and she was there and set up for the day. Dylan gave her a *hello* kiss. He didn't see any reason to hold back from how he wanted to act.

"You're selling this? I didn't think they had a distributor," Josh said.

Dylan turned to see him holding one of the C&C boxes.

Sydney snapped off a laugh. "You're kidding, right?"

Dylan added two and two, and got *royally fucked with a side of conflict of interest.* Why didn't he see it sooner? This wasn't someone else's game. It was Sydney's.

"No." Josh shook his head.

Sydney grabbed the box from him and set it neatly back on the stack. "It's *my* game."

Yup. Fuck.

"It's R.H. Pratt's game," Josh said.

"My maternal grandfather. I put his name on the company and the box, for credibility."

People wander the aisles, scoping out the goods for the last day of the con.

"Well, fuck." Dylan expected his career to conflict with his personal life at some point. He hadn't expected it to happen on his first real case.

Sydney's frown deepened, and she looked between them. "Care to share this bad news with me?"

Josh patted Dylan on the shoulder. "Your case. Your girl. Your news."

"I'm one of the lawyers negotiating the distribution deal between R.H. Pratt and the new publisher," Dylan said.

Sydney stepped back, arms crossed. This didn't look good. "You think that might have been important to tell me two days ago?"

Dylan winced. He didn't want to admit what his thought process had been, but he was going to have to. "It didn't occur to me that it was important."

"This game. This one, right here. That you've been selling all weekend." She patted the box. "You didn't figure it was crucial to mention your relationship to it?"

"Well?" Josh was enjoying this too much.

"I—" This was going to sound bad.

Sydney looked at him expectantly. "Yes?"

"I didn't realize it was *your* game. I thought you were working for the guy who created it, and you wouldn't care who he signed contracts with, as long as you still had a job."

Sydney scrubbed her face. "Nice. Wonderful. Un-fucking-believable. I don't even want to unpack the assumptions in that statement."

"I can still help you sell today. Our goal is the same—get your game in more people's hands." Dylan had no idea how to make this right. He didn't even know if he should try.

It wasn't that he thought his client would try to screw Sydney over during negotiations, but his job was to get said clients the best deal. He couldn't give them his full representation if he was worried about her on a personal level.

EIGHT

S ydney didn't sleep well last night. Seeing Josh again tugged at
something inside she thought was gone.

It should be. It needed to be. And now that she had time to prep
herself, she could ignore their past.

Except she was seeing his roommate. Was *dating* the right word?
Probably, if they were going to keep seeing each other after the
convention.

She didn't think Josh would tell horrible stories about her—
maybe she was wrong, but that wasn't like him. She was worried he
and Dylan would agree it wasn't cool for a buddy to date his friend's
ex.

It shouldn't have kept her up all night, worrying if she'd ever see
the guy again who she'd known for all of a weekend, but it did.

When both guys approached her booth and Dylan greeted her
as if everything was fine, some of her tension ebbed.

Until Josh dropped the big bomb.

And Dylan added a follow-up blow. Apparently her talking
about this being *her* company, *her* game, hadn't been enough of a
clue for him.

Because he'd assumed some guy created it.

Okay, so she used initials everywhere, to perpetuate that impression, but...

"Isn't sticking around a form of conflict of interest?" Sydney tried to keep her tone cool. "I don't want you to jeopardize anything by hanging out with the defendant."

"You're not the *defendant*. The goal is that both parties walk away from the negotiating table happy," Dylan said.

She looked past him, to Josh. "Does Ms. Hunter see it that way?" Sydney was certain the woman saw her as the competition even when a contract negotiation wasn't on the table.

Josh held up his hands. "I'm not on the legal team. She booted me to a new case."

Which probably meant the case wasn't significant enough for the boss's son to get his feet wet with it. Josh thought he didn't get any special attention in the firm, but Sydney had seen numerous indicators to the contrary, even pre-law school, when he was an assistant.

"It doesn't matter if I walk away now or in eight hours," Dylan said. "I'm not going to enjoy your company any less. Tomorrow morning, I'll recuse myself and ask someone else to take my place. I'm not a key figure."

And it wasn't a high-profile case. She hesitated to accept. That he'd offered warmed her from the inside out and automatically placed him another rung above Josh, who'd done the opposite when it came up. Several times.

But she also barely knew Dylan, and this was start of his career.

"No you won't." Josh broke in before she could respond. "You're going to woo this client and kick ass on their behalf."

"At least some things never change." This time the bitterness spilled into Sydney's voice. "Go enjoy the con. Both of you." She grabbed Dylan's hand and shook it. Might as well play it cool. "It was nice meeting you. Thanks for the fun. Have a nice life. Good luck with your job."

Dylan gripped tight, keeping her from letting go. "Hang on. He doesn't speak for me. Did you let him speak for you, when you were dating? His answer isn't mine."

She didn't know where to go from here. The distribution offer already had her on edge. She couldn't afford a lawyer for this negotiation. A friend had offered to go over the fine print. Josh wasn't going to point out places for her to be wary. She wished she could trust him for that, but he'd proven repeatedly that the law firm came first.

Dylan might tell her, but that put his job at risk. She wasn't his client.

"Listen." Dylan dropped her hand, but his tone kept her attention. "It doesn't matter if I walk away now. I already know you. I already like you. That conflict doesn't vanish if I abandon you for a few hours of booth work. And there's nothing I can do about it right this second. Let me help you finish out the day, and tomorrow I'll talk to the people in charge about next steps."

"Thank you." Sydney didn't think his talking to the boss would help, but she couldn't turn him down.

Josh's clenched jaw said he disagreed.

That hurt. If Dylan was a new lawyer, he wouldn't have a big impact on a simple contract negotiation. Did Josh hold that much animosity toward her?

DYLAN HAD HOPED that whatever bad feelings remained between Sydney and Josh would take more than two-point-five seconds to emerge.

"Don't go anywhere," he said to Sydney.

She raised an eyebrow. "This is my booth. I'm here the rest of the day."

"Right. Perfect. I'll be back, I promise." He grabbed Josh's arm and yanked him down the aisle. "What the fuck? Seriously."

Josh's scowl deepened. Apparently, that was possible. "This is the start of your career. You spent almost a decade in college to get here. You're going to start off on the wrong foot, for a girl you just met?"

Melodramatic much? "You mean this could be the start of *your* career. But you'll have other ways to get to know the publisher."

"Dylan." Sydney's plaintive tone carried over the morning chatter. "I'm sorry to interrupt…"

He glanced over his shoulder, to see a small crowd had gathered in her booth and she was telling three different people she'd be right with them.

"You're not changing my mind," Dylan said to Josh and turned away. He joined Sydney in the booth. "Who's next?" He called.

He'd expected it to be busier today. Attendance would be at its highest, and people had been saving their money all weekend and would spend today.

But it was different, experiencing the crowds from this side of the vendor table. Sydney's insistence on getting some rest last night made a lot of sense.

At one point, he looked up and realized Josh had stuck around and was helping customers too. He was even talking up the board game.

They kept busy most of the day. The five- and ten-minute lulls were enough for one of them to take a break but didn't leave any time for chatting. Even after the vendor hall closed, attendees dawdled.

Sydney dropped into a chair when the last person was gone. Her face was flushed, but her smile looked etched in place. "Thank you for sticking around. Both of you. If it comes down to it tomorrow morning, I'll pretend I don't know Dylan."

"You'd better not." Possessiveness surged inside Dylan. "Wait. Why just me?" That made it worse.

"Everyone there already knows at least a little of my history with Josh," Sydney said.

Josh shrugged and gave a half nod.

Of course they did. Something about the comment tickled the back of Dylan's mind. He reached for the thought, but it flitted out of his grasp. It would come back if it was important. "I'll recuse myself. It's not going to be an issue."

He expected a protest or at least a growl from Josh, but his roommate stayed impassive.

"When did the two of you meet?" Sydney stood and moved to the closest shelf. "And if you want to help me tear things down, Dylan, it all goes in the same boxes it came from during setup."

Dylan was happy to see this through. He moved to another shelf. He'd spent the day putting together the pieces of when his meeting Josh feel in the *breakup* timeline. It couldn't be a pleasant memory for Josh or Sydney. How much did he want to say?

"I needed a roommate. He was advertising," Josh said. He picked a third shelf and started unloading games into their boxes.

That was about as direct and clean as the answer to that question got.

"So, it was literally right after..." Sydney trailed off.

Josh nodded.

The story Dylan knew was that Josh and Sydney were going to move in together. She broke up with him after he'd already surrendered his old to live with her, and rather than argue with her over who would stay in the apartment they'd rented together, he let her take it.

"He's a great date, by the way," Josh teased. "The two of you will have fun."

Sydney looked surprised, and Dylan rolled his eyes. "Not like that."

She studied him. "How many ways are there to be someone's date?"

"We were..." What was the best way to phrase this? "Each other's *plus ones* when an uncomfortable situation called for it."

"Ah. If awkward at business meetings is your idea of a good date, I'll be a blast at firm parties." A hint of tension leaked into Sydney's voice. She finished boxing the items on her shelf and moved on to dismantling empty racks. "But I bet the two of you made an adorable couple." Flirting replaced her discomfort.

Dylan smiled. "We turn heads. No question." Something occurred to him. "You know all the deep, dark secrets about Josh that he's never told me."

Josh raised his eyebrows.

"You've met his mother?" Sydney asked.

Considering the woman was Dylan's boss. "Yes…"

"Then he probably has more secrets about me than I can tell you about him."

Odd answer.

"I do know a couple good ones," Josh said before Dylan could question further.

Dylan looked at Sydney. "Do I want to ask?"

"I can tell you a couple of her better fantasies," Josh offered.

Sydney turned bright red. "*No.* No, no, no. Don't you dare."

"You sure? Fifty-fifty chance of living at least one of them out…"

Dylan's curiosity was piqued. Given what he already knew… Memories from the hentai room rushed back. Of Sydney's body, molded to his. The show they'd put on for everyone else. How wet she was. The way she yielded to his touch.

He was definitely curious about what else she had to share.

It was also hers to share. It killed him to say it, but— "I don't want to hear it, unless Sydney wants to tell me."

Fuck, it sucked being a decent person sometimes.

NINE

Josh didn't know why he was here. He'd joined the mini caravan with Dylan, following Sydney back to her place, to help unload the rest of her merchandise.

Dylan's logic was that, if Josh helped, it would remind him this went beyond conflict of interest, and they could both be guilty at work tomorrow.

Josh caught the glance Dylan sent his say. The implied, *but you leave as soon as the heavy lifting is done.* They'd each driven their own cars, so Josh could leave the new sweethearts alone in peace.

Which didn't help him understand why he'd agreed to join them in the first place.

Because I'm having fun with them.

And because he liked watching Sydney move. And hearing her laugh. And the way she twisted her hair when she was distracted or nervous.

He shook the thoughts aside. Even if she did decide to spill to Dylan about her two-guys-at-once fantasy, it wasn't going to involve Josh.

They finished stashing her boxes in the second bedroom. She'd stayed in the apartment Josh found with her. They'd gotten a good price on it, so it made sense she stayed here.

The place radiated her personality. Display cases wherever there was space. A futon, and a TV on a cheap stand. Posters, wall scrolls, and merchandise from various fandoms decorated her walls.

He was trying his best not to think about how happy she'd been when she first saw the shower in the master bedroom. Big enough for three people to play in.

Josh wasn't going to be the cockblocking asshole. Not a second time, anyway. He'd let Dylan and Sydney get up to whatever they were going to get up to, and ignore the desire thrumming in his veins. He'd push aside the hedging fantasies of spending one more night stripping Sydney down and making her moan.

He couldn't believe Dylan had surrendered the chance to ask her for more details. The guy must really be smitten.

Dylan wandered toward one of the display cases in the living room. "What are these?"

Josh's thoughts stalled. Dylan was looking at painted figurines for a variety of tabletop games, and she had shelves of them.

"Where are the new ones?" Josh asked.

The look she gave him was difficult to interpret. "Work occupies most of my free time these days. I haven't touched the figurines in a while."

"*You* painted these?" Dylan hovered his hands over the glass, attention fixed on its contents.

Not all of them.

"More than half of them are Josh's," Sydney said.

"I can't believe you kept mine."

She jammed her hands in her pockets. "I couldn't get rid of them. You might be an inconsiderate ass, but you're a talented one."

"Thanks. I think." Josh didn't expect she'd forgiven him, but the reminder was still a painful dig.

Dylan turned back to them. "What class do you play? And don't tell me *it depends*. Everyone has a preference."

"You're not going to just assume I'm the healer?" Sydney asked.

Of course Dylan wouldn't. He knew better. "No, because Josh plays cleric."

"Busted." Sydney laughed. She had relaxed a lot since this morning, and even since they left the convention center. It was nice to see. "Give me two swords and light enough armor to keep me mobile, and send me to the front line."

Dylan looked surprised. "Sounds dangerous."

"She's very agile," Josh assured him.

"Is that a double entendre?"

Sydney stepped closer to Dylan. "If that fills your head with naughty thoughts, then yes."

"I miss those games." What Josh really wanted to say was, *enough with the flirting*, but that was petty. Besides, he didn't actually mind. He thought he would, but Dylan and Sydney looked good together. The one regret Josh had was being on the outside. If he was putting this much thought into the situation, he needed to say his *goodbyes* soon.

He didn't know how much longer he could hold the vivid images at bay, of having Sydney sandwiched between them.

"It wouldn't work now," Sydney said. "We'd make a lousy party."

Right. They were still talking about roleplaying. The not-naked kind. "Why not?" he asked.

"Because your tank would get in my way." Sydney poked Dylan playfully in the chest.

Not the answer Josh expected, but one that made him smile.

"You're the agile one." Dylan grasped her wrist, holding her captive. "You can figure out a way to dance around me with your *two swords*. And I'm flattered you didn't peg me for a bruiser."

Sydney shook her head. "Only when your team is in trouble. Then you'll rain fire down from above. Doesn't matter if it's in your skillset or not."

"Did you ever have a chance to try out the shower?" Josh's question slipped out without his permission. Wow. Way to make things awkward.

Sydney raised her eyebrows. "I use it on pretty much a daily basis."

"This is about *the secret*, isn't it? Do I need to make him leave before I ask again?" Dylan gestured at Josh. "Because I'm trying to behave and not push the issue, but I like knowing secrets. Especially when they're about things that make you moan." He kissed her fingertips.

Sydney fiddled with a loose strand of hair as she looked between Dylan and Josh. "Josh knows. It's not like asking him to leave keeps him from finding out."

SYDNEY WAS TRYING to ignore her body's reaction to Josh, and failing. Not that she was giving up on Dylan. Holy wow, she wasn't walking away from a guy like that. But was there really any harm in putting the information out there, to see how Dylan reacted?

It wasn't like she wanted Josh back. He was attractive. He was fun. And he still had the same habits that drove them apart. But this didn't have to involve him.

"We got the apartment with the extra-big shower because I like shower sex," Sydney confessed.

Dylan's hungry smile sent happy shivers racing down her spine. "So let's kick him out, and we'll go get clean."

Josh gave her a pointed look. "And?"

"And it's big enough for more than two people. For three, actually. Because I think it would be fun"—hot, sexy, incredible—"to be with two guys at the same time." *Please don't let this confession backfire.* It wasn't as though she was saying she wanted to fuck her ex-boyfriend.

She'd probably do it. But not at the cost of pushing Dylan away.

Dylan searched her face. "The shower implies it was more than just a passing fancy."

"We'd started to look for a third before we broke up," Josh said.

Dylan glanced at him. "You never told me that."

What kind of relationship did they have, that Josh would share something like this with Dylan?

Josh sighed. "I didn't have the same interest in it without Sydney."

The revelation clenched around her heart. She didn't expect that kind of reaction—from herself or from him.

Josh looked at her. "I still like the idea. But it was your fantasy."

What was she supposed to say? It hurt to leave Josh, but she'd convinced herself he walked away unscathed. At least part of her knew that wasn't true, but admitting he was affected as well cut deep. She didn't expect her own reaction.

"I kind of feel like I should have stayed out of this," Dylan said. "I'm not sure if I regret pushing for an answer."

Please, please don't let this turn him off or push him away. "Would you still feel uncertain if the fantasy wasn't attached to Josh?" Because it wasn't. She needed to say that aloud. The second guy, feeling her up from behind while Dylan kissed her passionately, didn't have a face.

"You don't want my answer." Dylan's tone had shifted to something she couldn't decipher. It wasn't flat or angry or unhappy.

Sydney frowned. This was falling apart fast. What did she expect? New boyfriend plus ex-boyfriend equaled disaster. But she didn't expect this would be the impetus. "I do. Want your answer, that is."

Dylan raised her hand to kiss her palm. It was such a tender, sweet gesture. It didn't comfort her.

"It makes it better, not worse, that Josh is part of it." Dylan's lips tickled her skin as he spoke.

"Oh." Way to sound intelligent. She should be bothered by his admission, but heat raced over her skin, and the images dancing in her thoughts solidified.

Dylan dropped her hand and traced her bottom lip with his finger. "Don't get me wrong. I don't like the idea of sharing you, in general. That's selfish of me, since we haven't talked about exclusivity, but there you have it."

"But?" Her voice cracked on the word. She needed to open a window. Turn on the air. Stick her head in the freezer.

319

"But in the hentai room——"

"The *what?*" Josh asked.

It was going to be a long night if this conversation didn't find a conclusion.

Dylan kept his attention on her. "That was hot."

"It really was." And with the memory added on top of desire, Sydney had to squeeze her thighs together, to mute the pulse between her legs.

Josh cleared his throat. "Details?"

Sydney had questions for Dylan. "Why does he matter? Why does he make the fantasy better?"

"Because he *does* matter to me," Dylan said. "I trust him. I like him. He's a fun date and a good lay."

She couldn't argue those last few words. She'd run out of reasons why this was a bad idea, beyond *ex-boyfriend*. She looked at Josh. "We got ourselves invited to a party the first night of the con. It turned out to be a bunch of people, watching anime porn and getting off to it."

"And you joined them." Was that jealousy in Josh's voice?

Sydney shrugged.

"I helped her put on a show," Dylan offered.

Josh stared at her, desire heavy in his eyes. *Fuck*, she missed that look.

She turned back to Dylan. "There's no universe where this seems like a smart idea. But it's tempting." What was she saying? *Shut up.*

She didn't want to listen to that voice, though.

Dylan searched her face. "It is, isn't it?"

"I'm offering fantasy fulfillment. One night only. I'll leave the two of you be, after," Josh said.

Fucking hell. Sydney was teetering on a sharp edge. Falling in one direction was safety and disappointment and boredom. And in the other direction was impulsive stupidity, with a high probability of a couple amazing orgasms and some fantastic memories.

Dylan cupped her cheeks, holding her gaze. "Are you okay with this?"

"I think that's supposed to be my question to you." Her throat was dry. She licked her lips and swallowed, but it didn't help.

"You have to tell me you're all right with all three of us together. Or I'll kick Josh out now. I'll leave too, if you want."

She didn't want either one of them to leave. Her answer froze in her throat. This was one more night with Josh, no strings, and living out one of her biggest fantasies with Dylan. She couldn't turn that down. "You should both stay."

Dylan crushed his mouth to hers, and her pulse soared. All of her doubt evaporated. He licked along her bottom lip, and she let his tongue in, to dance with hers.

A second pair of hands rested on her hips, and her heart slammed into her rib cage. And then Josh's lips were on the back of her neck, gliding up to the hollow behind her ear. The spot he knew drove her wild.

Yeah, this was a terrible fucking idea. And Sydney was going to enjoy every minute of it.

TEN

Dylan liked this whole threesome idea as a general concept—Sydney plus one more—but Josh was shattered by the breakup when Dylan met him, and it probably wasn't any easier on Sydney.

Sydney and Josh were adults. If they were okay with this, it wasn't Dylan's place to tell them they were wrong.

Besides, he liked Sydney's fantasies so far, he wasn't going to discourage them. Desires like this were a horrible thing to suppress.

He dragged his mouth down her neck and nudged aside her shirt collar.

"No." Her protest was weak. She rested a hand on his chest but didn't push him away.

He looked up to meet her gaze. Not the best time for second thoughts, but certainly her right. "What's wrong?" he asked. It was impossible to ignore the way Josh still gripped her hips.

"Nothing. I mean, not with what you're doing. But I'm all sweaty and gross from the convention. You may not want to be kissing all over me like this."

That was it? Fortunately, there was a solution in place. "Do you want to get in the shower, fully clothed?"

Sydney shook her head.

"Then the clothes have to come off." Dylan tugged her shirt over her head. "And it's up to me if I mind a little sweat or not." He lowered his mouth to her neck and kissed along the long curve while he dragged his palms up her sides.

Her bra fell away. In the wave of kissing and groping, his touch collided with Josh's several times. Another reason for Dylan to enjoy this. He brought his mouth back to Sydney's, to swallow her moans.

Josh cupped her breasts, and Dylan dragged his thumbs across her nipples. She whimpered and pressed into Dylan's touch.

The heat and desire flooding him set his thoughts ablaze. This didn't seem like one of those things people just fell into, but here he was... and *fuck*, he liked the potential rolling out in front of them.

He bit Sydney's bottom lip and dove deeper into the kiss. Each time he rolled her nipples between his fingers, pinched or pulled, she made another delicious sound and molded to his touch in a new way.

Josh's hands had traveled lower, to undo her jeans and tease along her waist. She squirmed her hips against the contact, and Dylan wasn't complaining about either of them brushing or grinding against him in the process.

Sydney broke the kiss with a breathless gasp and stepped away from them. She searched Dylan's face, mischief dancing behind her eyes. That playful look alone was enough to undo him.

"I want to watch the two of you strip." Her request was a combination of shy and bold that shouldn't work together. She owned it, though.

He exchanged a glance with Josh, who shrugged. "I'm not really a dancer," Josh said.

"Which I know is a lie. But I'm not expecting *Magic Mike* chore-ography. I do want to see some asses wiggling." Sydney fixed her attention on Dylan.

He kicked his shoes aside. "Do we get music?"

"I can hum the Jeopardy theme, but that might be a mood killer," Sydney teased.

Dylan was always up for a challenge. He swayed his hips and

slid his hands up his sides then back down, to tug up the bottom of his shirt. The way Sydney watched him—eyes wide, bottom lip caught between her teeth—made him harder than he thought possible and had his pulse hammering in his ears.

Her gaze drifted to Josh every few seconds. Dylan expected jealousy, but he was stealing the occasional look as well.

Josh was also going to make a show of this. He turned with his back to her. before stripping off his T-shirt, letting the stretch of his arms elongate his torso, and enjoying the heat of her attention flowing over him.

Dylan undid his jeans and let them drop low on his hips. The whistle he received in return was worth it. He liked to watch, but he'd never considered the thrill of being the one on display. It was exhilarating. As he spun back to face Sydney, he stole another glance at Josh, who was in a similar state of undress.

Wiry cords of muscle rippled under Josh's skin, showing off the athletic frame his clothes usually hid.

Dylan met Sydney's gaze again and pushed his jeans to the floor.

She twisted her mouth and raised an eyebrow, but it didn't hide her smirk. "Take it *all* off."

"You wanted a show." Dylan hooked his thumbs in the elastic of his boxers, inching them lower as he moved closer to her.

"I did. And I'm liking what I'm seeing." She covered his hands and coaxed them down. "But I want to touch, too." She pushed the rest of his clothes to the ground, and his cock sprang free. When she gripped his shaft, a low groan tore from his throat.

He knotted his fingers in her hair and claimed her mouth. His erection dug into her belly. She molded to him. And there was that third set of hands in there, Josh's, cupping her breasts as he pressed into her back.

"If you're not careful, we won't make it to the shower." Josh's warning was a low growl.

"He's got a good point." Dylan murmured against Sydney's lips.

She stepped from their grasp, and took them both by the hand. "I guess we'd better move, then."

FAMILIAR TOUCHES.

New ones.

More hands on her bare skin than there should be.

Sydney wanted to memorize every tantalizing brush of skin on skin.

Hot water poured over the three of them. Sydney was more scalded by Josh's open-mouth kisses up her spine and the way Dylan sucked along her shoulder hard enough to leave his mark.

She couldn't ignore Josh. Which made sense—he was drawing soapy trail along the inside of her thigh—but there was more to it. She liked this excuse to feel him again.

She was just as focused on Dylan—he glide of his hands along her torso, as he washed her clean and followed behind with hungry kisses. She gripped his cock loosely. He jerked against her hand each time she squeezed, spiking her desire.

Josh's erection dug into one ass cheek. A reminder of how good it felt when he was inside her. Each grip and grope made the need between her legs throb more insistently.

Dylan extracted the portable shower head from its socket. "This looks like fun. Not that a sweet girl like you would know about that." His tone was playful.

"It is fun. And I do know." Sydney was enjoying how easy things were with him. "A sweet girl has to entertain herself when there's no one around to help."

"Sweet and innocent?" Josh's question vibrated against her shoulder. He drew his fingers up the inside of her thigh, to tease along her slit.

She gasped. "One-hundred percent innocent."

Dylan flicked his thumb over the switch on the shower head, changing it to a massage setting. "And naive?"

"Let's not get carried away…" Her reply faded into a moan when Dylan lowered the nozzle and the water pounded her skin.

He parted her lower lips and moved the shower head forward. The stream hammered against her clit, stealing her breath.

Dylan claimed her mouth, holding the nozzle in place while he drank her whimpers.

Josh slipped two fingers inside her, and she arched her back, not sure which way to lean to feel *everything*.

Waves of pleasure rocked her body. Her thoughts swam on the crest as the men coaxed her closer to the edge of orgasm. Josh pumped, and Dylan didn't let up.

She came hard, screaming into the kiss and grinding against Josh's hand until it was too much. Her body shuddered away from the shower head, but she didn't want to let go of Dylan. Being pressed between the men was the one thing making it possible for her wobbly legs to hold her upright.

"*Fuck*, I missed making you come." Josh's whisper caressed her ear, so soft it was more of a suggestion than a sound. Did Dylan hear that? The words fluttered in her belly and clenched like a fist around her heart at the same time.

She shook aside the nagging regret. She wasn't going to second-guess her past because of a great orgasm.

Dylan replaced the shower head in its dock, then licked a path down her chest, to tease a nipple with his tongue. "All clean. I can nibble on whatever I want." He scraped his teeth over the sensitive nub.

She groaned and pushed into his mouth. "Okay." Her grasp of complex words had evaporated.

"Here's the thing…" Josh bit her shoulder, and she groaned. "This is a lot of fun, but I'm not sure the mechanics of actual sex are going to work in here."

He was right. There was plenty of room for three people, and a delicious hum still rolled over her skin from her climax, but she didn't know how anything complex could take place in this space. "What did you have in mind?"

"We dry off enough to not drip on the carpet, and move this into the bedroom," Josh said.

"I guess." Sydney let out an exaggerated huff.

Dylan shut off the water, then grasped her fingers and helped her step from the shower.

Being patted dry with a big fluffy towel was fun, but she was looking for a different kind of closure. One that involved feeling Dylan's thick cock stretching her out again.

He looked over her shoulder. "Condoms?"

"Don't have any," Josh said.

A twinge of something negative pinged inside Sydney, because she wasn't surprised he wasn't carrying protection. Josh was always Josh's priority. She ignored it.

"I do. In my wallet." Dylan kissed her fingertips. They made their way to the bedroom, with a quick detour for protection.

He stopped with his back to the bed, facing her. She couldn't help but notice he kept positioning her so she was looking at him, not Josh.

Not that Sydney minded. This was an easier way to keep things from getting more complicated.

So I'm just using Josh for the sex?

That was what they'd agreed on.

"What do you want?" Dylan asked. "Your fantasy. You drive."

Sydney liked the sound of that. "Does that mean I get to owe you a fantasy in return?"

"I have a feeling there will be a lot of give on that front. For both of us." He smirked.

She liked that even more. "I want you inside me. Both of you." She and Josh'd had anal sex several times, so she knew what to expect.

He seemed to remember too, since he didn't hesitate to grab the lube from the top drawer of her dresser.

Dylan settled on the bed and rolled on a condom. He crooked his finger and gestured for her to come closer. "I like the idea of watching you ride me. You make the most gorgeous faces when you get caught up in the moment."

A fresh wave of heat spread through her. She climbed up his legs and hovered over his length.

Dylan *tsk*ed and gripped her hip with one hand. "A guy can only take so much teasing." He fisted his shaft and thrust his hips up, plunging inside her.

His groan mingled with hers, as he filled her up and spread her open. So much better than fingers.

She rocked against him, letting him set a slow but steady pace.

Josh glided his fingers, slick with lube, along her ass. He teased her second hole. This was good. This was better than good, and it was just a hint.

Dylan paused, and Josh nudged her with the head of his cock.

Her breath hitched with anticipation.

Josh kissed the edge of her ear. "You okay?"

She nodded. A little sensory-overloaded maybe, but okay.

He eased in, pausing with every inch, to let her adjust and relax. The penetration seemed to take forever, and then he was inside her, chest pressed to her back.

It was different and incredible, being stretched out this way. With both men thrusting. Building up to a decent rhythm again.

The friction, the contact, being sandwiched between them—it short-circuited her thoughts. Dylan glided his hands up her stomach, to caress her breasts, drawing her further into the lovely clouds flitting around her thoughts.

Josh reached around to find her clit. Her body jerked away instinctively, but she leaned back in. His stroke was gentle and coaxing.

The sum of every touch and groan built in her veins, scorching her with a surging climax.

Josh still knew exactly which spot to hit, both inside and out, and Dylan read her cues without pause. She fell into orgasm, tumbling through the pleasure overload.

The familiar grunts, punctuated with long pauses, told her Josh was close. The way Dylan's face scrunched up said he was too. Thrusting became frantic pounding as they came.

As the frenzied pace slowed, then stopped, she slipped back from the edge. But part of her lingered in the haze. She rested her head on Dylan's chest and listened to the heavy thrum of his heartbeat as they caught their breath.

Josh slipped out of her, and a moment later, he collapsed next to them on the bed.

She rolled off Dylan but was reluctant to let go of him. He stripped off his condom and settled back next to her, arm around her waist.

"Everything you dreamed of?" He nuzzled her neck.

"The reality was much better."

She wanted to lie there all night, wrapped up between them, enjoying the afterglow.

Doubt weaseled back in. A question she'd been trying to ignore all night. The one that mocked her for months after she broke up with Josh. Did she overreact back then?

She was just starting things up with Dylan, and there was no way she'd jeopardize a chance with a guy this great.

Why do I have to choose?

Because that was the way the world worked.

"We should go." Josh's voice was quiet but hard, leaving no room for argument.

Dylan rested his forehead against Sydney's shoulder. "He's probably right. We have to work in the morning, and you have a meeting."

Ugh. That.

"Don't forget." Josh met her gaze. "Tomorrow you two don't know each other."

Ice flowed through her veins, and she clenched her jaw. There it was. That distinctly clear reminder of who Josh actually was.

"Don't listen to him," Dylan said. "I'll set him straight at home."

The reassurance didn't settle the churning in her gut.

ELEVEN

Josh was grateful to be making the drive home alone. It meant he could crank the radio and sing along, rather than listening to his own thoughts.

The last thing he wanted to do was dwell on what a first-class ass he was as they left Sydney's place.

Second-to-last was to remember the past.

Apparently the music wasn't drowning out anything.

Why did he say anything about work? What the fuck was wrong with him?

He didn't want admit the reality. Being with Sydney reminded him how much he enjoyed her company. He missed the sex, sure; she was fun, sexy, and delicious in bed. But he missed *her* more.

Sydney and Dylan clicked. It was easy to see that. They almost radiated sparks. Josh wasn't doing a great job of ignoring the part of him that seethed with jealousy at seeing them together.

Josh wasn't going to act on it, though. Tonight was fun. A one-off. He'd keep his distance. That was the one upside to his comment as he was leaving—it served to push him further away.

When he got home, he'd tell Dylan he didn't mean it and ask him to pass Josh's apologies along to Sydney. Not doing it himself would ring with insincerity. And Josh would suck it up and move on.

A fist clenched around his heart at the idea, and his mind decided now was a great time to traipse into his past.

The guy working the register at the comic shop shook his head. "You can't do that. In the two-point-five ruleset—"

"The secret we should never let the gamemasters know is that they don't need any rules." The woman talking to him was curvy, cute, and irritated. "Go ahead. Ask me who said it."

Josh paused a few feet back, to watch the conversation unfold.

Comic-store Guy pushed his glasses up on his nose. "No one said it. It's an unverified quote frequently attributed to Gary Gygax, with no verifiable source."

"Convenient, since that proves your point. How many unverified quotes do you spit out on a daily basis?" The woman crossed her arms, accentuating her breasts. The instant Comic-store Guy's gaze dropped, she shoved her hands in her pockets instead. "The point is, if you're not making the game your own, what's the point in playing?"

"You have to play the way the original creators intended."

Josh understood why the woman was annoyed. He stepped forward, to tell the hack to shut the fuck up.

"The original creators"—snideness dripped from the woman's voice—"intended people be creative with the game. If I want to say that werewolves can be killed by—"

"Everyone knows werewolves can only be killed with silver bullets." Comic-store Guy talked over her. He looked at Josh. "Am I right?"

Josh shook his head. "No. You're so very wrong. Shut up."

"Excuse me?" Comic-store Guy's retort came out weakly.

Half a smile flickered on the woman's face, like she was trying to hide her amusement.

Josh winked at her and turned to the guy. "I said, shut the fuck up. I'd like to hear what the lady has to say."

"Because you like her tits?" Comic-store Guy asked.

Josh's hand shot out lightning fast—his aikido training helped with the reflex—and he grabbed Comic-store Guy's shirt collar. He tugged him forward, half-bent over the glass display cabinet. "Because she makes more sense than you. Because she's obviously smarter." Josh let him go and wiped his hand on his jeans. "And because she doesn't have Cheeto dust or Doritos, or whatever the hell that is—dripped down the front of her shirt. I'd say apologize, but you wouldn't mean it."

"Fuckin' beta boy fag.'

Josh took a single step forward, and Comic-store Guy took several back.

Josh tossed his comics on the counter. "On second thought, I'll get these on Amazon." He strolled from the store, fury seething white hot under his skin.

When he stepped outside, he realized the woman was next to him.

"Thanks," she said. "Even if you didn't mean it, thank you."

"I absolutely meant it. Josh." He extended his hand.

Her grip was firm, and her skin soft and tantalizing. "Sydney."

"I'd love to hear about alternate rule sets. Can I buy you coffee?"

She ducked her head.

"What's wrong?" he asked. "No is fine."

Sydney twisted a strand of hair around her ear. "I'm just trying to figure out if coffee is a euphemism." Her clipped tone implied she'd rather it wasn't. At least right now.

"It's not." Josh was sincere. "I really do want to hear more. If you want to give me your number when we go our separate ways, that's up to you."

The ache in his chest snapped him back to the present. He'd thought he was over Sydney, but spending the day with her brought it all rushing back.

It didn't matter. Those were whispers of the past. He'd move on, like last time.

When Josh got home, Dylan's car was already in its spot.

In the apartment, Dylan's bedroom door was shut. There was a note scrawled on the whiteboard on the fridge:

You know how I feel. Conversation over.

That settled that. Dylan would do things his way, even if it meant fucking up his career.

And Josh would keep repeating that the matter was closed, until he believed it.

DYLAN SLEPT through his alarm and was rushed to get to work. It turned out working a convention all weekend, instead of just enjoying it at his own pace, was exhausting.

He was pretty happy with the way everything ended, too. Minus that one dark spot he called his roommate.

Josh was already on his way out when Dylan stumbled into the kitchen for coffee. Josh's, "Tried to wake you up. Glad you figured out consciousness. Tell Sydney I'm sorry," was halfhearted at best.

Dylan brushed it aside and finished getting ready.

An hour later, he sat across from Ms. Hunter, explaining that he wouldn't have pursued the creator if he realized her association with this account, but he had, and now he needed to recuse himself.

When he finished, she stared back impassively. One day, he was going to learn how she did that. It made her intimidating in a court room... and in an apartment at eight on a Saturday morning, when she was asking Josh in an eerily calm voice why there were takeout bags and beer cans everywhere.

In their defense, it had been finals week, and nothing was getting done except eating, studying, and test taking.

"I appreciate your honesty and professionalism." Her tone was kind but cool. "It's going to serve you well. For today, go ahead and sit in the meeting. You're in there to listen, not advise. After today, you can still be involved behind the scenes, but you won't meet with Sydney again. I trust you to not discuss the contract with her outside of work."

That was kind of permissive. Not that Dylan wanted to argue the best of both worlds scenario, but he had to cover his bases and his ass. "If there's something in the contract that's a threat to Sydney, I won't be able to not tell her."

"I wouldn't expect otherwise, regardless of the client. Have you seen anything that makes you hesitate? If so, I'd also like to know."

He hadn't. There was no language that stole her intellectual property or would take the game from her in any way. The biggest liberty they were taking was the right to edit the game manual, according to their grammar standards. "Her game is worth more."

"Noted, and not our decision. The client offers what they feel is appropriate. It's not your place to push her to ask for more, though I'd understand if you reminded her negotiation is expected when it comes to price."

Okay, well that went far better than his best case scenario. A thought tickled the back of his mind, and he struggled to grasp it. It flitted away. "All right."

"Wonderful. The meeting is in a few minutes. Is there anything else?"

"No. Thank you." He stood.

He was halfway to her office door, when the thought rushed back in. He looked at her again.

"Is there something else?" Ms. Hunter asked.

"You knew who I was talking about. Sydney's name is hidden from all the documents, and I didn't tell you she was who I'm seeing."

"I've done my research."

Which he expected and should have thought of earlier. "She's the reason you pulled Josh from the case. Why is it a conflict of interest for him and not me?"

Laurie Hunter gave him a thin-lipped smile that implied he'd crossed that line between employee and son's best friend, and he needed to step back. "You're reading too much into the situation. Best of luck today."

"Thanks." He'd push for more later, when he wasn't pressed for time.

It was a tiny observation, but it wouldn't leave Dylan alone. Did Ms. Hunter go out of her way to keep Sydney and Josh apart? Why was that necessary? Even if Dylan weren't dating Sydney, it seemed likely her name would come up in conversation at home.

Maybe Dylan *was* reading too much into it.

He grabbed his notebook and paperwork from his office, and joined Aaron Jorgenson and two client representatives in a conference room.

The other three looked up when Dylan entered, and then the editor turned to Aaron. "That's fine. If it's what you describe, I don't see an issue with it."

"Your appointment is here," the receptionist's voice came from behind Dylan, catching him off guard.

He'd have to ask Aaron for details after the meeting.

Aaron stood. "I'll go greet her, make introductions, and we can get started."

Dylan took a seat, a jumble of thoughts racing in his head. Something about this situation was off. He wasn't used to this type of doubt.

Aaron returned a moment later, with Sydney by his side. She was dressed in a simple black pantsuit that was professional and revealed another stunning side of her.

When she saw him, her eyes grew wide, but a tiny smile quickly replaced her surprise. Her shoulders seemed to relax a little.

Aaron introduced her to everyone, finishing with, "And I believe you already know Dylan."

News traveled fast.

Sydney nodded. "It's nice to meet you all."

Aaron gestured to a chair, waited for Sydney to sit, and took his own seat. "Will your attorney be joining us?"

"No. I'm representing myself." Sydney sat like someone had jammed a rod down her spine.

Dylan had known that would be her answer, but the apprehension racing under his skin didn't like it. Who did he know from law school who owed him a favor? Something he could call in for a few free hours of consulting for Sydney. An extra set of eyes, to look over the contract with her.

He'd told Laurie the truth, that he didn't see any issues with the contract, but his concern wasn't evaporating.

"Thank you for coming into the office today." Aaron launched into a smooth, friendly greeting. "I feel like it's better to do these types of meetings in person whenever possible. It lets everyone look each other in the eye, and helps all parties feel better about the process."

"It's not a problem, and I'm looking forward to it." Sydney was cool and collected. Her tension hovered under the surface. He saw it in the tight lines around her eyes, but she hid it well.

Dylan was impressed. And a bit turned on. This was another side of her he liked.

The group went through the contract, with Aaron giving an overview of each section. It was all boilerplate language. The same information Dylan read in preparation.

He still followed along on the copy on his tablet, making notes whenever Aaron used a phrase or definition that Dylan thought was important.

They reached the *Rights* section of the contract. Aaron read a number, but the information that followed didn't match what was in Dylan's document.

Dylan tried to be subtle about scrolling up and down in his file, to see what he'd missed. Why was he out of sync?

"Is there an issue?" Aaron's sharp question drew Dylan's attention from his tablet.

I have the wrong document. Dylan kept the reply to himself. That wasn't the kind of thing to admit in front of the client. "I'm fine. Please continue."

Within a few seconds, he'd located the portion Aaron was reading, but Dylan's copy was numbered differently.

The rest of the meeting continued without a hitch. Sydney asked a few basic questions—Dylan was impressed with the things she honed in on—and was on her way.

He wanted to run after her and give her a goodbye kiss. This didn't seem like the time to push the limits of his employer's leniency, though.

Instead, he headed back to his office, to pull the most recent contract from the file repository on the network.

As he flipped through the official copy, the concern hovering under his skin grew. It was identical to the file Dylan had, and that made it different than the one Aaron had read from.

He fired a quick email off to Aaron, asking about the discrepancy. He didn't have to wait long for a reply.

You're remembering the meeting wrong. Nothing is out of sync. It may be a good thing you're sitting the rest of this case out, if your girlfriend had you that distracted.

Dylan clenched his jaw. He knew what he'd heard. Confronting Aaron or taking things up the ladder hadn't done him any good in the past, since Aaron was fucking Laurie.

But this had the potential to fuck Sydney in a completely different way. Dylan needed to get a hold of the correct contract.

Or was he blowing this up into something it wasn't? Aaron wouldn't pull a bait and switch with a contract. He was an incompetent asshole, but he wasn't willingly performing ethics violations.

TWELVE

Sydney felt like she was watching the contract discussion from a hamster wheel. One someone else was spinning, and she couldn't figure out how to stop. She was used to representing herself in business meetings, when speaking with banks, and in a variety of other situations.

This was a new experience for her, and she hadn't expected to feel so tiny and isolated.

Having Dylan in the room helped a little, except that she didn't know why he was still there, and she didn't dare do anything that might cause him problems with his job.

So she smiled, nodded, and said *goodbye* when it was all over, and walked out the door.

When she reached her car, she sank into the driver's seat and let out a long sigh. Her stomach was tied in knots, and the muscles in her neck weren't doing much better.

The buzz of her phone startled her. She fumbled in her purse and fished it out.

Seeing Dylan's name chased away some of the butterflies, and she smiled.

You did awesome. I'll explain everything after work if you're free.

She was still getting used to him wanting to see her. The weekend hadn't been a dream after all. Her smile grew. *I am.*

Good. Before then, you're going to get a call from Liam. He's a friend from school, and he'll help you with the contract, free of charge. Talk to him. Have him give everything a once over.

More of her tension seeped away. *I will. Thank you. And I owe you.*

I'm sure we can think of a way you can make it up to me ;)

Heat raced over her skin at the subtle innuendo. She could think of a lot of things she'd do to thank Dylan. Some of them involved her being on her knees, and others included straddling his legs…

She squeezed her thighs together at the sharp pulse of need. Fantasy needed to wait until later. At least until she left the parking garage.

Twenty minutes later, she was home. The morning after a convention was usually unwind-and-decompress time. The meeting took that away from her, but she could make it up now. Shed the professional clothes. Spend a little time with her vibrator and memories of last night.

What was up with her? A weekend of getting laid, and now she couldn't get enough?

Not *just* getting laid. It was really good sex.

Tomorrow you two don't know each other.

Josh's sharp voice echoed in her memories, and anger surged inside. Mood. Killed.

She draped her nice clothes over the back of a chair in her bedroom, pulled on something more comfortable, and collapsed on her bed. The ceiling didn't have any more answers about what was wrong with Josh than she'd found anywhere else.

Her thoughts raced around in circles, chasing the reality of fantasy fulfillment, both in the bedroom and with her board game.

Why were both so complicated?

Sydney needed to step outside of her own head. She grabbed her phone and dialed her best friend.

"Hey." Kathryn's greeting was cheerful. "Perfect timing. I just finished a class." Kathryn taught marital arts. She was at least as good as Josh. "How was the con? What did I miss? Did you get laid?"

She asked that every time. She'd met her boyfriends at a convention, and kept insisting that, if she could do it, so could Sydney.

"Yes." Sydney couldn't fight her smirk.

There was a pause, and then, "*Ha.* I told you so. What's he like? Is he sexy? Of course he is. Did you use him and toss him away, or give in and give him your number?"

This was making Sydney feel better. "He has my number, but I made him beg for it just a little," she joked. "And he's got this room-mate..." No. *Fuck.* Why did she say that?

"Ooh. Did you...? I'm guessing, if you mentioned it... How was it?"

"It was good. Incredible." Sydney didn't want to share details. Those were hers. "But it was only a one-time thing. With the room-mate, that is."

"You never know." Kathryn's tone was playful. "But either way, at least you had a blast. So, give me details. What are their names?"

The answer stuck in Sydney's throat. When Kathryn met Dylan, the truth was going to come out. And it wasn't like Sydney'd gone back to Josh, so this wasn't a big deal.

"Why are you hesitating?" Kathryn asked.

Busted. "Mr. Has-My-Number is Dylan. His roommate is Josh."

Kathryn sucked in a sharp breath through her teeth, making Sydney wince.

"The name is a coincidence?" Kathryn's cheer had wilted.

Sydney pushed back a wave of defensiveness. Her friend was looking out for her. "No. It was him... And I know, but it was just once, and I didn't know Dylan knew him at first."

"I'm not saying anything." Kathryn's cautious tone implied plenty. "Because you *do* know. Okay, I'm going to say something. If Josh treats you the same way again, I'm grinding his balls into the dirt. I don't care what kind of black belt he has, or if I'm allowed to hit below it; I will."

"It won't happen again. No plans of that at all." Especially with the note he left things on.

A knock filtered in from the front door, and Sydney frowned. "There's someone here. Talk to you soon?"

"Always. But Syd… Please be careful with him."

"Always." Sydney's assurance came out too bright. She disconnected and went to answer the door. When she peered through the peephole, she didn't recognize the man on the other side.

Keeping the security chain in place, she opened the door a crack. "May I help you?"

"I have court papers for Sydney Brimhall." He held up several pieces of paper clipped together, showing her the court markings up top.

Was this the contract from this morning? She already had a copy of that. "Hang on a sec." She closed the door enough to unlatch it, then opened it wider.

He shoved the document at her. "Here. Phone number for questions is on the top. Contact the court or your attorney if you need. Have a nice day." He was walking away before he finished talking.

Not the friendliest guy. Then again, if it was his job to tell people the courts wanted to talk to them, he probably got yelled at a lot.

She leaned against her apartment doorframe, to flip through the paperwork. The *Cease and Desist* on the front page brought back her earlier tension. The *Patent Infringement* a little lower down made bile rise in her throat. What the hell was this?

"Tink? What's wrong?" Josh's voice startled her, and she looked up to find him standing in front of her, watching her with concern.

She should have stepped inside and closed her door.

The sound of his voice sent goosebumps racing over her skin, and at the same time was like nails on a chalkboard. Damn her body for the former. She wasn't in the mood for whatever he wanted. "Did you come by to insult, threaten, or belittle me a little more? Needed to do it in person?"

He raised an eyebrow. "I'm here to apologize. I was going to ask Dylan to intercede on my behalf, but you deserve better than hearing it from a messenger."

That was almost insightful and considerate of him. It didn't make up for the past, recent or longer ago. "Great. Good for you. See you around."

"Tell me what's wrong?"

Why did he care? Besides, she didn't need Josh's help. Dylan said Liam would call her. She could slip in a question about this at the same time. "Nah. I'm good."

"What is this?" Josh angled his body so his shoulder rested against hers, and he could see what was in her had. "Cease and Desist?"

She yanked the document and her arm away. Heat seared her skin where he'd touched. "Nothing for you to worry about. I'm going to discuss it with my attorney."

"You suddenly have a lawyer?"

"Dylan hooked me up with Liam."

Josh clenched his jaw, and his expression almost said *of course he did.*

She liked having news that bothered him but was none of his business. But that didn't erase her worry about the notice she held.

"Tink, you don't have to forgive me. I was a superior ass last night. But let me help you with this?" Concern and sincerity lined his voice. The use of her nickname didn't hurt either.

"This is technically company related. Are you even allowed to talk to me?" She wasn't letting him off the hook.

"If it's not related to your contract, I don't see how telling me could hurt."

She saw a lot of ways it could hurt, but the gnawing pit in her gut wanted her to deal with the issue. If nothing else, he could offer a second opinion. "It's indirectly related to the contract." Since it challenged her ownership of the property. Why was she still talking to him? Because he almost sounded sincere when he apologized, and because she needed answers.

She was going to cave anyway, if he kept asking. Might as well get it over with. She stepped aside. "I'm not saying things are good between us. They're not. But... please take a look?" She handed him the notice.

Josh lingered in the entryway. He scanned the paperwork quietly for a few minutes, then handed it back. "You're being trolled."

"What? Why? How?"

"Patent troll. And in this case, their claim is beyond ludicrous. It's for any board game using characters of a mythological origin."

She knew the term. Patent trolls were entities who filed broad patents, then used them to demand money from anyone who created a product that fell within their sweeping definition. "Do I pay them, then?" That was typically the result. Cheaper to pay them to go away, than to fight them.

"You take them to court." Josh didn't hesitate.

There was no way she could afford that. "I saw that episode of *Silicon Valley*. Once I pay attorney fees, I'll have been better off just writing these guys a check."

"Dylan will help you. I'll help you. I'll tell you exactly what paperwork to fill out, what you need to tell the judge in court, and everything else. You can ask Liam if he's willing to accompany you, but I'll give you all the knowledge you need, to feel comfortable with fighting this."

"Why? Because that keeps my contract cleaner for your family's law firm?"

A whisper of hurt flashed across his face. "Because this is a bull-shit move on the best of days, but especially when it's directed at you. People like this need to be shut down. Besides, I'm biased and don't want to see you miserable."

At any hands other than your own. The bitter thought surged forward without her permission. "When do you have time?"

"Right now. My afternoon is free."

Please don't let me regret this. She gestured to the couch. "Can I get you a drink? There's Mt. Dew."

"I'd love that." He grinned. "Grab your laptop or something, to make notes with. We have a few hours of work ahead of us."

She returned with soda and computer in hand, and settled in next to him.

For the rest of the afternoon, he shoved her head full of so much knowledge, she thought her brain might explode. But she was grateful for the information. What felt daunting and overwhelming when Josh arrived now looked manageable. Another inconvenience at the office.

Someone knocked, and when Sydney looked up, she realized how low the sun had set in the sky. "Be right back." She crossed the room.

When she saw Dylan through the peephole, flutters danced through her heart. She flung the door open, threw her arms around his neck, and kissed him.

He wasn't kissing back. Why was he just standing there?

She stepped back, to ask what was wrong. He wasn't looking at her; he was glaring at Josh, who appeared settled and completely at ease on her couch.

Well, fuck.

THIRTEEN

Dylan had a long day. The meeting with Sydney had left his mind whirring. He worked through lunch on a different project. And work kept him late.

Then to show up here, to find...

He wasn't jumping to conclusions. He also wasn't blind. Sydney was in a great mood when she greeted him. Josh looked entirely too at home in her living room. The two people who parted very bitter ways last night seemed to be getting along great now.

Dylan couldn't ignore the slap-in-the-face feeling that came with this. Worse, no one was saying anything. "Am I interrupting?" he asked.

"Not at all. Come in," Sydney said.

"Sure." He settled into a chair.

Josh's position on the couch and the paperwork spread out around him implied he and Sydney had been cozied up, doing... something.

Dylan fought the urge to be the possessive who flew off the handle. "What did I miss?" Either everything or nothing, given that there were no protests of *this isn't what it looks like.*

Sydney stood at the edge of the living room, looking between them. She crossed one arm across her chest, to grab the other. At least she had the grace to know this was an awkward situation. Josh didn't look fazed. "I was served a Cease and Desist for a patent infringement," she said.

The news worried Dylan on her behalf. He was also more than a little hurt she'd gone to Josh. "You could have called me. Or asked Liam about it."

"He hasn't contacted me yet."

"Oh." Dylan would deal with that later.

"And Josh was more or less here when I was served, so he got caught in the beam of my initial panic."

That didn't make the situation better in any way. "I'm sorry... Did I miss something? We ended last night with him telling you to pretend we don't know each other—not the least romantic thing to tell someone after sex, but probably in the top ten—and today he just happened to be here when you were served."

"I had the afternoon off, for the chiropractor." Josh finally spoke. "I stopped by, after—"

"Nope." Dylan snapped out the word. "I don't want to hear it from you." With Sydney, he didn't have the same gnawing concern she'd feed him bullshit. Which was a disconcerting feeling. He'd never mistrusted Josh before now.

"He wasn't here when I was served," Sydney said. "He showed up a few minutes after. I swear to God, it was one of those coincidences. He said he was here to apologize. I didn't want to hear it, but he saw me freaking out and offered to help. I might not trust him when it comes to keeping his commitments, but he grew up in that law firm, and if he says he's got an answer, I believe it."

Dylan didn't miss the hurt that flashed across Josh's face, and smugness surged inside. He could be the bigger guy here, but he wasn't up for that. He gestured for Sydney to come closer. "You should sit. It's been a long day." This setup still didn't sit well with him.

Sydney drew within arm's reach, and Dylan tugged her to sit in his lap. Her warm weight pressed against him. This might have been a bad idea, with the way his body was reacting. He didn't let his dick talk for him, though. Usually. "What was this about a C and D?"

"Patent troll is claiming Sydney stole their idea," Josh said, before Sydney could reply. "I was showing her why it wasn't a big deal."

So nothing was going on. That didn't stop Dylan's jealousy the way he wanted. "Why did you two break up?" It was a tangent, and it was a little manipulative. He wanted to remind them why they weren't together.

He'd heard snippets about their split. It wrecked Josh. He'd never pried for details before, though.

Sydney leaned into him. "Josh should tell you."

"You're the one who did the breaking, though. Am I right?"

"I was the one who said we were done. I wouldn't say I was responsible for all of the breaking. And after last night, I'm not sure he realizes even now why I walked away." Her sneer was audible.

Dylan wrapped an arm around her waist. Whatever happened this afternoon, he probably didn't need to worry about it. He still wanted answers.

"I *did* come over here to apologize." Josh sounded defensive.

"For…" Sydney dragged the word out.

Josh sighed. "She broke up with me because there was a really big moment—"

Sydney cleared her throat

"—and it wasn't the first one—that, due to a series of unfortunate events, I missed."

"You missed them *all*. After about three months of dating, you never made a single important date." Sydney's aggravation was growing.

Dylan wrapped an arm around her waist, for comfort, as much as to be possessive. He was building a bigger picture about her past with Josh, and he didn't have concerns about her intentions. Josh's, though…

Dylan would hate to choose between a friend and a woman, and he'd regret if the choice was obvious and he'd never seen it coming.

"It wasn't *all*." Josh's protest was weak.

Sydney clenched her fist. "It was all. My birthday. *Your* birthday. Our graduation party. Dinner with my boss at the time. Our anniversary. Every single one of them because something came up that Laurie Hunter needed help with, and it was so critical, it had to be Josh helping, and it couldn't wait."

"What was the final straw?" Dylan was morbidly curious. "Not that I'd blame you if it was waking up one morning and realizing he was an asshole.

Sydney focused her pointed glare on Josh.

He ducked his head. "We were supposed to go to dinner, and then ring shopping after.

Ring shopping? An invisible fist clenched around Dylan's chest.

"We'd agreed not to call ourselves *engaged* until I was wearing the ring," Sydney said. "Instead of picking one out, I sat in the restaurant alone for a fucking hour, nibbling on bread and drinking my weight in water. There was no call. No hint as to where Josh was. And no answer when I tried to get a hold of him."

"I was taking notes in a last-minute critical deposition that ran over. I wasn't comfortable interrupting."

Dylan was still processing that Josh and Sydney had been essentially engaged. "You couldn't say, *give me two minutes to call my all-but fiancée and tell her why I'm late?*"

"Or better, you couldn't have told your lovely mother to get another fucking intern to take the notes?" Sydney leaned forward, anger dripping from her words.

"It was an critical client." Josh's protest was stronger than it should be.

Sydney stood, face twisted in anger. "They were *all* critical, weren't they? Every time Laurie needs you to do something, it's a *critical* thing that she only trusts you to handle. And it happened frequently enough that you missed every important date we had across more than a year. You bitch that she treats you worse than anyone else there, but apparently her fucking firm would collapse if you weren't around to meet with every important client who walks through her doors. I guess that explains why you were pulled from my contract negotiation."

Actually, it probably did, just not in the way she thought. Had Laurie Hunter worked to keep Josh and Sydney apart, for some reason?

"It's my career." Josh's voice rose.

Sydney growled. "I was supposed to be your fucking wife." She was shouting now. "And it's not your career. You don't even want to work there."

She had a good point, but Dylan wasn't going to interrupt. Sydney had this on her own. It was sexy-scary in the best way possible. It was easier to lean in that direction, than acknowledge that her rage may mean she still had feelings for Josh.

"I'm not going to half-ass a job just because it's not my final stop," Josh said.

Ouch. Wrong answer.

"No. You're just going to half-ass a relationship with the woman you said you wanted to spend your life with." Sydney's face was red.

If Dylan didn't step in now, would this come to blows? He was having trouble finding any sympathy for Josh at this moment.

FOURTEEN

Josh was digging himself into a deeper hole the longer he talked. Any minute now, his ego would stop blocking that message from his brain, and he'd apologize and back down.

He'd been in the wrong with Sydney. There were so many better ways he could have handled things back then, without sacrificing his job or his work ethic. Now was his chance to own it.

"I fucked up. I'm sorry." That wasn't as tough as he expected. It only burned a little.

Sydney raised an eyebrow. It was the least angry thing about her blotched red face, clenched jaw, and narrowed eyes.

"You could have at least tried not to wince when you'd said that." Dylan's tone was flat.

Josh swallowed a growl, as reason warred with pride in his thoughts. "What do you want me to say?"

"Until about thirty seconds ago, I would have answered, *I just want an apology*. I'd like to amend that with, *it would be nice if you meant it*." Sydney gave him a thin-lipped smile.

Josh forced himself to take a deep breath and squash the obnoxious voice shouting, *she doesn't get it*. Because she did. Sydney was observant and intelligent and fun and creative. She'd never asked him to do something like quit his job or put it in jeopardy. She wanted his time for special occasions. He was the one who had been unreasonable.

"I'm sorry. Not for every single time. I won't say that, because it's not true. But you're right that I let work get in the way. Especially on those days like our anniversary, your birthday, our engagement. I'm sorry." That felt a lot better.

"Which ones aren't you sorry for?" Sydney countered.

Josh was prepared for that. "I never wanted to meet your boss. You didn't even go that night. I was the perfect excuse."

Sydney quirked her mouth in an unformed smile. "That's true. But it's not the point."

"How long do we do this for?" Dylan asked. His flat expression implied he wasn't going to forgive as quickly.

Wish I had your girlfriend back, and then feel like a dick for wanting to break you two up? Josh pushed the question aside. "Do what?"

"This back and forth, with the awkward running into each other. The arguing. The apologies. The hints of sexual tension." Dylan didn't sound amused.

Sydney leaned back into Dylan and gave him her full attention. "I'd suggest you and I spend more time here, but…"

"That's not the best solution." Dylan finished with a sigh.

Sydney shook her head. "Exactly. I can't ask you to never go home when you and I are spending time together."

Josh was doing exactly what he swore he wouldn't. He was coming between them. "I'm not…" What? The answer stuck in his throat. He wanted Sydney back. For the last few years he'd tried to ignore their past. Tell himself they were done.

After last night… he couldn't do that anymore. But he didn't want to come between her and Dylan. It was too bad they couldn't share.

Share had a nasty flavor to it. Sydney wasn't a piece of meat. It was too bad they couldn't all be together.

"You're not what?" Dylan hadn't loosened his grip on Sydney's waist, and his patience sounded thin.

"I'm not trying to come between you." That was about as true and real as this got.

Dylan looked skeptical. "If I were someone else, would you still say the same?"

Absolutely not. "If you were anyone else, Sydney would deserve better."

"Hi. Still here." Sydney waved her fingers. "I don't remember asking either one of you who I was or wasn't allowed to date."

"Technically... I have a say in that." Dylan nuzzled her neck.

She rolled her eyes, but her smile had broken through. "All right, *technically*."

Josh missed having that with her. An ache squeezed his heart. "This is going to sound weak, because it's so cliché, but... I'd like to be friends."

"Too bad..." Sydney frowned, then shook her head. "You're still an obsessive asshole about work. But tentative friends sounds good."

That hurt. He deserved it, but it stung. She also didn't finish the thought the way she wanted to. "What were you going to say?"

SYDNEY FELT Dylan's grip tighten on her hip when she said, *Too bad...* Did he know what she was thinking? Either way, she was glad he'd stopped her from saying too much.

What Kathryn had with her two guys was enviable in a lot of ways. Not just the not having to choose, but also the adoration. If Sydney trusted Josh, she might look for that with him and Dylan, but her mind was on the physical side of things. Diving into sex with Josh, just for that rush of being with two men again, was a bad idea.

And if she wanted to do any additional experimenting, she should be on the same page as Dylan. She needed to talk to him, anyway. Any sort of long-term relationship with him meant an agreement when it came to her ex and his roommate.

She stood and grasped Dylan's fingers. "Can I talk to you in the kitchen?"

"I can just cover my ears," Josh said.

Dylan climbed to his feet. "Privacy sounds like a good idea."

Sydney looked at Josh. This had gotten complicated fast. "Could you wait in the guest room?" It was the farthest room in the apartment from the kitchen, and the door closed. She'd ask him to leave, but they needed to work some of this out now. It was going to keep coming up either way.

"Sure." Josh frowned, but headed into the other room anyway.

The instant she heard the door latch shut, she pulled Dylan into the kitchen. The words wouldn't come, though. She paced, trying to organize her out-of-control thoughts.

Dylan stepped up behind her and rested his hands on her hips, interrupting her. He didn't pull her close, but the contact was comforting and helped her focus.

"Tell me what you're thinking," he said.

That was a bad idea. First of all, she'd have to put it into words, and then those words would need to form a coherent sentence. "You first."

"I don't think that's quite fair, but all right." He spun her to face him. "Josh is my best friend. He's been there for me, even though we've only known each other for a few years."

She nodded. That didn't change the way Josh had treated her.

Dylan guided her backward, until she collided with the counter. "Even though I've never seen the side of him that you did, I don't doubt you for a second, and you didn't deserve that. I'd like to think he's not that person, but apparently at least part of him still is," he said.

"Thanks for the support." She let out a strained laugh.

"Honestly, I kind of want to pound his face in, for treating you that way. I know how much it hurt him when you left, but that's on him, not you. I can also see he's still not over you."

Sydney didn't like the skip behind her ribs at hearing that. "I'm not giving him another chance. What he did was inconsiderate, but it wasn't abusive. Maybe he'll change, maybe not. I'm not looking at any of that. I'm concerned about you and me. I can't ask you not to talk to him anymore, and that means we'll all keep running into each other."

"You'd fuck him again."

She winced, but she wouldn't deny it. "It would be a mistake. There are too many blurred lines between then and now."

"So hook him up with one of your friends." Dylan pressed closer.

Jealousy jolted through her. "No. Not after what he did to me. My point is, I only see two options." *Please don't let this be a mistake.* She was trying to be reasonable. To look at the situation from a rational perspective.

Dylan raised his brows.

"I either go out of my way to avoid him, or I learn to be friends with him." That made sense, didn't it?

Dylan dropped his hands from her hips. "I can't believe you're considering friendship, after what he did." The low seductive understanding vanished from his voice.

Was she really hearing this? It took her a moment to process the words. Was it her, or was that a hint hypocritical? "But you were okay with me fucking him? Are you considering ending your bromance with him?"

"No." The refusal carried a sharp edge.

"Because you've never personally witnessed him being that kind of an asshole, until last night?" Sydney crossed her arms. She was willing to give Josh another chance, if he was trying. Not more than one. But Dylan was making it sound like she was wrong to consider forgiveness, where it was fine for him. That was bullshit.

Dylan jammed his hands in his pockets. "You make a fair point. I suppose that means there's a third option."

"What's that?" Her gut twinged, telling her not to ask the question.

"You and I stop seeing each other." Dylan made it sound like the simplest thing ever. "Then you don't have to worry about any of it."

Disbelief rang in her ears, and she swallowed back the bile rising in her throat. What just happened? How did they go from a reasonable conversation to this? "What?"

"It's been less than a week." How did he sound so fucking calm? Was this really the same guy who insisted over and over that he wanted to see where things went? "Don't misunderstand. You're sexy, fun, intelligent, and creative as fuck. But it's obvious you two aren't over each other. I can't compete with that kind of baggage."

Now this was her fault? "But—"

"Are you going to deny it?"

"I told you I'm not going back to him." Sydney couldn't keep the defensiveness from her retort.

"That's not what I said. Look me in the eye and tell me you're over him. Say that you don't wonder *if he changed, would I give him another chance?*"

Hadn't she said that? "Why are you turning this on me?"

"I'm not." His jaw was tight, and so were his words. He raked his fingers through his hair. "But this is how it looks from my perspective. You dumped this guy three years ago. He still wants you. And now you're asking me to watch and ignore all of that, so you two can *be friends.*"

"Is this about how Josh feels now, or about how he treated me then? Or are you looking for excuses, because you don't want to admit I have a past before you?" That was probably a low blow. She was taking focus off the original issue as much as he was. "Because *this is how it looks from my perspective.*" She couldn't keep the snideness from her voice. "You want me to back off and rearrange how I do things, so I can date you but never run into Josh. But it's okay for you to stay his friend."

"Because I never—"

"Never loved him? Never stood by his side while he did something asinine? There's no one in this room who can say that. But this isn't about you, right? It's all about me. Because he was cruel to me. Because he still carries a flame for me. It seems like I'm not the one whose perspective is clouded by my past with Josh."

"He treated you wrong."

And they were back to that. "Yeah. He did. And it's up to me to say if I forgive me. You don't get to tell me that, especially if you're doing exactly the opposite of what you're advising me of." This was so bullshitty, she couldn't process it. "You know what? You're right. I like your third option. We're done."

A voice inside her head screamed, *What are you doing?* She wouldn't take it back, but she did want Dylan to. Why didn't he understand? Or was she the one being unreasonable?

He nodded. "So we agree. Finally. Have a nice life." He turned on his toe and strode from the kitchen. "You can come out now," he called. "I don't care what you do after that."

A heartbeat later, the front door opened and shut.

Sydney's heart cracked. She leaned back against the counter, waiting for the tears to fall. But there was nothing to alleviate her emptiness, disappointment, and hurt.

FIFTEEN

Sydney's mind was a jumbled wreck. What just happened? She slid to the floor, unable to process how quickly the situation deteriorated.

Josh paused in the doorway, studying her with concern. "What's going on?"

"You need to go." She couldn't deal with human interaction right now. Especially him, being considerate.

"What's wrong?" He stepped toward her.

"Now, please. I won't ask again."

He held up his hands, palms out as if surrendering, and shook his head. "You know where to find me if you need me."

She did, and that was part of the problem. She'd ignored him all this time, and suddenly he was in her life again, reminding her of both the good and bad.

The front door opened and closed for a second time.

She summoned all the numbness she could find and forced it through her veins. Her eyes stung, and her stomach hurt, but tears wouldn't come. She could only stare at the floor and ask, *What happened?*

DYLAN DIDN'T MEAN for that to fall apart. He replayed the argument over and over, as he stalked to his car and headed home.

This was the right decision. Regardless of how hard his heart and body pushed back, he was doing what he needed to. There was too much baggage between Josh and Sydney. Too much of a past to get sucked into and bogged down by.

And you're jealous.

He rolled his eyes at the counter argument. Jealous of what? Of Josh?

And maybe Sydney, a little. That thing they have…

So?

He enjoyed Sydney's company and the sex. Maybe they'd fall in love, given enough time, and maybe not. But he wasn't doing this back-and-forth thing with her and Josh. He couldn't watch her go back to a guy who treated her badly.

You mean your best friend? The guy you're pretty sure knows better, so you're staying with him?

Dylan cranked the stereo, to drown out his thoughts.

If Sydney kicked Josh out after Dylan left, he wouldn't be far behind.

Would facing him at home be worse than Josh not coming home right away? Was he still at Sydney's?

If she thought it wasn't possible to ignore Josh while he was living with Dylan, Dylan would prove her wrong. At least for a few days. He needed to get his head on straight.

When he got home, he headed straight to his room and locked the door.

Less than five minutes later, Josh knocked. "Do you have a minute? Do you want to talk?"

At least he didn't stick around at Sydney's. Dylan saw no flaws with that.

"No and no," Dylan called. The best thing for him to do was get back to life as it was before.

He tried to read. Watch movies. Do a little studying for work.

His head was too busy arguing with itself, for him to focus on anything.

He left early in the morning, but not before writing Josh a quick note. *I need to process. Give me time.*

Dylan's brain countered with, *You couldn't do the same for Sydney? She's not the one who was an asshole.*

Sydney made her decision.

After you forced her hand.

He had a long day of work ahead of him. This was a bad time to fall onto an upgraded merry-go-round of mental arguing.

Dylan managed to avoid Josh most of the day, at home and at work. By lunchtime on Thursday, he was willing to admit Sydney had at least one thing right—it was almost impossible to not run into Josh while Dylan was living with him.

And now Sydney was back in his thoughts. The empty pit in his chest that he'd tried to ignore for days throbbed with longing.

It had only been a week since he met her. Why did her not being here gnaw at him so much?

Wrong question.

The right one was, *Why did I walk away?*

Because you're jealous.

He needed to get his work done. Before he could second-guess himself, he had his phone out. He sent Sydney a quick text. *I need to talk to you.*

When she didn't answer immediately, he dove back into the tasks he got paid for.

Dylan sifted through a stack of paperwork for one of Aaron's cases, making notes as appropriate. He flipped past one page, and a line of text caught his attention out of the corner of his eye.

What did he just read?

He scanned the paragraph several times, but nothing about it looked out of place. Nagging tickled his thoughts, telling him to look closer. That wasn't helpful without more information.

He moved on.

By Friday after work, he needed to crawl out of his head before he went insane. Between ignoring Josh and not hearing back from Sydney, his brain was a hazardous wasteland.

What was he going to do with his weekend? Most of the time, he'd game with Josh. Sometimes he'd hook up, but it had been a while. There was no reason to spend his time studying for the bar or for school.

Maybe he'd go out and get drunk. Get past this funk. If he and Sydney were over, there was nothing wrong with that. Hell, they'd never officially started.

Josh was gone when Dylan got home.

Dylan didn't care where. He changed into a more casual shirt and headed out.

He was so busy, avoiding his own thoughts as he drove, he didn't realize he was near Sydney's apartment complex until the sign came into view.

What was he doing?

Turning into the parking lot apparently, rather than heading to the club.

Not that it mattered. Her car wasn't here.

He continued on his original path. What would have happened if they hadn't split? He'd have to deal with these questions eventually. If he sorted through them, could he move on?

What if Dylan and Sydney had talked past the rough spot? What if he'd watched her try to be friends with Josh? What if he'd watched her deny they were more than friends?

He clenched the steering wheel until his knuckles ached.

They could do away with that denial. Admit up front that more was possible.

That would hurt. Dylan couldn't pretend otherwise. He didn't want to be on the outside of Sydney and Josh's relationship.

Would you rather be in the middle?

His own question caught him off guard. Was that an option? Because he should mind the idea, but it felt better than anything else he'd asked about this situation all week.

Could he share? Sydney or Josh?

The alternative was cutting at least one of them out of his life.

Fuck.

When he reached the bar, it was loud inside. Distracting. Impossible to think. Perfect.

He ordered a Sprite.

You're here to drink and get laid. You're already failing on Point One.

He didn't want to leave his car here. It meant either taking a cab or calling Josh for a ride.

One song bled into the next while he nursed his drink. The girl at the other end of the bar was cute and watching him over her glass. It would take minimal effort to wave the bartender over and order her another of whatever she was drinking.

She wasn't Sydney.

He pulled a ten from his wallet for drink and tip, and walked away. Most expensive Sprite ever.

The entire drive home, his brain rehashed the same old questions. Could he watch Sydney be friendly—more—with Josh? Was he willing to see how things went if the two of them resumed their relationship?

Not if it left Dylan out. But that wasn't what Sydney had asked. Never once. It might be what she meant, but she'd been honest with him so far. She'd only asked why he held his relationship with Josh to a different standard than hers.

Back home, there was a note from Josh on the fridge that he wouldn't be back tonight.

Thank God. Not that Dylan wanted him gone forever. But he needed to sort out his head.

The knock startled him. Who was visiting at nine at night?

He opened the door to find Sydney on the other side.

Her expression was unreadable, but she looked good. Sexy. Curvy. Fuckable.

He shoved it all down. "Hey."

"I wouldn't have come up if Josh's car was here. You wanted to talk?"

The text he sent yesterday. He did want to talk. There was so much to say. Impulse swept through him. He knotted his fingers in her hair and crushed his mouth to hers.

Sydney whimpered against his lips. She planted her hands on his chest and pushed him back. "I said *talk*."

"Right." Dylan still tasted her. Her scent drilled into his thoughts. Was he supposed to go first?

You could apologize.

Sydney crossed her arms. He didn't register his gaze falling to her chest until she cleared her throat and shoved her hands in her pockets instead. "You're right. I'm not over Josh. Maybe I'm dumb for hoping he's changed, but I won't apologize for how I feel," she said.

Nothing Dylan didn't already know. He met her gaze. "Okay."

She twisted her mouth. Did she expect something else?

"Now it's your turn," she said.

"I'm sorry." For the first time in days, his brain wasn't assaulting him with questions. "I know why you're mad, and you're right. I can't expect you to hate him for something I excuse. I want to make things work between you and me. I don't know how to get past this and back to where we were."

"We start by admitting this is a really convoluted situation. The kind of thing that gets called *implausible* in books and movies. The type of fucked up that only happens in real life."

Dylan nodded. He agreed.

"And then you promise me that if we finish that kiss, it doesn't lead to us fucking and then you kicking me out."

He twitched his fingers, wanting to grab her again. Feel her. Lose himself in her. "I'm not kicking you out."

"If I asked you to kick Josh out, would you?" Her expression was still unreadable, but her voice hitched.

Dylan was caught off guard by the question. He already knew the answer, though. "No. But I also won't ask you to do anything similar. I truly am sorry."

She twisted her mouth, then caught her bottom lip between her teeth. The shift made her that much more alluring. "All right. You can kiss me."

He didn't need to hear more. He gripped the back of her neck and nipped her lips before kissing her hard.

She groaned. Fuck, he missed that sound. She grabbed fistfuls of his shirt and pressed her body closer.

Dylan was so not ready to surrender whatever this was. He didn't care what they called it, as long as he was a part of it.

He tugged her into the apartment, never breaking the kiss, and kicked the door shut behind him.

She pressed her fingers to his lips, interrupting the moment. "So are we good?"

"We're wonderful." He drew one finger into his mouth and sucked.

Her groan drilled into his thoughts. Her softness teased every inch of his body.

"We can keep talking if you want," he said. He tried to push her away, to play, but his body refused to cooperate. "But I think we'll both be happier once I get you naked and I'm worshiping those gorgeous curves of yours."

Sydney tugged his shirt over his head. "You've sold me."

He shoved up her top, pushing her bra out of the way in the process, and lowered his head. He dragged his tongue over a nipple, before drawing it into his mouth to suck and nibble.

She groaned and ground into him.

"I missed you," he murmured against her breast. "How did you get under my skin so fast?"

Sydney's giggle was another high, mingling with the pleasant cloud in his head. She snaked her hand down his chest and traced his erection through his jeans. "Pretty sure I made my luck roll."

"You're so perfectly geeky." He claimed her mouth again. He couldn't get enough. "And delicious. Did I mention that?"

"It's the bubblegum glamour. It makes me yummy."

He nipped down her neck, to bite her shoulder. "Very tasty." He pulled her shirt and bra off the rest of the way and tossed them aside.

"Are we going to be okay?" A hint of hesitation slid into her light tone.

He hoped so. He couldn't promise, though. "I think we can get back to where we were, and keep moving forward."

"Diplomatic of you." Her teasing was back. "I should stop asking tough questions until you're not looking to get laid."

He kneaded her breast, enjoying the splash of emotions on her face. "You can ask me anything you want. Now or later." The conversation didn't diminish his desire. He wanted to explore her and talking at the same time.

Sydney dragged down his zipper and stroked him through his boxer briefs. The thin layer of fabric between her skin and his was maddening in the best way possible.

"I still don't know what to do about..." She ducked her head. "About Josh. About you. I just knew I needed to see you."

Dylan should be jealous that Josh's name was still coming up, while they were half-naked. He didn't mind, though. "No one ever said the other night can't happen again." What the fuck was he saying?

She pulled back, her furrowed brow reflecting his mental question. "What did you say?"

SIXTEEN

Sydney thought she was keeping up with the conversation and Dylan's attentions, until he threw that curve ball out there. It was good. Incredible even. But she didn't know what to do with his statement.

"I don't know if I can stand to see you with other guys, but..." He muffled his words by kissing along her shoulder.

Heat and electricity raced over her skin, and desire thrummed underneath. She wasn't sure she should ask. Turned-on plus trepidation made for an odd cocktail. "But what?"

"But Josh is different."

Her breath caught in her throat. Was she upset that Dylan brought the conversation back to Josh while he was feeling her up, or grateful that she didn't have to be the one to do it? She didn't dare make any assumptions. "I don't know what you're implying. You have to spell it out for me."

"I don't know what I'm saying either, except... the other night was a lot of fun." He trailed a finger under the band of her jeans, tempting her.

She sucked in a sharp breath when he traced along her hip. "If you were upset that I'm not over him, Round Two won't make things better."

"I understand. I've had a few days to think about it." Dylan unbuttoned and unzipped her pants. "I'm okay with it." He pushed her jeans to the floor, then teased along the crotch of her panties.

This was distracting and delicious. Was she thinking clearly? The hammering of her heart against her ribs made it hard to say. He didn't hesitate with his assurance. There was no, *I think…*

She pressed into his touch. She was wet and anxious. Did she want him to finger her or fuck her? All of the above.

The front door *snicked*, and her heart leaped into her throat.

Josh walked in and paused, gaze locked on hers. He twisted his mouth. "Well, *fuck.*"

Sydney should cover up, but she didn't want to stop. Desire pulsed in her veins. This wasn't the litmus test she would have picked, but it was an interesting way to see if Dylan meant what he said.

"So you're okay with things happening again?" She forced the question out, keeping it quiet enough for his ears only. She was about to completely destroy things if she pushed wrong. She was intensely aware of Josh watching them.

Dylan rested his forehead against hers. He murmured, "What if I say *no?* At least not yet?"

That was fair. More than reasonable. "He betrayed me, and there's a lot to atone for there. You didn't. If you say *no*, that's all I need to hear."

"And if I say, *let's see where this goes?*" He brushed his lips over hers, his volume normal again.

"Where what goes?" Josh asked.

What were the odds she could have something like what Kathryn had? Two guys, all the time? She shouldn't hope for that, or that Josh would redeem himself, but she couldn't help it. Why was she so willing to make dumb mistakes when it came to Josh?

Because she knew the good, as well as the bad. And if Dylan was okay with things…

"Do you want an audience?" Dylan's question interrupted her

off-the-rail thoughts but didn't erase them. His attention was fully on her.

She caught her bottom lip between her teeth. "*God*, yes."

"Since neither of you is speaking directly to me, I need to pick between staying and going." Josh's voice was thick, as he flicked his gaze between Sydney and Dylan.

Dylan raised his brows. "You're still here. Haven't you already made that choice?"

Josh shook his head. "No. But I don't have a problem admitting I'm enjoying the view while someone makes up their mind."

Memories joined the fantasy and heat racing through Sydney's veins—the way she felt in the hentai viewing room, with Dylan's hands roaming her body, while others watched. This was a show for one, but it made her heart hammer against her ribs harder than when they'd been interrupted in the hotel.

"You should stay," she said to Josh. "But you have to promise to keep your hands to yourself." Like that was going to make the situation less of a bad idea.

The thrum of need between her legs didn't care, and, neither did she.

Josh held up his hands. "I promise the only person I'll touch is myself."

He took a seat in the chair across from them. His half-smirk sent ripples of desire along her tender nerves.

Dylan pressed his chest to her back and glided his hands up her stomach, to cup her breasts. He kneaded gently as he kissed along her neck.

She groaned and pressed back into him. His hard length dug into her back, teasing and tempting. Between that and the way Josh stroked himself through his jeans, Sydney was squirming again.

Dylan pinched one nipple, and she gasped at the sharp sting. He rolled the swollen nub between his fingers, alternating between heavy and light pressure, while he slid his other hand down her stomach, to dip below her panties.

He slipped his fingers between her folds. "*Fuck*, I love how much this turns you on." His growl vibrated against her skin.

"Me too." Her laugh ended in a moan. She bucked her hips when he brushed her clit.

He moved away, teasing along her slippery skin, but not offering relief.

When Josh unzipped and worked himself free, a new shock of desire spilled inside and throbbed between her legs.

Dylan finally moved up to the center of her need, tracing circles around her clit. He teased and coaxed, edging away each time her groans grew more punctuated.

She hovered in the knife edge of pleasure, whimpering and grinding, needing release.

Disappointment mingled with desire and release when Dylan pulled both hands away. She didn't have time to process what he was doing, before he hooked his thumbs in her panties and dragged them down to her knees.

She wriggled to drop them further

"They're good where they are." Dylan slapped her ass.

The sharp sting amplified her arousal.

He wedged a foot between hers and twisted, widening her stance. It wasn't the same as being bound, but the stretchy cotton was a tantalizing restraint.

Josh watched it all, stroking slowly, lips slightly parted.

Dylan pressed a hand into the small of her back, prompting her to bend over the couch. He trailed his hand along her behind. "*God*, I love watching your ass. And all of you, but this view is pretty incredible." He slipped two fingers between her legs and dipped into her opening.

She clenched at the easy intrusion. No witty responses came to mind. Once again, he had her tongue-tied and her thoughts racing with anticipation.

He withdrew, and she heard the tear of foil.

Dylan nudged her opening with the head of his cock, then slipped inside easily. He stretched her out and filled her up.

She pressed back into his cock, wanting him buried deep.

"*Fuck*, you feel good." He gripped her hips hard and withdrew almost all the way, before driving inside her again. The slow tease built rapidly to a hard pounding, as he slammed into her.

The combination of everything—the lingering touches on her skin, Josh stroking himself quickly, Dylan hammering against her—built back to the cusp of climax.

Dylan pried his fingers from her skin, to reach around. He sought out her clit again. When he brushed the tender nub, she squeezed around his shaft. He rubbed on either side.

The caress was enough to coax orgasm from her. She came hard, clenching his erection and the back of the couch.

He didn't ease up, and she fell into the stars that danced behind her eyelids. She watched as Josh came. That she'd been his private show was enough to draw out her pleasure.

Dylan's grunts grew shorter and more punctuated, matching his hard pace. He let out one final groan and slowed to a stop.

She didn't want to climb down from this cloud. Up here it was amazing and warm, and her thoughts were fuzzed, and out there, she might have to choose.

For now, she was only focusing on this moment. What lay beyond was too uncertain.

SEVENTEEN

Josh should have turned and walked out the instant he saw Sydney and Dylan mostly naked in the living room. A feat easier said than done, when the view was so fantastic.

When they invited him to stay, there was no way he could say *no*.

"Do I dare ask what I missed?" He wasn't content to sit in his lonely seat anymore. He wanted to be part of the tangle of limbs on the couch.

He crossed the room, and Sydney scooted her legs without hesitation to make room for him. He sat and pulled her feet in to his lap.

Dylan glanced at her, brows raised in question.

Sydney shrugged. "Part of what we discussed was about him."

Now Josh was really curious.

Dylan wrapped an arm more tightly around Sydney. "We were arguing about why it was okay for me to be friends with you but not her. Did I get that right?"

"You did." The tiny smile on her face was the pleased, content expression Josh used to adore.

Fuck, he still did. But he didn't like the knot that grew in his throat at Dylan's words. He didn't want to lose that friendship.

Or more.

What was that supposed to mean? "And the conclusion was I can watch you have sex?"

Sydney wrinkled her nose. "It sounds a lot more creepy and a lot less hot when you put it that way. I want... wanted..."

Josh could guess what she was going to say, but he didn't dare.

"To restart from the last save point," Dylan said.

"That's catchy, but barely clearer. Are you going to start hanging a tie on the front door? Spending more and more time at her place?" That was the opposite of, *let's see where this goes*, but Josh needed them to say it. To vocalize that it was okay for him to be a part of their relationship, and to what extent.

The casual sex was fun, even only watching. But he didn't want to be a third wheel, and he had zero interest in being a sentient vibrator.

Dylan furrowed his brow. "Not unless that's what you prefer."

"I don't have more specific words for it." Sydney shifted her legs so more weight rested against Josh's. *"Let's see where this goes* doesn't rule anything out."

"But you're still dating him." Josh nodded at Dylan.

Sydney twisted her lips and was silent for a moment. "And you're still living together."

"It's not the same." Josh almost fumbled on the words. It wasn't. They were roommates.

"You sure? Because friends with occasional benefits sounds similar." Sydney held his gaze.

Okay, maybe he didn't want them to define it. No reason to take anything off the table. Sydney had a friend who dated two guys. It worked fine for them, regardless of how Josh felt about Kathryn on a personal level. "All right. I'm in for this ambiguous... whatever it is. Besides, I kind of like the idea of no rules."

Sydney and Dylan both laughed.

Josh didn't get the joke. "What?"

"You hate not having rules." A playful smirk danced on Sydney's lips.

God, she was so fucking kissable. Was that allowed?

Nothing was off the table.

He leaned in and brushed his mouth over hers. Familiar sparks. A desire he thought he remembered but had completely understated.

Sydney's gasp hummed through him, and she leaned into him, pressing more weight and hunger into the kiss.

Dylan's growl snapped them apart.

Josh had to fight, to keep from tracing the faint sting that lingered on his lips.

"Is that a *no*?" Sydney leaned back into Dylan, her question tentative.

Dylan brushed her hair from her neck and licked a path up to her earlobe. Her eyelids fluttered, and she sighed.

"It's not a *no*." Dylan's voice was muffled by her skin. "It's more of a, *Fuck, I liked watching that.*"

Josh's blood heated to scalding with need. This was going to be interesting in the best way. "*Fuck*, I missed you, Tink."

Dylan traced a path down Sydney's arm, to tangle his fingers with hers. "You're staying here tonight."

"Okay." She nodded. "I didn't come prepared for that, so I don't have any extra clothes."

Josh was going to push this a little more. Not too much, but enough to get a loose idea of boundaries. "Oh darn." He kept the teasing in his sarcasm. "You might have to stroll around mostly naked for the next couple of hours."

"Crude." Dylan didn't sound upset. He handed Sydney his T-shirt. "We don't want you getting cold."

She tugged the top over her head. It was hard to tell when she was seated, but it looked like it was barely going to cover her ass.

There was a sting of jealousy that she was in Dylan's clothes, but the sight itself made up for it. "I was wrong." Josh was willing to admit it in this rare case. "That's *much* better than nude. Leaves just enough to the imagination and is easy to take off."

"Not that I mind the attention. *Wow*, I really don't. I almost don't know what to do with it." Sydney's chuckle was playful. "But

I'm not a fuck-all-night kind of girl, so if you two are going to get it on tonight, I'm the one who gets to watch next round."

Josh gripped her fingers and kissed the tips. "I think we can behave for at least a couple of hours."

"I guess if you two are out, so am I." Dylan gave an exaggerated sigh, but he was smiling.

"In that case, I'm going to ruin the moment even further," Sydney said. "What am I going to do about this patent troll thing?"

"We'll write up a reply and hand it off to our friend." Dylan paused with a frown. "A different friend. One who will call you back."

Josh liked the plan, but it had a teensy, tiny, glaring flaw. "That's a huge legal gray area."

"We won't be acting against our client or the firm," Dylan said.

"Hence *gray area*." Was this another of those instances that had upset Sydney before? Putting work before them? No. This was actually toeing a line, not putting in a few extra hours at work. But Josh wanted to help, and they wouldn't handle the actual interaction, just point her in the right direction. "I'm not saying we shouldn't. We just need to draw that line, for everyone's safety."

"I'm grateful for all of it. Don't get yourselves in trouble, but thank you for everything," Sydney said.

Dylan grinned. "Good. We'll get you sorted in the morning."

They tripped from one subject to another, talking long into the night. When all three of them were yawning as much as anything else, Josh did something he was reluctant to do. "We should get to bed."

Which meant letting them vanish into Dylan's room, because they were the couple, and Josh would go sleep alone.

"I'm good here for a little longer." Sydney's protest was cut short by another yawn. She blinked several times. "I promise."

Dylan nodded. "Me too. Sleep is for the week, right?"

Josh remembered that mantra all too well, from the last several years of school. "Exactly." This was delaying the inevitable. For now, no matter how much he wanted otherwise, he was that third wheel.

He had another chance, though. An opportunity to earn Sydney's friendship again, even if it wasn't more, and he was going to reach for that for all he was worth.

JOSH'S NECK screamed in protest at the angle he'd slept on it, forcing him awake. He pried his eyelids open, his body sending mixed signals of pleasure and pain.

A warm weight pressed against him. Partly Sydney's and partly Dylan's.

They'd fallen asleep on the couch, in an awkward jumble. *Fuck*, he'd missed waking up with her bare skin next to his. The entire night lingered fresh in his thoughts. He'd known he wasn't over Sydney, but spending this kind of time with her was a reminder of just how much he missed her company.

And things were getting back to normal with Dylan. That was nice. A few days of not speaking was too much for Josh.

He couldn't get up without disturbing them, but he needed to be in a different position. He extracted himself as carefully as possible, not surprised when both of them moaned and stirred.

Josh left them to find their own consciousness. He took a quick shower with the water on as cold as he could stand. He needed to keep his head clear, until he knew how this morning would play out after last night.

He ventured back into the living room, to catch the tail end of Dylan talking.

"…home, pack an overnight back, and we'll pick you up in an hour for breakfast."

They were making plans for their weekend. *We'll…* that implied Josh was a part of those plans. He liked that. "What if I don't want to go for breakfast?" He couldn't help teasing.

Sydney glanced at him over her shoulder, mouth twisted. "Who are you, and what have you done with Josh?"

He struggled to keep his expression straight. "Maybe I've changed. A guy can't stay a diner-omelet junkie his entire life."

"Maybe not, but you haven't given it up yet," Dylan said.

Josh's smirk broke through. "Yeah, all right. I'm in."

They sent Sydney on her way, and Dylan vanished into his room.

Thank God Josh didn't have anything pressing today. He was focused intently on what happened last night. The sex. The words exchanged. What it all meant...

And the question that had nagged him for the last week, that he hadn't been able to resolve with Dylan avoiding him—what was going on with him and Dylan? Things were awfully rocky, for not letting this come between them.

Dwelling on things without talking them through wouldn't get Josh anywhere. Despite his arguments against helping Sydney with this patent-troll bullshit, he'd already looked things over with her. It would take ten minutes to type up a basic letter to the opposing party, and then he could hand it off to her.

Josh was wrapping up, when he heard doors opening from the direction of Dylan's bedroom. He padded to the room and leaned against the doorframe.

Dylan was pulling on a shirt. It was always an incredible sight.

"Are we good?" Josh asked.

Dylan grabbed a pair of socks from his drawer. "I don't know. We're not the same as we were a week ago."

Josh tempered his irritation. On the one hand, he hadn't done anything to Dylan. His actions three years ago shouldn't impact their lives now.

Then again, Josh had pulled that bullshit with Sydney the first night they were back together, and if he were in Dylan's shoes, he'd be furious to see someone else trying to force Sydney out of his life.

"Thank you for sticking with me," Josh said. "I won't make you or Sydney regret it."

Dylan finally paused to look at him. "That's what I'm banking on. No third chances."

Josh didn't care for the ultimatum, but there wasn't a lot of room for argument. "All right."

"Cool. So, last night. Hot, right?"

Except for the part where Josh was an outside observer. He didn't have an issue with watching; it was that there was no other option that he was wavering on. "Superhot."

"Gotta go get Sydney. Meet you there." Dylan clapped Josh on the shoulder as he brushed by.

How long was Josh willing to play third wheel, to figure this out?

Longer than a weekend. But only for Sydney... and Dylan.

EIGHTEEN

Dylan liked intertwining his fingers with Sydney's as he drove them to the diner. A light and constant thrum flowed between them.

He shouldn't be okay with the arrangement last night. Logic and a lifetime of living in reality said, if he kept seeing Sydney and let Josh be a part of their relationship, it would end badly.

There should be reservations. He should hesitate.

It all felt all right, though. Would that change if they continued? If he found himself in the same place Josh was last night —watching?

Desire lit along his skin at the thought of sitting back and observing while Josh and Sydney fucked.

He shoved the image aside. If he lingered on the thought too long, he'd be fighting an uncomfortable erection.

He and Sydney reached their destination. As he joined her on the sidewalk, his hand found hers again with little thought.

"I haven't been here in ages." Sydney's voice was soft.

Dylan wasn't surprised. He and Josh came here all the time. It was Josh's favorite place. "They have new menus."

"Did they add anything good?"

"They didn't add anything. They just printed new menus."

She laughed, and her posture relaxed. "At least I know what I'm getting, then."

Inside, Josh waved from the booth in the back of the dining room.

"New upholstery, too." Sydney bounced once as she slid into the seat. "I barely recognize the place."

As Dylan took the spot next to her, Josh passed his phone across the table. "I drafted you a response letter, for the Cease and Desist," Josh said.

"My hero." Sydney pretended to swoon. "Email it to me? Or this friend of yours? And thank you."

That almost made Dylan jealous. What happened to all the protests? But even with that thought, he was happier that Sydney was getting what she needed and Josh was involved.

Was that weird or normal?

Dylan didn't know anymore. He wanted this to be what it was. Could he have that?

"I've been wondering something." Sydney angled herself in her seat, one leg on the bench, so she was turned between them. Her leg pressed against Dylan's. "How do you go from roommates to, *Be my plus one at this important dinner?*"

Josh shrugged. "We just did."

"No. There has to be more to it than that."

"You did know he was into girls *and* guys?" Dylan rested a hand on her calf.

Her smile came easily. "That was part of what made the threesome idea more fun. But there has to be a story to it. You know I love a good story."

"There's really not." Josh leaned back as Mel, the waitress, brought them coffee and water. "I told her we all wanted our usual."

Mel looked at Sydney. "Lovely to see you again, dear. We missed you."

"I missed you too. And the usual is great."

Mel made sure they were set, and walked away.

"I'll give." Dylan prepared his coffee and took a tentative sip.

Perfect. "There's technically a story, but it's not the kind of thing that brings audiences to their knees in laughter or tears. He needed a date for some event Laurie set him up for, and didn't want to go."

Josh leaned in. "Dylan said, *I'll go. That ought to ruffle some feathers.* And I liked the sound of it."

"Which led to, *You know what else would raise eyebrows? If we slept together.*" Sydney watched them over the top of her mug as she sipped her coffee.

Dylan liked the amusement in her voice. "Not quite. That was more like, I was horny, he was horny, and it happened more than once." The explanation sounded too casual. Like a brush off. But it was the truth.

So why did Dylan wish there was more to it?

"You need to work on your storytelling skills," Sydney said. "Try this on for size. The strong, handsome warrior had suffered a long, hard day of work. His bones were weary—"

"And his bone needed attention." Josh smirked.

Sydney rolled her eyes and shook her head, but her smile never wavered. "Not what I was going for. You didn't want to tell the story before. Have you changed your mind?"

"He hasn't," Dylan said. "I'd rather hear your version."

"Because your bone needs attention?" Sydney leaned back in her seat.

Dylan followed her gaze to Mel, who had just arrived with their food. Kitchen-sink omelet for Josh, chocolate-chip pancakes for Dylan, and apparently a grilled-cheese sandwich for Sydney.

"My bone got attention." Dylan was sparse with the syrup, but glad there was a lot of butter for his pancakes. "I'm cocky enough to believe I can have the same again, whether or not Josh spins his Beavis and Butthead version of our sex life."

Sydney held up a finger, worked her jaw, then dropped her hand again. "So, one—pretty sure neither of them ever got laid. And two —which one does that make you?"

Dylan pulled his shirt up over the back of his head and stuck his arms in the air, bent at the elbows and out to his sides. "Are you threatening me?"

"Oh my God." Sydney laughed. "I don't know if I needed to know how good you are at that."

"You needed to know. Because even when he's being asinine, he still does it perfectly." Josh's retort almost sounded affectionate. It wasn't enough to hide his irritation, though.

Dylan would bet it was because people were staring. He didn't care. He straightened his clothes. Inspiration struck. Did he have a lightbulb over his head, like in a cartoon? "You know what we need to do? Put our conversation from the other day to the test. See whether or not the three of us make a good questing party."

Josh seemed to consider this. "Someone has to DM. I nominate Tink."

"I accept. But two people don't make for much of a party..." Sydney drummed her fingers on the table. "Ooh, I can call Kathryn."

Josh scowled.

That was curious. "Who's Kathryn and what did I miss?"

"She's my best friend. You'll love her," Sydney said.

Josh's scowl deepened. "And she doesn't care for me."

Sydney pursed her lips and narrowed her gaze. "Do you blame her? You were an ass to me."

Josh clenched his jaw.

"This is your chance to prove her wrong." A sweet hint wove into Sydney's reply. She looked at Dylan again. "I promise. And you'll love her boyfriends, too."

Wait. *Boyfriends?* Did Dylan hear that right? "Call her. You're right. Two isn't really enough for a big campaign."

"I have the perfect one." Sydney grabbed her phone, poked the screen, then stuck it to her ear. "I've been sitting on it for way too long. Hey, it's me." Her tone and attention shifted. "What are you all doing today? ... You up for a game? ... More than just us. You know how I told you about that guy I met?"

She'd been talking about Dylan?

"That's the one." She frowned. "Both of them... It's just a game... I'm dating his roommate. It's going to happen."

The laughter faded from Josh's eyes, and his expression went flat.

There was a lot implied in Sydney's half of the conversation. Josh being relegated to *roommate* was probably the most glaring.

This was getting complicated. The one thing Dylan wanted to avoid. But he wasn't interested in walking away. Not yet.

Sydney set up a time with Kathryn, and gave her Dylan and Josh's address.

After breakfast, they headed back to the apartment to meet up, with a quick stop to buy snacks and soda.

When everyone showed up, introductions were passed around. Kathryn and Josh glared at each other, and the guys with her didn't seem to care for him either. Kathryn was slender, with dark hair and light eyes, and there was a fluidity to her movement that Dylan recognized. It was similar to Josh's.

When Sydney said Kathryn was an Aikido blackbelt and taught at a local dojo, that explained that.

Evan was the all-American blond boy, solid wall of muscle. He looked like the kind of guy who'd be cast as *Perfect Rebound Boyfriend Number One* on any TV show. He also looked like he was deciding if he could take Josh.

Trevor stayed close to Kathryn, arms crossed. He had dark hair, a wiry build, and looked like he'd bite anyone who came near her.

Especially Josh.

Sydney wasn't kidding about tension.

"Should we roll out characters?" Dylan would love a little bit of small talk. Fun. Build-up. If he was reading the room right at all, they needed to skip those at least until the glaring died down.

Sydney's tiny frown caught him off guard. "Do you need to?" she asked. "We can, definitely. Everyone else has a favorite already, but we can give you some extra stats, to put you…"

At their level. "I have one. I just figured, with a new campaign and since we've never played together before, you'd want that."

She shook her head. "I'm good to use existing. I'll adapt the story as we go. I just need your stats."

Dylan was impressed. And a bit annoyed with everyone else that they seemed to expect that answer. He'd never played with a DM before who didn't put hours into planning a campaign. And then reminded the players every time they screwed with a carefully crafted tale.

They settled around the living room like there was a divider wall running down the middle. Kathryn, Evan, and Trevor were distinctly keeping to their side.

Dylan had a barbarian character he loved to play. Dumb as a sack of rocks, but built like a tank. He amused himself with that pun.

When Josh said he was playing a healer, Kathryn laughed, and another round of glares was exchanged.

Kathryn played a monk, Evan a ranger, and Trevor a battle mage.

None of this seemed to surprise Sydney.

"We ready?" Sydney asked.

There was a series of nods and grunts. Dylan wanted to knock some heads together at the lack of enthusiasm, but he was willing to watch and wait.

Sydney wove a stunning setting of the countryside their party traveled through. With each question she asked, she received a round of one-word replies.

Josh continued to exchange glares with Kathryn. Sydney's tone wilted with each passing minute. Half an hour in, Dylan could almost hear her asking herself, *Why did I think this was a good idea?*

He was sick of this. Not of her. He suspected Sydney's story had a lot of potential, if everyone would just play.

"You reach the edge of a forest." Sydney spoke in a near-monotone. "It stretches endlessly in front of you, as far as you can tell. The trees are green and dense and shit. You can continue on the road that goes around the forest, but you don't know how far the tree line extends." She gave a little sigh. "You can go through the forest, but the foliage is so overgrown, you can't see more than a few feet ahead."

"Can we camp for the night and wait to see if things are better in full sunlight?" Kathryn asked. It was the longest sentence she'd spoken since she arrived.

Josh shook his head. "I'm not camping with my back to that forest."

"What do you want to do instead?" Trevor narrowed his gaze. "If we go into the forest, more our backs are exposed."

"Then we'll backtrack enough to establish a perimeter." There was a bite in Josh's reply.

Evan made a disgusted grunt. "Do you even know what that means? We pushed hard to get this far this fast."

"No. We pushed hard because no one wants to make any decisions." Now Josh was just being snide. "I'm making a decision. I want to backtrack and set up where we have a good view of all of our surroundings."

Sydney's scowl deepened with each new retort.

This was so not better than the one-word answers.

Dylan was done. "I check for traps."

The swivel of heads in his direction was almost comical. He bit back the laugh.

"You don't have that skill in your character class," Trevor said.

"I can still look around, right? I'm capable of scanning the forest?" Dylan looked at Sydney.

"I…" She looked between the character sheets and him. "Your perception is three."

Dylan didn't care. "I want to check for traps."

"Where?" Sydney picked up the dice and rolled her thumb along them in her palm.

"In the forest." At least he could see that.

Kathryn furrowed her brow, but she wasn't glaring anymore. "The *entire* forest?"

Dylan nodded. "I'm also not a very bright barbarian." His intelligence was five. "Me check for trap. Keep safe," he said in a booming baritone.

Sydney giggled, and Trevor rolled his eyes. Everyone watched Dylan with either curiosity or amusement. Perfect.

Sydney rolled the dice and stared at Dylan, mouth slightly open, when it came up twenty.

She rolled again. Another twenty.

One more time, and this time it came back a one.

She puffed out her cheeks and blew out a long breath. "Okay. You may not be the brightest or most observant barbarian ever, but you do have a fighter's instinct and an intense love of gold. Something calls to you from the middle of the forest. The ancient lessons of your ancestors say it's probably gold. Or a dragon. Or a dragon protecting gold. Any of the above would pretty much make your month."

"Let's keep pushing into the forest." All of Kathryn's antipathy was gone.

"Agreed." Josh sat straighter, and his scowl vanished. "Are we rested enough to continue?"

Evan looked between them. "We should be good for a couple more hours. Are we certain?"

"*Yes*," Josh and Kathryn spoke in unison.

Dylan just wanted to make everyone laugh a little. He hadn't expected an instant one-eighty in their attitudes. What had them so eager to push ahead where they hadn't agreed before?

"How close is this dragon?" Trevor's shoulders relaxed, and he leaned in, elbows on his knees.

"He's in the forest." Sydney looked like she was fighting a smile.

So worth it.

Evan drummed his fingers on his knee. Whatever Kathryn and Josh knew, her guys didn't seem to. "If I check for traps, will I find him?" Evan sounded doubtful.

"You can try, but he's not a trap." Sydney was definitely enjoying this.

Josh laughed. "Because your barbarian is so dumb, he doesn't know the difference."

"Guilty as charged." Dylan knew the teasing was friendly, and Sydney's pleased look was worth anything that came next.

"Okay," Evan said. "The barbarian takes the lead. He can

follow his *ancestral instinct* and be the front line if anything ambushes us. Kathryn can watch our rear."

Josh quirked an eyebrow. "So, same as always."

Kathryn blushed. "It's a good view."

"Do you want to do any more prep before you go in?" Sydney asked.

Dylan's character might be stupid, but he wasn't *that* into the role playing. "Yes."

"No." Josh and Kathryn were in agreement again.

Sydney looked at Evan and Trevor, who shrugged.

"Apparently they know something we don't," Trevor said. "We side with the sexy monk."

Dylan knew when he was outvoted, and his curiosity was screaming for answers. "I'm in. Let's go."

NINETEEN

They wandered for what Sydney said was a couple miles, with Dylan in the lead. The sun was setting, and the longer they traveled, the harder it was to see their path.

And then a light broke through the trees. Dylan led them toward the glow. The group reached a clearing and squinted in the brightness.

Dylan was as on edge as Trevor and Even, as they waited for their eyes to adjust.

Kathryn and Josh were already striding forward.

"There's a building in the clearing that looks like a Disney castle," Sydney said. "Spires stretching toward the sky, and opaque crystal walls glinting at you. You've never seen a building so stunning or so completely impractical.

"A woman strolls around the corner. She's tall and slender, and it's difficult for you to determine her age. When you look closer, if you squint, her form seems to shimmer and fade, and you see the hulking shape of a grand dragon wrapped around the building, its scales the same color as her vibrant leather outfit."

It sounded stunning, but Dylan didn't see why this was enough to make Josh and Kathryn get along.

Josh looked like he was fighting a smirk. "I stroll forward and bow. Great and mighty goddess, we're here out of respect, and not to intrude."

"I join him." Kathryn nudged Evan and Trevor. "We all do. Thank you for gracing us with your presence, Mistress."

"Me too?" Dylan was almost bursting from curiosity.

Sydney's smile was mischievous. "Inside my home are wonders from around the universe. Technology, knowledge, weapons… Treasures you've only imagined. To gain access, you must each complete a quest. Because you're a group, if every single one of you doesn't pass your individual quest, you won't be allowed inside."

That sounded… vague. "What kind of a quest?" Dylan asked.

"It will vary from person to person." Sydney rattled the dice in her hand. She rolled. "And your mage goes first."

"I didn't agree to this." Trevor held up his hands.

Kathryn gave him a sweet, wide-eyed stare. "Please?"

"All right." Trevor's sigh was exaggerated. "What's my quest?"

Sydney rolled again, then checked something on her phone. "You have to sing us the song of your choice."

"What?" His tone went flat. "Why would I do that? What's inside that's so great? Are all the quests like this?"

"Do you forfeit?" Sydney studied him. "Because you cost your entire party if you do."

He looked at Kathryn. "You have some idea what's in there. What's so great that you're dying to do this?"

Dude was kind of a whiny dick.

She pursed her lips. "We don't know until we go inside."

"Of course she has an idea," Josh said. "But if you're not going to play, why are you here?"

Evan clenched his fist and glared at Josh.

Kathryn rested a hand on Evan's leg, but her attention was on Trevor. "Play the fucking game, please?" Her voice was sugary sweet.

Dylan wasn't sure how he felt about her boyfriends, but he could see why she and Sydney were close friends. Kind until the situation called for otherwise, and then the sweetness faded.

"We all have to do something similar." Josh's good mood was fading too. "Are you a coward?"

Trevor raised an eyebrow. "Are you the kind of asshole who thinks he can goad me into something by calling me names?"

"Are you done being contrary?" Evan asked.

Trevor shrugged. "I guess. It's roleplaying, right?"

Dylan doubted that was the real reason for the attitude. He was tempted to deck the guy.

"The dragon wants to know what song you choose, and if you'd like accompanying music," Sydney said.

Trevor shook his head. "I've got this. The song is a surprise."

He sang "Don't Stop Believin'" by Journey. It was acapella and amazing. Dude had an incredible voice.

Now Dylan really wanted to deck him.

Until Sydney clapped, glee on her face. It was worth the headache. "Your barbarian is next," she said.

And Dylan was going to do whatever it was he was asked, without argument, because doing otherwise was ridiculous. No one could follow an act like Trevor's anyway.

"You have to tell a joke," Sydney said.

He stared at her in disbelief. "A... what now?"

Kathryn let out a low growl.

Josh clenched his jaw.

"A joke. Tell a joke. That's your quest." Sydney didn't look fazed.

If he was going to do it, he might as well get it over with. "Uh..." His mind was a blank. He'd heard hundreds of jokes in his life, and some were even funny. It figured that only one came to mind now. Well, aside from a punchline he never remembered the beginning of. *You think I asked for a twelve-inch pianist?*

He sighed. "What did Cinderella say when she got to the ball?"

"What?" Sydney raised an eyebrow.

"Nothing. She just gagged a little."

Everyone groaned, except for Josh, who snorted with a tiny laugh. Thank God for him.

"I don't think that counts," Evan said.

Sydney fixed her gaze on him. "The dragon hears your complaint and wonders why you're making this more difficult for your own party. The dragon would also like to point out the requirement wasn't to tell a *funny* joke, and that you were trying not to laugh despite your protests. And by the way, you're next."

Evan had to recite a line from his favorite movie... in character. He did a fantastic Casper Van Diem impersonation, though Dylan wasn't sure how he felt about anyone calling *Starship Troopers* their favorite movie.

Kathryn had to dance. If Dylan had landed on that one after that stripper routine last weekend, he probably would have made Sydney prove that was really what he'd rolled.

There was a fluidity in Kathryn's movements that reflected her skill with Aikido. It wasn't a stunning ballet, but it was amazing to watch.

Dylan had been wrong. She definitely followed up Trevor's act, and blew it out of the water.

And then it was Josh's turn.

Sydney scrunched up her face as she stared at the dice. "Apparently, you've picked the wildcard."

"What does that mean?" Dylan asked. He could see why Kathryn and Josh wanted to visit the dragon. This was ridiculous, but it was fun. With Trevor's tantrum out of the way, the mood in the room was lighter.

"It's quester's choice... sort of," Sydney explained. "He has to pick from one of the tasks someone who came before him already performed."

Josh twisted his face in consideration. "What if I pick nothing?"

Sydney looked amused. "Then the dragon will get angry, point out you know that's not how this works, and eat you before letting the rest of your party in."

"I'll die?"

"If you're lucky." There was no irritation in Sydney's voice. Her smile never faded.

Josh looked around the room. "What should I pick?"

Everyone had a slightly different opinion.

Josh stood, stretched his arms over his head, and rolled his neck. "I pick the dance." He extended his arm toward Sydney. "But only if the dragon dances with me."

She shook her head and pushed his hand away. "The dragon doesn't dance."

Dylan had the feeling this particular quest hadn't come up before.

"Maybe the dragon shouldn't hand out quests she's not willing to complete herself," Josh teased.

Her smile grew. She grasped his fingers, and he tugged her to her feet. A few swipes on his phone, and a tinny dance beat filtered into the room.

Where Kathryn was like liquid given life, Josh was something rougher. He was just as graceful, but it was fucking dirty. Grinding, groping, and on top of it all, correcting for any misstep Sydney made, so she was part of the entire thing.

Dylan's skin hummed, heat pouring through his veins, as he watched the two of them. There was no jealousy. Only the desire to not have three other people in the room.

Trevor cleared his throat. "Will the healer be fucking the dragon in front of us, or can we see what this is all about now?" His tone was light and playful.

Sydney's skin darkened. Josh spun her one more time and held her hand until she was seated again, before returning to his own chair.

"The dragon is pleased. And appropriately humbled. She lets you in the building." Sydney was almost glowing. *That* was magic. "It's a library and a museum all in one. Vast and glorious, and liter-ally encompasses anything you can imagine. You're allowed to explore anywhere. There are rooms set aside for you to stay the night and rest in. When you're ready to continue your journey, you'll be given access to the armory, where you'll each receive a weapon or other gift, suited to your journey."

Evan's face lit up. "Can we go there first?"

"You can," Sydney said. "But remember, when you step through that door, your time here is done. You'll collect your reward, and be transported to another plane. So don't do it unless you're ready to leave."

They played for several hours, and the mood stayed light. They ordered pizza in the afternoon, and stayed immersed in the game until almost midnight, when Kathryn announced she had a morning class and really needed to leave.

Dylan didn't remember the last time he'd had this kind of silly, careless, incredible fun, playing a game.

"Should we do this again next weekend?" Kathryn asked.

He was ready to say *of course*, when he saw the whisper of a frown cross Sydney's face.

ONLY ONE THING was making Sydney hesitate to answer Kathryn's question. A *yes* was more than the start of a new gaming schedule with friends. If she kept hanging out with Josh like this, she wouldn't be able to ignore the pull. This was more than friendship. She didn't know why she'd thought she could pretend otherwise.

She landed on, "Probably. I'll let you know."

"Perfect."

Kathryn and her boyfriends said *goodbye* and were on their way.

Dylan closed the door behind them and turned back to Sydney. "Why did you hesitate?"

Of course he had to ask her that. She couldn't keep this in her head. It was the kind of decision she didn't get to make on her own. She knew how she felt, but that didn't mean Dylan would agree.

Or Josh.

Did she want to have this conversation with both of them at the same time?

That made more sense than not. The way they both stared at her made her brain stall.

"I can go wait in my room, if you need to discuss this." A whisper of hurt lined Josh's voice.

Sydney didn't blame him. She didn't want him to be here as just a back-up penis. She wanted…

She wanted what Kathryn had. It wasn't that easy, though. All of this was lessening the ache of why she and Josh broke up, but it wasn't erasing the memory.

And they were still staring at her.

"I don't have a problem with you saying whatever's on your mind in front of both of us," Dylan said. "There are so many blurred lines here, it would be nice to erase a few and draw new ones. Maybe... more inclusive ones."

Sydney summoned her courage—the words weren't forming, so hopefully this would work as an alternative—and looked at Josh. "I know you're sick of hearing this, but I still have doubts. You hurt me. When you say you won't do it again, you believe it. But I need to as well..." She bit her bottom lip. This wasn't what she wanted to say, but it was too late to change course. "I'd rather stop looking over my shoulder, waiting for a fuck up to happen."

"That does make friendship easier." Dylan's tone was impossible to decipher.

She didn't know Dylan well. They had fun together. He'd proven over and over that he was sincere, and the only time he'd let her down was with that damn blind spot he had for Josh. Which— Sydney had one too.

"What if we tried what Kathryn, Trevor, and Evan are doing?" That was both easier and far harder to say than she expected.

She swore her heart stopped when Dylan raised his eyebrows.

She didn't know to interpret that. *Please, don't let this be a mistake.* "What if all three of us were dating?"

"Why did you phrase it that way?" Josh asked.

She shook her head. "I don't understand."

"You didn't ask about us dating you. You said *all three of us.*"

"The two of you are more than friends." She couldn't ignore it. She didn't want to. "It doesn't matter what you tell me or yourselves."

"We're not..." Dylan trailed off.

Josh gave a scoffing laugh. "Aren't we?"

This entire idea terrified Sydney, but now that she'd said it aloud, it also raced over her with sparks of anticipation. There were so many places things could go wrong. Josh and Dylan could decide they only wanted each other. Josh could make the same mistakes he had before. She and Dylan might realize they didn't like each other as they spent more time together.

And at this moment, it all seemed worth it. Heartbreak would tear her apart—she already felt it—but if everything went right...

TWENTY

"Yeah, we are more than friends." When Dylan spoke, Sydney's breath hitched.

He crossed the distance to Josh in a few short strides, grabbed a fistful of Josh's shirt, and crushed their mouths together.

Sydney bit the inside of her cheek, and heat spilled through her at the intense affection they radiated. It was so obvious they cared for each other.

She didn't want to interrupt, but she did want to get in on the kissing. The push and pull between Dylan and Josh sang in her veins and danced on the tip of her tongue.

When Josh looked at her, the desire in his gaze clenched around her heart. He gripped her wrist tight and tugged her close. A sliver of apprehensive mingled with her desire.

She needed to give him enough trust to make this work. Not all of it. Not yet.

Who was she kidding? Regardless of what she told herself, her heart was already going to shatter if things went south again.

Might as well enjoy the ride.

The way he kissed her, hard and hungrily, teeth nipping her lips, made it easy to shove her doubt into a box and lock it in the back of her mind. God, she'd missed this with Josh. His mouth on her skin numbed the ache of longing that pinged behind her ribs.

He kneaded her breast through her shirt. She loved the rough intensity in each touch. The need. The frantic groping. She melted into him, wanting to be as close as possible, and his erection dug into her stomach.

This was what the dance earlier promised, but couldn't deliver on with an audience. This time, they didn't have to stop.

"This is better than watching the two of you dance." Dylan's words echoed her thoughts. He kissed along the back of her neck and shoved her shirt up, sliding his palms along her bare skin.

Sydney reached back to feel more of him, and he pressed into her touch, his cock jerking though his jeans against her hand.

Being the filling in this sandwich was becoming one of her favorite things.

Josh spun her away, startling her, and dragged his hands down her arms to capture her wrists, before she could question him.

She tugged, and he gripped her tighter. The resistance made her smile.

He nipped her earlobe, his breath hot on her skin. "You got to call the shots before. Our turn now."

Her pulse screamed through her veins with anticipation, and her heart hammered against her ribs. His throaty promise combined with the way Dylan studied her, like she was lunch, made her squirm in the best possible way.

Dylan undid her jeans, and tugged them and her panties down to her knees.

Apparently it *was* possible to crank her anticipation higher, because every time he did this, something delicious came next. And then so did she.

He knelt in front of her, and she whimpered before he even touched her skin. He kissed along her bare hip, her stomach, the top of her thigh.

When Dylan licked along her slit, she groaned and pressed into his face. Josh kept her from moving more, which increased her desire with each new swipe of Dylan's tongue.

He wrapped his lips around her clit, and sucked.

Her gasps grew louder, and the thrust of her hips more frantic, as he alternated touches.

She clenched her fists and toes when she came, grinding into Dylan's face until it was too much, then jerking away.

Dylan rose and leaned past her, sandwiching her again, while he kissed Josh.

Her body heated to flaming at them sharing her taste. She didn't know which of the three of them was moaning louder, but it was an amazing chorus.

Josh and Dylan broke apart, and Josh spun her back to him again. She'd worry about all of it making her dizzy, but the two men already had her head twisted and fuzzed in the best possible way.

"I don't like not being able to touch you." Josh stripped her shirt off, then kissed her. "I love seeing your gorgeous body," he shoved her pants the rest of the way off, "but hate holding myself back." He dragged his fingers up her back, pulling her into him. "Now that I have you again, you should know I don't ever plan to let you go."

His words and the way he held her tight spilled through her with love, but a whisper of fear. If she wasn't careful, she could fall into this and forget the last three years never happened. That they'd never been apart.

Was that a good thing or a bad one?

"Come here." Josh grasped her fingers, and led her into the bedroom.

She heard Dylan follow. She trusted him to join in or watch as he wanted.

And she was so wrapped up in Josh right now, it was scary.

He stripped out of his clothes, claiming a kiss between each discarded article, then scooted onto the bed and pulled her with him. "I want to watch you ride me," he said. "I want to see as much of you as possible as I slide inside you. When you come."

Sydney didn't have a witty response, or any at all beyond straddling his legs. He skated his palms up her thighs. The way he raked his gaze over her, she felt like the most beautiful woman in the world.

She tried to tease, hovering over him, the head of his cock nudging her opening.

He gripped her thighs, and laughed through clenched teeth. "We have so much time to play. Later." He thrust up, filling her up and spreading her open. "I've waited too long to feel you wrapped around me, knowing it would last."

Sydney lowered herself onto him, sighing with pleasure as he was buried himself inside her.

He set a slow, even pace, rocking against her. Holding her gaze with his own.

The mattress shifted with a new weight, and Dylan knelt next to Sydney. He'd shed his clothing as well, and his cock stood at attention. He crushed his mouth to hers while he covered her hand and lowered it to his shaft.

Sydney didn't need to be prompted twice. She stroked Dylan's hard length while she moaned into his kisses. Josh slid inside her, hammering harder and faster with each passing moment.

Dylan dragged a thumb over one of her nipples, and she gasped. She didn't know which way to turn, to enjoy ever touch. She tumbled into the blend of it all. Josh pounding against her. Dylan teasing and kissing her.

When Josh pressed his thumb to her clit, she whimpered. He stroked the still-tender nub, coaxing her toward another climax.

She lost track of who was doing what. All she knew was it was so much *everything*. She hovered near orgasm, falling into a delicious haze when Dylan pinched her nipple and rolled it between his fingers.

She screamed when she came, clenching hard around Josh, forgetting for a moment that she still gripped Dylan.

As the edge softened, her desire lingered. She resumed stroking Dylan, keeping time with Josh's thrusts.

Their grunts and groans were musical. Dylan's grip on her breast tightened, and his breathing grew more shallow. She squeezed just a little with each stroke.

He came hard, coating her hand, her thighs, and Josh's stomach.

Josh gripped her thighs tighter. He was close too. He hammered against her, skin slapping skin, squeezing her legs as he spilled inside her.

Everything slowed, except for the euphoria filling Sydney's head. She could stay here forever, wrapped in this fantasy-come-to-life, pressed between two incredible men.

And as long as the post-coital giddiness lingered, she could ignore the nagging voice that insisted it was only matter of time before Josh fucked up again.

TWENTY-ONE

J osh was still buzzing from the weekend. It was like it used to
be, but better. He was still having a little trouble believing it,
but it had been incredible.

"Mr. Hunter. My office, now." His mother's sharp tone as she
strolled by his desk caught him off guard.

Whatever she was upset about wasn't going to ruin his morning.
He grabbed a pen and notepad and followed.

"What's wrong with you?" she asked the instant the door swung
shut behind him. She set her coffee mug on her desk and her purse
in its assigned drawer, never making eye contact.

"Do you want a list, or is there a specific offense I've committed?" He kept his tone light.

She unpacked her laptop and set it on its docking station.
"Aaron forwarded me an email this morning. A response to a *Cease
and Desist* on the *Changelings and Caravans* game."

How did he have that already? Josh had only forwarded it to his
friend yesterday. Actually, why did Aaron have that at all? Josh kept
the question to himself. Admitting he knew anything was a confession of guilt. "Okay?"

"I've been reading your papers since you were old enough to

399

write. I've read a number of your legal briefs and letters. Her *lawyer* is one of your frat brothers." She finally sat and fixed a glare on him.

All circumstantial evidence. But also, *fuck*. "And?"

"Are you an idiot? You can't do things like this." The tight edge that wove though her voice spoke to every time she'd lectured Josh throughout his life.

He wasn't letting it get to him, and he wasn't admitting guilt. "Like what?"

Laurie Hunter scrubbed her face. "I'm not in the mood to play games with you. Let's assume you're going to continue to deny this and that I'm going to continue to not believe your bullshit."

Lovely. Not. Then why pretend? "Why does Aaron have a response sent to someone who isn't related at all to this firm?"

"Our client is licensing rights to publish a product someone else is making a claim on. This has everything to do with us."

"It doesn't." Josh didn't like this. "Sydney is handling it. It's not a legitimate claim. Why does Aaron have that letter?"

"Even if you don't care how this reflects on our firm, she's dating your roommate. It's time to move on."

"Right." Josh should counter her complete and total deflection of his question, but she'd tripped him up. He hadn't considered the fallout of their relationship this weekend. If they kept going long term, all three of them, how was he supposed to explain it?

"*Right?* Is she or isn't she?"

"She definitely is. Dylan is absolutely devoted to Sydney."

"Good. Great. Let her ruin his life instead of yours."

Anger surged inside, white-hot and obliterating any reason in its path. "Excuse me?" He didn't know what made him more furious— the comment about Sydney, or the complete disregard for Dylan. "Sydney is talented and creative and brilliant, and Dylan is one of the best fucking junior attorneys you've ever had."

His mother's eyes narrowed. "And here's the problem. *You* should be one of the best I've ever had. But that *girl* got under your skin and fucked with your head. She almost talked you out of law school."

Josh didn't try to suppress his growl. "No. *I* almost talked me out of law school. I didn't know if I wanted to spend another three years in a classroom, for something I wasn't going to use."

"And she left, and you figured out you were wrong."

"I wasn't wrong. I just had the wrong goal in mind."

She twisted her mouth in that sideways irritated way that meant this argument would only get worse. "And what goal is that?"

Working here. "Did you know she was the other party in this negotiation?"

"Yes."

Josh clenched a fist. "Is that why you pulled me?"

Now his mother was smiling. That eerie, cold kind of smile that didn't reach his eyes. When he was younger, it would have chilled him. Now it cranked the heat another notch higher on his anger.

"I've done everything to prepare you for this job. And that includes keeping her out of your path," she said.

The late nights of work emergencies. The missed, super important dates. No. She couldn't mean that.

"You could have trusted me to decide on my own."

"Not if that decision included throwing away your future for something frivolous. I've done all of this for you. We're having this conversation for you. So that you don't destroy your legacy."

Josh had been hearing that all his life. He'd taken it to heart. Sydney's voice echoed in his thoughts—*For a job you don't even want.*

But he'd done what he was supposed to. Gone to law school. Passed his bar. Put in the hours. Surrendered the woman he loved…

Sydney was right. It was all for something he didn't want to be doing. Not here. Not like this. "No. This wasn't for me. It was all for you."

His mother's face contorted with rage, and her skin was blotched and red. "You ungrateful, selfish—"

"No. I'm not." He stood. "I appreciate everything you've given me, and I agonize over every single decision I know will disappoint you. I also don't work for you anymore. Consider this my resignation." His thoughts fluctuated between anger and apathy. He should be nervous or scared by what he was doing. Instead, calm was settling in. "And not that it's ever been your business, but I am seeing Sydney again. So's Dylan. And we're all okay with that."

An icy mask slid into place, more concerning that her fury. "Clean your desk and get the fuck out of my office. *Now.*"

"Of course, Ms. Hunter. Have a lovely day." Josh didn't slam the door. He let it swing shut softly behind him as he strolled away.

He didn't know what to make of his thoughts…Which feeling to focus on. He could scream—at himself or his mother—or laugh at the sense of relief that threatened his thoughts. Cry. Curse three years in law school just to wind up here.

He swallowed it all for the moment. Any reaction would wait until he left the office.

Josh was shoving the last of his belongings into a box, when Dylan approached.

"What are you doing?" Dylan's voice was low.

Josh shrugged. Could he talk without unleashing the flood of confusion that roared inside? "What's it look like?"

Dylan furrowed his brow. He liked it here. There was no reason to drag him down.

"I'll text you." Josh grabbed his stuff and walked toward the stairs.

He was shaking by the time he slid into his car. The yell he expected to tear free wouldn't come. He pressed his forehead into the cool steering wheel and took several deep breaths.

The action didn't help him sort out his head, but it helped him unclench his fists.

Now what?

Go back upstairs and apologize? Beg for his job back? Reach out directly to the publisher and ask for a chance to work for them, despite the way he left his last job?

Start drinking at eight in the morning?

Josh didn't know. And the thing that scared him the most was he wasn't worried about it.

SYDNEY WAS DOING her best not to fidget, as she waited to be shown into a conference room.

She shouldn't be as nervous as last time—Dylan and Josh went over the entire contract with her yesterday. Not that she'd tell anyone about their help. That wasn't a relationship line they'd completely obliterated.

None of what they told her was unexpected. The offer was an advance against royalties, to distribute her game. It was a good advance, too. Enough to keep her solvent for a couple of years, and hopefully give the game time to earn out, and maybe she could pitch them her next idea as well.

And this was the big day. She was surrendering some of her control to this publisher. It meant more money, more support, and with a little luck, more contracts in the future. It was still new and scary, though.

Sydney wanted to wander by Dylan's and Josh's desks while she waited. Say *hi*. Chat for a few minutes and maybe take her mind off the morning.

She wouldn't put them in that position. They'd be available after work.

"Ms. Brimhall? They're ready for you." A man about her age showed her back to the same conference room they'd been in before.

She resisted the urge to crane her neck for a glimpse of either of her guys.

Her guys. The phrase was enough to let a tiny smile poke through the tension. This weekend had been incredible. In some ways, she had a hard time believing it was real. If she could keep the memories hovering in her mind without blushing through this meeting, it would help her stay calm.

Dylan wasn't in here today. Not that she was surprised.

After a round of handshakes and polite conversation, they got down to business. Aaron Jorgensen handed her the contract and a pen, and asked if she had any final questions.

She tried to read everything though again, telling herself

Aaron's fingers drumming on the table had nothing to do with her going slowly. Her eyes glazed over after two or three pages.

She settled for skimming the rest, mostly for show. It made her look more professional, didn't it?

And then it was over. Weeks of stress and worrying, just to be done with the final step in less than half an hour.

She shook everyone's hands again. Josh had told her that while it wasn't in the contract, and she didn't hear it from him, that she should drop the hint that she had more ideas.

She reached their art director. "I'm looking forward to discussing future ideas with you."

"That won't be necessary." His tone was cool, and his expression cold. "It was a pleasure meeting you."

Oh. Sydney's smile froze in place, and a response stuck in her throat. Was that a brush-off? From the company who was distributing her game?

"Thank you again for coming down here, Ms. Brimhall." Aaron showed her from the room and walked her to the elevator. "Have a wonderful day."

Why did she feel like she'd just been pushed aside in a not-good way? Was the clenching in her gut the tail end of nerves?

She checked her messages as she rode the lift down to the parking garage. One from Dylan said *Congratulations*.

The other, from Josh, said, *Call me when you're done. We'll get late breakfast*.

Shouldn't he be working?

She settled into her car. The churning in her gut was worse now. Something was wrong. Josh would have to wait a few minutes.

She pulled the contract from her briefcase.

The first few pages were what she expected. And that eyes-glazing-over feeling was back. This time, she was reading the whole thing.

When she got to the section about rights, her gut sank. *Work for hire*. The phrase glared at her like it was written in neon. She read the section over and over. There was nothing in here about an advance. About royalties.

If she was reading this right, it said she's just surrendered her game and its characters in their entirety to the distributors.

This wasn't what she'd reviewed with Josh and Dylan. She had to be reading it wrong. She wouldn't have signed this. She'd turned down similar offers in the past.

It didn't matter how many times she read it. It still said *Work for hire*.

This was bullshit. Confusion and doubt gave way to anger. They had her sign a different contract than the one she'd reviewed.

Sydney needed to undo this. She headed back upstairs.

"May I help you, Miss?" The same man who had shown her to her meeting was working the reception desk.

She'd be polite and cool about this. She wouldn't freak out without proof. "I think there's an issue with the contract I just signed. I'd like to speak to Aaron Jorgensen or someone else who can help me."

"I see. Are you a client?"

"No. But I was just here. You saw me."

He shook his head. "We can't offer legal advice to people who aren't our clients. I'm sorry. You'll need to speak with your own attorney."

"*My* attorney didn't prepare this contract." She struggled to keep her frustration from bleeding into something more intense. "I'd like to speak with the person who did."

"We don't do that. I'm sorry. You can have your lawyer schedule a time with someone here if there are concerns. We can't help you if you're not a client."

Was she not making herself clear? "This doesn't have anything to do with whether or not I pay someone here. I just want to speak with one of the people who prepared this contract." She could ask for Josh or Dylan, but she didn't want to get them in trouble.

"We can't help you." He turned back to his computer.

She slammed her palm on the reception counter. "Just let me talk to someone!" The shout came out without her permission, but she didn't want to take it back.

"You need to leave."

"You pulled a fucking bait and switch." Now that she was yelling, she couldn't stop. "I *need* to speak with someone here, or I'll sue your asses off." Which she couldn't even begin to afford, but it sounded good.

"Then your lawyer can call us." His voice wavered.

"Is there a problem, Ms. Brimhall?" Laurie Hunter's voice drew Sydney's attention. She stood a few feet away, watching Sydney with a venom-filled glare.

Sydney swallowed the impulse that was always there to cower in front of this woman. "This contract isn't the one I was given to review. It was swapped for a bullshit version I never would have signed if I'd known."

"Did you read this one before you signed it?"

Sydney clenched her jaw and struggled to ignore the embarrassed, awkward girl who wanted to emerge. "I glanced at it."

"Then you knew what it contained. We're not responsible for seller's remorse, especially when you're not our client. You need to leave."

"I just want you to hear me out." Sydney's retort came out as more of a plea than a demand.

Someone loosely grabbed her arm. A man in a security uniform had stepped up next to her. "Miss, please come with me."

Humiliation mingled with her fury. She wanted to break away and throw a tantrum until they listened. It wouldn't do her any good. "Fine. But we're not done."

"Yes we are, Sydney. Don't come back here. Next time, I'll call the police." A strong threat wove through Laurie's reply.

Sydney blinked back the tears that pricked her eyelids as she stepped onto the elevator for the five-billionth time that day, this time with Security by her side.

Josh wanted to meet up. He could help her figure this out.

Unless he was in on it.

She growled mentally at the doubt and refused to give it any attention.

Because you know it's possible.

No. She wasn't listening. La la la la.

They reached her car, and the security guy waited near the hood. Was he going to stand there until she left?

He crossed his arms.

Apparently so.

She was going to cry. And then be sick. And then cry some more.

TWENTY-TWO

I t was rare for Dylan to be so distracted, it got in the way of what he should be doing. This morning though, he had zero focus.

Moments after Josh walked out of the office and left an empty desk behind, he sent a text. *I quit. My choice. I'll explain later. Don't let this fuck you too.*

Dylan asked for details.

Josh's response was, *Tell you at lunch. Best said in person.*

Not reassuring.

Dylan's level of distraction doubled when the clock ticked up toward Sydney's meeting. She'd be fine. Everything would go smoothly. It was a basic contract.

He forced his head down… and stared blankly at his screen.

Nope. Nothing was getting done today. At least not until he had some answers.

He sent Sydney a quick text that said *Congratulations*. That helped a little, even if she wouldn't see it or respond until she left.

A loud noise carried from the lobby, and Dylan frowned. Sydney?

No.

There was another yell.

That was definitely Sydney. He was halfway out of his chair, when Laurie Hunter paused in front of his desk.

Rage radiated from her. "I swear to God, if you go out there, you'll never practice law in this city."

He sank back into his seat as she stalked away. Was she serious?

Did it matter, if something was wrong with Sydney?

He didn't know what was happening. Was he willing to risk Laurie's threat being real if this was something he shouldn't be involved in?

It was Sydney. If he could help, he would. If not, he'd be there for her.

At the cost of his career?

He was on his feet before the question finished scrolling through his thoughts.

When he reached the lobby, Sydney was stepping into the elevator with Security. She didn't look up before the doors closed.

What the fuck?

He whirled to face Laurie. Red splotches dotted her face, and she was watching him with poison in her eyes.

Well, *fuck*.

She closed her eyes, and her chest rose and fell. When she met his gaze again, her mask was back in place.

This was honestly more terrifying than her fury. It didn't matter. He was ready to run downstairs, to stop Sydney.

"Take the rest of the day off," Laurie said in a cool tone. "I'm giving you permission, because you're going to do it anyway."

He was sprinting toward the stairs before she finished speaking. Her words hit his back as the stairwell door closed behind him, and he wasn't sure he heard her right.

"Tell my son I'm sorry."

That couldn't be what she said. She never referred to Josh as her son in the office. And she *never* apologized once she'd taken a stand.

He'd deal with it later. As he reached the parking garage, the security guy who'd escorted Sydney out was heading back to the elevators.

"Where is she parked?" Dylan asked.

"The chubby girl? She's gone. Watched her leave."

Dylan clenched his fist. It was so tempting to deck the guy for the *chubby* comment. But there were more important things to deal with. Like finding out *what the fuck was going on.*

He needed to grab his stuff from his desk. On the trip up, he sent Josh and Sydney both texts that said he'd be at the coffee shop a block from the office, and that he'd wait for the next hour, unless they said they weren't coming.

Already there. Josh's reply came before Dylan was back on the ground floor.

There was no response from Sydney.

Dylan was both grateful for the short stroll to the coffee shop, and irritated it took so long to get there. By the time he walked in the front door, adrenaline hammered full force in his veins, and his body was wound tighter than a spring.

He didn't have to look, to know Josh would be at the same table they always sat at. He crossed the room without pausing, bent at the waist, and kissed Josh hard, pouring several hours of built-up tension into the connection.

This was the one thing that felt right about the morning. Like it should have been this way long ago.

When Dylan broke away, Josh wore a faint smile, but it didn't erase the lines etched in his forehead.

Josh nodded at the seat across from him, and the second cup on the table. "Got you a drink. Decaf."

"Probably smart." Dylan would have scoffed at the idea on any other day. He sipped the still-scalding coffee. Should he ask what happened to Josh first, or tell him about Sydney? He knew which he'd want to hear, if he was the guy with half the information—the other half.

"Why aren't you at work?" Josh asked.

"Your mom gave me the day off. I think between you quitting and Security escorting Sydney from the build—"

"What?"

Dylan shrugged. "I don't know much. There was yelling—Sydney's—and when I got out to the lobby, they were seeing her to her car. And then she was gone."

"Fucking... I'd say *unbelievable*, but let me guess. My mother was involved." Josh's laugh was bitter.

"She looked worse than I've ever seen her. Laurie did. Not just angry, but... stressed."

Josh's scowl wavered. "She brought it on herself."

"What happened?"

"I don't even know where to start." Josh sighed through his fingers as he rubbed his face. "She knew I drafted that letter for Sydney. She told me Sydney was going to ruin your career and better you than me. She implied pretty heavily that she'd worked hard to keep me away from Sydney..."

There was so much to unpack there, Dylan didn't know where to start. "And then you quit."

"Wouldn't you?"

Dylan's decision wouldn't be as straightforward as Josh's. He liked his job. Then again, he'd been willing to be fired less than an hour ago. "I don't blame you."

"I don't know what to do." Josh slumped in his chair. "I can't believe... The only part of this not devouring me is the actual quitting. Fuck, that felt good. Why hasn't Tink replied to my messages?"

Dylan had a similar concern. "I told her the same thing I said to you—that I'd be here for an hour." Did they wait here or try to track her down? See if she was at her apartment, or... Dylan didn't know where else they'd look.

But he was worried about her.

SYDNEY GOT Dylan's message before she was more than a few blocks from the law offices. She'd wavered about going to meet him. He could explain. Help her understand.

Or he could ask her what the fuck her problem was, and chide her for acting so unprofessionally in the place he worked.

No. That wasn't Dylan.

It was Josh.

He'd said he was sorry.

Less than two weeks after he'd pulled the same shit as when they were dating—picking work over her.

His apology was like every other time.

Dylan meant it, though. He was so close to perfect. Doting. Sweet. Understanding. Sexy as fuck.

Too perfect?

She let out a wordless scream in the car. It didn't silence the gnawing argument in her head.

Sydney headed home, instead of replying. She needed to get herself under control. There was a freak-out crawling under her skin. The kind of insecurity she could usually suppress with a few distractions.

Today it roared for her attention. When she got home, she shed her professional outfit, not caring where they landed, and yanked on her baggiest, most comfortable clothes. The sweats and T-shirt she'd lived in for a week after she broke up with Josh.

Was she an idiot? Was this all a joke on their part?

No. It was too elaborate for that. It was a misunderstanding. For some reason they'd gone over a different version of the contract with her than she was handed today. It wasn't their fault.

Unless it was.

No. She couldn't listen to that voice. She'd call them. Call Dylan. Even when they fought, he was honest with her.

Unless he's been making fun of you this entire time and you didn't see it.

She pressed her palm to her forehead, to squash the doubt.

Ignoring your instinct won't make it any less true.

No. Nonononono.

Her phone buzzed with two messages. Identical, from Josh and Dylan.

Worried about you. Leaving here in 15. Coming to find you.

Because they cared. Because they could make this right.

Because they want to poke fun at the fat girl who thought two sexy as fuck men not only liked her, but were willing to share. Who does that?

She sobbed and knotted her fingers in her hair, yanking until her skull ached.

You can't ignore this. Deal with it now, and it will hurt less.

It wasn't true. Dylan hadn't... Neither had Josh. That wasn't who they were.

You don't know Dylan. Except that he's been fucking Josh for the last three years.

That didn't matter. It might to some people. She was not only fine with it, she was great with it. They were happy together.

Without you.

No. She wanted to scream again, but would it do her any good?

"Sydney?" Dylan's muffled voice carried through the front door, followed by a knock.

She clenched her jaw, to hold back the surge of doubt-induced nausea.

"We want to know what happened," Josh said.

Because they cared.

Because the joke isn't done.

She wasn't listening to that voice. It was a liar and an asshole.

You're going to let them in, looking like this?

She smoothed her hair the best she could, ignored the question, and went to open the door.

Dylan's expression softened when he saw her. "Fuck, Syd. What happened?" He reached toward her.

She stepped away instinctively.

Hurt splashed across his face. Or a scowl.

He's upset that you're not playing along.

She hated herself when she got like this. Then again, that was the point.

"Can we come in?" Josh asked.

She was too frazzled to do anything besides open the door wider and step aside.

"Did you come here to reinforce Laurie's threat?" Sydney's question came out raw.

Josh frowned. "She threatened you?"

Maybe they didn't know what happened.

Of course they know.

She clenched her fist until her nails dug into her palm. "She told me if I ever stepped foot in your law offices again, she'd have me arrested."

"What? Why?" Dylan's shock looked genuine.

Sydney wanted to believe it was. "Do you really not know?"

"I quit before your appointment. I wasn't in the office. Dylan only heard the shouting." Josh stepped closer. He flexed his fingers.

She wanted to fall into comfort from both of them. It was so tempting. They could tell her this was all a big mistake.

They could lie.

She forced steel through her veins and grabbed her copy of the contract from the briefcase she'd discarded by the door. "Read the section about rights and compensation. It's not what we talked about yesterday."

Dylan grabbed the paperwork, and Josh read over his shoulder.

Their frowns deepened, and silence stretched through the room, until Sydney couldn't ignore the ringing in her ears.

They didn't expect you to catch it so soon.

They didn't know it was there, or they would have told her.

You should have read before you signed. What were you thinking?

That regardless of what she thought of Laurie Hunter, the woman ran a solid and reputable firm.

Either that's not true, or you're just stupid.

Sydney tried to yank herself away from the hole she was plummeting into.

Dylan finally looked up. "This isn't the contract you were supposed to have."

"I figured that out. Thanks." She couldn't keep the sarcasm from her voice.

He thinks you're stupid.

Shut. Up.

Josh flipped to the last page. "But you signed it."

"Figured that out too. We're all on the same page now?"

"This isn't right." Dylan alternated his gaze between her and the contract. "Did Aaron tell you changes had been made?"

"Yeah. And I signed my life's work away anyway." Bitter sarcasm oozed from her reply. "No, he didn't fucking tell me. No one did."

"Well make this right," Josh said.

Don't say it. Don't say it. Don't say it.

Say it.

"Was this all fun and games for the two of you?" She hated herself even more when the words slipped out. "Fucking with my head? Making me think I was special? If you wanted to fuck me without lube, there were other ways to go about it."

Anger splashed across Dylan's face. "We didn't know about this."

"Yeah. Okay. You just happened to run into me right before this negotiation. You just happened to not know who I was. You just happened to be willing to give me all sorts of free legal advice. That just happened to be a completely and total *fucking lie.*"

"That's not how it went down." Dylan's tone was turning hard. "I've always been sincere with you."

Bullshit.

Sydney didn't know anymore. She couldn't tell which of her thoughts hated her and which wanted what was best for her. Her chest ached, and her eyes ached, and her heart ached. "You need to leave."

"If that's what you want," Dylan said.

Of course he caved that easily. Because the game is over. He never cared.

Josh shook his head. "We're not going."

"*Get out.*" Sydney screamed so loudly, her voice cracked.

TWENTY-THREE

Josh didn't move, and he wasn't going to let Dylan go either. He'd seen this Sydney before, and a fist clenched around his lungs, squeezing his breath out, that she was falling into this.

The doubt. The disbelief. The years of external pressure, telling her so many things that weren't true. They'd worked through it when he and she first dated. He knew better than to ignore it or to walk away from her when she was like this, and he remembered how much it tore her apart both during and after.

Any other time she asked him to go, he would. This had to be the exception. "We're not leaving."

"Now." She spoke through clenched teeth.

"No." Dylan stood by his side.

Josh was a little surprised by that. Dylan didn't do complicated or drama. But Sydney was different.

Josh itched to reach out to her, but he wouldn't do that yet. She needed to believe his sincerity first. "We're staying until you feel better," he said.

"Why?" Her question came out in a choked sob.

"I can only speak for me. I'm staying because I love you. I'm not making that up. I'm not saying that to poke fun at you. I love you so much. I've never stopped." He poured his heart into the words. This was one of those things he should always mean, and he'd done a shitty job of showing it in the past. "I was wrong back then, to set you aside the way I did. You mean so much more to me than that. I took us for granted, and you deserved better. You still do."

Her eyes glistened, and she scrubbed a hand across her cheeks.

He wasn't done yet. Now that the words were flowing, he couldn't dam up three years' worth of regret and missed opportunities. "When I tell you you're stunning, I mean it. Gorgeous eyes. Amazing body. Beautiful mind. Enviable, fuckable brain."

"Liar." Her protest was weak.

"Whatever your mind is telling you right now, it's the one lying." He didn't know if it would work, to be this direct. It might backfire on him. She might not be in the mood to hear it.

"Takes one to know one."

"I broke so many promises," Josh said. "I'm sorry. It was never because of 'you. What you and I had was incredible. The best thing ever, and I surrendered it. I was wrong."

"Please stop." She was begging now. "Don't make this worse."

This time he reached for her, placing a finger under her chin to look her in the eye. "Sydney, I mean everything I'm saying. I'll repeat it from now until eternity if that's what it takes to make you believe it. I love you more than anything—besides Dylan, but there's no competition there—you have a special place in my heart that no one else will ever fill. Whatever this is that you're feeling, whatever happened today, we'll plow our way through it. I'm on your side. I don't care what *Ms. Hunter* has to say. We'll make this right."

She stared back, eyes filled with unshed tears.

He was out of words, but he'd start over.

"I signed the contract." When she finally spoke, he let out a breath. "I didn't even read it. I trusted you both that it was what you said, and it wasn't. I walked in there this morning and signed my game away. I'm such a fucking idiot. I thought..."

Josh wasn't going to let her finish the thought, because that was the tip of the slide. He brushed his lips over hers and pulled back to meet her gaze again. "We didn't know. I swear to you. This is all wrong. Everything about the contract. But it doesn't have anything to do with how I feel about you."

"Same for me." Dylan spoke up. "This doesn't change my feelings at all. I mean everything I've always said. You're not a joke. You're... amazing."

Josh glided his hand down Sydney's arm, to grip her fingers. He tugged her closer and brushed a strand of hair behind her ear. "You're not stupid. This isn't your fault. And we weren't involved."

"I don't..." She sighed. "I don't know anymore."

"I do. And you don't have to come up with answers right now. You need to pause. And think. And probably eat. You skipped breakfast, didn't you?"

She ducked her head. "I was too nervous."

"Come on." He tugged her into the kitchen, pulled out a chair, and nudged her into it. He knelt at her feet and kissed her knuckles. "One thing at a time. There's no reason to force any more than that."

"I guess." Most of the waver was gone from her reply, and exhaustion had moved in.

Every inch of him pleaded to wrap her up and hold her. Not until she was ready, though.

DYLAN WASN'T certain what he'd just seen, but he had some assumptions that felt pretty right.

There was one thing he was sure of—Josh and Sydney may think they broke up, but it was more like a three-year hiatus. Whatever flowed between them in her living room, while she stood on the ledge of doubt and Josh talked her down, was more real and sincere than anything Dylan had ever seen.

When she'd started screaming without giving them a chance to explain, instinct told Dylan to walk away.

The only desire he had with Sydney was to stay, though. It was equal parts because he cared, and because she was right to be furious. She'd just gotten fucked over hard.

Josh moved around the kitchen like it was his own. Knowing which cupboard the bowls were in. Where the spoons were. Where to look for the cereal.

They ate Corn Flakes in silence, with Sydney so drawn into herself, she looked like she wanted to hide in that oversized shirt.

Dylan could only guess at the rules of this, but the quiet didn't sit well with him. "This wasn't an honest mistake."

Sydney looked up from her food, eyes wide. Was she startled that he'd spoken or by what he said? She swallowed. "What do you mean?"

"Aaron Jorgensen is an incompetent asshole. We cover for him… always. Because he's sleeping with the boss." Dylan knew that didn't answer the question, but he was still sorting out his reasons for the declaration.

Sydney looked between them. "So the whole extreme-anti-nepotism thing stops at blood relatives?"

"Yup." Josh sighed. "But what Dylan's talking about… If Aaron did this, he'll be disbarred. He'll be shunned. This is career-ending shit."

Pieces were clicking in Dylan's head. "Only if he gets caught. What was wrong with that last contract we fixed for him?"

"Everything was out of order. The formatting was screwed up." Josh pushed away his empty bowl. "Do you think… Was he doing the same thing there?"

It was a big assumption to make. Dylan couldn't proclaim Aaron was fucking with contracts without proof. But he and Josh helped implement the current document management system. Could they find proof? "Maybe. If he did this on purpose with Sydney, it can't be the first time. He didn't wake up this morning and think, *I'm going to cheat the system for this single client.*"

"He might have." Sydney didn't sound as pained as she had even a few minutes ago.

Dylan gave her a half-smile. "It's possible. But I don't think you're the only victim here."

"If you're saying that to make me feel better, it's working." Some of the tightness in her face melted away. "But someone would catch him, right? You said disbarment. What's worth that kind of risk?"

"Typically money." Josh cleared away their dishes, rinsed them, and set them in the sink.

How perfectly domestic was this, in the midst of this fucked-up day? Dylan didn't want to linger on it, but the simple actions left a warm glow inside, where he expected jealousy.

"How do you prove it? How can I help? Can I get my game back? Can I..." Sydney's scowl was back. "How can I help?"

What else was she about to say? "I can go in the system and compare changes. You two can't. Non-disclosure and all that."

"Okay, so... while it seems like a weird time to start caring about that *conflict of interest* line, I also understand this is more than a little bit of on-the-side legal advice," Sydney said. "But why can't Josh help you?"

Josh leaned against the counter near the sink. "Like I said. I quit this morning."

"Why?" Sydney asked.

"Because..." He raked his fingers through his hair. "Because I've never liked working there. And because I choose you."

"Oh." Sydney puffed out the reply on a soft sigh.

It was certainly one way to drive home the *I'm sorry, and here's proof I'll never do it again* point. Dylan couldn't argue with Josh's logic.

"There is something you can do." Dylan wanted to get to the bottom of this. He also needed to make sense of his own feelings. Whatever was happening between the three of them was more than just a casual hookup. It wasn't a simple *let's all date and see where it goes.* Something changed this morning, and he had to process.

Sydney leaned in. "Tell me. I can't... Sitting here, wallowing, will drive me insane."

"If Jorgensen has done this before, it's probably been in other cases like yours. People who came in without their own attorney. Smaller companies or individuals who couldn't afford to fight. And someone has probably bitched about it online."

"You want us to go play on the internet while you compare documents? That sounds grueling for you."

"It's not." Josh kicked away from the counter. "The system does ninety-nine percent of his work for him. We have to sift through search engines and blog posts and Reddit forums for our answers. And if we find proof, we have to hope my mother is willing to listen."

Dylan didn't want to doubt that part of the plan, but their past history of complaints about Aaron spoke for itself. This needed to not be for nothing.

And he had to figure out how to give Sydney the next bit of bad news. Best case scenario here was the publisher said *whoops, our bad, we didn't know either* and had her sign the correct contract.

Aaron didn't do this on his own, though. There was no gain in that. This was a long-term client who he'd bill hourly regardless of how this one contract went.

If the publisher didn't back down, Sydney wouldn't get the money promised, and she probably wouldn't be able to touch her game, either. Not while the contract was in dispute.

There was no way around that, no matter how desperately Dylan wished otherwise.

TWENTY-FOUR

Sydney was grateful that Josh stuck around. She was on the other side of the emotional chasm now; this feeling was as familiar as the one that came before. Now that she'd moved past her doubt and self-loathing, there was a new voice.

You overreacted.

She was better at ignoring this one. It was typically accompanied by sanity. Josh's being here helped too. His presence was another reminder of the reasons she adored him, and all the things he'd said warmed her from the inside out.

"How are you feeling?" Dylan asked.

Not secure enough to spill her guts to him, but happy he was here. "Heading toward *better*."

He tugged her to her feet, wrapped his arms around her, and pressed his lips softly to hers. "I know everyone says this, but I mean it—if you need me, I'm always here to listen."

"Not everyone says it." But she still made those who did prove it. It was safer that way. "It takes a while to get there, but thank you." She could sink into his embrace, though, and that felt wonderful.

He held her a little longer, then kissed the top of her head before loosening his hug. "I'm going back to our place, to get our laptops. You're in good hands, and I'll be back soon."

"Thank you." She stole another squeeze and brushed her lips over his. After he left, she turned to Josh. "I'm sorry."

Josh crossed the distance between them in a few steps and pressed his fingers to her lips. "You know how I feel about that." He meant the apology.

"And you know I can't help it."

"In that case, apology accepted."

The only thing that would silence the voices was time. But when Josh pulled her close, it helped.

"Thank you." She gripped his shirt in her fists, enjoying having something to hold onto. "Thank you for not walking away today. For pulling me out. For sticking around after. And for whatever comes next."

"You'd do the same for me."

"Except you don't fall into debilitating spirals of doubt."

"But I am an inconsiderate dick sometimes, and you tend to be pretty reasonable, as long as I don't push my luck."

"I love you." She hadn't missed when he said it earlier. "I never stopped, and I don't ever want to."

He smiled that stunning, heart-stopping smile she adored so much. "I'm going to try not to give you any reasons to change your mind."

"I'm not giving up Dylan, though." She didn't want to bring it up now, but it needed to be out there.

Josh shrugged. "Me either. Since that seems to be an all-around sort of consensus, we're good. Hell, I'd say we're pretty wonderful."

With each moment that passed, she felt better. She led Josh to the couch and snuggled into his arms. This was comfortable and right and something she'd missed terribly. She was happy to stay here, curled up against him, feeling him run his fingers through her hair.

When the door opened a short while later, she didn't stir.

"Can I get in on that?" Dylan asked.

Sydney was great with that. "Of course."

He planted a kiss on her lips, and then Josh's, before dropping next to Josh. He tugged Sydney so she was lying across both their laps.

It was just awkward enough to make her giggle. That felt good. She tried to make it work, but gave up quickly. "I appreciate the sentiment, but nope. Not comfortable."

"We'll figure it out." Dylan spoke with so much confidence, she didn't question him.

She wanted to cuddle longer and maybe more. However, an edge of doubt lingered. She didn't want sex to become a way to mask her insecurities. That, and she wanted to find out what happened today with her contract.

"We should get to work." It took more effort than she expected, to say the words.

"All right." Dylan sounded as reluctant as she felt. They untangled themselves, and he grabbed the bags he'd brought back. He set one laptop next to Josh and shouldered the other one.

He set up in the kitchen and flipped his computer open. "Wi-Fi password?"

"You're asking me to make a big commitment with that," Sydney teased.

"I know. And I'm cocky enough to believe we've reached that stage in our relationship."

Sydney grinned. "I'm good with that." She gave him the login info.

"I don't get it," he said, as he studied his screen.

"There's nothing to get. It's a random mishmash of letters and numbers."

"So weird. I love it."

With him at the kitchen table, screen facing away from them, Josh and Sydney set up in the living room. It kept them all within view of each other and let Dylan hide sensitive information.

Dylan was certain about what they'd find, but Sydney had her doubts. If something like this was happening on a wide scale, someone would have uncovered it already.

She searched anyway. First for Aaron Jorgensen. Which, thanks to the Internet assuming she misspelled something instead of wanting exactly what she'd typed, returned pages of personal listings, social media accounts, everything—for anyone whose initials were A.J.

"Clients next," Josh said.

They used the list that was public on the firm website, to make sure he wasn't violating any NDA's. Those were the bigger-name companies anyway—the businesses more likely to have dozens of dealings, and several of them with smaller groups.

Sydney felt frustration sinking in. Everything out there was standard complaint stuff. A massive corporation pissed off a little guy as part of their business model, and the little guy was going to tell the world.

She wanted to reach out to every single one of the people who'd written the blog posts and social media posts, and tell them, *Me too. I feel you.*

And then she hit something that sounded suspiciously like her situation. A person who swore they'd read the entire contract, and when they signed, it wasn't the same.

Then there was another example, and another.

Josh fed the names to Dylan, who used them to focus his search.

It was dangerous, but Sydney felt a spark of hope glowing inside. "What does this mean for me? I might get my game back if this is happening, right?" She felt giddy, speaking the words.

Josh and Dylan's winces mirrored each other.

That was a bad sign.

"Best case scenario, you have your game back tomorrow." Josh's voice was strained. "We call Aaron and the publisher on this, and they say, *Our bad. Let's cancel that whole deal.* It's doubtful they'll still go through with the original terms, but they may."

Her heart sank. "What are the realistic scenarios?"

"Looking at the publisher records, this isn't the first time they've done this," Dylan said. "They'll deny any claim you make. And this will be tied up in court for months."

She could put pieces together from there. "So I can't touch the money, because if lose, I won't get to keep it, and I can't sell my game, because the rights are currently in question."

The downward spiral was rushing back, full force, squeezing like a fist around her lungs and stealing her rationale.

Dylan frowned. "I'm sorry."

"We're here for you, however you need us." Josh rested a hand on her thigh.

"I need to not lose the only source of income I have." She needed to not freak out again, but she might not be able to control that any more than the rest of this.

"Hey." Josh kissed her. "We'll figure it out." His touch silenced some of the voices, but it wasn't a solution.

"We'll take this back to Laurie and see if she's willing to discuss things," Dylan said.

Sydney didn't like that plan. "What are the odds she'll hear you out?"

"We can proceed with or without her. Dylan and I can file the complaint against Aaron. Her life will be easier if she listens and acts appropriately."

Sydney wasn't assured. Laurie obviously had a different definition of *professionally appropriate* than Sydney did. "And if she doesn't see things that way?"

Josh's laugh was strained. "Then she's almost prophetic. She told me you would ruin my career. Not listening to you—to us— could destroy her firm."

"She said that about me?" The ache in Sydney's chest grew. Everything they were doing was supposed to help, but she was feeling shittier and more helpless with each passing moment.

Josh cupped her cheek and held her gaze. "I told you, I choose you."

"Which is why you quit, which means she was right about me." Sydney clenched her jaw. She didn't want to cry. "I don't want to ruin anyone's career. Except the assholes' who screwed me over. I just wanted more of your time."

"I know." He stroked his thumb along her jaw. "This was my decision, not yours. You can't take the blame for it."

Experience said she could, and she would, but Josh made his argument sound so logical…

"I sent Laurie an email." Dylan's tone was kind. "I copied her assistant and asked to get on her calendar tomorrow morning. All of us. I made sure to tell her it was critical."

All of us. That terrified Sydney. At least the fear pushed her clawing doubt aside. "I'm not going to be able to sit still until then."

"Fucking is a good outlet for unspent energy," Dylan said playfully.

She appreciated his levity. She must not be as far down in the pit as she feared. "For the next sixteen hours?"

"Of course not." Dylan shook his head. "We'll need some sleep, and to shower before the meeting. Though, with that shower of yours…"

And she was smiling again. "I'm going to need a little more seduction and foreplay. And I still need answers about what I'll do if I can't have my game back."

"Make a new one," Josh said. He of all people knew that wasn't so easy.

"I signed away a lot of my intellectual property in that contract."

Josh shrugged. "But not all of it. There are things they can't touch, and you happen to be tight with the guys who can tell you what those things are."

"It's still not as simple as *make a new game.*" She hated to point out the obvious. Mostly because his idea was a nice fantasy, and she'd rather sink into it.

"But you have concepts." Enthusiasm bled into Josh's voice. "Dozens of them, and a lot of them are solid enough to grab and build on."

She loved that he remembered that. "I don't know how objectively good any of them are."

"Fortunately for you, you have a test audience." Dylan closed his laptop and joined them in the living room.

"You're so biased," she said.

He settled on her other side from Josh. "I'm glad you know that. We also want you to succeed. Tell us what you have, and let's make this work."

She twisted so she was half-leaning on Dylan, and Josh tugged her legs up, to drape over his. This worked much better than what they tried earlier.

For the next several hours, they bounced around a huge swath of ideas. Sydney wrote everything down. They'd build off a tangent, and then loop back to a previous idea. From fractured thoughts, a discernible image began to emerge.

Sydney found herself laughing more than not. It was easy to fall into this. The entire setting felt natural. How had she gone without this kind of support for so long?

"What about a sex game?" She tossed the idea out. It wasn't a real suggestion, but things were getting silly.

Josh raised an eyebrow. "Like those dice they sell?"

"But more intimate."

Dylan scrunched his face up. "It won't work with just two people, if it's DM driven."

She loved that he was thinking along those lines. "We have three people."

"Do I get to roll the dice, to see if I can enter your love tunnel?" Josh asked.

She winced at the bad phrasing, but she couldn't stop laughing. "With your spear of penetration?"

Dylan gave an exaggerated cough. "You two are horrible. It's *obviously* a pleasure cave."

"I don't know…" Sydney tried to look serious for half a breath, and failed. "*Your barbarian strolls through my pleasure cave*, doesn't sound quite right."

Dylan drew his fingertips lightly up her arm, to caress her neck. "Because you're putting too much thought into it." His voice dropped an octave. "I think it sounds incredible."

She could argue, but she didn't want to. His touch sent too many delicious thoughts racing through her head.

TWENTY-FIVE

J osh was surprised when Sydney pressed a finger to his lips, and pushed him back from kissing her. He quirked an eyebrow in question.

She was smiling though. That delicious, mischievous smile that had earned the nickname *Tink* all those years ago. She looked like a playful fairy waiting to stir up trouble and fun. "If I'm the DM, this is my story."

"So, is that a *no* on the love tunnel?" Josh asked.

"It's not. But I want something else, first."

"Like what?" Dylan looked as curious as Josh felt.

"Don't get me wrong, I love being on display, but I figure there's got to be something to watching, too." Sydney snapped her fingers. "So... get to it."

Josh stared at her in disbelief. "I'm sorry, what?" He finished the question with a laugh.

She waved her hand. "I want to see you two be all sexy and stuff."

"*Sexy and stuff.* Is that the clinical term?" Dylan untangled himself from the three person pile and stood.

Josh needed to put a little more thought into it. "Not that I *ever* would argue about fucking Dylan—sorry, getting sexy and stuff—but I've really got you on my mind, Tink."

She ducked her head, but couldn't hide her flush. "Then I guess you have to get creative about how you use your spear of penetration."

Josh could do creativity. He stood, gripped Dylan's shirt in his fist, and kissed him hard.

Dylan pressed back with enthusiasm, biting Josh's bottom lip, and holding his head captive.

Sydney's breathy gasp was the perfect accompanying music. Josh could see why she liked this being watched thing. At least, with the right audience.

As he deepened the kiss, need snaked along his skin, and chased away the lingering shadows of stress. He raked his nails down Dylan's chest, and received a low groan in return, that hummed against his mouth.

He loved having Sydney back in his life, but just as much, he adored that things were right with Dylan again. Better than right. The way they should be.

Dylan cupped Josh's semi-erect cock through his jeans. He stroked, and Josh hardened under his touch.

Some days, Josh was up for long make-out sessions. He could swap gropes and slide into mutual masturbation, and enjoy every drawn-out moment.

Right now, too much desire flooded his senses. He wanted to be immersed in everything at once.

Josh undid Dylan's pants as he knelt in front of his boyfriend—fuck he liked the sound of that. He worked Dylan free, drawing another delicious groan. When Josh licked along the head of Dylan's cock, he bucked against Josh's touch.

Josh's dick strained against his zipper, begging to be free. He needed release, but it would wait.

He took Dylan in his mouth. Layers of pleasure overlapped, from being responsible for Dylan's moans, and because he could almost feel the touch of lips on his own skin.

He wrapped his fist around the base of Dylan's shaft, pumping in time to the thrust of hips against his face. He flicked his tongue out every few seconds.

As Dylan's thrusts became more insistent, Josh responded with increased enthusiasm.

Dylan gripped the short strands of Josh's hair tight. He fucked without hesitation. He was lost in the pleasure, Josh could tell from his grunts and lack of abandon.

Josh stroked Dylan's sack. Dylan wouldn't last much longer.

Dylan tightened his hold on Josh's hair. Yanking. Pulling. He thrust hard, and a salty spray hit the back of Josh's throat.

Josh continued to lick and suck, until Dylan slowed. He eased up and pulled back, licking Dylan clean as he pulled away.

Dylan pulled him to his feet, still holding his head, and kissed him hungrily. Driving their tongues together. Molding their bodies into each other.

They finally broke apart. "How is that always incredible?" Josh asked.

Dylan chuckled. "Pretty sure that's my line."

"Was that what you were hoping for?" Josh turned to Sydney, who watched them with hungry eyes, her shirt pushed up above her breasts.

She licked her lips. "So much better than. I think we've got a lot of experimenting to do."

"Good thing we've got time." He and Dylan knelt on either side of her. Josh claimed her mouth, and Dylan lowered his head to her breast.

Sydney's whimper was delicious torture to Josh's already aching cock. He glided his hand down her stomach, under the waistband of her sweats. He nibbled her lips and dipped under her panties.

She was slick and wet when he slid between her folds.

"You didn't take care of this while you watched?" he murmured against her lips.

"I was holding out for something to do with a spear of penetration, and a pleasure cave."

Fuck, he loved this woman so much. "I remembered the condoms this time."

"No." She kissed him again. "You don't need to. Neither of you."

They'd had that in their relationship before. Both of them were clean, and she was religious about taking her birth control.

And Josh knew what kind of trust she was offering up in making the decision again.

Josh wasn't sure how they managed it, but her sweats and his jeans came off, while he and Dylan continued to cover Sydney with kisses.

She straddled his legs, and her gaze met his.

"You're so amazingly beautiful." He stroked her cheek.

She tried to look away, but he held her chin up, needing to see her eyes. "You're just saying that because you're getting laid."

"No." It was true, that feeling of being a third wheel was gone. But as long as he had Sydney in his life, he'd make whatever concessions he had to. "I'm saying it because it's true. You're beautiful and brilliant and loving and everything incredible."

She kissed him in response, devouring his mouth. He poured every bit of love he had into returning the feeling.

When she lowered herself onto his cock, he groaned and dug his fingers into her thighs. Feeling her wrapped around him, warm and tight... this was more than sex. He'd spent so many nights building up what they'd had to this impossible pinnacle.

And this moment was nothing like what he'd imagined. It was better. More pure and complete. It was perfect.

SYDNEY WAS DROWNING IN ATTENTION, in the best possible way. Dylan kneaded her breasts and sucked on her nipples. Josh slid inside her, rocking slowly. She didn't know where to turn. There was so much to taste and feel.

Josh pulled her face to his for another desperate kiss. It was like he couldn't get enough of her lips, and she was good with that. While he devoured her, Dylan nibbled on her ear, and dragged his fingers up her spine.

He broke the kiss to crush his mouth to Josh's. The sight, and the adoration that flowed between them, sent a spike of desire that tugged in her heart and pulsed between her legs.

Dylan turned back to her, nipping her lips before licking a path back down to her chest.

He slid his fingers around her clit, and she moaned at the new intensity that surged inside. He stroked her swollen button, and scraped his teeth over her nipple.

His touch, combined with the steady thrust of Josh inside her, sent her reeling toward climax. She tumbled into orgasm without warning, gasping at the onslaught of everything.

She didn't know if she wanted to squirm away, or take more, until it was too much.

Josh's groan filled her head. Her thoughts swam with bliss, and everything flowed into a wash of ecstasy.

Dylan didn't ease up on his attention, pushing her into a second orgasm.

She clenched around Josh when she came, no longer knowing where one of them ended and the next begin.

Josh's frantic thrusts and grunts told her he was on the verge of climax too. He squeezed her legs hard, and for a heartbeat, everything in the world paused.

Then he slammed inside her as he peaked. Filling her up. Leaving her in a blissful haze.

They slowed to a stop, and she rested her forehead against Josh's chest. Dylan trailed his lips along her shoulder.

Whatever came next, the three of them would confront it. And in between, they'd explore each other. Physically. Mentally. All of it.

Sydney was looking forward to each and every new moment.

DYLAN WAS glad Sydney was sleeping soundly. It had been a long, stressful day.

Which was probably a large part of why he was still awake. He couldn't afford to be bleary eyed in the morning, but knowing that didn't help him shed the tension that thrummed through his body.

He extracted himself from Sydney and Josh, and wandered into the living room. Maybe sitting out here would help him unwind.

His mind looped over the day's revelations. Why he'd stuck around this morning—because Josh meant so much to him. Because he already didn't want to imagine life without Sydney.

This was all so fucked up. That was what logic said. He shouldn't be involved in this. He shouldn't be willing to share.

Does it matter?

No. Logic didn't matter here. He felt what he felt, for both of them.

"You all right?" Josh's question drew Dylan back into the room.

Dylan glanced at the clock. Had he really been here for more than an hour, just thinking? "Yeah. I'm good." And he was. "Really good."

"Whatcha thinking about?" Josh dropped onto the sofa next to him, pressing his leg to Dylan's.

"A lot of things. You know, if the two of you hadn't broken up three years ago, I probably wouldn't be part of this now."

"Not that I'd know in that case, but I wouldn't want that. There's a weird kind of ambivalence here. I hated that time away from Tink, but I wouldn't give up my time with you."

Dylan agreed. He hated that Josh and Sydney had been hurt, but he wasn't willing to surrender either of them. "So if you could go back in time…" He wasn't sure where the question was going.

"Would I tell myself not to be an asshole? Probably. But if I have a chance to go back and fix things, I'm not only telling me to treat Sydney better, but also to go find you."

"I was going out of my mind this morning, trying to figure out why you'd quit."

Josh sighed. "I didn't mean to add to your stress. I needed time to process."

"And when we got here, you helped Sydney process, too." There was a spark of jealousy over that. Dylan liked seeing it, but he didn't care for being on the outside.

"Your being here, sticking around, helped too."

Dylan smiled. "I love you. I don't know why it took me so long to put words to it, but I want you in my life, long term. I need you here."

"Me too."

Dylan raised his eyebrows, waiting for something a little more heartfelt.

Josh laughed. "I love you too. I'm glad we're in this together— and by *this*, I mean life." He leaned in, searching Dylan's face, then crushed his mouth to Dylan's.

One of the groaned—or they both did.

Dylan cupped his face, searing the moment into his memories— the hard press of Josh's mouth, the heat that flowed between them... He couldn't count the number of kisses they'd shared in the past, but this was different. It was sweeter, and stronger, and promised everything, and didn't deny them anything.

Desire and expectation roared in his veins as Josh's tongue danced with his. He never would have guessed meeting the perfect woman would land him with the perfect guy as well.

The shuffle of feet on carpet drew his attention, and they broke apart.

"I didn't mean to interrupt." Sydney stood in the doorway, wearing an oversized T-shirt that hung just low enough to cover her ass.

"You're not. Ever. Come here." Dylan gestured.

She approached, and when she was within arm's reach, he grabbed her hand and tugged her into his lap. He was in the mood to bare his soul tonight. There was no reason to stop with Josh.

SYDNEY LEANED into the kisses Dylan laid along the back of her neck. His touch was casual and light, but it sent intense tingles racing over her.

"I love this," he murmured against her skin.

Love. It was an easy word for her to use with Josh. Saying it after so long was scary, but they'd said it before. Then again, she was overthinking this moment. Dylan hadn't said the magic combination of three words.

"Love what?" she asked.

"All of this. What we're doing right now. Having both of you so close. Hearing you laugh when you're happy. Seeing you light up with enthusiasm. I love this, and…"

She frowned at the way he trailed off. "What's wrong?"

He shifted her to the couch and stood.

Emptiness rushed in behind her, at the loss of his touch, despite Josh's still holding her hand and listening quietly.

Dylan crouched in front of her, which put him at eye level with her. "Nothing's wrong." He searched her face. "Everything is incredibly right. Except for this bullshit with your game. But us, here and now… It's perfect. I don't want to say this to the back of your head, though."

Her heart lodged in her throat, and she raised her brows, not trusting herself to respond. Could he hear her pulse? She could. It hammered in her ears, muting other sound.

"I love you, Sydney." He kissed her fingertips. "I know it's only been a couple of weeks, and they've been messy ones. And yeah, a lot of people make fun of love at first sight, and this wasn't that. But it was lust, and it's become so much more. I've wanted you since the moment I met you. The more I get to know you, the more I fall into how incredible you are."

The confession sank deep into her, filling her with a warm glow and making butterflies dance in her gut. She wanted to say it back, but she couldn't. Not until she knew she meant it.

"It's okay. You don't have to be there yet." There was a hint of sadness in his tone, but understanding muted it.

"It's okay?" She couldn't leave it at that.

He winced. "It stings a little. But I say that to be honest, not to manipulate you. I hope you get there, and if you don't, I understand."

She believed the assurance. That was comforting. "I want to get there. I like you a lot. A whole lot. I'm miserable, thinking about you, not being here. I want you in my life. I want to be on your arm and in your bed…"

"The rest will happen as it happens." He brushed his lips over hers.

If he kept that up, love would happen quickly. She kissed him back. There was a tiny stone of longing that asked why she couldn't tell him now. It whispered, *what if he leaves?*

She ignored it more easily than she thought possible. He was here to stay. She believed him and Josh when they said that.

They had enough to worry about, with their meeting tomorrow, without her causing more drama.

TWENTY-SIX

Josh should be dreading the day ahead—the meeting with his mother, the lack of employment...

Instead, he felt lighter than he had in... He couldn't remember, but it was while he was still with Sydney. Before law school. Before the reality of expectation fully caught up with him.

Even sitting in the law firm lobby, with Sydney clutching his hand, him having no idea what they were about to walk into, he felt like everything was going to be all right.

"Ms. Hunter will see you now." Her assistant led them to the conference room attached to Laurie's office.

Dylan was seated at the round table. Josh's mom stood at the front of the room, wearing a scowl.

Josh held out Sydney's seat and pushed it back in as she sat, which earned him a deeper scowl.

Good. He picked the chair next to Sydney, which sandwiched her between him and Dylan.

"The *only* reason I'm seeing you is because I know the two of you don't throw around panicky terms like *this is critical* lightly." Mom's voice was tight. "You don't have much time to prove I made the right decision."

Josh was ready to take the heat for this. "Aaron Jorgensen is manipulating contracts. Bait and switch—"

"Stop." Laurie slammed her palms on the table. "I shouldn't have to say this. I thought after my conversation with Dylan, a week or two ago, I didn't need to. The two of you can't be involved in Sydney's contract. I don't care what she told you."

"We know." Dylan nodded. "Conflict of interest. We've been working hard not to cross any lines."

Mom barked a laugh. "*Everything* about this is a crossed line."

"And not just for us," Josh said. "She's not the only one Aaron has done this to. We have proof. Dylan has proof, since I'm not supposed to be in those files anymore."

Dylan slid a manila folder across the table. It contained several of the altered contracts—showing before and after—and associated complaints they'd found online. "All of these tell a similar story to Sydney's. This isn't a one-time mistake. He's got a history of this."

As Laurie Hunter flipped through the printouts, she paled. "Fuck me." She sank into her seat. "How long... I can't believe... You've tried to tell me he was a problem."

"I thought he was just incompetent." Josh had said it before, but it bore repeating. "This is worse. I stopped pushing, because you weren't listening."

"This could ruin the firm." She scrubbed her face. "I've been sleeping with him. I never..." She exhaled through her fingers, then met Josh's gaze. "I'm sorry for being blind to this. For yesterday. For everything that led up to it. And I'm so grateful you brought this to me, instead of going around me."

Josh wasn't as certain she'd listen as Dylan had been. "I'm glad we didn't have to go around you."

Mom turned to Sydney. "I still don't know that you're a good influence—"

Sydney cringed.

"—but I apologize for the way you were treated yesterday. And that you got caught up in this. I want to make this situation right for you. You can't touch the money or the game, and I can't change that. I can offer other things, though. While Josh's law-school friends may be clever, this isn't a *get your feet wet* kind of case. I'll get you a real attorney, as long as these two promise to step back from this completely. I can't have any more blurred lines." She gestured to Josh and Dylan.

Sydney's smile was tight. "Thank you."

It wasn't peace, but it was a decent ceasefire.

"Now if the two of you will excuse me, I need to talk to my son alone," Mom said.

Dylan and Sydney shook her hand, then Dylan tangled his fingers with Sydney's and led her from the room.

Josh would much rather join them, but this conversation needed to happen.

Mom turned to him again. "Does this mean you're coming back to work?"

"No." The answer flowed out easier than he thought possible. "My quitting wasn't about this thing with Aaron. You know I've never been happy here."

She frowned. "You spent all that time in law school for nothing?"

"No. I'll still use it. I'll still practice somehow. I haven't figured out the details yet." He definitely wouldn't be working for the publisher he'd been eying. Not if this was how they fucked over people they bought from. "Besides, I paid for the schooling. I can waste it if I want."

Laurie almost looked like she was in pain.

"I actually enjoy law," he said. It might not reassure her, but it helped him feel better to say it aloud. "I have to do it for me, though. I can't do this for you anymore."

"I see." She stood, and he did the same. "If you ever change your mind, you're welcome to apply again. And promise me something."

"All right." He shouldn't agree blindly, but he had a feeling it wouldn't be an issue.

"I need you to swear to me you'll step away from this case of Sydney's. Hands off. You know how I feel about her—prove me wrong. But don't fuck her out of her life's work by interfering."

440

"I promise." That was something he could do with certainty. And maybe, by walking away like this, he could rebuild a healthier relationship with his mother at some point in the future.

———

SYDNEY WAS grateful the morning's meeting didn't end in a worst-case-scenario, but things were still pretty bad. They left Dylan at the office, and Josh dropped her off at her apartment, before heading home.

He promised they'd be back tonight.

She'd need to book more conventions. At least she had her other merchandise—toys, models, clothes—even if she didn't have her game to sell. She looked at the boxes stacked in a closet, her gut churning. Acid rose in her throat.

She swallowed it down. The situation was what it was. She wouldn't get anywhere stressing about things she couldn't change. What she could do was make adjustments. Hell, she'd start doing freelance, or even get a part-time job if she had to.

By the time Josh and Dylan showed up that evening, she'd made a billion lists, but doubt lingered inside.

Sydney didn't have a guaranteed next paycheck. She'd lost half her revenue stream. All the plans in the world might act as a band aid, but they wouldn't fix the core problem.

She kissed both guys as she let them in.

Dylan drew his thumb across the lines in her forehead. "What's wrong?"

She spilled everything she'd kept bottled for the last several hours. It felt good to let it out.

"I have another item to add to your list of things that may help," Josh said.

She liked the confidence in his words. "I'm listening, because I need something."

"Having one or two people to share the rent with would take a huge financial strain off you."

His meaning sank in immediately.

She smiled. "Are you inviting yourself to move in?"

"I am. Not just me, but my roommate too. We're kind of a package deal."

Dylan waved.

Her smile grew. "Here, right? After all, that's why we got the place."

"Here." Dylan pulled her close. "We're not giving up that shower."

She sighed happily and relaxed back into him. Maybe things would be all right after all.

Over the next couple of weeks, Josh and Dylan moved into Sydney's apartment. It felt right having Josh here again. And incredible having Dylan here.

Sydney added more nearby conventions to her schedule—smaller locations she could get to inexpensively and still earn.

Josh didn't have any trouble finding a new job. His mom offered a great recommendation, and he had his pick. He chose a small charity that wanted an on-staff advisor who wasn't looking for a partner-level salary. It meant he worked more nights than he did days, but they were also willing to give him time off, to travel with Sydney.

They were also planning their next game. Getting into the details and building something. Sydney and Josh would have a handful of new samples to take with them for sale in a few months.

Dylan shared all sorts of stories of the fallout Aaron was dealing with. His name was showing up in legal journals. He was facing disbarment. His life was falling apart.

Sydney wished she could have been there, to see Laurie rip him a new one when she confronted him. Dylan assured her that, if the conference rooms weren't soundproofed, the entire office probably would have heard it.

Josh was working late tonight, leaving Dylan and Sydney to hang out at home. The two were cuddled on the couch, half paying attention to the TV.

"Wash," Dylan said. "No contest."

Sydney hadn't seen that coming. "I'm glad you didn't say Jayne. That might be a relationship ender," she teased. "And Wash is fun and all, but that's who you'd be if you could be any one of them?"

"*Were I unwed, I would take you in a manly fashion.*"

She laughed. "'Cause I'm pretty?"

"'Cause you're pretty."

"So, you like him for the one-liners?" Sydney was trying to make sense of this.

Dylan shrugged. "That's a lot of it, yeah."

She twisted in her seat so she could see him. "You know you're a way smoother talker than he is."

"You take that back. No one has better lines than Wash." His scowl would have carried more weight if he weren't fighting a smile underneath.

She shook her head. "Nope. I said it. I meant it."

"I can make you take it back." He lunged and tickled her, trailing his fingers up her sides. Hitting every sensitive spot he'd discovered in the last several weeks.

She squealed, but didn't try to break away. His touch was as enticing as it was giggle-inducing. "You'll never change my mind," she managed between laughs.

"Fine." His sigh was exaggerated. He brushed his lips over hers and rested his hands on her hips instead. "You've got it all figured out, which *Firefly* character would you be?"

"Inara."

He raised his brows. "Not what I would have guessed."

"Kaylee is awesome, but I'm already an adorably optimistic genius in my own way."

"No arguments here."

"And Mal looks good in a dress, but if I'm going to be someone else, I want to shed some of the emotional baggage."

Dylan seemed to consider this. "You've put a lot of thought into this."

"I'm swapping my life for a fictional character's. It's got to be right," she said.

"If you were Zoe, you could be my girl."

She had to correct him there. "If I were Zoe, you'd be my guy. Which you already are, and I'm not giving you up. Even to be with Wash. But Inara... She's beautiful and exotic and strong. She's confident and knows what she wants and goes after it..."

He kissed her forehead, and her nose. "Sounds like you're already there."

"I'm not—"

Dylan brushed his lips over hers, silencing her protest. He deepened the kiss, and her insecurities flitted away. Each caress of his hands on her skin, or his mouth on hers, danced through her on fairy wings.

She let the conversation fade away in favor of kissing him back. They had so many nights like this. Everything was easier with Dylan.

"God, I love you," she murmured against his lips. It was the first time she'd said it, but the words tasted as incredible as he did.

He grinned against her mouth. "Say it again."

"I love you. So, so much." She liked the sound of it too. It was better each time she said it.

"I love you too." He sucked a line up her jaw, to her ear, and nibbled her earlobe.

A knock on the door interrupted. She groaned in disappointment.

He planted another kiss on her forehead, extracted himself, and went to answer.

"Ms. Hunter." His voice was abruptly professional.

Tension clawed through Sydney, and she sat up straighter on the couch.

"*Laurie* is fine outside of the office."

Since when?

Dylan stepped aside and opened the door wider. "Josh isn't here, but you can come in if you'd like."

"No, thank you." Laurie looked at Sydney and gave her a tight smile. "Good evening, Sydney."

"Hi." Sydney was pleased her reply—brief as it was—didn't come out as a squeak.

"Happy housewarming." Laurie handed Dylan a basked wrapped in cellophane. She stepped past him and approached Sydney. "I've been thinking a lot. About you. About my son. About this entire situation. I haven't treated you right, and it's nearly cost me a great deal."

Sydney's response died in her throat. She couldn't say, *that's all right*, because it wasn't.

Laurie gave her a real smile. "I hope, someday, you can forgive me."

Sydney did have an answer to that. She stood and met Laurie halfway. "I think it's a distinct possibility. And thank you for the gift, for everything you've done, and for raising an incredible son."

"I'm still not down with all of this"—Laurie waved her hand—"but you both look happy, and Josh does too, when I see him. So it's me, who has to figure that out."

They made a little more small talk, and then Laurie was on her way.

The basket was filled with wine, crackers, and cheese. Sydney and Dylan set it aside for when Josh got home.

Sydney settled back against Dylan, on the couch. "Life isn't that bad," she said.

"My life is fucking incredible."

She grinned. "All right. I can't argue that." Affection surged inside—a potent and delicious mixture of love and security and rightness. "Thank you. For sticking with me. For everything you've done. For loving both of us."

He looked at her, brow furrowed. "You don't have to thank me for that."

"I do. Because I'm grateful. I never want to take either of you for granted. And I also want you to know I love you. Truly and completely. For everything that you are, that you bring out in me, and that you make possible in the future."

"I love you too." He squeezed her tight.

God, this was never going to get old. This here, with Dylan and Josh, was incredible. She loved everything about it, and she never wanted to go without either of them.

It tuned out life could be better than fantasy, and the three of them were the perfect proof, as far as Sydney was concerned.

TWENTY-SEVEN

Sydney couldn't believe she'd met Dylan at this same convention a year ago. Talk about a life-altering encounter.

Day One was winding down, and she hadn't stopped smiling or talking for most of it. She'd also been on her feet almost that entire time. She was sore and tired, but energized.

"Good opening day." Josh slid up behind her and wrapped his arms around her waist.

She leaned back into him with a smile. "*Fantastic* opening day."

Their new game was selling amazingly well. Even better, last week she'd gotten the official news that *Changelings and Caverns* was hers to sell again. When people saw the board game was available, she'd sold through half her stock.

At this rate, they'd be out before the end of tomorrow. "We'll need to start taking pre-orders for the next print run," she said.

"There are worse problems to have."

"How *dare* you?" A loud gasp cut through the waning chatter in the vendor hall.

Sydney's grin grew, and she scanned the faces for Dylan.

He approached, his scowl wavering. "My best friend and my girlfriend... I can't believe this."

"Knock it off, Mr. Melodramatic." Sydney playfully smacked his arm.

He grabbed her wrist, stepped closer, rather than pulling her away from Josh, and pressed his mouth to hers.

She groaned and sank into the kiss. That still hadn't gotten old, and she couldn't imagine it ever would.

This was the perfect life. It didn't matter what anyone said, or that the three of them had the occasional bump. Sydney wouldn't have things any other way. She couldn't have written a better ending if this was the conclusion to one of her games.

THANK you for reading my 3d20 series.

Make sure to check out my Three Player Co-op Series Anthology as well. It's got geeky heroines and the possessively sweet heroes who will stop the world for them.

Grab the THREE PLAYER CO-OP SERIES ANTHOLOGY today

www.ingramcontent.com/pod-product-compliance
Lightning Source LLC
Chambersburg PA
CBHW051553100726
47898CB00001B/77